capture *the* wind *for* me

Other Books by Brandilyn Collins

Cast a Road Before Me
Color the Sidewalk for Me
Eyes of Elisha
Dread Champion

Book Three of The Bradleyville Series

capture
the wind
for me

BRANDILYN COLLINS

ZONDERVAN™

GRAND RAPIDS, MICHIGAN 49530 USA

ZONDERVAN™

Capture the Wind for Me
Copyright © 2003 by Brandilyn Collins

Requests for information should be addressed to:

Zondervan, *Grand Rapids, Michigan 49530*

ISBN 0-7394-3381-4

Interior design by Tracey Moran

Printed in the United States of America

For Amberly, my wonderful thirteen-year-old daughter.
May we ever chatter away with each other,
go to concerts, and remain great friends.
And may you never stray from Christ your Savior.
As for your first date — let's talk again when you're twenty-five.

Acknowledgments

My thanks to these folks who helped make *Capture the Wind for Me* a better book: Melanie Panagiotopoulos, for teaching me about Greek accents and language, and the country of Greece. Niwana Briggs, for her keen eye in critiquing the manuscript. My daughter, Amberly, for coming up with a great name for a singing group. And as always, my editor, Dave Lambert, and my agent, Jane Jordan Browne. For all they do.

Forgetting what is behind
and straining toward what is ahead,
I press on toward the goal
to win the prize for which God has called me
heavenward in Christ Jesus.

Philippians 3:13–14

~ *1996* ~

prologue

I remember how even the sky mourned with us, hanging in shades of gray, chilled and fitful. How the wind moaned through the red-leaved trees in the cemetery. I was only fourteen. Nature's sorrow seemed right to me, for surely the world could not go on as usual, undisturbed and blithe, in the face of our tragedy. Vaguely, I wondered if others in my family shared the same transcendent thoughts. Now, at twenty, I know they did. Seems to me such self-absorption is common to the grieving. Every act of nature shouts our loss—the merest drop of rain a tear for the deceased, a stream of sunshine hailing some bright memory.

My family and I huddled together, trembling more in soul than body, as we faced my mama's casket. White and gleaming, it rested on wide strips of green fabric above an open and hungry grave.

"Should we lower it?" the funeral director quietly asked.

No!

Daddy's cheek muscles froze, tears glistening in his red-rimmed eyes. He nodded.

The wizened cemetery worker stretched gnarled hand to metal gear and started cranking. *Chink, chink. Chink, chink.* Slowly, the casket began to descend.

Daddy gripped my shoulder, grief bubbling in his throat. My brother, Robert, age ten, leaned against me, solemn, wooden. *Chink, chink.* Seven-year-old Clarissa clutched her coat around her, as if to wrap herself against the sound. I watched the bottom of the casket disappear, the blunt cliff of earth edge up its side.

Mama, I cried. *Mama!*

Memories pierced me like shards of glass. Saturday morning pancakes. Softball game cheers. Suppertime laughter. The way she hugged Daddy. Our talks of first love.

Cancer. Pain. Dulling eyes. Final words.

Lifeless head on a satin pillow.

Chink, chink.

Grandma Westerdahl wailed for her daughter.

The top of the casket disappeared. Still the man cranked. An errant leaf, brittle and worn, skittered across the ground to snag on his wrist. As if to say, *Stop! Stop your turning; crank the other way, up and up. Turn back time!* He flicked the leaf away.

Chink, chink. Chink, ch—

Silence, save for the wind. The man rocked back on his heels, task done.

The ceremony was complete. Time now for us to go home. To leave Mama behind. My mind numbed. I could not grasp it—my mama's warm brown eyes, her voice, her love, her *life* now stiffened, silenced. Covered by a casket, soon by soil. Her light, her dreams, her energy— a sputtering candle now spent.

We stood, bewildered refugees, staring sightlessly at the open earth. Grandpa Delham put his arm around Daddy. Grandma Delham reached for Clarissa, but my little sister pulled away. Carefully, she inched to the edge of the grave, then peered down. I can still see Clarissa, her blue coat flapping against lace-topped socks, her weight tilting forward on one foot, neck craned. I knew she had to see the casket, had to have a mental picture to take with her, to remember after dirt covered all.

Grandpa Westerdahl held his sobbing wife.

Clarissa took her time, then sidled back to us, bleary-eyed and pale. Daddy grasped her hand.

I, too, had to see. Approaching the grave as if pulled by an unseen hand, I braced myself and looked down. Expectation did not lessen the shock. The pure white of the casket screamed against black earth. I reminded myself that Mama was not really there. That her soul flew in heaven, hovered at Jesus' feet.

Little comfort the thought gave me.

We had to leave. I had a family to take care of—a grief-stricken father, siblings who needed a mama. *God*, I cried, *I can't do this!*

I took a step back, willing myself to say goodbye to Mama. Willing it and willing it. Somehow I managed a second step. A third. Then I forced myself to turn around. Rejoined my family. I hugged Robert, slipped my fingers around Daddy's arm. Clarissa still held his other hand.

As a group, we began to make our wearied way toward the car. To our home and life—without Mama. I clutched Daddy and trudged forward, even as my mind screamed, *I can't leave her, I can't leave her, I can't leave her!* I told myself to not look back. That I *had* to go on, all of us did. That my family needed me to be strong. I focused on my feet, one step at a time. Forward.

But a piece of my heart jagged loose and took a manic leap down the grave.

~ *1998* ~

chapter 1

When Katherine May King set foot in Bradleyville she brought a tornado with her.

It happened on a Monday afternoon in mid March—a year and a half after my mother's funeral. I'd hurried my brother and sister home from school through a blustering wind and darkening sky. Clarissa dropped some spelling papers, and I had to chase them up the sidewalk as they dipped and soared like drunken butterflies. We blew in through our front door just as the downpour started.

"Whoa." Robert set his books on the kitchen table with his typical nonchalance. "It's sprinklin' a might."

"Winnie!" Clarissa opened the back sliding glass door. Our black-and-white spaniel shot inside, already drenched, and danced grateful paw prints around our legs.

"There goes my clean floor." I grabbed a rag from under the sink and started drying her off. Then crab-walked around the wood, swiping at the tracks. "You two make sure all the windows are shut. This is gonna be a bad one. Then come back in here. Might as well start homework."

"But I haven't had my hour of TV," my sister pouted.

I pushed to my feet. "You can't watch television during a storm, Clarissa." And I hurried into the family room to unplug our set.

Although being on the phone wasn't a great idea either, I made a quick call to Daddy down at the bank to tell him we were home safe. He instructed me to do everything I'd already done. I told him to wait the storm out if he had to before driving home, even though the bank was only a mile from our house.

The wind wailed like a banshee as I hung up. Clarissa high-tailed it back into the kitchen, eyes wide. "I'm scared."

I hugged her, rubbing the top of her light brown head. Clarissa was small and immature for age nine, a frail body and a frail soul. Often I despaired that she needed more mothering than I could give her. "It'll be okay," I soothed. "Come on, I'll get you a snack. Then we'll tackle your math." Clarissa and math were not the best of friends.

"Oohh." My sister could drag out those two letters like no one else. Her tone would rise about four notes, and she'd add a little "uh" on the end. "I *hate* math!"

Before long we huddled at the kitchen table, Winnie at our feet. Robert had retreated to his bedroom, supposedly to study. My theory held that he cultivated dirty socks behind that closed door. I swear they grew from the carpet.

Clarissa and I could barely concentrate. Gusts rattled the windows, and our trees creaked and groaned. We struggled through six problems, Clarissa's eyes flicking warily to the backyard.

Then—silence.

Our heads snapped up. I stared through the glass door, frowning, then rose slowly from my chair.

"Jackie, what happened?" Clarissa's voice tinged with fear.

"I don't know." I placed a palm against the door and peered out. Everything seemed deadly still. Not a drop of rain. Not the tiniest breeze.

The sky had turned pea green.

The silence roared in my ears. My skin tingled. Something was coming.

"Clarissa," I said quietly, "stay right here."

Before she could protest, I pivoted through the kitchen and toward the front door. Carefully, I opened it. Stepped outside on the porch. An eerie calm bathed our street. On shaky legs, I made my way down the sidewalk, then tipped back my head to view the sky.

In the distance, I saw a whirling black mass.

A moment passed before the sight registered. "Tornado!" I screamed.

I flew back into the house, locking the door with fumbling fingers. "Robert! Clarissa!" I pounded down the hall to my brother's room. He yanked open the door, gaping at me. "Come on." I grabbed his arm and pulled him toward the kitchen, my thoughts flying in a dozen directions. We didn't have a basement. I'd never been in a tornado before. Where was the safest place to go, what should we do? Clarissa met us in the hall, already crying from the fear in my voice. I forced myself to sound calm.

"A tornado's coming. Get into the front closet." I pushed her toward Robert.

"I'm scared," she wailed.

"Just go, Clarissa! I'll get Winnie."

Wordlessly, Robert led her away. There were times when my brother's understatedness came in handy. I ran toward the kitchen, calling for Winnie. She trotted out, ears back. "Come on, girl, let's go."

Robert flung the closet door open, and we shoved coats aside. Outside a distant freight train rumbled. Clarissa hung back. "It's gonna be dark in there."

"*Go*, Clarissa!" I pushed her inside, then Winnie, all four paws sliding beneath stiffened legs over the floor. Robert jumped in and I followed, pulling the door closed. I couldn't see a thing.

"Get down on the floor," I commanded, feeling for Clarissa.

"Jackie!" she wailed.

I caught her shoulders and nudged her down. The freight train grew louder. "Robert, where are you?" I groped until I hit something solid.

"Ow, that's my head."

"Well, get down, you idgit."

I knelt down, folding myself over top of Clarissa. The train fumed. "I want Mama!" Clarissa sobbed, and I shushed her with a quaking throat.

"Jesus, help us," I prayed.

The freight train turned into the roar of a thousand waterfalls. I could scarcely breathe.

Strange, the visions that blew through my head. I pictured our bodies broken and dying, our spirits ascending to heaven—to Mama. For a brilliant moment I felt intense, almost heartrending peace. Then thoughts of this world swept the vision away. We couldn't die and leave Daddy alone. Besides, I was only sixteen and had yet to be kissed. Couldn't God allow me my deepest longing on this earth—to fall headlong into a perfect love like Daddy and Mama had?

So much for noble thinking.

We trembled and prayed. Clarissa cried. Then the roar receded. Finally, all grew quiet.

Cautiously I opened the closet door, not knowing if we'd have a house around us. We did.

I laid my head against the front door, listening, then eased outside. Branches littered the street like dominoes. Paper fluttered among the treetops. I saw a dark shape lying on the road a ways down, and my heart clutched. Who was it? I ran down the sidewalk toward it, neighbors spilling out of their own houses. Fleetingly, I wondered about Mr. and Mrs. B next door. They were elderly and couldn't move very fast. My vision jerked up and down as I ran, feet slapping against wet pavement. I realized what the shape was, and I slowed, unbelieving. A dead horse in the middle of our street. The nearest farm lay across the tracks and outside town. If the tornado could pick up that heavy animal light as a feather and drop it near our house . . . I turned and sought the wayward pieces of paper, now sifting to the ground.

Then sprinted to our house, heart hammering, to call the bank.

Which brings me back to Katherine May King.

At the time, I didn't know everything that had happened, of course. Only much later, through secretive smiles and quiet revelations, would I piece together the details.

Katherine rolled into town that afternoon, expected by no one, chased by the storm. By the time she passed the handmade sign on Route 622 that read "Welcome to Bradleyville, population 1723," rain poured in buckets down her windshield. She inched her way toward the first of the town's two stoplights on Main, no other cars in sight. I can just picture her now, long red nails gripping the steering wheel and a defiant tune humming in her throat. The rain ceased and the world stilled about the time she hit the light. She stopped in the middle of the intersection, got out of her car, and studied the sky. And spotted the tornado.

That was enough to make even Katherine May King jump. She threw herself back into the car and gunned down Main in search of a safe building. The post office she passed up. Didn't look like it had changed a bit in the past eleven years, and she knew it would offer little shelter. She passed the IGA grocery as well—a wise decision in retrospect, because a corner of its roof ended up blowing off. Spotting the bank on her left, she screeched to a halt at the curb and fought to open her car door. The tornado was closing in, and the force blowing down Main did everything it could to keep her from crossing the street.

Inside the bank, Daddy had received a phone call about the approaching monster and ordered everybody into the vault. He tried to call home, but nobody answered. He'd just shooed the last person into the vault when something made him turn around. Through the front glass doors he saw a sight to behold. A woman in form-hugging jeans and a ruffled blouse, raven-black hair flying about her face, staggered toward the door. "Lord, help me," Daddy murmured, and practically flew across the bank. He crashed into the door and pushed with all his might before it opened. Reaching out both arms, he dragged the woman inside as the tornado screamed overhead. The bank shook. They had no time to reach the vault. "Here!" he shouted over the rumbling, and pulled the woman toward the nearest desk. He pushed her underneath and climbed in after her. The rumble turned deafening. She shot a wide-eyed look at Daddy, then buried her face in his chest, fingers clutching his sleeve. He threw both arms around her and held on.

A loud *crack* reverberated through the bank. Something exploded, followed by the sound of crashing glass. Daddy held the woman tighter as wind buffeted through the bank, sure they would both die, praying to God for us kids.

Finally, silence.

Daddy relaxed his grip. The woman raised her head. They faced each other in the dimness, listening. Daddy had the vague thought that she looked familiar. She blinked large brown eyes, as if thinking the same about him. Then, cautiously, they crawled out from under the desk.

The bank was a mess. People emerged to find the glass doors shattered, papers and supplies littering the floor. A purse balanced crazily on the edge of the counter. Daddy would eventually find his suit coat torn and crumpled against the back wall. Sick with fright, he stumbled to find a phone to call us. The woman pivoted after him, tugging at his shirt.

"Goodness, I must've looked a sight," Katherine told me later, "my blouse all untucked and my hair in a million different directions."

Maybe. But I can picture what Daddy saw. Katherine, all tanned and slim and fiery, basking in gratitude until it welled in her eyes. Not that I think she didn't appreciate what Daddy had done. It's just that she knew how to use it.

"Thank you, *thank* you," she said. "You probably saved my life."

Their eyes held for a moment. He nodded at her, then reached to snatch a telephone up from the floor. Katherine picked her way over glass, intent on seeing what was left of her car. Of course, she looked back. Daddy was saying hello to someone on the phone.

Me.

But his eyes were fixed on her.

chapter 2

Bradleyville is a tiny burg in the shadow of the Appalachians in eastern Kentucky. Its nearest neighbor is Albertsville, over twenty miles away by winding road. Albertsville seems huge in comparison. Meaning it's about four times bigger.

To the town denizens, Bradleyville is a sacrosanct little microcosm, nestled on the banks of the Columbia River by the finger of God himself. In 1998 the town was not quite one hundred years old, but what history it had was told and retold, like the annals of the Israelites. God might have chosen the Israelites first, but the folks in Bradleyville ran a mighty close second.

During the tornado, God protected our town. Some of the downtown businesses sustained damage, but nobody's home lay flattened, no one dead. Most of all, the sawmill wasn't touched. As employer for over half the men in town, the mill's condition remained a major issue. The Clangerlees immediately set about repairing their IGA grocery store, and Daddy busily saw to the bank. Grandpa Delham helped out. He'd managed the bank for years before passing the reins to Daddy upon his retirement the previous year and knew what to do.

For the next few weeks, talk of the tornado shared equal time with only one other subject: the return of Katherine May King. I first laid eyes on Katherine in church on the Sunday following the storm. What an auspicious day that turned out to be.

"Glory," my best friend, Alison, nudged my arm when the unknown woman slid into the end of the Kings' usual pew—across the aisle and down two rows. "Who is *that?*"

"Got me," I whispered back, amazed. The woman looked like she'd stepped from the pages of a magazine, with an aura of confidence as sleek as her shoulder-length black hair. She wore a bright yellow dress that fitted her just so, and high black-strapped heels. Her fingernails gleamed long and bright red—the same color as her lips. I blinked at that. Nobody wore that color lipstick to church.

I raised questioning eyebrows at Daddy over the heads of Robert and Clarissa. His gaze at the woman crinkled into puzzlement, then smoothed into surprised recognition. And then came the look that would change our lives. A flicker of undeniable pleasure tugged one corner of my daddy's mouth.

I remember that look as if it were yesterday. For me, it carried a lifetime of meaning. I'd seen the look often enough on the faces of my girlfriends as they admired some boy. I'd felt it on my own features whenever Billy Sullivan came into view. The expression bespoke eye-tugging attraction—caged only by social graces.

Four years have passed since that day. One thing I have learned since then: the bonfires of change start with the merest spark. Sometimes we see that flicker. Sometimes we blink in surprise at the flame only after it has marched hot legs upward to fully ignite. Either way, flicker or flame, we'd better do some serious praying. When God's on the move in our lives, he tends to burn up things we'd just as soon keep.

When it came to Daddy and Katherine May, I saw the spark right off. I knew my daddy too well. I stared at him, air catching in my throat.

He caught me watching and gave a little shrug. With purpose, he turned his head toward Pastor Beekins, who approached the pulpit to announce the first hymn. Half dazed, I stood with the rest of the congregation to sing, fumbling for the correct page in the hymnbook. But my eyes slid back to the woman, who held half a book, sharing with Derek King. Now that was a contrast. Derek King was a year ahead of me in school and the weirdest person I knew. He looked like a scrawny chicken next to a panther. I'd have laughed if my brain wasn't so busy scrambling for equilibrium.

I heard not a word of the sermon. I tried to focus on the pastor, but my eyes kept drifting left. A couple of times I stole glances at Daddy. He appeared to be listening with intent. But somehow I knew his thoughts were elsewhere. I could *feel* it.

After the service, I slipped quickly into the aisle, Alison on my heels, then stood waiting for Daddy like a protective guardian. I planned on turning him aside from this woman. But she was too clever for me.

"Well, *there* you are," she said, holding out a slender arm. "You're Bobby Delham, aren't you."

The name tripped off her tongue as if she'd said it a thousand times. I darted a surprised look at my father.

"Yes." Daddy took her hand in his. "Now that you're with your family, I recognize you. Katherine King, right? It's been a while since you've visited."

"Far too long." She smiled at him a suspended moment, then glided her eyes to Clarissa. "And who's this beautiful young lady?" She bent over and studied my sister's face. "Yup, I thought so."

Clarissa stared up at her with wide green eyes. "Huh?"

"The Pretty Fairy visits you every night, and every night she kisses you right here." She ran a finger down Clarissa's nose and tapped the end. "That's why you're so lovely. And you'll get lovelier every day."

Clarissa considered Katherine as if amazed that a grown woman would tell her such a tale. Then she grinned, captivated. "My name's Clarissa," she said.

"A perfect name for you," Katherine replied.

I put an arm around Clarissa's shoulders and drew her to my side. Katherine turned her eyes on me. "And you must be her sister."

I could only nod, mouth pressed.

She seemed undaunted at my coldness. "What's your name?"

I hesitated. "Jackie."

"And this is my son, Robert," Daddy broke in, as if embarrassed at my attitude. "And Jackie's friend, Alison."

"Hi." Alison nearly gawked. I could have strangled her. Katherine King did not deserve any kind of awe. Not at all.

"Wonderful to meet you." Katherine smiled again at my daddy. He smiled back.

"Are you visiting for a while?" he asked.

"Yes. I expect I'll be here for some time, staying at my parents' house."

I tightened my fingers on Clarissa's shoulder. "Ouch!" She frowned at me.

"That's nice to hear. I imagine they will be glad to have you around." Daddy stood awkwardly then, as if trying to think of something else to say. "Well." He cleared his throat. "We'll be seeing you, I'm sure."

Oh, no, we won't.

Our families parted ways.

Daddy was quiet as he started the car for our short ride home. "Who is she?" I demanded.

"You heard who she is—Jason and Connie King's daughter."

"But where's she been?"

He shrugged. "Don't know. Now that I think about it, she probably left town after she finished high school."

The rhythm of his name from her lips beat in my memory. "Did she go to school with you?"

"Not really. She was probably"—he thought a moment—"five or six years behind me. So I didn't pay all that much attention to her."

"Well, she certainly paid plenty of attention to you," I retorted. "And where did you see her before, anyway?"

Daddy gave me a look, clearly perturbed. "I saw her outside in the wind just before the tornado came. I pulled her inside the bank."

Oh, great, he'd saved her, like some knight in shining armor. I narrowed my eyes at the road. "She could have at least thanked you."

"She did."

Ah. Clearly, there were details he wasn't telling me.

"Isn't she married?"

"Apparently not."

"I like her, Daddy," Clarissa chirped from the backseat. "She's real pretty."

Such timing from my innocent sister. I pressed back against the seat and folded my arms. "Her lipstick's too red."

A teenage girl's bedroom is her haven. At that time in my life, my room was as much a part of me as my right hand. Its doorway symbolized the threshold between my two lives—ersatz mother and trembling young girl. Within the rest of our house responsibilities weighted me. I cooked and cleaned and cared for my siblings, sweeping my fears and self-doubts into a safe pile in the corner of my heart as surely as I swept dust from the kitchen floor. But in my room, closed off from the wearying demands and expectations, I could be sixteen. There, I exchanged secrets on the phone with my friends. Amid those four walls I begged God for help countless times. I rested there. Stewed and complained and cried there. I daydreamed of love there.

And in that year of 1998, through all the elation and heartache that would grip my family, I would grow up there. While growing up is a much-sought prize, I would feel no satisfaction at the time. In truth, I would feel like a feather caught in a whirlwind. Only later would I realize what had happened: the dual parts of me had become one.

Somewhere along the way, the once definable threshold of my room, my life, had faded into nondistinction, like photo development in reverse.

After church on that day in March, I sat at my bedroom desk, trying to study for a history test, but my thoughts had other plans. The scene from church echoed until my head rang with it. I tried to read, yet could only see that look on Daddy's face, and Katherine King's poised perfection as she spoke his name. Disgusted, I turned away from my book only to catch my reflection in the dresser mirror. I gazed at myself.

Why had I never noticed how plain I was?

Everybody said I looked just like Mama—a high compliment. Like me, she was short and slim, with light brown hair and wide-set, almond-shaped brown eyes. She had an oval face and lips that turned up at the corners. It was true, Mama had been beautiful. But suddenly her looks on my face didn't translate so well.

I told myself it had nothing to do with Katherine King. What a betrayal that would be, comparing her looks to Mama's and finding them superior. The mere thought sent such a pang through me that I shoved it away right then. Even now that thought disturbs me.

No. I was not plain, I told myself. I was just a lost cause. I'd turned the magic age of sixteen the previous month. Finally old enough to date but too burdened with being "mama" of our family, a weary woman in a teenager's body. Mama and I had talked about my dating since I was twelve. "You're lucky times have changed in Bradleyville," she once told me. "When I was young, we couldn't date until seventeen. And even then, the whole town watched us."

"You went out with Daddy right from the start, didn't you?" I asked.

She smiled one of her secretive little smiles, tinged with sadness. "Yes. I did."

Mama had never loved anyone except Daddy. She told me so many times. He was her first kiss and her last. A perfect romance.

How easy love seemed when I was sixteen.

My gaze drifted to the glossy posters on my walls, photos of the music stars I listened to constantly on the radio. I especially liked the boy bands: 98 Degrees, Backstreet Boys, and 'NSync. What lives those singers must lead, I thought. What perfect romances they must have seen to enable them to sing such love songs.

They might as well have lived in a different world.

I closed my eyes and envisioned Daddy's smile of pleasure. *How could he have looked at some other woman that way?*

It won't go anywhere, Jackie. Stop thinking about it.

I turned back to my history book, rubbing my forehead, and tried to concentrate. But before long, my thoughts drifted back to the telltale flash of delight on my daddy's lips as he beheld Katherine King.

chapter 3

It doesn't take much in Bradleyville to cause a stir. No matter where I went that week, folks talked about Katherine King's sudden appearance. At the grocery store on Monday, Edith Bishop was yakking away to Shirley Clawson. Their voices fell to a whisper as I pushed my cart by, but I could still make out their words. Besides, at the mention of Katherine's name, my ears pricked. I stopped not too far away and pretended to consider the prices on canned beans.

"Connie tol' me she feels like it's Christmas all over again, havin' her daughter back," Miss Edith said.

"I can only imagine." Miss Shirley's voice dripped empathy. "But land sakes, where's the girl been for eleven years?"

"Too many places, apparently. And she's only visited her parents a few times. But except for her grandma's funeral, she'd refuse to come to church—even on Christmas Eve or Easter."

"Don't sound right to me."

"Well. At least she come Sunday."

"True, true."

The conversation paused. I could almost feel the women's suspicious glances at my profile. I made a point of sighing at the beans and shaking my head, then moved reluctantly on down the aisle. The voices resumed.

The next day I popped into the hardware store, and two other women were talking, these from the Baptist church. They'd apparently heard how Katherine's red lipstick and nails fired up the Methodist sanctuary. And glory, had the other woman seen Katherine May just that mornin', wearin' those tight jeans? It's a wonder she got a leg in 'em.

Katherine May. That was the first time I'd heard her full name. I did not like the ring of it.

Even at home I could not escape from the topic. That night at supper Clarissa asked, "Is that girl Katherine gonna be at church again Sunday?"

"Don't know," Daddy said.

"Probably." Robert shoved mashed potatoes into his mouth.

I blinked at him. "Like how would *you* know?"

He swallowed. "I saw her."

"Saw her? Where?"

"When I was walkin' home from softball practice yesterday."

My brother had the maddening habit of saying the least words possible. "Well, what'd she say?"

"She said she'd probably see us in church Sunday."

I scorched him with a look. "Do tell, Robert. But what else, like why'd she talk to you at all?"

He eyed me, forehead creasing. "Like I said, I was walkin' home. She drove by and saw me, so she pulled over and said hi."

I narrowed my eyes. The only reason Katherine King would pull over to say hi to Robert was that he was my daddy's son. Had she no shame?

Robert shrugged. "She said, 'You're Bobby Delham's son, Robert, right?' and I said, 'Yes, ma'am.' And she said even if she hadn't a met me in church, she'd a known me for a Delham, seein' as how I have the same thick dark hair and handsome face as Daddy."

My jaw dropped. "She told you *that?*"

"Uh-huh." Robert resumed eating.

I turned a shocked gaze on Daddy, as if daring him not to disdain this madness. He tipped his head with an "Oh, well," expression, then took a drink of iced tea. His little charade didn't fool me one bit. I could tell he was pleased. Anger plinked up my spine.

"Goes to show folks are right," I declared, cutting my meat with ferocious intent.

"About what?" asked Clarissa.

"All they're saying about Katherine King." I took a prim bite of chicken.

"Jackie, you know you shouldn't listen to gossip." Daddy frowned at me. A moment passed. "What do they say?"

I told him every detail.

Daddy nodded slowly, pressing his full lips together the way he did when he was thinking. "Here's what I say. One, don't believe everything you hear. Two, even if you hear somethin' awful about a person and you know it's true, best be forgivin', like Jesus told us to be. Everybody makes mistakes, and some day, you might need some forgivin' yourself."

How true those words would prove to be. But at the time I focused only on Daddy. Something about his words pulsed with personal experience. My fork paused midair as I studied him. Daddy had never done wrong his entire life, far as I knew. Anyone in Bradleyville would have said he was one of the most respected and liked men in town. He continued eating as if nothing were amiss. After a moment, I returned to my chicken, but I still felt unsettled.

As I did the dishes, I remember thinking that the mere mention of Katherine King's name in our house set off disturbing repercussions.

That school year, Derek King attended one of my morning classes. The following day, drawn like some crazed moth to flame, I found myself staring at the back of his angular head. Derek sat like no person I'd ever seen, with one shoulder way lower than the other and his head crooked, kind of like a hunchbacked bird listening for a worm. But his odd posture barely registered in my mind at the time. I was wondering if he'd heard his sister say anything about Daddy.

"So you gonna tell me what's up?" Alison plopped her tray down across from me at lunch.

"Yeah," I sighed dramatically, "but you have to promise not to tell another soul."

"That bad, huh." Her large brown eyes goggled. "Well, everybody else is on their way over here, so we won't be able to talk."

"Everybody else" meant our friends who always sat with us—Nicole and Cherise and Millicent. Yes, there really is a person named Millicent, and in high school she lived up to it. Straight back, arched eyebrow, and an attitude of wisdom beyond her years. Well. If she sported pockets of maturity, I wore a whole dress of it. Millicent still had her mama. Enough said.

"Hurry up and eat," I urged Alison. "Then we can hang outside."

"Whoa," Alison exclaimed fifteen minutes later. "Sure sounds like she's hot for your daddy."

We sat outside on a worn bench, looking across the yard toward the buildings for first through eighth grade. Somewhere in those classrooms my brother and sister toiled away. I'd meet Clarissa by the big elm near the street after school to walk her home. Robert would stay for softball practice, then walk home by himself. *Without* interference from Katherine King, I hoped.

"Well, not if I have anything to say about it," I told Alison. "Who does she think she is? Besides, can you just imagine my daddy with the sister of *Derek King?*"

Alison laughed. "No way." She tucked her blonde hair behind her ears, thinking. "She sure was nice to Clarissa."

"So what, *everybody* likes Clarissa. Sweet little waif Clarissa, who wears her heart on her sleeve? Who's nine but looks like she's six and a half? People just *look* at Clarissa and want to hug her."

"I got it!" Alison exclaimed. "Just let Katherine King have your brother, seein' as how he's so 'handsome.'"

I snorted. "Yeah, right. My brother's so twelve. Just wants to play softball, watch TV, and be left alone."

"Wait till she sees him hit a home run—that oughtta make her heart pound."

"Oh, good, Alison," I retorted, "keep it up. You're just sayin' the most helpful things."

"Sorry."

It was true about my brother, however; he did know how to play softball. He'd plant his feet just so, wrap loving fingers around the bat, and give it a few graceful swings. His eyes would half close as he watched the pitcher let loose the ball. Then time would warp into some kind of strange suspension. Robert would wait to swing until you thought surely it was too late. Next thing you knew, you'd hear the *crack* of wood meeting ball. He'd streak the bases, elbows bent and arms pumping. And all the fans would be out of their seats.

"Oh, well," Alison sighed, "guess she'll have to settle for your daddy."

"No way. I want her *out* of here," I declared, firming my mouth.

"Sounds like your daddy may have other ideas."

"Daddy doesn't know what's what," I shot back. "He's just still grievin' over Mama, and his mind's all messed up. I've got to get him back on track."

"Shh," Alison whispered. "Derek's comin' this way."

"Oh, great. He'd better not say anything about all this."

I could picture Derek, with his long-legged amble, large black shoes kicking through the grass. His hands would be hanging limp at his side, thumbs rubbing across his fingers. Derek walked with his ash blonde head slightly atilt, though not as badly as when he sat. Probably because he needed to see where he was headed. In my most charitable of mindsets, I'd have allowed that his face wasn't all that bad. He had a strong nose, a wide forehead, and close-set gray eyes behind silver-rimmed glasses. His mouth would slip in and out of a smile so quickly you'd doubt that you'd seen it at all. Most of the time, you had no idea what he was smiling about. Probably some brilliant new computer software concept.

We sat in silence until Derek listed into view. He blinked and veered away from us, as though we'd just parked ourselves in the center of his path. I rolled my eyes at Alison.

To this day, I can't tell you why I opened my mouth.

"Hi, Derek," I called, amusement lilting my voice. Alison threw me a look.

Derek slid to a halt and jerked his head in our direction. It took him a moment to focus. "Hi." He stared at me, waiting. I stared back. "What's up?"

I dropped my gaze to his ankles. "Just wondering what color your socks are today."

"Oh." He lifted his pant legs. "Brown and blue."

It could have been worse. I'd seen him with one orange foot and one green. "Derek." My tone sounded peeved. "*Why* do you wear different colored socks every day?"

Alison laughed in her throat.

"Who said socks have to match?" Derek countered.

I gave him one of my for-heaven's-sake-Clarissa looks. "Like maybe the people who made them the same in the first place?"

He considered that. "Those people," he declared, "have no imagination."

And with that, he took his leave.

Alison shook her head, watching him go. "That is one strange guy."

Well, good for him, I thought. I'd asked a perfectly logical question, given Derek's odd little dress mannerism. So why did I feel like he'd cut me down? "You know what makes him really weird? That he's *proud* of his stupid socks."

"I know." Alison twisted her mouth. "You think he wears 'em to work?"

Derek had been working at a computer store in Albertsville ever since he'd gotten his driver's license the previous year. His parents, who apparently doted on him as their "surprise" child late in life, had bought him an old car to get him back and forth.

"Guess so," I said. "He goes after school, right?"

"Maybe like his boss doesn't care?" Alison offered. "I mean, as long as he does the work. He's supposed to be this computer genius."

I frowned at her, inexplicably perturbed that she'd said something favorable. "Well, hoo-fah." My voice dripped sarcasm. "He thinks he's so hot, but no way. I mean, a computer freak, how original."

Honestly, with Bradleyville's history of independent thinkers, you'd think our generation could have coughed up something better than Derek King.

I stewed about him for the rest of the school day.

That evening Miss Connie phoned to invite us to their welcome-back "at-home" for Katherine on Sunday afternoon. Do not think for a moment that I was fooled. Something told me the idea had been conceived by Katherine herself, not her parents. And that, although many would be invited, the only guest that mattered was Bobby Delham.

That did it. I sensed a Rubicon in our path. And I knew that somehow, some way, I had to put a stop to this thing on Sunday, or our family would face real trouble.

chapter 4

Sometimes even now I look back on that spring and summer and wonder how I made it through. On one hand you could say if I'd survived the death of my mama, I could handle anything. There's a lot of truth in that. The difference is that Mama's death brought one all-encompassing emotion—grief. Granted, the palette of grief is multi-hued, depression in grays, purpled anger. But these all swirl into the undefinable color that coats the world of loss. In my sixteenth year, however, I would endure emotions as varied and distinct as black from white. Exhilaration and despair. Self-absorption and guilt. Love. Indifference.

And for the next few days of that week, obsession.

I simply *had* to find a way to keep Katherine May King apart from Daddy during the at-home. Alison and I discussed the issue in low tones at school. Then Thursday afternoon Alison's life scudded into glory, and I was left on my own. She called me that night, breathless with the news.

"Jacob asked me out! My first date!"

I sucked in air. "Wow, really? Tell me everything." I trotted into my bedroom and shut the door.

Jacob Keeley had talked about this and that before cranking up the courage to ask Alison to go bowling in Albertsville the following night. After the standard lecture, her mama had agreed to let her go.

"Alison," I said, "that is so cool." And I meant it. Alison had liked Jacob for a long time.

But she noticed the snag in my tone. Only a best friend could have done that. "Oh, Jackie, don't worry. Next thing you know, Billy will be askin' you out."

Billy Sullivan was the hottest guy in the junior class. I'd liked him for as long as Alison had liked Jacob. But I didn't stand a chance. He was already going out with Mary Breckenridge, who had blonde hair and a knockout figure.

"Oh, forget him," I retorted. "Just call me Saturday. I want to hear everything."

She said she would.

In such moments I would feel as if the world whirled merrily before me, a carousel of colors and motion, while I dragged my feet over sandy ground. When I punched off the phone, I lingered on my bed, disappointment and vague longing settling like kicked-up dust in my chest.

"I couldn't believe it when your daddy started comin' to call," Mama once told me. "We were so different that I never thought he'd want me. He was quiet and serious. And tall. I was short and giggled all the time. But one day there he was, at my door. Handsome Bobby Delham, with his doe-brown eyes."

I could picture Mama's face so clearly as she'd said those words, recapturing the magic of that time. Now here I was, her age. If it could happen to my mama and my best friend, I thought—couldn't it happen to me?

Friday night as Alison went on her dream date, I hurried about the kitchen doing dishes, cradling the telephone between my shoulder and ear. Through the sliding glass door I could see Clarissa and her much larger and athletically built friend, Alma Sue, tearing about the backyard, Winnie barking at their heels.

"Okay," I said to Mrs. Crary, the wife of my brother's softball coach. "I'll be sure Robert gets to the game on time."

I hung up the phone, mentally checking my list of my remaining to-dos. Help Clarissa with her math. Work on my social studies report. Better to do that now than have it hanging over me on the weekend. I sighed and stepped through the back door to call Clarissa inside. She slowed, swishing hair out of her eyes. "I don't wanna come in yet."

Winnie flung herself on the grass, panting with fury. Alma Sue placed hands on her hips, almost as if defying me to stop their fun.

"Come on, Clarissa."

She surveyed me dolefully. "Five more minutes."

"No. Now."

Defeated, she dragged herself into the kitchen while Alma Sue turned on her heel toward home. Clarissa slumped at the table, where her books awaited. I sighed into a chair beside her.

"Hey, girls, homework time?" Daddy entered the kitchen. "Jackie, don't you have work of your own to do?"

"Yeah, a report."

"You go on then; I'll help Clarissa." He pulled out the chair across from me.

I hesitated. "You sure you're not too tired?"

He smiled. "I can handle it."

"I know, but it's the end of the week for you, and—"

"Jackie, go. This is not a suggestion."

Daddy's favorite phrase. Which meant the discussion was over. "Thanks, Daddy." I padded out of the kitchen, stopping to check on my brother.

"Robert?" I tapped on his door, then opened it. He lolled on his brown carpet, fists stacked on top of each other and supporting his chin as he read a sports magazine. His books were scattered around him, along with the ubiquitous dirty socks and numerous other pieces of clothing. I made a point of ogling. "What is this, the city dump? And why aren't you doin' your homework?"

"I got all weekend; stop raggin' on me." His eyebrows knit, and he spread his full lips even wider, just like Daddy would do.

"Oh, I won't bother raggin'," I retorted to Robert. "You bring home a bad report card, it won't be me they kick off the softball team." I started to shut his door. "By the way, Mrs. Crary called. The game's at 2:00 this Saturday. You should be there by 1:30."

I left him to his poor choices and retreated to my room.

Some time later, a knock on my door made me jump. I snapped off my radio. "Yes?"

Daddy eased inside. "Jackie, I need to talk to you."

My eyes fell on the clock. "Good grief, it's 9:30! I have to put Clarissa to bed." I started to rise.

"It's done."

"Oh." I blinked at him. He usually tucked Clarissa in bed, but I was the one who made sure she got ready on time. "Did she brush her teeth?"

Daddy half smiled. "Yes, Jackie, she brushed her teeth."

"Okay."

He sat on my bed. "That's what I wanted to talk to you about."

I frowned. "Clarissa's teeth?"

"No, I mean . . ." He raised a hand and let it flop back down. "You've taken care of us all so well, Jackie. I know this last year and a half hasn't been any easier for you than for the rest of us. I've been proud of the way you've grown up so quickly. But it's also made me sad to see you change so much. All the things you used to love—the gymnastics, the cheerleading—you don't do them anymore."

"I don't have time."

"I know. That's just it."

My heart twinged, both for him and myself. "It doesn't matter, Daddy, I don't want to do those things now anyway. Like you said, I've grown up."

"You're only sixteen."

"Well." I straightened my back. "Sixteen's not a kid."

He laced his fingers, nodding slowly. "Jackie, I want you to understand me. I'm grateful for all you do with the house and kids. With my havin' to work to support the family, I couldn't have made it without you."

He paused. I remained silent, not sure where he was headed.

"But lately," he continued, "I've begun to feel how unfair this is to you. Now you mention at supper that your best friend's goin' out on her first date. I don't want you to feel that you're tied to this house every Friday and Saturday night. Your mama and I said that you could date when you're sixteen, and nothin' about that's changed. You understand? Even with all the work you do, I still want you to *feel* like you're sixteen."

"Okay, Daddy," I managed. How awkward, talking to him about going out. Hurt seared through me. I missed Mama so much! She was supposed to be here to help me with guys and romance. How could I possibly play her and be sixteen at the same time? "Nobody's asked me out yet anyway," I added with a little shrug.

He smiled. "They will."

I looked at my lap, wondering why we were having this conversation. A suspicion, dark and ugly, niggled at my brain. "Daddy," I said abruptly, "why did you tell the Kings we'd go to their at-home?"

He blinked at the change in topic. "Why shouldn't we go?"

I lifted a shoulder. "Have they invited lots of people?"

"Probably. The Kings know lots of townsfolk, between their relatives and all the men that work with Jason at the mill."

Exactly, I thought. "So why did they invite us?"

"Well, I did help Katherine King the day she arrived in town. And she did meet you and Clarissa and Robert at church."

He held my gaze, crinkling his forehead. Somehow I knew he feigned the puzzlement.

"You like her, don't you," I accused.

He drew a breath. Now I'd done it. I'd crossed the line from unspoken to spoken, and he'd have to answer.

"What makes you say that?"

I pursed my mouth. "That's not fair. Taking my question and turning it back on me."

"Okay." He drew out the word, stalling for time. The sudden strangeness between us hung in the air. As if I were the parent, questioning the ill-advised plans of the teenage child. "Tell you the truth, I don't really know her."

I looked away. That's not what I meant, and he knew it. You didn't have to know someone very well to be attracted to that person. "Oh, forget it." My voice sounded tight. "It doesn't matter."

Daddy opened his mouth, then shut it again.

"Jackie," he would tell me much later, "I couldn't help being pulled toward Katherine. Surely now you can understand my loneliness at that time. Do you know how many nights I couldn't sleep in my empty bed after your mama died? I slept on the couch. Time and time again I'd force myself to be patient with Clarissa and her math, when all I wanted to do was scream my frustration that I didn't have a wife to help. Coworkers at the bank would complain about small things, and I'd think, 'You think *you* have problems.'"

Yes, Daddy, I understand now what I could not then. Now I know what it is to fall in love. To feel the giddy swirl of cringing anticipation and sodden hope. I know what it is to have your heart want to burst from your skin with longing. I know what it is to lose.

"Well." I shifted toward the open book on my desk. "I have to get back to work."

"Sure." I heard the bed creak as Daddy pushed to his feet. When he reached my door, he hesitated. "Jackie, I really am grateful for everything you do. Your mama would be proud."

I squeezed my eyes shut at the words. "Thank you," I said softly.

He closed the door and left me.

chapter 5

No doubt Bradleyville will never see another "at-home" the likes of the one for Katherine May King.

Katherine did not come to church that morning. She'd stayed home, her mama explained with embarrassment, to get things ready. This raised more than a few eyebrows, as Bradleyville folk wouldn't think of so overtly putting a party before worshiping Jesus. Martha had made that mistake in the Bible, and look where it got her. Forever branded as a woman with skewed priorities.

However, it didn't seem to matter to Katherine. "I tol' her we could just keep it simple, put things out soon as we got home," her mama confided to Mrs. B before the service. "But you know Katherine; she plants her feet in concrete, and that's that."

Mrs. B chuckled as she laid an arthritic hand on Miss Connie's arm. "Don't forget, I raised a stubborn one myself. But Jessie came 'round, and so will Katherine. You just got to keep prayin'."

Miss Jessie is Mr. and Mrs. B's niece, raised by them since she was sixteen, after her mama was killed. She's married to Lee Harding, Miss Connie's brother, which makes her Katherine's aunt. Miss Jessie was mighty helpful and sweet to me after my own mama's death, urging me to trust God, telling me that believe it or not, I'd get through the days with his help, just like she had. I couldn't imagine she'd ever once been stubborn. Miss Jessie was one of the best people I knew. Still is. And my family owes a whole lot more to her than we can ever repay.

We dawdled after church, giving the Kings time to get home first. Katherine didn't appear to be the homebody type, and hearing that she was in charge of her own welcoming, I lowered my expectations of the food several degrees. I figured if she managed to spread peanut butter on celery, we should be thankful. This assumption raised my spirits significantly. Daddy would not be able to deny Katherine's shortcomings in the kitchen. Pretty as a woman might be, a man had to eat.

Life does throw a few curveballs.

My thoughts swirled as we parked down the street from the Kings' house. First, of course, I worried about keeping Katherine away from Daddy, although I had no idea how. My lack of a plan made me feel about as confident as a kitten plotting the demise of a wildcat. Second, Alison's awe-tinged report of her date with Jacob taunted me. He'd kissed her at the end of their date. She'd been practically beside herself ever since. Surely spring fever had twirled through the air when I wasn't looking, I ragged to myself. My daddy had inhaled it, and now my best friend. I must have been doing laundry.

And third, I was about to enter Derek King's house. I'd never been there before. Would I have to talk to him? I have to admit that I felt somewhat curious to see him in his home. Kind of like spying on a rare species in its own habitat.

"What are we gonna do here?" Clarissa asked as Daddy knocked on the Kings' door.

"Eat," Robert replied. Daddy chuckled.

"But there's no kids here that I know."

"Maybe there will be." I combed her hair with my fingers, and she pulled impatiently away. "Tell you what, as soon as we go in, you see who you can find."

I glanced at Daddy, searching for the slightest hint of anticipation on his face. I saw none but felt no less edgy. Ever since our conversation Friday night, I'd sensed he was doing his best to prove he held no interest in Katherine King. As if he fooled me.

"Come in, come in." Miss Connie beamed as she pulled back the door.

"Hey, Bobby." Mr. King greeted us as we stepped inside.

"Thanks for includin' us, Jason, Connie." Daddy and Mr. King shook hands.

Katherine was nowhere in sight. I looked into the crowded dining room and caught a glimpse of the food. My jaw nearly dropped. Before I knew it I'd wound my way through chatter and bodies to stand before the table, gaping at the delicacies. Tiny puffed pastry baskets with handles, filled with cheese and mushrooms. Chocolate cups with strawberry-colored thick cream. Thin, lacy cookies sprinkled with powdered sugar. Dainty open sandwiches with all sorts of different accoutrements. Fruits cut in unusual shapes. In the center of the table sat a gorgeous flower arrangement, trailing greenery that curled around flickering candles in multiple colors. I'd never seen lit candles in the middle of the day.

"Have you ever beheld such a pretty sight?" a familiar voice asked. I turned to see Miss Jessie at my side.

"No." We both admired it for a moment. "Who did all this?" I asked, praying that some angel had miraculously taken over the Kings' kitchen.

"Katherine." Miss Jessie tasted a cookie with utter delight.

My heart skidded to the floor. "But how did she—I mean—where did she learn it?"

Miss Jessie brushed powdered sugar from her lips. "Katherine's done a lot a different things since she's been gone. Workin' for a caterin' company, for one thing."

A lot a different things. I felt immediately suspicious. "Oh, really. What else has she done?"

"Oh, I don't rightly know everything," she said vaguely. "Maybe Katherine will tell you."

Miss Jessie was close to her sister-in-law, Miss Connie. I'd have bet whatever the Kings knew about Katherine, Miss Jessie knew. I pursed my mouth. "Why'd she leave Bradleyville in the first place?"

Miss Jessie eyed me for a moment. "Aren't you the curious one. Oh, well," she laughed, "seems most a the town's curious about Katherine." She reached for a tiny sandwich and examined it. "She left to go to college."

Not so unusual. "Where'd she graduate from?"

"Actually, she didn't. After a semester she decided she . . . wanted to do other things." Miss Jessie gave a little shrug, as if to say it didn't matter. But somehow I got the impression it mattered a good deal to her and the rest of Katherine's family. I started to probe some more, then realized I'd been doing a poor job of keeping an eye on Daddy. "Where is Katherine, anyway?"

"In the livin' room, talkin' to folks."

"Folks" could mean Daddy. "I'd better go say hi," I breathed, then scurried off.

I heard Katherine's laughter before I rounded the corner—rich and tinkling at the same time. I spotted her in the midst of a gathering, mouth wide open, head tilted back. Her hair was pulled into a French twist, giving her a regal look. She wore pants—black, silky, and wide-legged, yet clingy to her curves. And a red silk blouse. Men and women alike—although I have to admit the males outnumbered the females three to one—hung on her every word.

"Land sakes," she teased wizened old Mr. Luther, "how could I *possibly* forget you? You still pass Tootsie Rolls down the pew when you're supposed to be singing hymns?"

Mr. Luther blushed and silently drew a Tootsie Roll from his pocket. Everyone around him burst into laughter.

"Oh, you!" Katherine rested her hand on his shoulder. "The best things never change."

I checked around for Daddy, happy to see him engaged in conversation with Mr. Clangerlee. Probably discussing all the cleanup they'd both had to do after the tornado.

"Jackie." Clarissa appeared from nowhere. "I have to go to the bathroom."

"Um, okay. It's probably down there." I pointed with my chin.

Clarissa eyed all the people she'd have to wade through. "Come with me."

"Oh, good grief, Clarissa, you can go by yourself."

"No, pleeeease."

I let out a martyr's sigh. "Oh, all right."

I steered my sister around Katherine and entourage, then led her down a hallway until we found the bathroom. "Will you wait for me to come out?" she asked.

"Yeah, yeah, just hurry."

I sidled toward the wall, watching Katherine intently through the doorway as I waited.

"Hi," a voice said behind me.

I jerked around. Derek peered down at me, a video game box dangling from his hand. "Oh," I said, feeling quite stupid. "Didn't know you were there."

"I wasn't."

I puckered my forehead.

"But now I am." A smile flashed across his lips, then disappeared.

We stared at each other.

"I was just . . . waiting for my sister in the bathroom." I gestured vaguely toward the door.

"And spying." He said it with not the least bit of accusation.

I felt my cheeks go hot. "I was not."

"Yes, you were." He sniffed. "But it doesn't matter. Sometimes I catch myself watching her, too."

"Spying on your own sister?" I blurted, then could have kicked myself. What was I doing talking to Derek King anyway?

He pushed his glasses up on his nose. "First of all, she's my half sister."

I tried not to react. I never knew Miss Connie had been married before.

"Second, I really don't know her very well," he said with matter-of-fact ease. "I mean, she left when I was six."

I groped for something to say. I hadn't stopped to think what that would be like—a stranger whisking into town and claiming your own family. For a moment I felt an odd alignment with Derek, which rattled me all the more. Then irritation settled in. Why was he telling me all this?

"I'm sorry," I mumbled.

At that opportune moment, Clarissa emerged from the bathroom. She looked up at Derek and smiled her trusting Clarissa smile—the one that always made the older women at church press her to their bosoms. "Hi."

"Hey, Clarissa. Wanna see some computer games?"

"Sure!"

"Your brother here?" Derek asked me. "He's probably bored as all get out."

The perfect excuse to make my exit. "Probably. I'll find him and send him on back."

"You can come back, too."

Oh, right. As if I wanted to be in Derek King's bedroom. Besides, I had more important things to do. "I'll see."

I found Robert near the food, stuffing his face. "Go see Derek," I told him. "He's got a bunch of games on his computer to show you."

Robert considered the invitation. "Okay." He took a handful of cookies to carry along.

I returned to the living room. Daddy still talked to Mr. Clangerlee. Katherine said something cute to her admirers, then glanced sideways. At that moment, Daddy turned aside from his conversation. Their eyes met. Katherine smiled at him, slow and sultry.

Uh-oh. I had to act fast. As Katherine edged toward Daddy, all I could think to do was beat her to her destination. Trotting past her, I caught Daddy's hand. "Come check out Derek's computer!" I cried. "We gotta get one."

"Uh, okay." He looked at Katherine with an apologetic smile. He must have questioned my motives, but he didn't show it. Good grief, I'd never been interested in computers before in my life.

Soon we hung around Derek's computer, watching Robert play a game about landing a spaceship on Mars.

"What do I do?" Robert demanded as a warning flashed that his craft was low on fuel.

"Go over here"—Derek pointed to the corner of the screen—"and fuel up. While you're there, pick up some extra ammunition 'cause your enemies are gonna show up in a minute."

Before long the room filled with the sound of laser guns and dying aliens. Robert's fingers jabbed and jerked over the controls. Daddy and Clarissa started shouting, "Watch out, over here!" and "Get that one!" Even I began to lose myself in the game. Derek's long fingers jumped here and there across the screen, warning of pitfalls, his body taut with concentration.

"Shoot, shoot, shoot!" he cried. Robert streaked his ship through asteroids, gunning until all enemies fell away.

"Okay, super." Derek punched Robert lightly on the shoulder. "Now go dock to get more fuel."

We all took a deep breath in the momentary lag. "This is some game," Daddy said to Derek.

"Yeah." Derek snatched his glasses off and wiped the lenses with his shirt. "Games like this can teach stuff too, you know. All the math involved in the calculations of time and distance."

"Let's get one, Daddy," Robert said, his eyes glued to the screen.

"Do you have a computer?" Derek looked from Daddy to me. "It'll need to have lots of memory and a pretty decent graphics card to play this game."

Vaguely, I heard Daddy answer that like most of Bradleyville, we were behind the times and still hadn't bought a home computer. But I could only stare at Derek. I'd never seen him without his glasses before. Suddenly his small gray eyes loomed large and warm. He looked so different. Not only normal but actually *good*.

For a split second, his gaze locked with mine. His fingers stilled. I blinked away and focused again on the screen, wondering at the level of craziness to which I'd just descended. Glory, my brain must be overloaded. Out of the corner of my eye I saw Derek consider his glasses as if seeing them for the first time. Then he cleared his throat and jammed them back on his nose.

"Okay," he said to Robert, "ready to go at it?"

Within minutes, we hollered like idiots again.

I didn't even see Katherine enter the room. I'd turned my back to the computer to clack through Derek's games, which sat in a plastic holder on a bookcase. Naturally, Katherine chose that moment to make her stealthy entrance.

"Hi!" I heard Clarissa sing, but it didn't register. By the time I turned around, Katherine stood behind Clarissa and next to Daddy, one long-nailed hand resting on my sister's shoulder as if it belonged there.

"That's it, Robert, you got it!" She turned to Daddy. "Derek's been trying to teach me this game all week. I keep getting killed off."

"Reverse, reverse!" Derek yanked back an imaginary control stick.

"I wouldn't have thought you were the spaceship type," Daddy remarked.

"Are you kidding?" Katherine's eyes sparkled. "This stuff's a blast!"

Daddy's lips curved. Suddenly I thought that computer game must be cursed. Look at the strange things happening around it. Katherine's gaze slid past Daddy to me. She offered me a smile of tentative friendship, without the slightest hint of complicity. And I disliked her even more for it.

"Don't we have to go, Daddy?" I abandoned the box of games.

Daddy turned to me, clearly annoyed with my lack of subtlety. "Jackie, be still; we have a while yet. Besides"—his tone lightened—"I'm hopin' Derek will give me a chance to play."

"Oh, sure," Derek replied, eyes on the screen. His chin jutted out. "There, Robert, go there!"

Today, I understand Daddy's remark as a mere indication of his attraction to Katherine—and nothing more. But at the time his words cut right through me. *How could he put me down like that in front of her?* I thought. I knew he'd made the final comment for her sake—as flimsy proof that he, too, knew how to have a good time. In other words, caught between Katherine and me, Daddy had chosen her.

What that thought did to me, after how close Daddy and I had been since Mama's death. Something heavy and dull balled in my stomach. I swallowed hard.

Katherine didn't look at me. But in the tactful turning of her attention to Clarissa, I knew she understood. The thought that she, a stranger, could so easily see through my daddy—and through me—only made me feel worse. As Daddy focused on the computer, seemingly unaware of what he'd done, my muscles turned wooden.

"I should get back to my other guests," Katherine said quietly and slipped away. Even after she left, the glisten of her presence lingered.

We were among the last to leave.

Daddy and Clarissa had each played the game. Derek offered me a turn, but I would have none of it. By the time we left Derek's bedroom, Robert had persuaded Daddy to buy a computer. My laconic brother talked a blue streak, asking Derek which other games we should buy and on and on.

"Games are just the beginning, Robert," Derek told him. "Wait till you see all the cool stuff you can do on the Internet."

"I don't know a lot about settin' computers up," Daddy said to Derek. "Any chance you might lend some help?"

"Sure." Derek rubbed his thumbs and fingers, his head cocked at that odd angle. He hadn't looked me in the eye since that moment his glasses had been off.

Great, I thought. *Just great*. Derek King in our house. Most likely with Katherine on his heels.

I watched as Daddy said goodbye to Katherine, giving her a brief hug, complimenting her on the food. Her smile at him dazzled. I took my leave of her with stiff politeness, grazing her face with the barest of glances. As the four of us walked to our car I remained silent, aware of how miserably I'd failed and knowing deep within that it would cost us dearly.

chapter 6

In case you hadn't guessed, change in Bradleyville flows at the pace of thick syrup. And most in Bradleyville would say they like things that way.

As long as I can remember, the bench outside the post office has been a favorite resting spot for the older folks. The IGA has sported the same brickwork over its entrance, although some of the new bricks that repaired damage from the tornado stood out lighter in color. The bank still has the sign in one window that reads *Banking with us makes cents*. The hardware store offers a sale on gardening supplies every spring and lightbulbs every winter. And to this day Bradleyville customs and folks' way of talking depict an odd conglomeration of the present and many years past.

All the same, one of the biggest life changes in Bradleyville happens amazingly fast and typically at a young age. Love. Which leads to marriage.

In Bradleyville, folks don't go out with one person this week and someone else the next, not even teenagers. Flirt, perhaps, within respectable boundaries. But then, if you care at all about your reputation—a mighty important thing in Bradleyville—you'll choose the apple of your eye and start polishing. When all is nice and shiny—usually not long after you graduate from high school (unless you go off to college)—you marry. And that's that.

By Bradleyville standards, a twenty-nine-year-old single woman was an old maid. Something had to be sorely wrong with her. Too bossy, too temperamental, or maybe just plain mean. And she wouldn't look so great, either. Which is why you'll find few unmarried men that age in town—the female pickin's fall off at a morbid rate.

And then came Katherine May King.

If she'd stayed in Bradleyville, she'd have married long before. She'd have two or three children by now, teach a Sunday school class, and make heart-shaped cookies on Valentine's Day. Even I would grudgingly admit that Katherine seemed destined for more than Bradleyville could offer. And apparently, she'd managed to collect a wide range of experiences in the great big world. So I had to wonder—*why* had she returned?

Nobody else seemed to be asking this question. In the snatches of conversation I heard, an assumption carried the day: the prodigal daughter had finally come to her senses. For the townspeople, the question wasn't why she'd returned, but why she (or anyone else, for that matter) would ever want to leave Bradleyville in the first place.

If anyone else did wonder, their doubts were apparently silenced by Katherine's staying after church one Sunday to talk to Pastor Beekins. Tears ran down her cheeks as the pastor and she disappeared through a door and into his office. "After long years on my own, I needed to get right with Jesus," she told folks later, her face radiant, "and I'm glad to say he welcomed me back."

And so, despite her bright lipstick and nails, the whole town soon embraced Katherine. The older ladies fawned over her like shepherdesses finding a lost little lamb. "I just know how *glad* your mama is to have you back!" The younger married women subconsciously began to imitate her in ways that ranged from subtle to flagrant. They seemed to stand a little straighter, capture some of her glide in their walks. I saw Miss Ellie Hawkins carrying her baby downtown on an ordinary weekday with her hair done in a French twist. I stood behind Miss Mary Lell at the dime store checkout and watched her count out dollars with painted pink nails. Apparently, red still proved a bit much.

The men remained another matter. The elderly ones flat out flirted with Katherine. The younger ones slid sideways glances at her during church when their wives weren't looking.

And then there was Daddy. The man who'd lost his beloved wife and now struggled to raise three children. The Christian man who remained kind and gentle, and ever ethical in his dealings at the bank. The man who so deserved a beautiful, loving partner after all he'd endured. The man who, apparently, found Katherine May King remarkably attractive.

Bradleyville saw. Bradleyville knew. A few lingering glances between Daddy and Katherine, their few brief touches, and townsfolk assumed it wouldn't be long until Miss Jessie sewed another wedding dress.

Most astounding to me, in the weeks following the Kings' at-home, Daddy didn't stand up and say the town had it all wrong. I just could not understand. Yes, he'd endured much. Yes, he'd lost Mama. So had I.

And no one could ever replace her.

To me, who straddled the worlds of teenager and adult, thirty-five seemed *far* too old to think about dating. There I stood, yearning for my first kiss, while Daddy and Katherine exchanged lingering glances the likes of those between Alison and Jacob in algebra class. I could not grasp this. The world had turned upside down—and no one but me seemed to care.

"Come on," even Alison said one day, "she's so pretty, and she looks so *fun*. Just think of all the things you could do together." Clarissa openly adored Katherine. As for Robert, a few words from him about how "cool" she was spoke volumes.

I wish I could say that my fear of Daddy's being hurt is what fueled me most in those first few weeks. I did carry suspicions—a vague sense that something sat amiss. But looking back, I readily admit that I, full of dreams and desire for passion in my own right, could not accept the unfolding of romance in my daddy's life while it cruelly passed me by. What's more, Katherine's presence always left me feeling that God must have created me in an uninspired moment. The shining star of Katherine May King dimmed whatever luster I possessed.

But Daddy, in those halcyon days of new attraction and the beckoning of promise, found pleasure in allowing his subtle but sure pursuit by Katherine May King.

And the town looked on, smiling.

chapter 7

All four of us wanted the computer in our own bedrooms. Which left Daddy with no choice but to put it on a desk in the corner of the family room. Daddy unpacked it on a Thursday evening, and Derek came over to help with the setup. Katherine did not trail along, although I suspected she wanted to. I had to admit to her sense of propriety. Talking to Daddy at church, smiling at him when she came into the bank, was one thing; crossing our threshold quite another. This was *my* turf.

I made a point of studying in my bedroom while Derek worked in our house. I'd felt awkward around him ever since the at-home. Not because of that fleeting moment of weirdness between us; that I'd long since chalked up to the surrounding anxiety of the moment. But because of the obvious growing attraction between his half sister and my father. What had Derek and I to say to one another? What *could* we say?

"Jackie." Daddy stuck his head in my door around nine o'clock. "Derek's all done. You need to come say thank you."

"Don't worry about it," I heard Derek mutter as I pushed back from my desk. He stood in our hallway, head tilted, one hand shoved in his pocket.

"Thanks so much, Derek," I offered, meaning it. I knew he'd probably come straight over from work. "I don't know when you'll have time to do homework tonight."

"Or eat a full supper for that matter," Daddy added.

Derek lifted a shoulder. "I'll be okay. Don't need that much sleep anyway." He glanced at me, then considered the floor. "Well." He turned to Daddy. "Thanks again for the sandwich."

"Hey, the least I could do." Daddy opened the door.

"And if you run into trouble, just give me a call." Derek threw me a shadow of a smile and stepped out onto our porch. Daddy and I followed to see him off.

"He's a nice kid," Daddy remarked as we watched him drive away. "Mighty smart."

"Mighty strange, too."

Daddy focused on something in the distance. "Not strange, Jackie. Just different. He's—himself. That takes a strong person."

"Uh-huh." I pursed my mouth, irritated at his defense of Derek. I couldn't help but think he'd said it just because Derek was Katherine's brother.

An hour later in my bedroom I sang along to "I Want You Back" by 'NSync. I'd already seen Clarissa and Robert to bed. Daddy knocked on my door, saying he needed to talk to me again. Instinctively, I knew what the topic would be. *No, no, no,* I thought. Couldn't we talk tomorrow? How about next week, next year? How about never?

"Okay," I mumbled and turned off my radio.

Daddy lowered himself to the edge of my bed and crossed his ankles, hands clasped between his knees. I waited. He regarded me with an expression of love and sadness that sent darts through my chest.

"I suppose you've guessed what I want to talk to you about."

A stillness gathered within me. I nodded.

He inhaled slowly. "I don't know if I can do this very well. Just hear me out, okay?"

"Okay."

He focused on his thumbs, lining them up side by side. "It's been a long road for me since your mama's death, Jackie, as it's been for you. In the last few weeks, I've felt an anticipation about life that's been gone for a long time. Katherine . . . is an unusual person. She has many fine qualities, and I would like to start spending some time with her to get to know her better."

He paused, awaiting a reaction. I remained silent, denials humming through my head.

"You kids are the most important thing, though; I hope you know that. Robert and Clarissa like Katherine a lot. I'm mostly concerned about you. I'd like you to be honest with me about what you're feeling. And I want to tell you that I don't know where all this will lead. I simply want the chance to explore where it may go, and I can only do that by spending time with Katherine. Not that I need your permission. But

I do want your understanding. Mostly, I don't want you to be hurt. This doesn't in any way mean I love you less. And it doesn't mean I loved your mama any less. Do you hear me, Jackie? *No one* will ever replace your mama. If I could have her back right now, believe me, I would." His voice dropped. "But at the same time, after her death, I have to go on. Our family has to go on. Any future we may find does not take away from the past."

My eyes flicked around the room, over the posters of singing groups and my schoolbooks stacked on the desk. A framed certificate from my cheerleading days hung crookedly on the wall, and before I knew it, I'd moved across the floor to straighten it. My gymnastics trophies sat slightly askew on top of my bookcase, and I straightened them too. A hair clip lay on the floor. I picked it up and tossed it into the butterfly dish on my dresser.

"Jackie."

"This room is so messy." I threw my shoes into the closet. Shoved a sweater into a drawer. My hands shook, hovering before me as I searched madly for something else to do. I glanced in the mirror and saw Daddy watching me, tension pulling at his lips. Left to no other device then, I turned and dropped back into my chair.

"Okay," I said, defeated. "You want to go out with Katherine King? Fine. Why talk to me about it; what do you want me to do? Watch the kids at night while you're gone, is that it? Like that's a problem. I take care of everything around here anyway."

"Jackie—"

"All my friends are startin' to date now," I rushed on, my voice turning tinny, off-key. "You wanted me to go out, too; remember how we talked about that? 'Course now I won't have the chance. But maybe *you* could double-date with my friends, wouldn't that be nice."

Sadness filled Daddy's eyes. "Jackie," he said quietly, "I hoped you could be happy for me, knowing that I have healed enough from grief over your mama's death to become attracted to someone. I know that I'm speaking very plainly to you of adult things, when you're just a child yourself. But because you're far more mature than most girls your age, and because you've taken care of this family so well—I thought we might be able to talk about this."

Anger sucked up my veins. No fair, the way he trapped me. Using my very maturity to tell me I should understand. "We *are* talking about it."

He nodded. "Okay. That we are."

Part of me rose to another plane then, looking down at myself, miserable and rooted in my chair. I gripped its armrest until all energy and offense drained out my fingers. *God, I hate this! You can't let this happen!*

"Okay, Daddy," I managed, "I'm sorry. I'm . . . I *am* happy that you're happy."

"Thank you. I know this is hard for you."

I focused on my knees, pinpricks in my eyes.

"I thought it might be easiest if we first invite Katherine to supper Saturday. Just an informal meal so we can all get to know her a little better."

My face muscles froze. Come to supper. I knew what that meant. Everybody in Bradleyville my daddy's age and older knew what that meant. It would signal to the town that their dating had officially begun, just as it had in the days when Daddy went out with Mama. Daddy seemed to read my thoughts.

"It's not the big deal it used to be." He spread his hands. "Times have changed. I'm only suggesting it so that all four of us can be with Katherine. It's best for all of us."

True, the days of "coming to supper" were over. I only knew the term's meaning through stories from Mama. But it remained part of Daddy's history. Ancient meanings of the heart didn't change.

"I'll cook," Daddy offered, wheedling me with a little smile.

My throat tightened. "Oh, Daddy, you couldn't cook if your life depended on it."

He feigned hurt. "Well. We'll have frozen dinners, then."

"Like *that* would make a great impression," I replied with bitterness. "Especially after she's displayed such talent."

"Is that what this is about? You worried about cooking for her?"

Yeah, right. I shot him a look.

"Okay, okay." He sighed, dropping all pretense. "Will you do this, Jackie? Will you just . . . give it a chance?"

I gazed at Daddy, wanting so much to be happy for him, but too steeped in my own hurt to feel anything else. His eyes pleaded for my understanding. Fleetingly, I wondered what he would do if I told him I could never, ever accept Katherine King. Then I thought of his siding with her during the at-home and told myself I didn't want to know.

"I'll make a nice supper." I tried to smile.

"Thank you for tryin'." He started to say more, then apparently thought best of it. Instead he rose and crossed to my chair to hug me. "Just keep it simple, all right?"

I closed my eyes. *Nothing* about this would be simple. "Yeah, Daddy. Sure."

chapter 8

Pork medallions with orange glaze. Wild rice. Broccoli and cheese casserole topped with dried onion pieces. Spinach salad and fresh-baked herb bread. Peach cobbler and whipped cream. No matter that I'd not made even one of these recipes before. I merely chose the most exotic dishes I could find, poring Friday afternoon over Mama's cookbooks.

Herein lay my fallacious A+B=C logic: A—I would demonstrate that my skills in the kitchen could stand up to Katherine's. B—Katherine would realize there was neither room nor need for another female in the Delham family. C—Through sheer intimidation, she'd quell her pursuit of my father.

Such colorful rationale that strutted before me, fluffing its plumage.

I realize now the underlying, driving need to this logic—the need that Katherine's appearance in my life had wrought. The need that, at the time, had anyone dared name it, I would heatedly have denied.

In proving myself to Katherine, I would prove myself to me.

After supper on Friday, I drove to the IGA to buy all the ingredients.

"I thought we decided you wouldn't go to any great trouble," Daddy said when I told him where I was headed.

"Don't worry, I'm not. But I still need a few things." I wouldn't look at him. "Oh, Daddy," I said as I turned to leave, "would you fetch the bread machine down from the cabinet above the fridge?"

Half an hour later as I lugged two bags of groceries into the house, Robert met me in the kitchen. "Where's Daddy?" I asked.

"In the backyard, pullin' weeds." He rescued a bag from my lagging arms and dropped it on the counter.

"And Clarissa?"

"Playin' with Della."

Winnie trotted across the floor, ears up. I petted her quickly. "Go on now, out of my way." She paced to her favorite spot between the table and wall and huffed down, tags clinking against the floor.

"Maybe we oughtta let Katherine bring the dessert," Robert offered.

"I'll make my own, thank you very much."

"Well, you'll have to work pretty hard to beat her cookies."

"Thanks a bunch, Robert, but I am *not* working hard to 'beat' her at anything." I pulled a package of cheese from a bag. "Any other wise remark you'd like to add?"

He regarded me with mild perplexity. "No."

"Good." I turned away from him. "Now get lost. I have work to do."

"Like what?"

"Like cooking."

He peered into the other bag. "But we just had supper."

"I'm cooking for tomorrow night, you idgit."

I bustled about, too busy to look him in the eye. He sidled in front of me. "I thought you weren't workin' to beat her."

"I'm not." I pulled the tenderloin out and plunked it in the sink.

"Then why are you actin' like the Queen a Sheba's comin'?"

I fisted my hands on my hips. "Would you get out of here? Go play on the computer. Better yet, take Winnie outside and brush her."

"So what are we havin', caviar?"

"Out!" I shooed him away like a pesky animal.

After my brother's departure, I finished unpacking the groceries, then stood in the kitchen thinking, fingers pressed to my lips.

"Need any help?" Daddy stuck his head through the back kitchen door. Sweat dribbled down his forehead, the knees of his old jeans stained with dirt.

"No, Daddy," I said quickly. "Just do your weeding; I'll be fine."

He eyed the food spread across the counter. "You sure? I could look mighty good in an apron."

"Uh-huh."

He wiggled his eyebrows, then pulled his head back out the door.

"Jackie!" Clarissa banged in through the front door, Della at her heels. "Can I spend the night at Della's house? Her mama said it was okay."

I looked to Della for agreement, and she bounced her curly head up and down. At normal size for a nine-year-old, Della stood a good head taller than Clarissa. "Is your room clean?" I asked my sister.

"Yuh-huh." She jiggled on her toes. "Pleeeease."

Perfect, I thought. Get her out of my way for the evening. "Okay."

"Yay!" both girls cried, then flitted toward Clarissa's room.

"Come show me what you've packed before you leave," I called after them.

My thoughts immediately scudded back to the task at hand. I could mix the casserole tonight. And whip the cream. And fix the table. Also assemble the spinach salad and make its dressing. That was about it. Everything else would have to wait till tomorrow.

I never dreamed that anything might go wrong.

As I cooked feverishly on Saturday, by 1:30 I still had everything well under control. Clarissa played at Della's, and Daddy prepared to leave with Robert for his softball game. Normally we'd all have gone, but I informed Daddy that he couldn't possibly expect me to set supper on the table at 6:00 when the game would run until 5:00.

"Jackie." He regarded me askance. "Are you sure you're okay?"

I busily peeled an orange. "Of course, Daddy, what a question."

"I just want you to *enjoy* this supper. Katherine won't mind if everything's not perfect, you know."

No kidding.

"Well, I'll just do the best I can." I looked up at him, struck by his anxious expression. My fingers stilled, the tangy sweet scent of the orange wafting through the kitchen. Quickly, I turned back, intent on my work. "You'd better fetch Robert; he's supposed to be there now."

Daddy ran a gentle hand down my hair, then disappeared.

"Oh," I muttered. I needed to put the ingredients for the bread in the machine. It would take four hours to bake. Time was of the essence; a delayed supper would hardly display the utmost of culinary talent. Hurriedly, I assembled the flour, salt, and the rest, measured them into the machine, and flicked it on. Then back to peeling and squeezing oranges for the glaze.

By 3:00 I'd fallen into a mild state of panic. Making pie crust was hard! The first batch felt like rubber when I tried to roll it out. I threw the whole mess into the trash and started over. The second batch of crust still seemed tough, but it would have to do. I floured a cutting board and rolled and rolled for the bottom of the cobbler, then cut the remains into thick strips for the top. The peaches were bubbling in a pan. I had to assemble the dessert and pop it in the oven right away so it would be done in time to slide the meat in at 4:30. The kitchen looked like a train wreck—flour on the counter, over my apron, on the floor. I brushed hair out of my eyes with the back of my hand and feverishly assembled the cobbler. I yanked open the oven door, leaving white fingerprints on the handle, and shoved the pan inside.

That's when it occurred to me that I hadn't allowed time to fix myself up before supper. I could hardly serve a dignified meal with flour in my hair. I'd planned on cleaning up the kitchen too. The rest of the house already shone.

Well, I'd just have to decide—kitchen or me.

I took a deep breath and checked the time. I should call Clarissa home. She'd have to put her things away, take a bath. Which I had no time to oversee.

I washed dough off my hands and dialed Della's number. She huffily told me that Clarissa had gone over to Alma Sue's.

"Why'd she go there?" I demanded, piling pans and utensils into the sink.

"Why does she always go to Alma Sue's? To eat candy, that's why."

Oh, great.

For some reason God places a flaw in even the most adorable of creatures. To this day, Clarissa's is her love for candy. She's learned to curb her desires, I'm happy to report. But back then no matter what plans she might hold in her pretty little head, dangle any sugary concoction before her, and they'd melt away like ice on a hot brick.

"I *hate* Alma Sue," Della burst out. "She steals Clarissa away from me all the time."

"Sorry, Della. Clarissa shouldn't have gone."

"I told Mama. She said, 'Don't worry. When the candy's gone, she'll be back.'"

Ouch. Bad enough I knew my sister's weakness, but to hear a neighbor peg her so well. The thought incensed me. Just wait till Clarissa got home. Didn't she find it even the tiniest bit demeaning that she allowed herself to be enticed away from her most loyal friend week after week?

"When she comes back, Della, send her home, okay? We're having company for supper, and she needs to get cleaned up."

Clarissa dragged in at 4:25, sticky-cheeked and frowning. I took one irritable look at her and declared she was headed for the bathtub. She balked, saying her stomach didn't feel so hot. "Wonder why," I retorted. "How much candy did you eat?"

"Don't be mad at me, Jackie." Her face crumpled.

Brother. I hauled her to the bathtub and turned on the faucets. Behind schedule or not, I couldn't let her do that herself. Our hot water could scald in no time flat. She lay down on the floor, holding her belly. As the water ran, I coaxed her out of her clothes. She climbed into the tub, and I rubbed her forehead, like stroking a kitten.

I really can't blame the burnt cobbler on Clarissa. Truth is, I'd forgotten to set the timer. Back in the kitchen, as I languished over the sight of blackened crust, I realized I hadn't put the pork in the oven. I shoved the meat in and banged the door shut.

Well, fine. We'd have ice cream for dessert.

I started in on the glaze. Stir and stir, don't let it burn. Then the rice. I wondered how Clarissa was doing in the tub. The kitchen clock happily ticked past 5:00. That's the last I remember checking it.

Clarissa crept out to the kitchen and lay down on the hard floor near the table, holding her stomach. No doubt so I could have an unobstructed view of her suffering. I moved her to the family room couch, letting Winnie into the house to keep her company. I dawdled over my sister for a moment, making sad faces at her discomfort, covered her with a blanket, and gave her some medicine. Then rushed back to the kitchen. Stirred the glaze, watched the rice. Slowly, the burnt smell from the cobbler faded, replaced with the scents of the meat, bread, and orange sauce.

The phone rang. It was Mrs. Crary, home from the softball game, saying their team had won, 3–2. But Daddy had asked her to tell me they'd be delayed getting home thanks to Robert's fighting with a player on the opposing team.

"Robert, in a *fight?*" I couldn't imagine my mellow brother fighting about anything.

"I just don't know what got into 'em," she declared. Anyhow, Daddy wouldn't bring Robert home until he'd made up with the boy from Albertsville and apologized to the boy's father, to boot, Mrs. Crary continued. And when they did get home, I'd better have some ice ready for Robert's bruised cheek. "It'll swell sure as you're livin'."

I hung up the phone, dazed.

When I heard the garage door open, I was just about to trash the cobbler. Daddy strode in, grim-faced, Robert trailing him with the same expression. My brother's left eye was purpling, his cheek already swollen.

I wanted to strangle him. "You picked a fine day to take up fightin'."

"Now, don't start in, Jackie." Daddy's voice sounded tight. He jerked open a drawer for a plastic bag and began filling it with ice.

"Fine, then, I don't have time anyway. I'm tryin' to get supper on the table, the cobbler burnt, and Clarissa's got a stomachache 'cause she ate too much candy at Alma Sue's."

Daddy's shoulders dropped. If I hadn't been thinking of myself so much, I might have realized how anxious he felt, Katherine soon to arrive on our doorstep, and the household falling apart.

"Here," he commanded Robert, handing him the ice bag, "put this on your cheek for five minutes, then go take a shower."

Robert sulked down the hall, and Clarissa called for Daddy. He went in to commiserate with her. I whirled about, trying to clean up the worst of the flour, telling myself I'd just have to keep Katherine out of the kitchen. And somewhere in that process, the orange glaze started bubbling, which it wasn't supposed to do. Seeing how thick it turned, I madly peeled an extra orange—the one I'd planned to use for garnish—and squeezed the juice into the pan. Then I took it off the burner. By the time I remembered to rescue the broccoli casserole from the oven, its onion topping resembled the crust on my cobbler. For the second time that afternoon, a burning smell seeped through the kitchen. The meat looked done. I turned off the oven.

The bread machine dinged. I opened it to take out the loaf. *Please, God, let one thing be right.* Flat as a pancake. I could only gape, arguing with it in my head. *Why didn't you rise, what's the matter with you, stupid machine?* Until it hit me that I'd forgotten to add yeast.

"Aaah!" I stood in the middle of the kitchen, digging fingers into my scalp.

"Everything all right in there?" Daddy called.

"*Nothin's* right! This is a total *disaster!*"

And then, in the next five seconds, Daddy said he'd be in to help; Clarissa protested; Robert rounded the corner from the hall, half his face bulbous and his nose wrinkling at the burnt smell; the doorbell rang; and Winnie pounded toward the entryway, barking her fool head off.

chapter 9

Katherine May King swept across our threshold, chin high and a stunning smile on her lips. If she smelled burned food, she didn't let on. "Hello!" she cried, as if entering our presence defined the most anticipated moment of her life. She wore navy blue pants and a white ribbed top, somehow splendid in their simplicity. A slim golden bracelet shone on her arm as she reached for my hand. "Jackie, thank you so much for having me."

I took her hand briefly, willing the surprise not to show on my face. For a moment, my dislike of her wavered. She had so easily recognized me as hostess, the one in charge of the home. "You're welcome," I replied a little stiffly.

Katherine's sleek black hair brushed her cheeks as she bent to pet Winnie, who welcomed her with wiggling stubby tail. "Well, hello there," Katherine cooed. She straightened and laid a hand on Daddy's arm. "Hello, Bobby."

The way she touched him, said his name. My fingers curled into the front of my dirty apron.

Robert sauntered into the entryway to smile lopsidedly at Katherine, then dropped his gaze to the floor.

"Oh, what *happened* to you, Robert?" Katherine tipped up his chin to get a better look, concern on her brow. I fully expected Robert to do what he normally would—mumble something unintelligible and turn aside. Instead, he raised his eyes and considered her for a moment. She waited him out.

"Got into a fight after the game."

"That I can see." Her tone sounded dry. "But why?"

Lots of luck, I thought. I doubted Daddy had even gotten an answer to that question.

Shame flicked across my brother's forehead. Then he shrugged. "He called Bradleyville a dirty name."

My eyes bugged. I flicked a look at Daddy, who apparently thought the moment so monumental that he dared not move.

"Ah." Katherine nodded sagely. She pulled her fingers away from Robert's chin. "I take it you beat his team."

"Uh-huh."

She gave him a knowing look. "No wonder he felt small."

I watched the amazing insight smooth my brother's features. He made no response. But his shoulders squared, and he abandoned attempts to hide his battered face.

Katherine turned to me with an unassuming smile, as if she hadn't just orchestrated a minor miracle. "The house smells wonderful. Your daddy said you've been cooking since last night."

I blinked at news of such betrayal. It hadn't occurred to me that Daddy would spoil my veneer of insouciant chef. "I've just learned to space out my work so that everything gets done on time," I said coolly. "Would you please excuse me now? I need to finish getting things ready."

I turned and took my leave. The silence fairly echoed behind me. I pictured Daddy and Katherine exchanging adult glances and hoped I was wrong. I could not bear to think that they saw right through me.

In the kitchen, I leaned against a counter and took a deep breath. I had to salvage what I could of my ruinous efforts. Time no longer mattered. If we didn't eat until 7:00, so be it.

From the family room drifted the sounds of Katherine greeting Clarissa, who still languished on the couch. After her flawless performance with Robert, I could only imagine the encore she'd saved for my sister. For all I knew she already sat on the couch, Clarissa bundled and breathing like a contented bunny on her lap.

I threw a wooden spoon into the sink none too gently.

A good dose of resolve can make up for lack of experience, especially when you're feeling as cantankerous as I was. In the next half hour, I climbed to a whole new level of skills. First, I peeled the burnt crust off the cobbler and discovered the fruit in the middle to be perfectly fine. I spooned the usable portion into five bowls and set them aside. When dessert time came, I'd add a spoon of ice cream and a dollop of whipped cream, and no one would be the wiser. But what to do with the telltale glass pan? I certainly had no time to clean it. Frantically, I looked around, then shoved it into a cabinet.

Next, I ditched the blackened onion topping from the broccoli, then took a taste. None the worse for wear, though no longer hot. Well, I'd nuke it.

The bread tasted good but was hard and looked like it had been run over by a truck. I stared at it, willing it to tell me what to do. The idea drifted into my head like a cool breeze on a sizzling day. Wasn't expectation often three-quarters of the problem? With some force, I sliced the loaf into small pieces of "homemade herb crackers."

To the orange mixture I added a bit of cream for thinning. No longer a glaze, but it proved an intriguingly flavored sauce.

Katherine materialized from the family room. "May I help?" she asked.

"No," I said a little too forcefully. "Thank you." I continued working, the competent homemaker preparing for the guest. She left without a word. I heard her voice, then Clarissa giggled. My, hadn't my sister recovered in a hurry.

Little left to do but fill the glasses and set out salads. When that was done, I bustled into my room to brush my hair and check my face. I'd wanted to put on a little makeup, but no time for that now.

By 6:40 we sat at the dining room table.

Daddy said a fervent prayer, thanking God for Katherine's presence. The way Robert smiled at her afterward made me feel sorry I'd placed her on his side of the table. Clarissa ogled her as well. And Daddy looked . . . I couldn't put my finger on the word. And then felt sorry when I did.

Expectant.

The whole family had obviously gone crazy. Even Winnie forgot how to act. She trotted up to the table and nudged Katherine's arm with her long nose, begging for a pat.

"Winnie!" I said sharply. "We're eating. Go lie down."

Winnie had something in common with Clarissa. They both couldn't hide an emotion if their lives depended on it. Winnie's ears went back and her head hung. She turned away with a doggy sigh and dragged herself theatrically from the room. A few seconds later, we heard her flop upon her bed near the laundry room.

"Oh, how cute," Katherine exclaimed. "She knows just what you said."

I managed a little smile, inordinately pleased that our dog had displayed her awareness of who was boss in the house.

My meal turned out amazingly well. Katherine voiced her pleasure over every dish without sounding placating. That threw me, I can tell you. I'd have had a much easier time disliking her if she'd oohed and aahed with abandonment. Instead, she asked me questions, one competent chef to another. How long had I cooked the orange sauce? Was that mushroom soup she tasted in the broccoli casserole? And which herbs were in the crackers?

"Katherine worked as a caterer for how long, five years?" Daddy offered. "She could probably talk to you about recipes all day."

"Miss Jessie told me," I replied. Suddenly I wondered if Katherine would see my dessert as a reconstruction.

"Are you able to eat, honey?" Katherine asked Clarissa. "You don't want to miss your sister's wonderful meal."

"A little." Clarissa's forehead etched with martyrdom as she picked at her food.

I gave my sister a pointed look. "I don't know when you're going to learn not to stuff yourself with candy." I turned to Katherine. "I watch how much she eats here. But when she's at a friend's house . . ." I sighed.

Daddy shot me a glance. I pretended not to notice.

The conversation lulled, and Katherine began asking questions. She pulled more information out of us than I'd ever have imagined. She asked Robert about school and softball. He answered her queries and more, adding details about his friends and not-so-favorite teachers. And by the way, did she know that today was the first time he'd ever gotten into a fight? Clarissa alternately giggled over her games with Della and complained of how Alma Sue always got her way.

"Why is that?" Katherine wondered.

"Well, for one thing"—Clarissa twisted her mouth—"she's a lot bigger than me and my other friends. All her older sisters and brothers are big, too. And she's better at stuff than anybody. She runs faster and jumps higher and kicks balls farther, and everything."

"Yeah," Robert added, "and she's got a much bigger mouth."

Katherine raised her eyebrows at Daddy. "She does tend to boss the other kids around," he said.

"Especially Clarissa." I shook my head. "Alma Sue towers over her, and she's not above using her height to get what she wants."

Clarissa took a tiny bite of meat and shrugged.

Daddy told stories about various customers at the bank. How old Mrs. Watlin, who lived in the country, came in wearing a different outlandish hat each time, and how Mr. Hetherbockam always had his miniature poodle prancing around his feet. I listened to Daddy tell his tales with growing dismay. We hadn't talked this animatedly at the table since ... well, since Mama had been with us. Now here he was, unfolding in Katherine's presence like some hearty blossom in the sun.

The pork tenderloin and sauce lost its flavor. I set my fork down.

"You done eating?" Daddy asked.

"I did a lot of sampling in the kitchen."

Before Katherine could start pestering me with questions, I turned to her with a hostess-polite smile. *Know thine enemy*, as they say. "So tell us about you."

Katherine swept a lock of hair behind an ear. She leaned back in her chair, one forearm on the table. Although I could feel the chilly vibrations rising off my shoulders, she didn't seem to notice. "There's not a great deal to tell. You knew my grandma Wilma, I'm sure. And you know my parents and brother."

Miss Wilma had been a prayer warrior in our church until her death five years ago. This family information was hardly what I cared about, but since Katherine had brought up the subject ... "You're really Derek's half sister, aren't you?"

I didn't dare look at Daddy, after such a rude question.

Katherine didn't miss a beat. "Yes, that's true. Mama married Jason King when I was six months old, so he's been the only dad I've ever known. They didn't have Derek for another twelve years."

I forced as much friendliness as possible into my voice. "What about when you left Bradleyville? You went to the University of Kentucky for a while, right? But then you started working? What all have you done since then?"

"Bet you didn't know we'd play Twenty Questions," Daddy remarked to Katherine with a frowning glance at me.

"Oh, no matter." She played with the bracelet on her wrist, pushing it toward her hand, letting it fall, pushing it up again, letting it fall. "I don't mind answering." She shifted in her chair, then offered me a small smile.

I can't say what it was exactly. Maybe the way she toyed with the bracelet. Maybe her self-conscious smile. Whatever the reason, for the first time I glimpsed a hairline crack in the smooth sheen of Katherine's poise. I'd hit on something. She didn't like to talk about those years outside Bradleyville. Now here's the surprising part. Given my attitude, you might assume I felt glad for her discomfort. But I didn't. In fact, I felt something far different. The moment I sensed her anxiety about proving herself to me was the moment Katherine May King became human.

"Well, I'll be honest," she began. "I left Bradleyville to go to school. But I soon discovered that I really just wanted to experience *life*."

Funny how she made that word breathe with longing and dreams and . . . passion. I understood all that. Suddenly, I realized that Katherine was speaking of when she'd been eighteen, not much older than I. What a thought—that she and I would have something in common.

After only one semester at the University of Kentucky, Katherine took a job in the office of a radio station. She worked there for two years, loving the music (top forty hits), and even getting free tickets to concerts. Then she worked as a caterer for another two years. At twenty-three, she moved to California with a girlfriend, working in San Diego as an office assistant, then again as a caterer. After that, she worked for the City of San Diego in the tourism department. Finally, she just got tired of it all and wanted to go home. She returned to Bradleyville.

Mighty short story, I thought. What about boyfriends? Surely Katherine had been pursued by hordes of men. There had to be things she wasn't telling us. Important things.

"Are you gonna stay here now?" Clarissa pressed. "'Cause I don't want you to go."

Robert took a purposeful drink of iced tea, as if Katherine's answer concerned him not in the least.

"Yes, I am," Katherine told my sister firmly. Maybe a little too firmly. "I've seen enough of the world, Miss Clarissa. I'm ready to settle down."

The moment the words left her mouth, Katherine realized their dual meaning. She blushed. Lowering her eyes, she worked at placing her knife just so across her plate.

"I can understand you're wantin' to do all those interesting things." Daddy sprang to her rescue. "But I know what you mean about bein' back here, near family. I never even wanted to leave, myself."

My throat tightened at that. He'd never wanted to leave because Mama had been here. Every state in the country could have beckoned with golden opportunities, and he wouldn't have been tempted to go. Now Mama was gone, and Katherine King sat at our table, talking of her adventures, declaring them behind her. And Daddy nodded his head, saying he understood when I knew he didn't, not at all. What adventure had he ever pursued in his life? What had he done, other than be completely, achingly, content to live in Bradleyville, married to Mama?

At that moment, I didn't know who I understood more, Daddy or Katherine. My sudden confusion made me feel as if I'd been buffeted by some wild wind into unfamiliar territory. I didn't like that feeling one bit. Abruptly, I pushed away from the table. "Time for dessert."

With concentrated efficiency, I stacked plates and whisked them into the kitchen.

chapter 10

Mama knew this day would come.

I pushed that thought away easily enough as I served dessert. As I played hostess and poured coffee. As I whirled through the kitchen, wiping every sticky square of tile and cleaning every dirty dish. Including the blackened glass pan I'd shoved into a cabinet. I even managed to block the thought as we bade Katherine goodbye and watched her glide down our sidewalk to her car. I saw Clarissa to bed, accepted Daddy's gratitude and accolades for supper, shook my head over Robert's shiner as I bade him good night. Finally, then, I had nothing to do but retire to my room and slump, exhausted, upon my bed. I did not bother to turn on the light but did turn my radio on low. One of my favorite songs played.

If only you would see me for all my soul can bare,
The inside of me, the best of me, the part I long to share . . .

Picking at my bedspread, I stared vacantly at the posters of singers on my wall, my mind elsewhere. Thinking, *Mama knew.*

Some things in this world cannot be adequately described. One is watching your mama, bubbly, full of life, waste away into a rag doll of pain and sedation. Through the summer of 1996 she went in and out of the hospital. Finally they sent her home to die. When the pain tied her face in knots, we gave her extra medication and prayed for drugged sleep to hurry. Other times, Mama would be more lucid. I think she saved her most important thoughts for those moments, spilling them like picked blossoms from an apron. During one of those times she called me to her side—alone—to prepare me for this day. I did not want to hear what she had to say.

"Mama." My throat pinched as I sat beside her on the bed. "Don't talk now."

"I know it's hard." Her voice rasped. "Hard to talk about rebuildin' when the tearin' down's not even through yet. But hear me out, Jackie, then you can set these words aside. They'll come to you again when you need them."

Mama laid frail fingers over mine. "I've watched you, Jackie. I know what's happenin' to you. You used to be full of laughter, never a care in the world. Now that's gone, and you're busy with cares you shouldn't have to face. Cookin' and cleanin', watchin' your brother and sister." She stopped to swallow. I reached for the glass of water on her night-stand and put the bent straw to her lips. She drank with strained concentration.

"After I'm gone," she continued, and I began to shake my head, *no, no, no*. Mama patted my hand. "Listen to me, Jackie, you've been actin' like a grownup; now I'm goin' to talk to you like one." Her face blurred. "I know what you'll do. You'll keep on carin' for the family, takin' over my place. You will grieve, and so will your daddy. It will take a long time, but slowly your daddy will get better. Stronger. And one day, he's goin' to find someone else."

I could not talk to her about this, I could *not*.

Mama gave a little smile. "He has my blessing in that; I've already told him so. Your daddy has much to give, and I don't want him bein' alone the rest of his life. Robert and Clarissa are young enough to be all right with that, I think. What I'm afraid is, it will be hardest for you."

I could find no response.

Her eyelids slipped shut, and she fluttered them open. Her words fell to a mere whisper. "God will send your daddy who he needs. Don't fight his choice. Just pray a lot and try to look to the future. Give her a chance."

These words will come to you again when you need them.

"How could you know?" I moaned that night Katherine came to supper, nearly two years after the horrible conversation. Was I really supposed to be glad Katherine May King had entered our lives? Would Mama expect me to just welcome her with open arms, despite my mis-givings? Part of me wanted to like her. The other part of me wondered about those eleven years, and what she hadn't told us.

Please, God, help us. I tipped my head toward the ceiling. *Please help me know what to do. And don't let Daddy be hurt. None of us can stand any more hurt.*

I prayed more and cried some. Finally, after midnight, I crept beneath the covers, leaving my radio on to rock me to sleep.

Not until I awoke Sunday morning did I realize I still wore my apron.

chapter 11

Over the next two weeks as my brother's bruised face slowly mended, Katherine visited our house six times, her luminosity filling the rooms. Clarissa took to asking Daddy when she'd come next. At Katherine's arrival, she'd bound to the door like a wayward fawn prancing into an open field. Even Robert's face lit up when Katherine hugged him. And Daddy stood back and watched them both, an ancient happiness gleaming in his eyes. Then he'd turn those eyes on me, on my ambivalent smiles and cautious acceptance, and the light would falter like some sputtering lamp.

Katherine seemed unfazed by my chilled response, allowing me my space. She never forced hugs, yet was warm. She asked me about school without seeming to pry. We talked about music, my favorite groups and songs. She'd try to help in the kitchen, but did no more than I allowed. I couldn't find fault with anything she did, really. Still, I could not allow myself to embrace Katherine King.

I walked around feeling confused and out of sorts. I wanted to be happy for Daddy. I *was* happy for him. But I also felt scared to death and, admittedly, somewhat jealous. Why did this sudden happiness and excitement in our home have to be because of Katherine? Why did we need an outsider to show us what joy we had lacked?

And, of course, I had to deal with my emotions while the whole town watched, for Bradleyville being Bradleyville, the news of Katherine's visits spread quickly. The desirous glances between Katherine King and Bobby Delham were leading to exactly what everyone had hoped for. Well, almost everyone. Grandma and Grandpa Delham were thrilled, but at church Mama's parents treated Katherine with reserved politeness. I'd never been as close to them as Grandma and Grandpa Delham, but for once I leaned more toward their sentiments.

"Jackie!" Mrs. Clangerlee beamed knowingly at me one day as she checked out my groceries. "How are things going at your house?"

"Fine."

"Well." She picked up a bag of frozen corn as if it were a wondrous thing. "I'm surely glad for y'all. I surely am."

I managed a tight little smile.

At school the boys teased me no end. Billy Sullivan waited until a crowd had gathered to drape a muscular arm around my shoulders. "Hey, Jackie, I hear Derek's available." He leaned in close, and in spite of my irritation, my heart did an odd little dance. "Y'all might as well keep it in the family."

I shrugged away, disdain on my face. The problem with Billy, I told myself as my ankles trembled, was that he knew his own good looks.

"What's the matter, Billy?" I looked at him out the corner of my eye. "Afraid I'm too much for *you* to handle?"

"Oooooh." His friends sucked in a collective breath and exploded into laughter. Billy blinked, then recovered by pretending to faint at my feet. I flounced away without looking back. But my shoulder still tingled from the warmth of his hand.

"Oh, my," Alison sighed later that day. "Guess the cat's totally out of the bag."

"Yeah, and it's got claws, too." I shoved a book into my locker and yanked out another.

"Well, things could be worse. I mean like Billy practically *hugged* you."

I banged shut my locker and shot her a look. "I wasn't talking about things here at school, Alison. I was talking about *her.*"

"Oh." Alison's shoulders rose. "Sorry."

We headed down the hall toward our next class. "But you like her some, right? And Clarissa and Robert still think she's great? And isn't your daddy happy?"

"Yes, to all of that," I said glumly.

"So what's up, Jackie? I don't get it."

I skidded to a stop, fingers pressing into my books. "What if she's not like she says she is, huh? What if she . . . disappoints us?"

I wanted to say the rest of it but couldn't admit the depth of my pettiness. Even then I recognized that Alison's very empathy bared the darkness of my soul. I, who worked myself silly serving my family, now begrudged their joy, partly because I felt left out. Everyone, including my daddy, was falling in love but me. It didn't help matters any that Alison was now officially going out with Jacob. I didn't even have a close friend to commiserate with over my loneliness.

Alison peered at me, forehead wrinkling with concern. "Things will be okay, Jackie, you'll see. Just—be thankful. After losing your mama and everything bein' so horrible, finally you and your family have a chance to be happy again. I know," she added quickly, "that Katherine will never replace your mama. But she can give y'all new things to look forward to." Alison sucked a portion of her lower lip between two teeth. "She can be a friend to you, Jackie. Don't look at her as tryin' to replace. Look at her like a new friend."

I forced a nod. Alison's words reminded me of Mama's. "Yeah, you're right. Thanks."

She gave me a lopsided smile, then headed for her seat.

Only Derek seemed completely unfazed by the budding relationship. Even as my girlfriends whispered questions and the boys slid meaningful gazes between him and me, he said nothing. Perhaps he didn't know what to say. Perhaps he simply didn't care about the teasing. He always had seemed immune to such comments. He did smile at me when we passed in the hall, and he asked me once if our computer worked okay. I felt conspicuous talking to him at all, aware that two words passed between us would only fuel the fire.

I mulled about Derek as I walked Clarissa home from school one Wednesday afternoon, only half listening to her chatter about how Alma Sue and Della were fighting again. Most likely over her friendship. Robert had stayed behind for softball practice. The sun warmed my skin, and a light breeze dipped the leaves on our maple trees as we climbed the steps to our porch. "Well, try to keep out of their fight," I told Clarissa.

"The phone's ringin'," she said.

"Oh, yeah." I unlocked the door and trotted into the kitchen, reaching the phone just before the message machine kicked on. "Hello?"

"Hi, Jackie, it's Katherine." She sounded excited.

"Oh. Hi." I dropped my books on the counter, panting. "Um, sorry. Had to run to get the phone."

She laughed. "I knew you might not be home yet, but I couldn't wait to call. I just heard some news that I thought you'd like to know."

Oh, really. Katherine had never called just to talk to me. I leaned against the tile, firming my lips. "Okay."

"Do you know the singing group LuvRush? They're new to this country. They have one hit song called 'Hung Up on You.'"

"Yeah. They're hot." The group's song had climbed the charts in a hurry. I'd read something about them in the last issue of my *Teen Dream* magazine but couldn't remember the details.

"Well, guess what. Their lead singer, Greg Kostakis—his brother grew up in Bradleyville and is related to me."

That stopped me cold. I gazed out the glass door, trying to register the news.

"Jackie? You still there?"

"Uh-huh."

She laughed again, a tinkling sound that could have come from one of my friends. "Guess you didn't know either."

"Tell me," I said tersely, giving myself over to the moment. I scuffed out of the kitchen and toward my bedroom to find the magazine.

"Who is it?" Clarissa wondered as I passed.

"Nobody." I waved a hand to shush her.

"Who *is* it?"

"Katherine, okay? Now beat it."

"Lemme talk to her, lemme talk to her!" Clarissa jiggled on her toes, trying to grab the phone.

I jerked it away. "Clarissa! You can talk to her when I'm done!" Hurrying into my room, I shut the door in my sister's face.

"Don't hang up without letting me talk to her," Clarissa's muffled voice filtered through the wood.

So obvious now, isn't it—how easily I changed. Fighting with Clarissa over talking to Katherine merely because she'd dangled a carrot before my nose.

"Sorry." I jerked open my top desk drawer and pulled out the magazine. "Go ahead."

I flipped through the glossy pages as Katherine explained. His brother's name was Danny Cander, she said. Actually, half brother. Danny's father had been a first cousin to her mama, making Danny and Katherine second cousins. Since Greg had a different father, she wasn't really related to him at all. "But it's sure close!" she exclaimed.

"You just found this out?" I couldn't believe what she was telling me.

"Yes, Aunt Jessie happened to tell me about him. She's never met Greg, but she's stayed in contact with Patricia, Danny and Greg's mama."

The article lay opposite a full-page picture of LuvRush. Greg Kostakis posed in the middle, the other three singers around him. He looked so hot. "It says in this magazine that the group's from Greece."

"Yes. Danny left Bradleyville at eighteen, just like I did. He ended up working for a cruise line that's headquartered in Greece. His mama went with him. His daddy had already died. His mama married a man over there, and Greg is their son."

Just like I did. I couldn't help noticing the comment, almost as if Katherine sought to justify her own choices through the success of someone else. I ran my finger over Greg's picture. "I can't believe it," I murmured.

"There's more." Katherine paused. "Danny Cander recently married Celia Matthews—your mama's best friend all through school."

"Oh," I breathed, staring at Greg's oval face, his dark hair cut short on the sides, thick on top, shaggy over his forehead. His deep-set brown eyes stared almost *through* me, a tiny smile playing around his naturally upturned lips. This new star had ties to my hometown. To my mama. Practically to *me*. We were *connected*.

My eyes fell on another paragraph of the article. "Oh, wow. This magazine says they're startin' their first tour in the States soon!"

"I know, that's how Aunt Jessie and I got on the conversation. The group's going to be in Lexington, at Rupp Arena. I used to go to concerts there when I worked for the radio station."

"Lexington!" A *concert*. I closed my eyes and dreamed of it. I'd never been to a concert in my life. I wondered if Daddy would let me go. I wondered if I could possibly meet this guy.

"One more thing. The real reason I called."

"Uh-huh." My voice wavered. I wasn't sure I could take any more.

"Well, I want to tell you. But first I have to say that it's a very big secret. So you have to promise not to breathe a word."

"I promise." I hunched in my chair, muscles taut.

"You sure? I mean, it'll be tempting, but it's really important."

"I'm sure, I'm sure."

"Okay." She took a breath. "Greg's coming here to Bradleyville."

I stared at my carpet, expecting to sink right through it. Took me a while to find my voice. "You're kidding."

"I'm not! The group's already in California, practicing for their tour. But Aunt Jessie just heard that Celia and Greg are going to visit here before it starts. Celia wants to visit her parents, and Greg wants to see where his brother grew up. Plus he wants a place to rest for a few days."

"When are they arriving?" I asked, now floating somewhere near the vicinity of my ceiling.

"Next week."

"Next *week!*" The news pushed me to my feet, across the room and back again. "Can I see him? Can I meet him? Oh, I can't *believe* it!" I brought a fist to my mouth.

"Yes, you can meet him," Katherine exclaimed. "That's why I'm telling you. It's just that he wants it to be a quiet visit, which is why all the girls in town can't know. He's already having to deal with fans recognizing him, and he doesn't want that here."

"Okay, sure, sure." I ran fingers through my hair, trying to *think*, trying to believe this was really happening. "So, how do I—what do I *do?* I mean, what if he doesn't want to meet me?"

"Don't worry, he will," she assured me. "Aunt Jessie will be talking to Celia again. They're very good friends. I'll make sure she tells him about you."

"Katherine, thank you, *thank* you. I—." My throat swelled, and I couldn't continue. A part of me knew that she did this as a way to win my favor. For the first time I realized just how important my acceptance must be to her. Still, who but Katherine May King could have come up with something so wondrous? Suddenly, I felt very glad for those eleven years Katherine had spent outside Bradleyville.

"Jackie." Her voice filled with warmth. "You are so welcome."

We talked a few more minutes, planning, imagining. I still could hardly believe the news. Finally, I had to go. Somehow I remembered to give the phone to Clarissa. As she giggled her "hello" to Katherine, I returned to my room to stare at the face of Greg Kostakis before the chore of monitoring my sister's homework pulled me from my heavenly daze.

chapter 12

I was dying to tell Alison, but for two days I flipped back and forth on whether I should. After all Katherine had promised to do for me, I owed her *my* promise of silence. Still, as I daydreamed my way through classes and listened to the talk of boys at our lunch table, I could hardly keep from pulling Alison aside. By Friday afternoon, I thought I'd burst with the news.

"What *is* it with you?" she demanded as we met at my locker after the bell had rung. "I swear like you've been walkin' around in a fog the last two days."

I clamped my teeth down. "Oh, nothin'." I took my time pulling out my geography book.

"Don't give me 'nothin',' Jackie Delham, I know you better than that." She leaned against the locker next to mine, hugging her books to her chest. "Has Billy Sullivan been talkin' to you or somethin'?"

"Oh, right." I closed my locker. "With Mary right beside him, swingin' her hips." We headed together down the hall toward the exit. I could not keep Clarissa waiting.

"Well, what's up then?"

I threw her a meaningful look out the corner of my eye. She caught my arm. *"What?"*

So much for promises to Katherine. The news spilled out of me like frothing milk from a bottle. Alison nearly tripped over her jaw. "Oh, glory!" she exclaimed over and over, digging her fingers into my arm. "Do you think like maybe one of the other band guys will come with him?"

"No," I replied, surprised. "And besides, you're goin' out with Jacob, so why should you care?"

"Oh, I know! But a singer, Jackie! This is so cool!"

"You can't tell a soul, Alison, and I mean it." I slid to a halt and eyed her squarely. "I promised Katherine. I'd feel terrible if this got all over town. She wouldn't trust me anymore."

Alison raised her eyebrows. "Listen to you—all of a sudden worried what Katherine feels." She smiled wickedly. "You just don't want to share Greg Kostakis with anybody else, *I* know."

"That's not true. Well. Maybe it is. But it's also true that Katherine deserves for me to keep my promise."

"Uh-huh. So why didn't you?"

Ooh, touché. "You know I couldn't hold out on you." I spotted Clarissa waiting impatiently for me by the corner of the school yard.

"You managed to hold out for two whole days." Alison's tone tinged with accusation. "You never would have done that before."

"Like I've never exactly been in this position before."

"Like you've never exactly had Katherine to talk to before."

I gave her a look. "I thought you wanted me to get along with Katherine. You've told me more than once what a 'friend' she could be to me."

"I know." She furrowed her brow. "It's just that—I mean, usually I'd be the first to know, and—"

"You *are* the first to know. And the last."

She blew out air. "Okay, okay. Sorry. I should just be happy for you."

"Jackieeee!" Clarissa waved an arm. "Come on!"

"All right, all right," I said under my breath. I shrugged at Alison. "Duty calleth."

Smiling ruefully, Alison pushed her hip against mine. I pushed back. "I'm jealous," she pouted.

"Well, don't be. Just think about it, Alison, you've got Jacob for good. Greg's only here a week, and all I get to do is meet him anyway."

My anticipation drained away as we reached Clarissa. Why hadn't I realized that before? A few special moments with a guy whose picture now hung on my wall, and then it would be back to reality. How awful that would be.

For a moment, I almost wished Greg wouldn't even come.

Telling Daddy about Greg's arrival proved another matter entirely. Katherine had left that part up to me. "You know him better than I do," she'd said Friday afternoon on the phone. Then asked almost anxiously, "You don't think he'll mind, do you?"

"No, he won't mind." I opened the pantry and pulled out Winnie's large bag of dry dog food. "Just a few weeks ago he was tellin' me he wanted to see me start goin' out, for heaven's sake. And this is just meetin' somebody."

"But Greg's a singer. A new star. And this *is* Bradleyville."

I heard an underlying judgment in her tone. Fine time for her to be second-guessing. "It'll be fine, Katherine."

Leave it to a parent to be full of surprises.

After supper, with Robert and Clarissa doing the dishes, I sidled up to Daddy as he sat at the computer.

"Whatcha doin'?" I pulled a footrest from the couch over next to him and sat down.

"Oh, just lookin' at some stuff on the Internet." He tapped the "enter" key. "You need somethin'?"

I crossed my ankles and wiggled them, suddenly self-conscious. "Not really."

He nodded, eyes still fixed on the screen. I sat silently. After a moment, he turned to look at me. "What is it, Jackie?"

I shrugged with slow animation.

"Okay." He pushed back from the computer and twisted in his chair to face me. From the kitchen came the rattle of dishes. "I'm listenin'."

I bit the inside of my mouth, suddenly worried. All my visions of meeting Greg, the hours I'd lain awake the last two nights thinking about him, jumbled in my head. What if Daddy said no? I mean, I knew he wouldn't, but what if he did?

"Katherine and I have something to tell you." Such wiles I had not known I possessed.

"*Katherine* and you?" Pleasant surprise marched across his face. "Let's hear it."

I took a deep breath and told him the bare-bones details of Greg's visit. Then sat practically trembling as I awaited his reaction.

"Whoa." Daddy pondered the news. "A singer, huh. One of those guys in your magazines?"

"Yeah. Can you believe it?"

He shook his head. "Amazing. How did Katherine find this out?"

"Greg's sort of almost related to her."

"To the Kings? How?"

"He's somebody's half brother. I forget the name. But it must be somebody you went to school with. The guy married Mama's old best friend, Celia, and they live in Greece."

Daddy's smile went limp. He sat very still, staring at me.

I felt my insides grow cold. I wanted to ask what was the matter but couldn't find my tongue. I waited until I could wait no more. "Daddy?"

"The guy's name is Danny Cander," he said, his tone flat.

"Yeah, that's right," I whispered.

"Danny Cander's brother." Daddy spoke the words to himself with disbelief. Abruptly, he swiveled back to the computer. "I don't want you seein' this boy." He jabbed at the keyboard.

"Why?"

"Because I just don't."

I'd never seen Daddy that way. Terse and irritated and . . . totally unreasonable. "But all I want to do is meet him!"

"I don't want you meetin' him, Jackie. He can't be good for you."

"What do you mean, 'good for me'? It's not like I want to marry him or anything. I just want to talk to him, see what he's like."

"I can tell you what he's like." Daddy kept his eyes on the computer screen. "Is he nice-lookin'?"

Hot would be the operative word. "Yeah."

"Don't you think he'll have all kinds of charisma? After all, he's a performer, isn't he?"

"So?"

"So how long is he here?"

I swallowed. "A week."

"So what if you—" Daddy cut off his rising voice. He turned to me. "What if you like him?" he pressed. "What if you meet him, and you really like him. And you see him the next day, and the next. And then after a week—he leaves. How hurt will you be then?"

My mouth dropped open. Such a simple thing, meeting a guy. I went to school with guys every day. Why was this one suddenly so threatening? "I really don't think that will happen," I said evenly. "But, Daddy, this means so much to me. Imagine if someone famous you wanted to meet came to town, and you couldn't even go say hello. Wouldn't you think, like, what a chance I missed?"

"Jackie." He leaned forward, clasping his hands between his knees. "It's a chance that can't possibly get you anywhere. Either it'll disappoint you from the start, or it'll disappoint you when he leaves. Whichever way, I don't want to see that happen to you."

I focused on the floor, pulling my upper lip between my teeth. I felt too stunned to argue any further, and Daddy said no more. But I knew he watched me.

"Why can't you just find a boyfriend in Bradleyville?" he finally asked.

"Daddy, I'm not talking about 'finding a boyfriend.' I just want to *meet* him."

"But you never know where meeting him might lead."

This was insane; what did he think, I planned to elope with the guy? Tears bit my eyes. I pushed myself up to stalk away. "I'm not you, Daddy!" I retorted. "I don't meet someone and instantly fall at their feet."

"Hey!" He stood and caught my arm. His finger raised, pointing at me. "I will not have you talk to me that way."

I squeezed my eyes shut. "Sorry." The word shook.

He held on to me. A dish clattered in the kitchen. "Jackie ..." Air escaped his throat. His fingers loosened and fell away from my arm.

I thought my rigid jaw would break. "I want to go to my room now, if you don't mind."

He waved a hand, letting me go. Stone-faced, I strode down the hall. Greg's photo smiled its charm from my wall as I locked the door and sank with bitter disappointment upon my bed.

chapter 13

Daddy and I spoke no more that night. Never had we treated each other that way. The next morning we silently made our own pieces of toast, pulling boxes of cereal from the pantry with chilled indifference. "Want some orange juice?" I asked Clarissa when she wandered in, wiping sleep from her eyes. Her nightgown ended below her knees, exposing skinny legs and tiny bare feet.

"Uh-huh." She sidled over to Daddy and hugged him with one arm. "Mornin'."

"Hi, Punkin." He smiled at her almost sadly.

She peered at him. "What's wrong?"

"Nothin'."

What *was* wrong with him? I'd gone over and over our conversation, trying to figure it out. I poured orange juice into a small glass and set it on the table for Clarissa. Only one thing to do, I figured—tell Katherine. Somehow she'd fix this. She knew how much I wanted to meet Greg.

"Robert!" Daddy called. "Better come eat. We have to leave for your big game in an hour."

"Katherine's goin' to be there," I told Clarissa, watching Daddy.

"Yay!" She plopped into her chair, suddenly awake.

I wanted to call Katherine after breakfast, but Daddy sat at the kitchen table, reading the newspaper. The only other phone lay in his bedroom. *Drat.* I went into my bedroom to get dressed. And stare at Greg's picture. I knew every inch of that face by now. The warm eyes, the blunt cut of his jaw. Just looking at him sent longing through my veins. No way he'd be in this town without my meeting him.

By the time I returned to the kitchen, Daddy had disappeared. Stepping out on our back deck, I dialed the Kings' number. Winnie bounded over and panted up at me, begging for a pat. I scratched behind her ears.

Katherine did not sound happy at the news. "Oh, what have I done?" she moaned. "I didn't mean to cause problems."

"You didn't cause the problem; Daddy did. Can you talk to him while we're at the game? Please?"

She hesitated. "That may not be the best time."

"Just try. He's not gonna be himself anyway; you'll see that something's wrong." I paced to the edge of the deck and turned around. "Katherine?"

"He may have a point, you know."

Oh, no, not her too. I raked a hand through my hair, glaring at our rooftop.

"I mean, after Greg leaves and all the excitement dies down, Bradleyville could seem pretty boring."

"It's pretty boring now," I retorted. I swung toward our back fence, blowing out air. I did not want to argue with her. "Look, I don't know what the big deal is. Besides, I don't think it's Greg at all. Daddy didn't get all weird till I mentioned his brother. So would you just . . . help me out here?"

Katherine sucked in a breath, as if she'd realized something momentous.

"What?" I asked.

"Nothing." She fell silent for a moment, then sighed. "I'll try to help." She sounded reluctant. "But . . . I'm still not sure we can talk about it at the game."

"Why don't you two go out tonight, then? Isn't it about time y'all had some time alone?"

"Well, now, Miss Jackie," Katherine commented wryly, "that's quite a change of opinion."

I winced at my lack of subtlety. "I'll get Daddy to ask you at the game. I'll offer to watch the kids." Really. Had I no shame?

She laughed. "I see. You help me, and I help you, is that it?"

"Something like that."

"Fact is, I do need to talk to him, and we've not had much chance."

"See? So go for it."

And there you have it. How easily we slipped into our new roles. With one phone call, Katherine May King moved from tentative friend to cohort.

Oh, the power of rationalization. The more we need it, the mightier it proves to be.

As we drove to the school ball field, windows down and a warm breeze blowing hair into my face, I told myself that my intentions were more for Daddy's sake than mine. Hadn't he wanted me to accept Katherine? Well, now he had what he wanted. He'd been right about her; I'd been wrong. How mature I was to admit it.

We piled out of the car, Robert loping to join his team in warm-up practice. The sun beat down on our heads as Daddy and I settled on the third row of the bleachers. Soon every seat would be filled. Robert's team had a great record for the season, and today's winning team would advance to the playoffs for the best school teams in the region.

Daddy and I still hadn't spoken. He'd fallen into one of his brooding moods—thanks to me, no doubt. Well, hoo-fah. At the moment, I didn't feel all that great about him either.

"I don't wanna sit down till the game starts," Clarissa complained. "The seats are too hard."

"Okay," I said. "Just stay out of the way of the players."

My sister skipped away.

Other families greeted us as they found their seats. Grandpa and Grandma Delham took seats beside Daddy, Grandpa's eyes twinkling as always. Grandma smelled like coconut sunscreen. She forever watched her weight, which looked fine to me, and protected her skin from the sun. "Where's my Robert?" She shaded her eyes, turning to look out over the field.

"Way back there, catchin' balls." Daddy pointed with his chin.

"Did he get a good sleep?" Grandpa stuck his thumbs in the waistband of his pants. "A boy needs his sleep before the big game."

I managed a smile. "Yes, Grandpa, he got his sleep."

"How 'bout breakfast, he have that too?"

"Oh, Ed, for heaven's sake." Grandma waved a hand at him. "You sound like an ol' hen."

"Don't call me a hen, woman, you know what a fine rooster I am." He poked her playfully in the ribs.

"Now, now," Mr. Clangerlee commented as he moved his large frame past us up the bleachers, "we'll have none of that kind of talk in front of the children." He grinned at Grandpa.

"Can you spread out a bit?" Daddy asked his parents. "We need to save a place for Clarissa and Katherine."

Grandma's face lit up. "Katherine's comin'?"

"Said she would." Daddy tried to sound nonchalant, but I knew how much he wanted Katherine beside him.

Before long Grandpa Westerdahl showed up alone.

"Betty not with you?" Grandpa Delham asked.

"She's feelin' a bit under the weather today. Decided to stay home."

His gaze wandered to the empty spot beside Daddy and hung there. I watched the knowledge of who the seat was for move across his face. My heart went out to him. I knew he and Grandma Westerdahl loved us and wanted the best for our family. They would never stand in the way of Daddy's finding someone else. But surely every time they saw him with Katherine, they reeled with the pain of remembering when their daughter had stood beside him.

Grandpa Westerdahl raised his eyes to Daddy's. He nodded slowly, working his mouth.

"Lou," Mr. Tull spoke from the row in front of us, "set yourself down here, there's plenty of room."

"I thank ya kindly." Grandpa took a seat beside him.

Practice heated up. The *smack* of balls meeting leather and shouts from the coaches and players rang through the air. Daddy hunched forward to watch every move Robert made, arms on his knees. I knew I should talk to him before Katherine showed up, but my irritation with him stayed my tongue.

My nostrils filled with the smell of warmed dirt and faint honey-suckle, thanks to the vines trailing a patch of fence at the corner of the lot. That ten feet or so of fence has been there as long as I can remember, linking with nothing, serving only to hail the edge of the softball field. I gazed with distraction at the honeysuckle, and the strangest thing happened. A wondrous anticipation crept over me until I fairly tingled. Even remembering it now, I can almost feel it again. Something was going to happen to me. I just *knew* it. Something new in the air as heady and wild and enticing as that wafting honeysuckle scent. I closed my eyes, reveling in the sensation for as long as it would last, my entire being filling with a longing I couldn't even name.

The feeling melted away as inexplicably as it had come.

I blinked, bringing myself back to reality. Katherine might arrive any minute, and I still hadn't broached a particular subject with Daddy.

At that very moment I saw her car drive into the gravel parking lot, kicking up dust. She got out, clad in jeans and a blue T-shirt, her hair tied in a ponytail with a bright red ribbon. Only Katherine could look so stunning in such a casual outfit. Clarissa ran over, throwing both arms around her waist. Katherine hugged my sister effusively. The passenger door of the car opened, and low and behold, Derek unfolded his lanky frame.

Oh, great. What was *he* doing here?

I turned to Daddy, suddenly pushed for time. "You know, I don't like fighting with you."

He flexed his back and eyed me, the practice momentarily forgotten. "We're not fighting."

"Really. What would you call it, then?"

He considered his hands. "I told you no to somethin', and you got mad and attacked me personally. That's what I'd call it."

"I didn't mean to attack you personally."

"Well, you did."

"Oh, Daddy, I'm sorry. I'm sorry for everything; I didn't mean it."

"Jackie, I think you did mean it. You blurted what was on your mind."

"No. Really. I'm glad about you and Katherine. I don't want to get in the way of that anymore."

Daddy regarded me warily. "I wonder. Would you be sayin' that if she hadn't told you about that boy's comin'?"

"Of course I would."

"Hey, Katherine!" Grandpa and Grandma Delham exclaimed at once, and our conversation abruptly ended.

"Hi!" responded a honeyed voice. Daddy swiveled around. I watched his profile as his lips spread in their wide, slow smile. Katherine held Clarissa's hand, Derek behind them.

"Hello there, pretty lady," Mr. Buckley boomed. Katherine played the coquette, turning aside her head and swishing her hand in an "oh, my" gesture. Mr. Buckley laughed, his stomach jiggling.

"Hi, Bobby," she said as Daddy stood up and held out a hand to help her climb up.

Clarissa clambered after them. "I wanna sit by Katherine," she announced, and promptly flopped down. She hugged Grandpa and Grandma Delham, then snuggled against Katherine's arm.

"Hey, Derek," Daddy said, "glad you could come."

Derek mumbled hello, then stood looking at us, wondering where he'd sit.

Katherine leaned forward, searching for places. "Squeeze in on the other side of Jackie." She reached across Daddy to graze my arm with her fingers. "Hey, there." She held my eyes for a split second, as if trying to read any unspoken signals. I gave her a crooked smile.

Derek climbed over the bleachers awkwardly, his pant legs pulling up to reveal one green sock and one yellow. The sight of them irritated me no end. He plunked down, knees akimbo, large shoes pointed outward. "Hi, Jackie."

"Hi." Oh, for the life of me I hoped none of my friends showed up. Millicent's brother played on Robert's team, but I hadn't seen her. I studied Robert's teammates, trying to think who else might have an older brother or sister.

"Uh, you been on the computer much?" Derek tilted his head and squinted down at me, making his glasses rise up on one side.

"Not really." Good grief. Was there anything besides computers this guy could talk about?

"Plaaaay balll!" the umpire called, and the game began. Henry Sythe, a short, stocky kid on Robert's team, strutted up to home plate and struck it twice with the bat. Across the field, parents of the opposing team filled the bleachers. They'd had to drive all the way from a little town on the other side of Albertsville.

"How come you came today?" I asked Derek.

He shrugged. "Important game. And it's earlier than usual. I don't have to be at work until three. Plus Katherine was comin', so I figured why not." He surveyed the field. "You don't mind, do you?"

"'Course not."

The two teams fought neck and neck through the first five innings. Robert batted two other players in with a home run and caught three outs. Daddy seemed to have forgotten his disappointment with me as he yelled and clapped. Katherine yelled right along beside him. I couldn't help thinking how familial she and Daddy seemed, shouting for Robert like two parents.

Derek surprised me with his excitement. "Yeah, way to go!" he'd yell, stomping his different-colored feet. "Man, can your brother play," he said with a grin.

In the sixth inning our team was down by one run. "Whooeee!" Mr. Tull called as Jeb Cranksley came up to bat. We all stomped and hooted, then fell deathly silent, watching the ball. The pitcher let loose. Jeb swung with fury. And missed.

"Oh!" A roar of disappointment rose up, then fell away as we awaited the next pitch. Jeb let it go by.

"Strike two!"

Derek's head dropped. "Oh, man."

"We'll do it, we'll do it." My eyes fastened on Jeb. The pitcher threw what seemed to be a perfect pitch, and he swung hard. *Crack!* The ball flew toward left field, and Jeb tore out for first base.

We all jumped to our feet, shouting, punching the air. But the left fielder caught the ball just as Jeb neared the base. Jeb slowed, then swung back toward home, kicking at the grass.

Robert remained the most likely player to hit a home run. We craned our necks to watch as his two coaches conferred.

"What're they doing?" Derek asked. He leaned close to me, long neck extended, as he followed my gaze.

"Deciding whether to put Robert up now or not." I shifted away from him. "It would be great to have someone on base in case he hits a homer. Then we'd be ahead. But it's a gamble at this point."

A flash of red nail caught my eye. I glanced over to see Katherine's hand resting on Daddy's knee. The sight jolted me, like touching metal in dry air and getting shocked. I stilled, then turned my gaze aside. Only I made the mistake of turning too far, and for some reason, my eyes pulled to Derek's. He watched me, solemn faced, as if he read my every thought. I blinked away.

The coaches ended their conference. "Theodore," one called, "you're up."

"Go, Theodore!" Daddy yelled. Katherine's hand lifted off his knee as she clapped.

Theodore connected bat to ball on his first swing. An outfielder fumbled the ball and Theodore made it to second base. We jumped to our feet, screaming.

Robert came up to bat. "Ro-bert, Ro-bert!" we yelled as one.

"That's my grandson!" Grandpa Delham declared above the din.

"Go, little brother," I whispered.

Robert took a couple practice swings, then assumed his batter stance, his profile cut out against the green field. I saw the firmness of his mouth, his hard stare, the veins in his arms standing out as he gripped the bat. Robert in his element. He was made for moments like this.

The pitcher wound up, and the ball flew. Robert didn't move.

"Ball one!"

I blew out air, hands against my lips. Another pitch.

"Ball two!"

"Oh!" Katherine exclaimed, "I can hardly stand this."

The pitcher wound up once more, then let fly. The ball streaked toward Robert, and again he didn't move. *Come on, come on,* I breathed. At the last possible second, he swung. The *crack* split the air.

"Aahh!" We jumped and hollered, willing our energy to flow into that ball, watching, watching as it arced up and over every player's head. Robert streaked toward base, arms pumping, hair flying in the wind. The ball peaked and began to fall. "Go, go!" we cried. Theodore tore around third base and cut home.

The ball landed at the very edge of the field.

"Get it, get it!" came the cries from the opposite bleachers. An outfielder ran to the ball, snatched it up, and threw wildly toward second base. Robert hit that base and turned toward third. Theodore flew across home plate so fast he couldn't stop and bashed into his teammates, knocking two of them over. The second baseman caught the ball and let it fly toward third.

"Don't look back, Robert! Run!" Daddy's arms pumped the air.

The third baseman leaned out, one toe on base, reaching, reaching for the ball. Robert lowered his head, gunning with every ounce of energy he possessed. The ball would not reach the baseman. He jogged two small steps, jumped high, and caught it. Robert neared his goal and threw himself into space. Swiveling, the other player leapt to beat him.

They collided midair.

"Ungh!"

To this day, I can hear the breath of those two boys whooshing from their lungs, the *smack* of their bodies. Robert careened into the ground, his shoulder cutting a ridge through the grass. His right leg flew up. The opposing player crunched squarely on top of it.

Robert cried out. I froze. I'd never heard such a sound from my brother.

"Robert!" Katherine yelled. Clarissa screamed.

Daddy shot off the bench, practically knocking folks below him aside. The coaches ran toward third base. Katherine followed. The next thing I knew, I ran across the grass as well, Derek and Clarissa and my grandparents behind me.

"Get back, get back!" Robert's coach waved his arms as we neared. Daddy ignored him, falling to his knees beside my brother. The other boy had rolled off and slowly pulled to his feet, gasping for air. Robert gripped his leg below his knee, eyes squeezed shut, mouth pulled back and rigid.

Daddy reached for him. "Robert—"

"Wait, let me check him," Coach Crary said.

I slapped a hand over my mouth, heart scudding.

"He'll be okay," Derek murmured, "he'll be okay."

"Can you move your ankle?" Coach asked. Robert jerked his head in a no. Coach touched the leg, trying to examine the damage, but Robert pulled away in pain.

"We'd better get him to a hospital." Coach Crary shook his head at Daddy. "I think it may be broken."

"Oh, no, Robert!" I cried. The Albertsville hospital was a good forty minutes' drive away. I couldn't stand to think of my brother in such pain for all that time.

Everyone swung into action. Coach Crary and Daddy carried Robert off the field and laid him in the backseat of the car. Derek and Katherine, Clarissa, my grandparents, and I all followed, with half of Robert's teammates trotting anxiously behind.

"Oh, poor Robert," Grandma's voice trembled. She turned to Grandpa Delham. "Let's follow them to the hospital."

"N–no," Robert managed to say. "Stay and watch the game. I wanna know who won."

"Okay, Robert, they'll stay." Daddy pressed a shaking palm to Robert's cheek. "We'll get you fixed up." My brother's eyes glistened with pain, but he would not cry.

"*I'm* going with you," Katherine insisted, her face white.

Daddy nodded. He turned his shocked gaze on me, and my throat nearly closed with love for him. How awful I felt for Daddy at that moment. How small and selfish I'd been, concerned with only myself when Daddy loved his family so much. He deserved better treatment from me. Wordlessly, I hugged him.

He wrapped his arms around me quickly, then pulled away. "He'll be okay, Jackie. Derek will have to bring Katherine's car. He can drive you and Clarissa home. I'll call from the hospital as soon as we know anything."

"Uh-huh."

Katherine pulled her car keys from her pocket and shoved them into Derek's hand. Clarissa wailed beside me. I drew her close. "It's okay, honey, it's okay."

Everyone stood back as Daddy started the car. "We love you, Robert!" Grandma called. Derek gripped my shoulder as we watched them drive away. I felt too distraught to care.

We wandered back with the coach and players, still shaken, wanting to hear whether the game would continue. The teams were now tied. The coaches announced, "Play on."

"We'll be prayin' for Robert," folks on the benches called down to us.

"Thank you."

Clarissa and I hugged our three grandparents. I insisted on going right home to wait by the phone, even though I knew we could not hear soon. "Would you call us?" I asked Grandpa Delham. "Let us know who won."

We hurried away then, Derek and Clarissa and I. When we pulled up to our house, Derek turned off the car. "I'll stay until I have to go to work. I want to know how Robert is, and maybe I can help keep Clarissa busy."

He spoke with such quiet firmness, as if he knew what I needed. Honestly, if he'd asked whether or not he could stay, I don't think I'd have been able to reason through an answer. For all Derek's strangeness, I felt comforted by his presence. "Okay. Thanks."

Clarissa still cried. Derek rubbed her head as we dragged up the porch steps. "How about I teach you some cool tricks on a computer game?"

She leaned into me, sniffling. "Okay."

We went inside and began our waiting vigil.

chapter 14

The next hour seemed more like ten. Derek pulled up a chair beside Clarissa at the computer to play her "Rising Creek" game. He discovered all manner of ways for Clarissa to jump the tadpole from one rock to another without drowning. Before long, her tears turned to giggles.

"Jump higher," he chided. "You wanna swim the whole way like some drowned cat?"

"I'm not a cat; I'm a tadpole."

"Tadpoles look like cats when they're drownin'."

She let out a small *tsk*. "You're silly."

I wandered back and forth between the computer and my bedroom, not quite sure what to do with myself. My thoughts skipped about as erratically as Clarissa's tadpole, all of them negative. The vision of Katherine's hand on my daddy's knee still made me wince, even though I told myself it shouldn't. Hadn't I wanted them to go out tonight? Which, of course, would not happen now. I stared at the photo of Greg and LuvRush, wondering if I'd ever meet him at all. I ran a finger over his face, imagining what it would be like to stand this close to him in person. After looking at his picture so many times and thinking about him so much, I felt as if I knew him. But I really didn't. Maybe he wouldn't even care about wanting to meet me. Maybe he was stuck-up and rude.

Maybe I'd never meet him.

Maybe I'd never fall in love in my whole life.

Ever.

Sighing, I sauntered back into the family room, straightening a pillow on the couch and the magazines on our coffee table. In the corner, Winnie wagged her stump of a tail, then sighed back into sleep.

Derek glanced at his watch. "I have to go in fifteen minutes. I should take Katherine's car home and get my own to drive to work."

I swept imaginary crumbs off a cushion. "Maybe we'll hear by then."

Ten minutes later, Katherine called. "What happened?" I demanded.

"Thank God we got in to see a doctor right away." She sounded tired. "Robert's leg is broken. They're puttin' a cast on him now. Your daddy's with him and wanted me to call."

"Oh, no." Tears bit my eyes.

"He'll be okay, Jackie. They've given him something for the pain. We should be home in, I don't know, a couple of hours."

I rubbed my forehead. "I'll have supper ready. You'll stay, I hope."

"Sure. Thank you." In the background, I could hear a doctor's name being paged.

"How long is he going to be in a cast?"

"Six to eight weeks. No more softball for him this year, I'm afraid. He's already asking who won the game."

I had to smile. It sounded so like Robert. "Don't know. It must have gone into extra innings, because Grandpa hasn't called yet."

"Ooh. Maybe I'll call back in a little while. Robert's anxious to hear. I think he's using that to keep his mind off things."

"Okay." I shifted my feet. "And thanks, Katherine. I'm glad you're with them."

"I am too," she said softly.

I told Derek and Clarissa the news, and he rose to leave. I walked him to the door. "Thank you so much," I told him rather formally. "You've been very kind."

He smiled at me lopsidedly. "You're easy to be kind to."

I could think of no response. It was one of the nicest things anyone had said to me in a long time.

I watched him lope to the street. Derek folded himself into the car, then ducked his head down to wave to me. I saw in the gesture his self-consciousness. I waved back, smiling, as he drove away.

※ ※

Robert looked pale as he shuffled into the house awkwardly on his crutches, the right leg of his softball uniform cut away to reveal a bright blue cast.

"Whoa." Clarissa's eyes grew round.

Winnie pranced around, sniffing at the plaster. Her anxiety frayed my own nerves. "Come on, you're in the way." I opened the sliding glass door and pointed outside. She looked up at me with the eyes of a martyr and slunk onto the deck. When I closed the door, she sat peering through the glass as if she were the most abused canine on earth.

I turned back to my brother. "That's quite a color," I remarked, trying to sound like he hadn't frightened me out of my wits.

He puckered his chin, surveying the cast. "White's kinda boring."

We all hovered as he made his way to the couch. Clarissa hugged Katherine for moral support. Katherine assured my sister in hushed tones that he would be okay.

"You sure you feel like lying here instead of in bed, Robert?" Daddy piled three pillows on the end of the couch.

"Yeah." Robert pulled up to the couch, then stood staring from it to the leg he couldn't bend, his expression muddled.

"Maybe it would be easier if you turned around so it's on your left," Katherine suggested. Her ponytail lay askew, the red ribbon practically pulled out of its bow. Her shirt puffed around her waist untucked, as if she hadn't given herself a thought in hours. She put a hand on Robert's shoulder to urge him the other direction, then helped him lie down, his good leg on the couch and the heel of his cast resting on the floor. Carefully, she eased up the leg and moved it onto the couch. "That better?"

Her actions sent a pang through me. Mama would have done the very same thing.

Robert nodded. We all looked at him. I wondered what on earth he'd do in this condition for six weeks.

He wiggled his left ankle as if already bored. "Least our team won," he said tersely.

"Thanks to you." I scruffed his hair.

He snorted. "Lot a good I did."

"You brought Theodore in, sounds like a lot a good to me. Grandpa told me once you were hurt, your team wasn't about to lose. By the eighth inning, they were practically beside themselves. Then Chuck stepped up to the plate, declarin', 'This is for Robert,' and hit the ball clean out of the park."

"Amazing." Daddy raised his eyebrows at Robert. "Chuck's never hit a home run in his life."

"Guess I oughtta break my leg more often."

We laughed. Muted though it was, the laughter felt clean in my throat, renewing.

"Somethin' smells mighty good." Daddy gave me a weary smile. I saw forgiveness in his eyes.

"It's spaghetti." A favorite of both Daddy and Robert.

"I'll help you get it on the table," Katherine offered, and for the first time I felt glad to let her. The concern for my brother that glinted in her eyes meant more than I could say.

By the time we called the family to supper, Robert had fallen asleep on the couch, fingers spread over his stomach and faintly twitching. Most likely dreaming of the home run he never completed.

chapter 15

For the first time in Katherine's presence, we sat around our kitchen table instead of the more formal dining room. Mama's kitchen chair had been in the garage since a few months after her death. Every time I'd gone in there, my eyes had been drawn to it. The vast emptiness of that chair, the loneliness it represented. Now here was Daddy, fetching it and bringing it back to the table. My throat tightened as I watched him seat Katherine. She settled into it far too easily for me, with no apparent thought to its significance. Yes, she had been kind to Robert, and I was grateful. But *this* . . .

We'd managed to wake Robert up and get him to the table, but he remained groggy from the pain pills. He ate a fourth of what he usually would, trying his best to keep a placid expression. I could tell his leg still hurt. Not much conversation that night. Plenty on all our minds, I suppose. As soon as we finished, Daddy helped Robert into bed, which took a while. The cast made him awkward, and the pain pills rendered him nearly useless. Clarissa cleared the table while Katherine and I did the dishes. Winnie flopped on her back in her usual corner and fell asleep, all four legs splayed wide apart, her head sticking out at a funny angle. I had to laugh. With her neck twisted that way, she reminded me of Derek.

Robert put to bed, the four of us watched television. My sister lay happy as a clam with her head in Katherine's lap and her feet in Daddy's. Katherine stroked her hair. I knew Daddy and Katherine wanted some time alone. If they couldn't go out on a date and talk, at least they could talk here. I kept an eye on the clock.

"I'm goin' to run your bathwater," I told Clarissa at 8:30.

"I don't wanna go to bed." She pouted at me.

"Yeah, so what's new?" I headed for our bathroom to fill the tub.

"But I wanna stay till Katherine leaves."

"Now, Clarissa," I heard Daddy reply, "you know I won't let you stay up late, especially after everything that happened today. You need your sleep; we've got church tomorrow."

Half an hour later Clarissa stood clad in her frilly pink nightgown, ready for bed. She lingered in the family room for extra good-night kisses, then sighed her way down the hall.

"I'm tired myself," I told Daddy and Katherine. "I'm gonna read in bed after I get her settled."

Daddy shot me a grateful look. Katherine stood up, and we exchanged our first hug. "Good night," she said. I gave her a self-conscious smile.

I fully intended to leave them alone. Really. Eavesdropping had never entered my mind. It's just that once I got Clarissa to bed and changed into my pajamas, I remembered I hadn't brushed my teeth. As I exited the bathroom, I heard the quiet drone of voices, and something pulled me toward them.

Knowing what I do now, sometimes I wonder—if I could go back and change that evening, would I do it? Would I slip into my bedroom and firmly close the door, never to hear the words that would cut me so deeply? And then I think of God and his mercy. How he uses even our mistakes to hone us. How he allows the wind of our past to blow us into the wisdom of our future.

But at the time, I merely followed my curiosity. Creeping over the floor, I eased down the hall and around the corner. I stopped a good length from the next corner to make sure I couldn't be seen, even if one of them looked back from their seats on the couch. Not for the life of me would I have allowed myself to be caught. I'd never live down the embarrassment. Pressing my back against the wall, I listened.

They commented on the game and Robert's leg. Daddy said something, and a long pause followed before Katherine spoke. I sensed in their stilted tones the newness of the conversation, as if they'd turned off the TV only minutes before and feigned chitchat. The thought surprised me. Two adults as tongue-tied as I might be on a date?

"Katherine," Daddy said at length, "you've been wonderful today. Thank you."

"I wouldn't have wanted to be anywhere else."

"It must be hard, being thrown in the midst of a family like you have been. Always a lot goin' on. 'Course today was rather unusual."

"Your children are wonderful, Bobby. All three of them are a joy to be around."

"Jackie's . . . taken her time warmin' up to you."

"She's the oldest. She's had to fill in the role of mama. It's understandable."

"Seems like you two are gettin' along better now, though."

A pause. I heard the sound of someone shifting position. "Did I do wrong, Bobby, telling her about Greg Kostakis? I'm so sorry if I did."

Daddy hesitated. "I suppose you did it to reach out to her."

"Of course I want to reach out to her, but it's more than that. She's sixteen, Bobby; she's at that age of hopes and dreams. Then here's this boy she listens to on the radio, coming here! I know how crazy girls get over meeting these singers. I saw it often enough when I worked at the radio station. What an exciting thing to happen for Jackie. How could I not tell her?"

Silence. It seemed to last forever.

"Please tell me what you're thinking. Do you not want her to meet Greg?"

"I just . . . don't want her to get hurt. I can understand that meetin' some star would probably be a dream come true for her. That's just it. What's she goin' to do when he leaves?"

"He won't be here that long," Katherine said. "I didn't think we'd be doing much more than giving them a chance to get acquainted."

"What if that's all it would take?" Daddy retorted, an edge in his voice.

I pressed my palms together, surprised at the intensity of his tone.

"Bobby," Katherine said softly. "What is this about?"

Silence again. Finally Daddy spoke, the words almost worn. "Come here."

Clothes rustled. Katherine still must have sat a Clarissa-length away. In the protracted stillness that followed, I knew they were kissing.

How to explain all the things I felt? I remember leaning my head against the wall, a desperate ache rising in my throat. Part of me wanted to flee to my bedroom, both to block the knowledge and to leave them be. I had no right to spy on them like this. Another part screamed *no, no, no* at the boundary now crossed, my mama's memory betrayed and dimming on the other side. Did Daddy not care that our last family photograph watched them from the mantel? Did Katherine not care?

And the rest of me looped and knotted with undeniable self-pity. I was the teenager, "full of hopes and dreams," the one ready to fall in love. This was supposed to be happening to *me*.

Katherine laughed quietly. "If we were disagreeing, maybe we ought to do it more often."

No response from Daddy. Perhaps emotion held his tongue.

"Bobby, there's so much we need to talk about. So much I need to say."

"Me too." Daddy paused. "But you go first." I heard a smile in his voice.

"Oh, thanks, put me on the spot. How much time do I get?"

"All the time you need."

"Okay." Pause. "Suddenly, I'm . . . scared."

"Not any more scared than I am."

A whisper of movement, as though she pulled back to gaze at him. "Why are *you* scared, Bobby?"

He didn't answer immediately. When he did speak, all teasing had melted from his tone. "Because I'm falling in love with you."

The word seeped like simmering water into my chest. I squeezed my eyes shut.

"I won't play games, Katherine. I don't have the energy, and I've been through too much. So I'm tellin' you outright. I have only loved twice in my life. My first love hurt me badly, and I made some terrible mistakes. The second with Melissa brought me years of joy, then nearly killed me when I lost her. I tend to be a quiet person, but I feel things deeply. People look at me and see someone they think is strong. I have to look that way for the kids. But they don't know how weak and fearful I feel inside."

Oh, Daddy. My heart turned over at his words. But what was he talking about—*two* loves? Daddy had never loved anyone but Mama.

"Bobby—" Katherine's voice caught. "I love you."

The sibilance of movement, then quiet. I tried to steady my own breathing.

"Want to hear my confession?" Katherine finally said. She inhaled audibly. "I came back here because of you."

"Me? I don't . . . You'd been gone for eleven years."

Katherine breathed a laugh. "You don't know, do you? You never had any idea. But then, why should you, being so much older. I had a crush on you when I was twelve years old. You were a senior in high school and dating Melissa. I used to dream of getting up the courage to tell you to wait for me."

Twelve years old. Robert's age. I couldn't imagine it. Daddy said nothing. He must have been beyond words.

"I know what happened just before you graduated," Katherine said softly, "your fall from grace. I heard the talk. But I didn't care what everyone was saying. Then I ran into you one day down at the IGA. You looked so forsaken, so sad. You could hardly hold your head up. I gathered my nerve and walked up to you. Do you remember this, Bobby?"

"I'm . . . not sure."

"Oh, some thanks I get. You *should* remember; it got me grounded for a whole month, and with summer just beginning."

"Wait. I do," Daddy drew out the words, as if a vague memory had surfaced. "How could I forget? You reached out when everyone else was shunning me."

"I did more than that. I swept aside every Bradleyville expectation of a young lady, especially given how young I was. I can see it now, Bobby; I must have gone over it in my mind a million times. You were standing before the rice section, staring stupidly at it, like your mother had sent you on an errand, but you couldn't remember what she wanted. At first sight of you, my heart nearly fell out my toes. Then I felt so bad, watching you. Somehow, I wanted you to see that not everyone in the entire town was against you. I didn't even notice old Mrs. Schwartzbocker coming around the corner. I marched right down the aisle and threw my arms around you. Stood on tiptoe and kissed you on the cheek. And I said, 'I love you, Bobby.'" Katherine chuckled. "You were so shocked, you couldn't move. I mean, you barely even knew who I was. And then, dear God, I'll never forget this—a look of sheer terror crossed your face, and you shoved my hands away and stepped back, looking around like you were scared to death that someone had seen and you'd be blamed for it. I saw Mrs. Schwartzbocker then and realized what I'd done to you—that this was all you needed to turn the town on its other ear. I felt so horrified, I just ran. Left you standing there—alone with that woman."

Disbelief weighted my limbs. I could not even begin to imagine what they were talking about. What could Daddy possibly have done to turn the whole town against him?

"It's all comin' back to me now," Daddy said. "I guess I'd forgotten because of all the trouble in my life at the time." He paused. "I have to admit somethin'. I can remember now Mrs. Schwartzbocker glarin' after you, hands on her hips. I remember how I shook when she turned her eyes on me. And then she declared very firmly, 'It wasn't your fault, Bobby. I saw the whole thing.' I could have fainted with relief. Not very noble of me, after what you'd done."

"She saw it all right. Took her all of about five minutes to call my mama. Probably didn't even stop to buy her groceries."

Daddy laughed quietly. "Grounded a whole month, huh."

"Oh, you don't know. Daddy liked to near kill me. Told me he'd better never catch me speaking to you again. So I didn't. And then you eventually got back with Melissa. I sat in my room crying the day you got married. Thought I'd go to hell for sure, liking a married man, but I couldn't help it."

"Katherine. I never dreamed . . . I just had no idea."

They were silent for a moment.

"So what does your father say now?" Daddy wondered. "How funny, after all these years, here you are—with me."

"Well. You've grown up a bit. And changed your evil ways."

"I see."

"Bobby, the whole town loves you, and you know it. Everybody wants you to be happy. Which scares me to death. I feel it every day, the pressure. If I did anything to hurt you, I think I'd be run right out of this town."

"You won't do anything. Will you?"

The vulnerability in his voice made me want to cry.

"No, please God!" Katherine's tone tinged with desperation, almost as if she were afraid she would. Later I would remember that tone. "Did you hear what I said, Bobby? That I've gone over that scene a million times? Not just while I grew up here in Bradleyville, but while I was gone. Through all the jobs and places and boyfriends, I never forgot you. Then I heard about Melissa. When the time was right, I came back. Thinking maybe . . . And then I could hardly believe it— the first person I saw in town was *you*. Protecting me with your arms underneath that desk. Do you know at that moment I wanted the tornado never to end?"

"Oh, Katherine."

They spoke no more for a long time. I leaned my head against the wall and silently cried. I could not sort the tears of happiness and relief for Daddy from those that mourned my mama.

"Bobby," Katherine finally spoke, "I need to tell you other things about me. But first I should explain something. When I told Jackie about Greg, I didn't stop to think about . . . you know, your old tie to Celia. And how you must have felt about Greg's brother."

My hand stilled as I wiped a tear. Old tie to Celia?

Daddy emitted a sigh.

"I'm really sorry if I've done something wrong."

"You didn't do anything wrong. That's ancient history. And I'm ashamed at myself for reacting the way I did."

Katherine made no reply.

"It's just . . . . You were too young to know everything, Katherine. I do believe Celia and I would have ended up together if it hadn't been for Danny. Of course, now I'm glad things didn't turn out that way. But at the time, it near killed me. Even while I was dating Melissa, I went to Celia on my knees more than once, asking her to change her mind. But no. Even when Danny left, all she wanted to do was graduate and go after him."

Something slick and oily rolled through my stomach. I could barely assimilate Daddy's words. When he'd dated Mama, who loved him so much, he'd really wanted her best friend?

"So, you're right. I didn't like Danny Cander. In fact, he was my enemy. When he was gone, his presence was still here, stealin' what I wanted. That's how strong he was, how magical he apparently was. And whatever he did from afar, Katherine, whatever he said, caused Celia to come to me that night. Not because she wanted me. But because she wanted revenge. Danny, hundreds of miles away, had the power to do that to her."

Came to me that night. Fall from grace. No. I shook my head, denying the words, what they must mean. No.

"Oh, Bobby, I'm sorry," Katherine breathed. "I didn't know how it all happened."

"No one would ever have known if I hadn't confessed to Melissa," Daddy said almost to himself. "But I couldn't bear the guilt. Anyway, it doesn't matter now. I hadn't thought about it in years. But see, all of a sudden, it's *my* daughter who's sixteen. And I hear that Danny's half brother is comin' to town. What's more, he's some singing star. And

Jackie, my daughter, the jewel of my life, wants to meet him. I know I overreacted. Maybe I'm even carryin' old resentments I didn't know I still had, which is hardly the Christian thing to do. But the situation just . . . scared me. I can't stand to think of anything that could lead to Jackie bein' hurt. God knows she's been through enough already."

"I know," Katherine soothed. "Jackie's a special girl. I don't want her to be hurt either. But, if I could just say—I think this will be okay. Jessie says all she's heard about Greg is that he's a terrific kid. His parents are strong Christians, and he's been raised that way."

"Uh-huh. Terrific kids can get into trouble, too."

"Oh, Bobby." Katherine sounded almost exasperated. "I do understand everything you've said, but—you really need to lighten up."

Daddy managed a chuckle. "Probably. I have a feelin' you're goin' to help."

Silence.

They were probably kissing again, but I could not think about that. Daddy's talk of Celia Matthews echoed too loudly in my head. I pictured Mama on the mantel, smiling down at him. How could Daddy have done to her what he did? With her *best friend*. How could Celia have done it? I couldn't begin to imagine Alison's doing something like that to me. They had both betrayed Mama. Daddy had betrayed her, when she loved him so much.

I could hear no more. Sick to my stomach, I turned toward my bedroom. But when I rounded the corner, a loud crash rang from Robert's room. My breath caught.

"What was that?" Katherine cried.

I scurried to throw open Robert's door, searching the dimness. From the family room came the sound of running feet.

"Robert?" I flipped on the light, rushed inside. My brother had collapsed on the floor, his crutches scattered like two pickup sticks. Softball trophies lay askew on the carpet. He squinted in the sudden glare.

"What are you doing?" I crouched at his side.

Daddy and Katherine ran into the room. "What happened?" Daddy sank to his knees. "Robert? Say something!"

Robert batted bleary eyes into focus. "Howdy."

"What—" I threw out my hands. "What did you do?"

"Just tryin' to go to the bathroom. One crutch got away."

"Oh, Robert!" Katherine slapped her hand to her chest. "You scared us to death!"

"Sorry."

"Come on." Daddy pulled the crutches together. "Let's get you up. I'll help you to the bathroom and back into bed." He looked over his shoulder at Katherine. "I think he's just woozy from the pain pills."

It was all too much. Spindly fingers snatched the air right out of my throat. My eyes pricked with sudden tears.

"It's okay." Katherine rubbed my back. "He's going to be fine."

I nodded, my whole insides trembling. But I wasn't crying in relief. I couldn't push their conversation from my head.

Daddy shot me a glance. "Help us, Jackie."

The three of us tugged and lifted and straightened until Robert stood swaying on his crutches, Daddy's hands under his elbow. "Okay, champ, let's go. Then it's back to bed."

I didn't want to say another word to Katherine. I couldn't look at her, too afraid she'd see the truth on my face.

"Jackie? Are you okay?" She touched my arm.

I focused on my feet. "Uh-huh."

She surveyed me. "No, you're not." She reached out, lifted my chin. Fresh tears tumbled from my eyes. Her lips parted. "What is it?"

I shook my head, my chin quivering. She drew me to her, and I leaned against her shoulder, silently hiccuping. She stroked my hair.

I had to get hold of myself; no way could I let Daddy see me cry. How would I explain? Forcing down the ball in my throat, I pulled back.

Katherine gazed at me, frowning. Then slow dismay crept over her face. "Oh, no. Our talking. Don't tell me you heard us."

I made no move to deny it.

"Oh, Jackie." She ran a finger down my cheek. "*Why* did you listen?"

I heard the toilet flush. "Please don't tell Daddy."

"Telling's not the issue; you heard things you don't understand."

I twisted my pajama top.

"We'll have to talk about this," she said. "When we have some time, okay?"

The bathroom door began to open. I jumped at the sound. Without a word, I fled to my room.

chapter 16

I slept little that night, I can tell you.
Robert did not feel up to attending church the next morning. Neither did I, but I had no excuse to give. I volunteered to stay home with my brother, but Daddy wouldn't hear of it. "No," he said, "you go with Clarissa. I'll keep an eye on Robert myself."

All my grandparents except for Grandma Westerdahl, who was still sick, clustered around me and Clarissa before the service, asking how Robert had fared the night. I managed to put on a good front. I told them of Robert's fall, how he'd blinked up at us and said howdy. Grandpa Delham hooted at that, and everyone laughed along with him.

"You want to sit with us?" Grandma tweaked Clarissa's nose.

I glanced across the small sanctuary and saw the Kings entering. "I think we'll sit with Katherine."

Grandma smiled, clearly pleased. "Gettin' along with her, are you?"

I nodded, wondering how much Daddy had said to her.

"Hi, Katherine!" Clarissa threw herself into Katherine's arms. I watched them, wishing I could do the same thing. I still hardly knew how to feel that morning, and only Katherine could guess what I was going through. No way would I tell anyone else the shameful things I'd heard. Not even Alison.

"Hey, there, squirt." Jason King bent down and made a face at Clarissa. She made a face back. Miss Connie hugged my sister, then me. Almost as if they were family.

Derek ambled in, head tilted. His eyes cruised the sanctuary and fell immediately upon me. He smiled almost self-consciously, then leaned against the end of a pew, talking with Grandpa Westerdahl. I blinked at that. Not that they weren't acquainted, but I'd never known them to say much to one another. Derek focused upon my grandpa, but I felt a vague emanation from him, as though he were highly aware that I watched.

Katherine pulled me aside. "How are you?" She ran her hand down a strand of my hair.

"Okay."

"You look tired."

"I didn't sleep all that well."

"Me either." She shook her head. "Way too much to think about. I worried half the night about you."

I could find no response to that. After everything that happened between her and Daddy, she thought about me?

The service would begin soon; we needed to sit down. Clarissa and I followed the Kings to their pew. I did not want to end up beside Derek, but that's exactly what happened. "Come on." Katherine beckoned to him. She urged Clarissa into the pew before her with sheer innocence, then followed with me behind. If I hadn't known better, I'd have thought she did it on purpose.

I focused on my lap as Derek slid into his seat on the end. He took his time getting settled, his knobby knees nearly hitting the hymnal rack of the pew in front of us. "Hi," he said.

"Hi."

I couldn't see his socks.

He drummed his fingers on both legs. "Robert's okay, I hear."

"Yes." I felt like an idiot, finding so little to say. I did not want him to think me unfriendly after all he'd done yesterday; he didn't deserve that. "Thanks again for your help with Clarissa, Derek. I really appreciate it."

He nodded. "You're welcome."

Well. If Pastor Beekins didn't preach an appropriate sermon that day—"Forgiven, But Not Forgotten." What had he done last night, I wondered, been a fly on our wall? "What do we do," he asked, "when God has forgiven us of a sin, but the natural consequences of that sin remain to trouble our lives, maybe even the lives of those we love?" Pastor Beekins leaned over the pulpit. "Because I'll let you in on a little secret. God will forgive you, but nature won't."

Derek shifted in his seat, his arm rubbing against mine. He drew it away.

My mind wandered back to Daddy and Mama. And Celia. For the hundredth time I wished I'd never listened to that conversation last night. Never, ever. Vaguely, I heard Pastor talk about God's turning even the negative consequences of sin in our lives to good. But I could not concentrate on his words. Over and over again I heard Mama's voice, telling me how she'd always loved Daddy. Never once letting on that she'd been so hurt. I'd thought their relationship so perfect.

How could he have done it?

... So I'll stay
Hung up on you,
That's all I can do.
I just keep on dreamin',
My thoughts on you schemin'
To make you my own,
My love for you's grown.
I'm nothin' but hung up,
You just got me strung up,
I'm nothin' but hung up on you.

Tiredly, I hummed along with Greg and LuvRush as I changed the sheets on my bed Sunday afternoon. Katherine had come over and sat in the family room with Daddy and Robert. Clarissa played with Alma Sue. My mind still reeled with thoughts of Daddy and Mama and Celia and Katherine, and I just wished it would *be quiet*. Then I happened to glance out my window and spotted Clarissa, kicking through the front lawn, arms pumping, chin in the air. Mad as a hornet.

Oh, great. Something else I'd have to take care of.

The door banged open. I met her in the hall. "Trouble with your friends?"

"Yes!" Her eyes blazed. "Alma Sue won't let me do *anything* I want. She always has to be the boss of everything. Plus, she cheats!" She stomped away from me and back again. "We played checkers, and I had to go to the bathroom, and when I got back, she'd moved the *whole board* around. Sayin', 'Look, Clarissa,'" my sister's voice mimicked in singsong, "'I can jump this man, and this one and this one.'" Clarissa breathed hard, tears filling her eyes. "Sometimes I just *hate* her!"

Daddy appeared. "What's goin' on?"

"She's fightin' with Alma Sue again." I patted my sister empatheti-cally on the head. "Just stay here, sweets, you don't need to play with her anyway. What about Della?"

"She can't play this afternoon." Clarissa crossed her arms and pressed them against her chest. "Oooh, Alma Sue makes me so *mad!*"

"Well, make sure you stay that way." I couldn't resist the dig. "Don't go easin' up on her just because she offers you a bag of candy."

Clarissa seared me with a look, as if to ask how could I possibly *think* she'd stoop so low.

"Come on, Clarissa, Katherine's here." Daddy urged her down the hall. "She's playin' with Robert on the computer. I'm sure they'll give you a turn."

"I don't *want* to play on the computer! I don't *want* to see Katherine. I am just too *mad!*"

Clarissa humphed her way into her bedroom and slammed the door.

Daddy and I looked at each other. "Must have gotten your mama's temperament," he commented.

Katherine materialized in the family room doorway. "Did I just hear a tornado blow in?"

"Yup." Daddy eased to her side. "Wanna get under a desk somewhere?"

They smiled at each other secretively, forgetting my presence. I swung away toward my bedroom, irritated and weary and hopelessly sorry for myself. Couldn't even summon the energy to finish making my bed. Instead I found myself dawdling before the LuvRush photo, staring with longing at Greg's face.

Some fifteen minutes later I sat at my desk, flipping halfheartedly through the pages of *Teen Dream* when I heard scraping noises on the porch. I tried to ignore them, but they did not stop. *Now what?* Sighing, I tossed down the magazine and went to investigate. Only to find Clarissa, with creased forehead and a determined jaw, setting our lightweight outdoor folding chairs around the perimeter of the porch.

"Clarissa. *What* are you doing?"

"Guardin' our property."

"Guardin' it? From who?"

"Alma Sue." She made a *tsking* noise, as if I were an idiot to have to ask.

I gazed at the chairs, which weren't much heavier than the wind. "Hm. Looks like a real fortress."

"I know she won't be happy to stay in her own house and leave me alone," Clarissa said in a rush. "She'll come over here with her big self, sure as you're livin'. And if I'm not out here to watch things, no tellin' *what* she'll do."

I forced my mouth not to smile. "I see." I leaned against the door, clearing my throat with all seriousness. "You gonna just sit out here?"

"Yyyup."

"Anything I can do?"

"Nnope." She puckered her chin at me. "I got it all under control."

"Okay." I left her to the war.

I didn't see what happened next. Suppose that's a good thing, because I'd surely have wrung a neck. But, as Clarissa poured out her sordid tale not one hour later, I could well envision the scene.

At first, Clarissa played the good soldier, sitting cross-legged on the porch and keeping watch. She soon found this quite boring, however. No harm in keeping occupied while she guarded, she thought. Quickly fetching a brand-new coloring book and a box of crayons, she lay on her stomach on the porch, soon absorbed in filling out a picture. The warm air made her more than a little sleepy. Besides, coloring always did tend to demand her utmost concentration.

Somehow, she let down her guard.

Next thing she knew, Alma Sue stood on the top step, glaring down at her, water pistol clutched in her hand.

"What's this?" she taunted. "A little girl coloring?" And with that, she swept her athletic body through the folding chairs. Clarissa faced a moment of unadulterated terror as she stretched her neck up to view the dreadful apparition towering above her, complete with the barrel of a gun.

Pffzzzt. A stream of water shot out of the pistol onto her page. A second shot, and a third, and before Clarissa could even react, the coloring book lay in utter ruin. Alma Sue, coward that she was, turned and ran. Wailing to the heavens, Clarissa picked up the book by one soggy corner and hightailed inside in full retreat.

"I'll *never* talk to her *again!*" Clarissa sobbed, her coloring book leaking blue-and-yellow drops onto the hall floor.

"That—that Amazon!" I pried the evidence from my sister's hands, holding a palm under it to catch the water. "We should call her mama right now." I marched to the kitchen and dumped the book into the trash. By the time I returned, Clarissa sat in Daddy's arms, crying into his shoulder like a toddler.

"What are you going to do about it?" I demanded.

Daddy rubbed Clarissa's back. Katherine's hand rested on her shoulder. Robert had hobbled over on his crutches and looked on in empathetic silence.

"Maybe we oughtta break Alma Sue's leg," he offered.

Daddy tossed him a look.

"All right, Clarissa." Daddy slid her down to the floor. "You're gonna be all right. Not the nicest thing to happen, I know. But you just stay inside now for the rest of the day. Let Alma Sue cool off."

Clarissa sniffed. "But now I don't have anything to color."

Katherine watched her mournfully. "Maybe tomorrow we could buy—"

Daddy held up a hand, stopping Katherine in midsentence. "You have other coloring books, Clarissa. And you have plenty of games, and books to read, and the computer."

Before long, Clarissa and Katherine were playing dominoes on the coffee table. I watched for a while, a tirade of accusations against Alma Sue running through my head. That girl was nothing but a big bully. Somehow I had to teach Clarissa to stand up to her. Without getting creamed.

One of these days, I promised myself, Clarissa was going to learn to fight back.

Katherine carved out a few moments to talk to me in my room that afternoon, but we found ourselves at an impasse over the eavesdropped conversation. I did not want Daddy to know I'd listened. He'd be so disappointed, and he'd lose some of his trust in me. Katherine gently insisted that it wasn't her place to talk to me about what had happened in Daddy's personal life so many years ago.

I knew I'd put her in a difficult position. In a way she betrayed Daddy by not telling him, yet she'd betray me if she did. She'd chosen me, and for that I felt grateful. I just wasn't sure why.

That evening Katherine suggested that she and Daddy take a drive. Well. Guess I couldn't listen to any conversation that way, could I? As they left, I avoided looking at her, imagining the hint of a knowing smile on her lips.

I don't know how Katherine finagled it. Except through pure use of her charm. But somehow during their talk that night, she convinced Daddy to allow me to meet Greg. After he got home, Daddy came into my bedroom and told me he'd changed his mind.

With all that had happened, I needed some good news. I nearly went nuts.

"Oh, are you sure?" I cried, bouncing up and down. Then instantly thought, *What a stupid thing to say! Like you want him to take it back?* "Oh, thank you, Daddy, thank you, thank you!" I threw my arms around his neck.

He hugged me back almost wearily, as if he wondered what on earth he'd let himself be talked into. "Yeah, well, thank Katherine," he said as he nudged me off of him. "You've got a friend in your corner, that's all I can say."

For the second night in a row I hardly slept, this time due to sheer excitement. You might wonder how I managed to so quickly push aside my pain over what I'd heard about Daddy's past. Looking back, I realize my confusion and hurt were deep enough that subconsciously I sought a diversion. Well, I'd certainly found one, and I would use it to its fullest. A naïve thought, as I would discover. Diverted pain does not magically disappear. It merely sinks to a deeper level, flowing like a hidden stream beneath the bedrock of one's soul.

Katherine called Monday afternoon, and I thanked her profusely for what she'd done. "Do you know anything more?" I prodded. She wasn't sure when Greg and Celia would arrive, she replied. They'd be driving in from Lexington in the next day or two.

The next *day* or two? That really sent me over the edge. I could hardly enter my room without ogling Greg's picture. Clarissa caught me swooning over it more than once. Each time, I swung away as if caught at something. I taped Greg's song "Hung Up on You" from the radio, then played it over and over and over again. I knew every word, every nuance and note of harmony in that song. I read the article on him ten times, forming questions to ask. Telling myself that when we met I'd be calm, cool, and collected, full of charm and grace.

So much for realistic thinking.

chapter 17

I dreamed my way through school the next three days, Alison bugging me constantly with, "Do you think he's here today, do you think he's here?"

"Would you chill?" I whispered to her furiously at lunch Thursday. "You're makin' me crazy!"

She feigned a pout. "I'm just like tryin' to be a best friend, show I'm all excited for you."

After school, Grandma Delham waited near the elm tree to give us a ride home, which she'd committed to do until school let out for the summer. No more softball practice for Robert, and he certainly couldn't walk home on crutches.

I set my books on the floor of her backseat, then helped Robert ease his way inside the car, his casted leg stretched across the seat. Clarissa clambered in front. "Grandma," I said, "I brought some money with me today so I could stop by the dime store. I'll just walk home. Robert and Clarissa will be fine until I get there."

"You can stay for a while and see our computer, Grandma," Clarissa chimed in. "I'll show you how to play 'Rising Creek.'"

"Oh, that would be fun." Grandma grinned at her, then turned to me. "I can take you by the store if you'd like."

"That's okay, I want to walk." I needed some time to be with my own thoughts. Plus, I didn't want to explain to Grandma why I could not wait to buy a certain bottle of perfume. I shut the car door and waved as they drove away.

What a beautiful day. On that fourteenth of May, the sodden humidity of summer had not yet descended, and a light breeze ruffled the trees. I set out walking downtown, thinking of Greg, enjoying the sun on my arms.

I entered the relative coolness of the dime store and turned down the personal items aisle. A guy stood in one-quarter profile, checking out the shampoos, one hand reached out and resting on a bottle. He looked up distractedly as I neared him. And my heart stood still.

I knew every inch of that tanned face. His brown eyes, deep-set, and utterly captivating. His upturned mouth that carried a hint of mischief. Dark hair, tumbling over his forehead. It looked even thicker than in the LuvRush photo. He stood before me, about five inches taller than I. Real, dressed in jeans and a red T-shirt. In the Bradleyville dime store.

My mouth creaked open. My mind raced for something, anything, to say. I stared at Greg Kostakis, and he stared at me. I thought, *I'm an idiot; he's going to think I'm a total idiot.*

And still I couldn't move.

He gave me a smile that nearly sucked the breath from my body. "Hi." His fingers fell away from the shampoo bottle. He looked at me almost expectantly.

"Hi," I stuttered. "I'm . . . you're . . ."

Vague recognition spread across his features. "You are Jackie?"

He said my name in a glorious accent, the sounds all softened and warm. It came out more like "Tsoky." My name! I managed a nod.

"Hi." He took a step toward me. I fully expected to die right there and then. Collapse on the tile floor. Mrs. Wedershins would have to leave the counter and come clean up the mess.

"Glad to meet you." The "meet" sounded like "mit." "Jessie and Celia tell me about you." He held out his hand. He wore a gold ring with a dark blue stone.

I slipped trembling fingers into his. My shake must have felt limp as a fish. He squeezed briefly, then let go.

Words would not come. He cocked his head and regarded me with amusement. "You can talk?"

I laughed then, a shaky, amazed little laugh that bubbled right up my throat. "Yes." The next thing I knew, words gushed from me. "I've been wanting to meet you too. I just didn't expect it to be here. I love your song; I listen to it all the time. When Katherine told me you were comin', I could hardly believe it—"

My eyes widened. What was I doing, going on like this? "Sorry," I mumbled. "For babbling."

He frowned. "'Babbling'?" He said the word like "bobbling." It sounded so cultured, coming from his mouth.

"Um. You know, goin' on and on about somethin'."

Greg raised his chin in a slow nod. I hoped because he understood the word, not because he agreed with it. "In Greece, we learn English in school, but I do not speak it much until I write songs in English. I have many words to learn."

"You speak it great," I assured him. We stood there, trying to think of something else to say. I cleared my throat. "How long are you staying?"

Oh, good grief, did that sound too ... something?

"Until Tuesday." He smiled again, almost shyly. "I just arrive a few hours ago. Nice to meet you so soon."

How to respond to that? Surely he hadn't been thinking of me. "Why did you come?" I flicked my eyes toward the ceiling. "Sorry. Am I asking too many questions?"

"No." He laid a hand on the back of his neck. I gazed at his arm muscles, then blinked away. "We are in the States for our first tour. We practice twelve hours a day. Now we have some time to rest. My brother's wife says to come with her here. She says it is quiet."

Twelve hours' practice a day. For the first time it occurred to me his life may not be all ease and roses. "You must work really hard. I can't imagine it. I used to be in gymnastics, but I never practiced so many hours in one day."

He nodded.

"Well. I'll tell you one thing about Bradleyville—it's real quiet, all right. Believe me, you'll get rest here. In fact, by the time you leave, you'll probably be bored to death."

"Oh, I don't—"

A blonde woman appeared around the aisle corner. "Greg, did you—"

She took one look at me and stopped dead in her tracks. Her cheeks paled. For a moment, everything seemed surreal, as though I were the famous person causing someone to nearly faint. My cheeks warmed under her stare.

She brought a hand to her chest. "Oh, I'm so sorry. For a moment I ..." She moved toward me. "You must be Jackie." The words pulsed with emotion.

"Yes."

She took my hand in hers. Suddenly, I realized who she was. I almost wanted to pull away.

"You look exactly like your mama. I suppose you've heard that many a time, but it's true." Her blue eyes misted. The sight shocked me. "I'm Celia Cander. Your mama was my best friend all during school. The last time I saw her, she wasn't much older than you."

"Hello," I managed. She loosened her grasp, and I slipped my hand away.

She seemed to pull herself together. "I see you've met Greg."

"Uh-huh."

I wanted to dislike her. I *did* dislike her. Just thinking of her and Daddy made me blush again. And what she'd done to Mama!

"I'm so glad we ran into you," Celia said. "Until I came back last year to help my father after his stroke, I'd been away from Bradleyville since high school. I was so sorry I never got the chance to see your mama before she passed."

I nodded. Greg gave me a sad smile.

Celia shifted her attention to him. "So. Did you find what you need?"

"Ah. Yes." He picked up the bottle of shampoo. He hesitated. "You need a ride home?" he asked me.

"Thank you, no." The offer amazed me, but I just couldn't. Even to be with him, I couldn't bear another moment in Celia Cander's presence. "I can just walk."

"I walk with you then? Okay?"

I stared at him, surprised out of my wits. "Okay."

I forgot all about the perfume.

Oh, the memories of that walk. I can still picture the dappled shadows on Greg's shoulders as we passed under maple trees. I can hear the timbre of his voice as he told me about his life in Greece, his mother and father. "Mamma" and "baba," as he called them, emphasizing the last syllables. The faint, spicy scent of his sun-warmed skin. The way he watched me out of the corner of his eye as I talked. Greg had given his purchase to Celia to take home and so walked free-handed, running his fingers over a flowering bush as we passed, tapping someone's mailbox. As if he paid attention to everything around him.

He's really here, I kept telling myself. *Walking me home.* I don't think my feet touched the sidewalk once.

A couple times acquaintances from school drove by and gawked, trying to figure out who this hot stranger might be. From the passenger seat of her mama's car, Millicent nearly twisted her neck backward, trying to see. Our eyes met for a split second. *Oh, great,* I thought. Questions would abound at school tomorrow. All the same, I didn't expect any of the girls to recognize Greg. They simply wouldn't dream of such an impossibility.

Our walk took no more than fifteen minutes in measured time. But I couldn't begin to measure what happened inside me. Greg seemed to be everything I'd dreamed of. Friendly, nice. "Stuck up" couldn't begin to apply to him. What's more—and this I could hardly grasp—he seemed to like me. His glances lingered, and now and then he leaned toward me, just the slightest bit. *Maybe that's just the way Greek guys treat girls,* I told myself. *Maybe they're all flirts.*

We reached my sidewalk. "Well. This is where I live."

He gazed at our house. "It's nice."

Grandma's car sat in the driveway. I took a deep breath. "Would you like to come inside? My daddy's still at work, but Grandma is here visiting, so it'll be all right."

He smiled, as if impressed that I would not have invited him in otherwise. I wondered at that. Surely, he had plenty of girls who would give anything to be alone with him in a house. My cheeks grew warm at the thought. Would Greg do that?

What if Greg had been with a dozen girls? I thought suddenly. What if he saw me as just one more?

"I like to see your house," Greg said.

Fleetingly, I wondered how Daddy would react when he heard. He'd said I could meet Greg, not exactly bring him trailing home like a lost puppy. Oh, well. Too late to back out now.

Grandma sat next to Robert in front of the computer, watching him play the spaceship game. Clarissa had gone out to play with Alma Sue. Apparently they'd hit on some sort of truce. Most likely, it involved a bag of candy.

Seeing Greg, Grandma rose in surprise. Robert said hi without even taking his eyes off the monitor, as if this weren't the most auspicious moment of my life—bringing Greg Kostakis into my home.

"Good to meet you." Greg took Grandma's hand with such gallantry that she seemed taken aback. Not half as much, however, as when he answered her questions about his visit. At the mention of his sister-in-law, Celia, startled recognition flicked across her face. My eyes jerked to Greg, hoping he hadn't noticed. How odd it appeared to me—this ancient and disastrous tie between our families.

Grandma quickly recovered. "It's wonderful to have you," she said in all graciousness. "Would you like something to drink?"

"Ah, I—"

"Now don't you mind; it's the Bradleyville way." She waved a hand in the air. "Jackie and I'll just get somethin' in the kitchen."

She pulled me out of the room, still smiling.

"Looks like a good game," Greg said to Robert as we exited. I heard him ease into the chair next to my brother.

In the kitchen, Grandma put her hands on my shoulders. "Your daddy know he was comin' over?" she asked quietly.

Oh, boy. "Not exactly. He said I could meet Greg, but I didn't expect to run into him today."

"You'd better call him right now."

"Grandma, I wouldn't have brought him in if you hadn't—"

"I know that, Jackie. Still, your daddy should know."

I almost wondered whether she'd be so insistent if I'd brought home anybody other than Danny Cander's brother. Derek had spent over an hour here with just Clarissa and me, and nobody seemed to care. Irritation niggled up my spine at the thought. "Okay." I turned away toward the phone. Grandma reached into the refrigerator for some soft drinks. "By the way," I said, baiting her, "do you know who Greg is?"

She eyed me around the refrigerator door. "Whatever do you mean?"

"He's a singer. His group's name is LuvRush. I have a picture of them, torn from one of my magazines, hangin' on my wall."

She pushed closed the refrigerator door, a soft drink in each hand, and gawked at me. "You're kiddin'."

I effected a shrug. "Go look at the posters in my bedroom. He's the hottest guy of 'em all."

"Well," she breathed. "My." She set down the drinks and reached into our cookie jar. "My."

Her reaction proved vindication enough for me. With a little smile, I picked up the telephone. Then hoped like crazy Daddy couldn't talk. And he couldn't. His assistant told me he was in a meeting.

"At least you tried," Grandma said. "I'll vouch for you."

We took the drinks and cookies into the family room, setting them on the coffee table. For the next hour, we all talked, Greg proceeding to charm the socks off my grandma. Even Robert paused his game to listen as Greg described the food delicacies of Greece, their pastries, their strong coffee. About the city of Athens, where he lived. How the Parthenon was bathed in golden light at night as it overlooked the city from the Acropolis, and how outdoor chairs from cafés lined the narrow stone streets of the Plaka marketplace. The smell of spinach pie and roast potatoes drifting from the Byzantino Restaurant. Red-orange sunsets over the water at Cape Sounion.

Seemed to me such a romantic place could not possibly share the same planet with Bradleyville.

"Do you stay in touch with your family?" Grandma asked.

"Yes. I have a laptop computer, and I e-mail them." He turned to me. "You have an e-mail address?"

"Sort of. Daddy set one up for me, but I haven't used it yet. Haven't learned how."

But if it meant being able to write Greg, I'd certainly learn in a hurry.

With reluctance, Grandma announced she needed to leave. She offered to drive Greg to the Matthews' house. "Wouldn't want you to get lost in our major metropolis," she commented. He accepted her offer.

The glass door off the kitchen slid open, Clarissa and Winnie panting in tandem as they trotted inside. Winnie sniffed Greg's legs with curiosity, and he hunkered down to scratch behind her ears. Pure bliss half-closed her eyes, her mouth pulling up. If any dog could almost smile, it would be Winnie.

Clarissa's face looked red and sweaty, a strand of hair sticking to her cheek. I brushed it off. She pulled her head away, staring at Greg.

"Hi." He grinned at her. "You are Clarissa?"

She continued to stare most rudely.

"Clarissa." I nudged her. "Say hello."

She frowned. "I've seen you before."

Greg stood up from petting Winnie. She nosed his hand, begging for more. "Think so?"

"Yuh-huh." Distractedly, my sister rubbed sweat from her forehead. Then her face lit with sheer amazement. "I know! You're on Jackie's wall. She stares at you all the time."

If the floor had opened up and swallowed me right then, I'd have been forever grateful. Heat rose to my cheeks.

Greg nodded, looking embarrassed. "Oh." He bent down again and gave Winnie his full attention.

Robert snickered. I could have strangled him.

"Well." Grandma rescued me. "I really must be goin'. Come on, Greg, I'll take you home."

With a searing look at Clarissa, I ushered them to the door. Grandma stepped out onto the porch. Greg touched my arm. "I can call you tonight?"

Surely my cheeks were still flushed. What he must think of me. Just one more groupie who swooned over his picture. "You don't have to do that." My voice sounded flat. I wrapped my fingers around the edge of the door.

Disappointment flickered across his brow. He turned to leave, then stopped. "I can do it anyway?"

A sunray glinted one side of his hair, faintly dusting it with bronze. He smiled crookedly, and my heart surged.

I nodded.

Briefly, he laid his hand over my fingers and pressed. "I will talk to you then."

And he was gone.

chapter 18

When Greg left I whirled through the house, scrubbing a bath-room, folding laundry, brushing Winnie. I accomplished not one lick of homework. What a laugh it would be to even try. Sitting at my desk with Greg's picture looking over my shoulder, trying to con-centrate on social studies? After a busy hour I tripped into the kitchen, where I banged pots and pans, and mopped the floor while the rice cooked. When I heard the garage door open, I pushed the mop against the wall and hurried into the hallway. Daddy entered, briefcase in hand. I nearly knocked him over, determined to beat Clarissa in blurting the news. My sister had done enough damage for one day.

"Daddy, I have somethin'—"

"Daddy, Daddy, Jackie had a boy here—"

"Hush, Clarissa!" I swished my hand at her in fury.

He swung his head back and forth, perplexed.

"Anyway, I wanted—"

"And he's in a picture on her wall!"

"Clarissa!" I stomped my foot at her. "Will you be quiet!"

She folded her arms. "Well. It's true."

I shot her a look to kill. "Go. Now."

With a humph, she tromped away.

I turned back to Daddy, trying to calm my breathing. He set his briefcase down and raised his eyebrows at me, looking none too pleased.

"You tryin' to tell me Greg was here? In this house?"

"I tried to call you, but—"

"In this house?" He spaced each word. "With just you and the kids?"

"Grandma was here." I bit the inside of my cheek. "She thought he was great."

"Really. You didn't tell me he was arriving today."

"I didn't know."

"How did he end up with you? So fast?"

I told him, my heart sinking more with each question. This was just because Greg was Danny Cander's brother, I thought. The unfairness of it thickened my lungs. Daddy would not have been concerned if it had been somebody like Derek.

Daddy looked away at nothing, ambivalence clear on his face. I knew he regretted having allowed me to meet Greg. But he *had* said yes.

"He wants to call me tonight, Daddy," I ventured. "Please say that's okay."

Daddy's expression softened. He reached out his hand and cupped the side of my face. "It's a hard time in life, Jackie," he said quietly, "bein' your age." He dropped his hand, picked up his briefcase. "I'll make a call to the Matthews' house tonight before I let this go any further." He started down the hall, and I followed. "I plan on askin' Celia a few questions about her young brother-in-law. If he's a troublemaker, she won't lie to me about it."

I thought of Celia, her misty eyes as she'd greeted me. Daddy was right; she would not lie to him. Apparently she felt a debt to him—and to Mama—that she didn't think she could pay.

Back at the stove, I stirred the lima beans and rice, then checked the chicken in the oven. Daddy greeted Robert, asked Clarissa about her homework, and petted Winnie. Without a word then, he looked up a number in the phone book and dialed. He meandered toward the table, looking out at the backyard as he waited for an answer.

"Hi. Is this Celia? Well, hey there. It's Bobby Delham."

I reached inside the freezer for ice cubes. Something inside me cringed, just hearing him talk to her. What was he thinking, even as his voice sounded so unaffected? What was she thinking? Suddenly, I realized I was reacting just as he had a few nights back—dwelling on some situation that had happened years ago. My hand stilled on the ice cubes until my fingers grew cold. If I could think such things, how much more understandable for Daddy to do the same.

"I hear congratulations are in order," Daddy said. "You and Danny married last December, right?"

I dumped a handful of ice into a glass. Reached into the freezer for more, my heart doing an odd little *rat-tat*.

"That's true." Daddy lingered over the kitchen table, tapping it with his knuckles. "Katherine King. She was just a little squirt when you and I were in school."

I filled a second glass with ice. Then a third.

"Listen, that's what I wanted to talk to you about." Daddy turned to walk through the kitchen. He passed me without a glance and headed down the hall toward the master bedroom. "He was over here today . . ."

His voice faded. I heard the click of his door.

My hands nearly shook as I poured the iced tea. Turned off the stove and slid out the chicken. Then I stood waiting, leaning against the counter, clasping and unclasping my fingers. It seemed forever before Daddy returned, phone in hand.

I studied his face.

He sighed. Laid the phone down on the tile. "Well, from what Celia says, he's a very nice boy." Daddy kept his voice low so Robert and Clarissa wouldn't hear from the family room. "Says he's been raised by strict Christian parents, and that for all his singin' in a band and makin' a name for himself, they've kept strong watch over him. Apparently, he hasn't dated much himself. Celia says he seems to have taken a real likin' to you."

My legs weakened. I sank my fingers into the counter.

"So I'll let him call you. And I'll let you see him this week. But remember, Jackie." Daddy grazed my cheek with his finger. "He won't be here long. Be careful. When I was a teenager, I watched someone go through terrible pain because the one she cared for had to leave. Granted, they'd had a lot more time together than you and Greg will have. But I know the heart of a teenager—how quickly you can fall for someone. As old as you think I am, it really hasn't been that long."

"It was Celia, wasn't it?" I blurted. Then couldn't believe what I'd done.

Surprise moved across his face.

The sound of lasers fired up from the computer. "I wanted to play!" Clarissa fussed at Robert.

"Too bad, I got here first."

"Why do you ask that?" Daddy hedged.

How to back out now? I wavered between protecting myself from the suspicion of eavesdropping and the desperate need to understand.

"You loved her," I heard myself say. "For a long time. You even loved her when you dated Mama."

Ping, ping, the lasers shot.

Daddy stood back, drawing in a breath. "Who told you that? Your mama?"

I made no reply.

"Jackie, I loved your mama more than life itself. You know that."

Yes, I did know. But I wasn't talking about their marriage, couldn't he see that? All those years of hearing stories from Mama about their dating—now I realized she'd told me only the best, glazing over the bitterness like icing on sugarless cake.

"But you loved Celia first. Mama was your second choice."

"Mama was God's choice for me," he retorted. "The only right choice. If I had to do it all over, even with losin' her, I'd marry her again. Don't you ever doubt that."

"I don't, Daddy. I don't."

His expression lightened. "You're just wonderin' how it all works, aren't you. No mama to talk to, and now ready to date yourself. Just remember, Jackie, God watches over his own. If I could end up with your mama, who loved me in spite of all my stupidity, you can trust him as well."

I nodded, unable to talk about it anymore. I pushed away from the counter. "Better get supper on the table."

Every time the phone rang as I did dishes, I jumped. First Grandma Delham was on the line, wanting to put in her two cents about "that nice boy, Greg." Daddy shook his head as he hung up the receiver. "He must be some kid to get Mama so tickled over him."

Next Katherine called. She'd heard the news from Miss Jessie, who'd talked to Celia. "Oh, Katherine," I whispered, not wanting Daddy to hear our conspiracy, "Greg's *unbelievable*. And he's gonna call me tonight, so we'd better get off the phone."

"Is that Katherine?" Daddy wiggled his fingers at me, urging me to hand over the receiver.

"Don't stay on long!"

"Hi." Daddy's lips spread, his voice full of warmth. Such a little word. But the way he said it spoke volumes. "Why don't you come over for a while?"

Yes, yes! I nodded with vehemence. *Just get her over here so you can hang up!*

I hovered about the family room, trying to think straight. I'd still done no homework, and Clarissa needed to finish her math. She made a beeline for the computer. "Oh, no, you don't." I caught her by the shoulders and turned her toward the kitchen table. "Homework time."

"Just fifteen minutes."

"No."

"Ten."

"Clarissa, this is not a suggestion!"

"Please." She wriggled away from my touch.

"Why do we have to go through this every night? Do I ever let you off the hook?"

She pulled her mouth down. "Well, there's always a first time."

I glanced at Daddy. He still talked on the phone, not paying the least attention. I sidled in front of him, folding my arms. Shot up my eyebrows as if to say, *Would you please.*

He held up his hand in surrender. "Gotta go," he told Katherine. "Jackie's expecting an important call."

I marched Clarissa to the table and sat her down, wondering to myself how in the world this house could stand two generations dating at once. The whole thing was just downright strange.

Winnie flopped down in her corner with a sigh, as if empathizing with Clarissa. Soon she was snoring.

We made it through three problems before Katherine arrived. Which, of course, called for multiple hugs and numerous other means of procrastination on Clarissa's part. In time, Katherine settled on the couch with Daddy. Robert crutched his way into his bedroom to do his homework. I sat down again with Clarissa.

Two minutes later the phone rang. I nearly jumped out of my chair. Daddy made a point of answering. It was Greg. Daddy introduced himself and they talked for a minute while I shifted from one foot to the other. Katherine watched me, lips twitching. Apparently satisfied with what he'd heard, Daddy finally handed the phone to me. "Half an hour," he whispered. "It's not a suggestion."

I slid out of my tutoring chair, Daddy taking my place. Katherine sat on the other side of Clarissa.

I took the phone and headed for my bedroom, trying to think of something witty to say. "Hi." I clicked my bedroom door shut. Sank upon on my bed and stared at his picture.

"Hi." He sounded amused. "You are, what do you say, the Queen of Sheba. Today I answer to Celia, her mamma, Miss Jessie, and your baba just to talk to you."

Oh, good grief. "I'm sorry. That's Bradleyville for you. The adults are always really protective."

"That's okay. You should hear my parents. Mamma says do not look at girls until I am thirty."

I laughed, loving the way he said things. "That is pretty bad."

"She says this because she marries so young. To my brother's father, I mean. And they are . . . not good together."

"Oh." I gazed at his picture, wondering. "How did Danny and your mama get to Greece?"

"Danny's father dies just before he finishes school. Danny and Mamma leave Bradleyville soon after that and work on cruise ships for a year. Then one goes to Greece, and they stay there."

I played with the fringe on a throw pillow, thinking. Danny. Leaving town. Leaving Celia behind.

"Did . . . I mean, your brother must have known Celia when he was here, right?"

Greg hesitated, almost as if we'd hit on an uncomfortable subject. "Yes. They . . . love each other."

"Then why did he stay in Greece?" I blurted. None of this made any sense to me.

Greg's silence drew out even longer. "I don't know. Things happen."

Suddenly everything fell into place. Things happened, all right, as in Celia and my daddy. Like cold water in the face, another realization startled me. Greg's brother couldn't possibly like my daddy any more than my daddy liked him. I closed my eyes, trying to imagine it. Did Greg know all this? Is that why he sounded so uncomfortable?

An old car rattled by on the street. A neighbor's dog barked. I tried to think of something new to say.

"So tell me—"

"I want to—"

Our words tumbled over each other. "You first," he urged.

"I was just going to ask about you. I want to know everything about LuvRush. How you started. How you got where you are."

"Oh. You have all night?"

I wished. "But first I want to tell you again how much I love 'Hung Up on You.' It's my favorite."

He thanked me. "That is good to hear. Most of the time we hear from our coaches that we are bad. Our singing is horrible, and our steps are wrong. We work all day, try to improve. That is why we like the fans. They say good things."

"You must have lots of them. Fans, I mean." I didn't like the thought. All those girls. Most of them prettier than I. "So how did LuvRush start?"

I lay on my bed and listened as Greg tried to explain a desire so deep that he'd clung to it for years, even when everyone told him his band would never make it. He'd received a guitar for his eighth birthday after much pleading with his father. The feel of those strings under his fingers, the polished wood in his hands, had filled him with excitement. He took lessons and practiced constantly. His mamma loved the music. Baba just shook his head.

The other three singers in LuvRush—Alexei, Lysander, and Demetri—were older than Greg. When they were fifteen and sixteen, they formed a band. Greg proved he could play guitar well, and they asked him to join. He was only twelve. They played rock songs, imitating American groups. Greg graduated to an electric guitar. Then he started singing and surprised everyone. Slowly the band made its way into small dance clubs for teens. Greg's mamma would always go to keep an eye on him. They played at wedding receptions, in cafés on weekends. Greg spent all of his time either in school or with the band. He kept his grades up. He had to. One slip, and his father would have taken away his guitar.

One day they met a nightclub owner who knew someone who knew someone in Europe. The man made some phone calls. Months passed. Then the band was invited to send a tape of their music. After hours of practice and retake after retake, they sent the tape with much fear and trembling. More weeks passed. A month. Two months. Finally a phone call came. Could they travel to Europe? No guarantees, nothing paid. But they faced the chance of a lifetime—an audience with a real agent.

Greg's father wouldn't let him go. He was too young. His mother interceded, saying she would go with the band. Watch Greg every minute. His father relented.

Their audition proved a success. The boys could hardly believe it. Their heads spun with thoughts of making it big.

"We don't know how hard it will be," Greg said. "Even if I do I still would do it. I have the dream for so long. No one can take it away."

They had talent, their new agent told them. But their music was all wrong. They needed more of a pop sound. And if they intended to make it in America, they had to sing in English. Plus they needed a name that would appeal to young girls.

Back in Greece, they worked night and day around school. Greg and Demetri tried and tried to write new songs. They worked on harmony, dance steps. They practiced until their patience wore thin. They argued about lyrics, stomped around and kicked walls in their frustration, quit three dozen times. After months of work and very little guidance from their agent, whom they'd come to realize was small-time, they had three songs. These they taped and sent to their agent. He said they had "raw potential." In other words, try again.

The other three band members quit. For the last time, they said. Greg paced his room, tunes and snatches of lyrics running through his mind. He'd fall asleep to the music in his head, wake up to it. The band members drifted back, unable to let go of their dream. They worked for another three months, and finally taped four new songs.

One of them was "Hung Up on You."

"It is not like you hear on the radio," Greg said. "Lots of things have to be added. Like the seventh chords. Make it more interesting. It's much better now."

Greg and his friends were finally finding their sound. They wrote more songs and settled on a name. Eight months ago LuvRush traveled to Europe to cut their first CD. Greg's mother went along to supervise.

I laughed at that. Greg, with his picture in my magazine. A new star. And his mama looking over his shoulder all the time. Who would ever guess?

LuvRush signed with a manager. Their CD was a hit first in Europe, then it jumped to the States. "Hung Up on You" made it to number five on the American charts.

"So we are here. We are in America for six weeks, practicing. Mamma is with me. She goes back to Greece when Celia comes to bring me here. She does not like to be away from Baba that long. Baba says she has to go on tour with me." He laughed. "She does not want to go. I am glad to say Danny helps change his mind."

"Wow, all that's amazing," I gushed. "You've worked so hard. But what do you do about school now?"

"I have studies I do and send to Greece. Lysander and Demetri and Alex—they are fortunate to be out of school. I have much work to do this week."

"What's it—" Someone knocked on my door. "Just a minute." I cupped my hand over the mouthpiece. "What?"

Daddy stuck his head in. "Half hour's up."

I checked my clock radio and sighed. "Okay."

"Sorry," I said to Greg, "I have to go."

"Oh." He hesitated. "I can see you tomorrow? After school?"

My heart leapt at the thought. "I have to take care of my brother and sister. But let me see what I can work out. I'll call you when I get home."

"Good. And, Jackie?" *Tsoky*. My name would never sound the same to me again. "I want to say—I'm glad I meet you today."

My eyes drifted to his picture. This had to be a dream. Any moment I would wake up. "I'm glad I met you too."

I hung up the phone and pushed to my feet, half surprised to feel the solid reality of the floor beneath me.

chapter 19

"All right, out with it," Millicent demanded as she plunked down her lunch tray. "I've been waitin' all morning to hear, and so has everybody else."

True, thanks to her big mouth. I scooted my chair up to the table, flicking a sideways glance at Alison. She'd kept her promise and hadn't said a word. She was doing her best to feign dying-to-know interest along with the rest of my friends but couldn't begin to match their animation. Across the table Millicent stared at me almost accusingly. With a prim flick of her wrist, she opened out a paper napkin and placed it in her lap. Nicole blinked at me through her bangs, fingers dangling a bite of bread. Cherise mixed her corn and mashed potatoes with a vengeance.

"Yes, do tell," Cherise said, eyes on her food. "I heard he's really hot."

"Is he from Albertsville?" The bread disappeared into Nicole's mouth.

"No." I took a nonchalant sip of water. Truly it would be a miracle if I could keep Greg's identity a secret. The adults who knew would keep quiet for the Matthews' sake. Celia's parents certainly didn't need every local female between twelve and eighteen banging on their door. As for my sister and brother, I'd threatened them with death if they told. Robert caused me little worry; he couldn't understand what the big deal was anyway. But Clarissa—I didn't trust her one teeny bit. I could just see her now, bragging to a friend.

All I could do was stall things for a while and hope for the best.

"He's from Greece." I picked up my fork.

"Greece!" Nicole and Cherise echoed as one, then proceeded to volley me with questions.

Millicent held up her dainty hands. "Girls. How is she supposed to say a word with all your yakkin'?" She waited for quiet, then turned one hand palm up, as if to give me the floor.

I told my friends as succinctly as possible about Greg's relation to the Matthews and Kings.

"That's why you got him first—Katherine told you." Cherise eyed me askance. "You gonna see him again?"

Wouldn't she like to know. Matter of fact, I'd scored a major coup with Daddy the previous night. I asked him, with Katherine still around, if Greg could join us for supper the following evening. At first Daddy said no. Surprise, surprise. I'd cast a pleading look at Katherine. She turned her gaze purposely out the back window, as if to say, *I'm staying out of this one.*

"Please, Daddy?" I begged. "What could it hurt? Seems to me you'd want to meet him."

The irony of the situation was not lost on me. Hadn't it been mere weeks ago that Daddy had come to me with a similar question?

"This is way different than when you asked me if Katherine could come," I declared, "'cause you knew I'd have to cook for her. But I'm not askin' you to do a thing."

Katherine's lips twitched. She pressed them together and remained silent.

"Let him come, Daddy," my sister said.

"Clarissa, this is not your business." Daddy eyed me straight on. No question he saw right through my tactics of so innocently mentioning Katherine. Well, so what? Fair was only fair. Meaningfully, I looked from him to her and back again. There he sat with his new love. The one for whom I'd cooked a special supper. Now he was trying to say no to me?

He cupped his jaw with fingers and thumb. Rocked his knee back and forth.

"Come on, Katherine," I appealed, "say something."

"Don't put her in a position between you and me," Daddy countered.

Katherine remained silent. But she did lean forward to give him a very pointed look.

"Oh, for heaven's sake." He raised his hands, palms up. "Two against one's not fair."

"Three against one, Daddy." Clarissa folded her arms.

Daddy surveyed the ceiling. He knew when he'd been bested. "All right, Jackie," he said wearily. "He can come."

"Hello." Nicole rapped the table, making me jump. "Earth to Jackie. I asked like what does he do in Greece?"

Good grief. Talk about twenty questions. "Like what would any boy do in Greece, Nicole? Go to school."

"Oh, listen to you." Millicent raised her chin. "Miss Sarcasm."

"Sorry. But there's really not much to tell."

"I think there's a great deal to tell," she drawled. "Or you wouldn't be so possessive about the whole thing."

"I'm not bein' possessive."

"Yes, you are. If you went out with a guy from here, you'd be gab-bin' our heads off about now. Didn't I tell when I went out with Randy? Didn't Alison tell when she started goin' out with Jason?"

"That's different."

"Yeah? Why?"

"Because . . . well, for one thing I didn't 'go out' with him." I pushed my tray away. Pressed my back against the chair.

Millicent watched me, thinning her lips. "What's his name?"

I hesitated. "Greg."

"Greg what?"

"Don't know."

"Yes, you do."

"Why are you makin' such a big deal out of this?" I retorted. "I told you he'll only be here a few days. When he leaves, you'll still have Randy, and Alison will still have Jacob. And I'll be have-nobody Jackie." I stopped abruptly, surprised at the hurt in my voice.

Millicent eyed me like a wise counselor. "Oh, I see. I get it." She drew out the words, then offered me a patronizing smile. "Don't worry, Jackie. You'll find a boyfriend soon."

For a friend, Millicent could be downright annoying. I had a choice. Either strangle her right then and there, or go take a walk and cool off. I rose and picked up my tray.

"You haven't eaten anything," Cherise protested.

"I'm not hungry." I looked across the cafeteria and spotted Derek dumping the remains of his food in the trash. He slid his tray on top of the stack, then ambled toward the door. Something about him caught my eye. I had to look twice before I realized what was different.

"Derek's not wearing his glasses."

Millicent and Nicole turned as one to look. Cherise took a large bite of her brownie, then craned her neck, chewing.

"He hasn't had 'em on all day," Alison said. "I saw him in third period."

I'd been in a class with him that morning, too, but hadn't paid attention.

Millicent shrugged back to the table. "Probably broke 'em." She looked up at me questioningly, as if amazed I'd noticed.

I left the table without another word.

Between fifth and sixth periods, I passed Derek in the hall, my mind still stuffed with little but Greg. Derek smiled at me but didn't slow. For some reason I touched his arm, stopping him.

"Hey." I pressed against a locker, away from the flow of bodies. His gray eyes looked just as I remembered from that day at the Kings. Warm. Round. "Where are your glasses?"

"Oh." He creased his face in surprise, as if to assure me the topic had been the furthest thing from his mind. "I got contacts." He shuffled his books from one arm to the other.

"Hi, Jackie," Shirley Crane sang as she passed from behind, tapping my shoulder.

"Hi," I said with distraction, still looking at Derek.

He scratched his head, clearly put on the spot. "Guess I better get to class."

My heart went out to him. I hoped he'd gain some self-assurance through his improved appearance. If he'd just stand up straight, quit tilting his head. "You look really good, Derek."

His eyelids flickered. "Thanks."

We couldn't seem to find anything more to say. He mumbled "see ya" and went his way while I went mine.

Within seconds, my thoughts had drifted back to Greg. Just a few more hours, I told myself, and he'd arrive at our house for supper. As voices chattered around me and lockers slammed, I pictured Greg at our table. Katherine next to Daddy. And suddenly the unfolding events in our household didn't seem as strange as they did wondrous.

How ironic now to look back on that moment. I can almost hear the scuff of my feet across the dusty tiled hallway, feel the schoolbooks in my arms. I remember thinking, as I entered the classroom and slid into my seat, that life was finally improving, and the Delhams had much to anticipate. That Daddy had found happiness, which he so deserved.

That I couldn't *wait* for supper.

Not in a million years would I have dreamed how disastrous it would prove to be.

chapter 20

Katherine came over that afternoon to help me cook. She looked smashing in a pair of tan slacks and a short-sleeved silk orange top that hugged her curves, the gold bracelet gracing her wrist. I glanced down at myself, wondering what on earth I could change into for supper. The way things stood right now, Greg would more likely have eyes for her than for me.

We stood in the kitchen, canned laughter from a cartoon show drifting in from the family room. I'd seen Clarissa flop down on the couch, one hand scratching Winnie's ears.

Katherine stared at the floor, deep in thought.

"What is it?" I asked.

Her head jerked up. "Nothing. I was just . . ." She waved a dismissive hand. "So. What are we cooking?"

"I'll show you." I began happily pulling out recipes from my file.

"Wait a minute, though. Shouldn't you be doing homework first?"

At a time like this? "Oh, come on, I've got more important things to do."

"Huh-uh." She laid a hand on my recipe file, stopping my busy fingers. "Come to think of it," she said knowingly, "did you manage to do any homework yesterday?"

I winced.

"Ah. Thought so. Go on then. I'll make supper."

"I don't want—"

"Go, Jackie. What do you suppose your daddy would think if he knew Greg was costing you schoolwork? Not to mention making sure that your brother and sister do theirs."

Still I hesitated. I wanted to take the credit for making a bang-up meal.

Katherine placed a hand on her hip. "Look. Are you planning on seeing Greg again this weekend? If so, you'd better not let anything slide around here. I've gone out on a limb for you; now don't blow it."

What was this—all the sudden she was boss in our house? A retort sprang to my lips. I bit it back. Katherine was right; she *had* been a big help.

"Okay. I'm in my bedroom, doing homework. And on my way, I'm checking out Robert. How's that?"

She studied me, as if trying to figure if I was being smart. Then she flicked her eyes. "Listen to me, telling you what to do. Sorry. I'm . . . I just want the best for you."

"It's okay. Thanks."

Before holing myself in my bedroom—probably to do little more than daydream—I looked in on Robert. He sat propped against pillows on his bed, good knee up, reading a magazine. In the last few days school friends had covered his cast with get-well scribbles. Adults had signed it, too, as they'd stopped in to say hello, most of them bearing gifts. Grandma and Grandpa Westerdahl had brought Robert a new computer game, and Coach Crary had presented him with a stack of sports magazines he hadn't read. Seemed most of them were now scattered across his bed.

"Studying hard, I see."

He grunted.

"Robert, just 'cause your leg's broken and you're the town hero doesn't mean you can let your studies slide."

As if I had room to talk.

"I'm done with homework."

"You are not."

"Am too."

I sighed. Amazing how my life could continue in such banality when pure magic had entered it. "Fine, Robert, do what you want."

"Why not? They can't exactly kick me off the team for low grades now, can they."

The bitterness in my brother's voice stopped me short. Suddenly I realized how self-centered I'd been the last few days. All caught up in Greg, not pausing to think how disappointed Robert must be in losing the rest of softball season. I slipped into his room and sat beside him. Brushed the hair off his forehead.

"I'm sorry. This must be awful hard for you."

He let the magazine fall closed and stared sightlessly across the room.

"Robert. You helped win the game for your team. And your leg will heal. You'll be able to play next year."

"What if it won't?" He turned toward me, pain in his eyes. "What if it's messed up, and I can't ever run right again?"

"From what I've heard, that's not what the doctor said."

The faint sound of cabinets opening and closing filtered in from the kitchen. Robert ruffled the pages of the magazine with his thumb. "But what if he's wrong, Jackie? What if one stupid move will cost me for the rest of my life?"

My fingers stilled on his head. What a horrible thought. Surely God would not let that happen. "Robert, I honestly don't think that will be the case. You can't let fear of the future keep you from doin' the things you should be doin' now, while you're in the cast. And you know you've got people prayin' for you."

He nodded solemnly. "Yeah."

I gave his shoulder a squeeze, then stood, sensing he'd said all he wanted on the subject. "Suppose I better do my own homework."

He gave another grunt. "You're not doin' homework; you're starin' at that guy's picture." He picked up his magazine and flipped to where he'd been reading.

Oh, fine, that's the appreciation I got. "Thank you, dear brother, for your learned opinion."

I closed his door firmly on my way out.

Two hours later, my homework done, believe it or not, I stood in the kitchen with Katherine, making a salad. Clarissa sat at the table, miraculously working on her math by herself.

The phone rang. Miss Connie was on the line, sounding worried. I handed the phone to Katherine.

Apprehension darted across her face. "Hi." She disappeared into the family room, her voice lowering. I frowned at her back. Something wasn't right, and I did not like the unsettled feeling that kicked through me. Nothing could go wrong tonight. Nothing.

I slipped out of the kitchen toward the entry hall, then eased toward the open archway door of the family room, listening.

"How many times has he called?" Katherine hunched over the phone, her back to me. Who could she be talking about? Couldn't be Daddy.

"All you can do is say the same thing we've been saying—I *don't* want to see him."

She paused.

I heard the dog flop down in the kitchen. "Get off my feet, Winnie," Clarissa complained.

"What makes you think that?" Katherine gave her head a disgusted toss. "If he keeps calling and harassing us, I'll report him." She ran a hand through her hair, sighing. "Okay. Thanks, Mama. Have a good time at the Clarks' tonight."

Katherine hung up the phone and stared at it mindlessly. I sidled back into the kitchen. By the time she appeared I stood before the salad bowl. I stole a look at her profile, apprehension coiling through my stomach. *I don't want to see him.* The words sounded so threatening, so frightening for Daddy, that I could only push them away. Whatever this was from Katherine's past, she'd handle it. Her past didn't matter now, I told myself. She'd come back to Bradleyville for Daddy. It didn't affect us. It did not.

Besides, I thought, tonight was hardly the time to worry about it. In half an hour, Greg would arrive.

❧❧

"Somebody put Winnie out!" I called when the doorbell rang. I drew myself up, closed my eyes. I could barely breathe. *Calm, Jackie, be calm.* Quickly, I slipped into my bedroom for one last look in the mirror. I'd changed into a skirt and one of my favorite shirts—a lacy white cotton with bell sleeves. The front part of my hair was pulled back away from my face. I'd dabbed on a bit of blusher and lip gloss. Now I wondered if I'd overdone it. Well, too late.

With a deep breath, I went to answer the door.

Greg stood on our porch looking rather sheepish, the crinkle-wrapped bottom of a flower bouquet clutched in both hands. He wore khaki pants and a bright blue silk shirt that set off his dark skin. I caught a whiff of spice-scented cologne. He smiled at me, and the corners of his eyes creased.

Celia sat in their rental car at the curb. We waved to each other, and she drove away.

"She says to call when I'm ready to go back, and she can pick me up," Greg explained. "I don't have a driver's license for this country." He pronounced the word almost like "cowlty," with the "l" drawn out.

"Okay." I pushed back the door, ushering him inside. Knowing the last thing I wanted to do was call Celia to pick him up. I fully planned on driving Greg home myself.

"These are for you." He held out the bouquet.

"Oh!" My first flowers. "Thank you."

Katherine came from the kitchen, Daddy by her side. I introduced them. "You are the one who is almost my cousin." Greg grinned at Katherine.

"Yes, it's about time we met." She hugged him briefly. "I hear you're going to meet my whole family tomorrow."

Greg said hello to Daddy and shook his hand with solemn respect. If not for his accent, with all Greg's politeness he could have been a Bradleyville boy, born and bred.

Please, Daddy, please like him.

While Daddy and Greg talked, I hurried away to put the flowers in a vase.

At supper, we sat at the dining room table, Katherine in Mama's seat at the end for the first time. Greg helped me get seated, his hand grazing my shoulder. My skin tingled at his touch. Robert sank awkwardly into his chair opposite me and placed his crutches on the floor. He had to sit half-turned, with his broken leg sticking out beyond the table leg.

"Mm." Clarissa sniffed appreciatively.

Katherine had made a wonderful dish of chicken in a rich sauce, plus rice and herbed peas. All the same, I felt too nervous to eat much. Daddy said the prayer, and we began passing the bowls around the table.

Greg, naturally, fell into the center of attention.

"Tell us about how you got started in your band," Daddy urged. Oh, brother. I wondered how many times Greg had been asked to tell that story.

But he told it again, this time peppered with interrupting questions.

"Is your picture in magazines where you live?" Clarissa wondered.

Greg laughed. "Yes, more than here. How can I explain? In my country we are like one big family. We are very proud of someone from Greece who becomes known, particularly in other countries. People from Athens give us much attention when we say we come to the U.S. They give us a big party before we leave. Many people come."

"That must have made you feel very proud," Katherine said.

"Yes, proud for Greece. We want to . . ." He searched for a word. "Represent our country. When we are interviewed here, we always talk about Greece."

Greg's humility amazed me. All of his success, and just look at him. To think I ever could have liked an egomaniac like Billy Sullivan. Never would I dream of him again. I glanced at Daddy. Surely he could see how wonderful Greg was.

Katherine reached for her iced tea, her bracelet reflecting in the light. "Where do you go next when you leave Bradleyville?"

"Back to California to practice. Then we start the tour."

"I hear you're coming to Lexington."

Greg nodded. "I don't know when. I don't know the names of cities enough to . . . keep them straight." He scrunched his face. "Keep them straight? That is right?"

I smiled. "Sounds right to me."

Greg looked to Daddy. "You like to come to the concert? I can get tickets for you all." He grinned. "Seats in the front."

"Please, Daddy?" I blurted, afraid he'd say no. I *had* to go to that concert.

"I wanna go," Clarissa declared. Robert just grunted. I knew he couldn't care less.

"I don't know," Daddy said slowly. "We've never been to something like that."

"I can give you our CD if you don't have it. You can listen to the songs."

Katherine's smile teased. "Come on, Mr. Delham, you just might enjoy yourself. The concerts are a lot of fun. Loud music. Girls scream-ing." She winked at me.

"Sounds awful," Robert commented, then caught himself. "Oh, sorry."

Greg laughed good-naturedly. "That's okay."

"We do thank you, Greg," Katherine said. "I know tickets down front are expensive." She glanced meaningfully at Daddy.

Daddy scratched his cheek, caught by Katherine's ploy. I knew he didn't care a whit about going, but neither did he want to seem impo-lite at the offering of an expensive gift.

"*I* know, Bobby!" Katherine exclaimed. "You stay here with Robert and Clarissa. I'll take Jackie."

Clarissa made a face.

Yes! I didn't want my whole family with me anyway. Katherine would be perfect. She'd probably be really fun at a concert.

Greg's eyes lit up. He smiled at me, and my heart nearly melted. Would I be able to see him personally before the concert? I wondered. Or after?

"Well," Daddy hedged. "That's a thought."

"I will get two tickets for you," Greg put in. "On the front row."

Katherine raised her eyebrows at Daddy. "You have any idea how hard it is to get front-row seats?"

He gave her a look. "That sounds very nice," he replied to Greg. "Let me know when it is, okay? Then we'll see."

"But, Daddy," Clarissa protested, "I wanna—"

The doorbell rang.

Daddy frowned. "Now who can that be?"

Supper in Bradleyville is a sacred family time. Folks just don't show up on one another's doorsteps anywhere between 5:30 and 7:00. Even Clarissa's friends didn't come asking to play during that time.

My chair sat closest to the open archway leading into the hall. "I'll get it." Still thinking about Greg's concert, I blithely rounded the corner, my steps hitting the wood floor, and opened the front door.

A stranger slouched on our porch, one hand shoved in the pocket of his jeans. Brown hair in a buzz cut. Dark green, piercing eyes. I caught a whiff of alcohol.

"Hey," he said brusquely, jerking his head. "I'm looking for Katherine King. I asked somebody on Main Street back there, and they said she might be here."

I ogled him, instantly wary. "Who are you?"

He dragged in a long breath, his nostrils widening. "Her fiancé."

chapter 21

I couldn't move, thoughts tangling in my head.

He stood wide-legged, staring down at me, almost as if enjoying my shock. "Hasn't told you about me, has she?" He emitted a bitter laugh. "Can't say I'm surprised. Katherine has a way of keeping secrets."

My spine tingled. A surreal aura stole over me, as if I'd just tripped onto the stage of some foreign play. All I could think to do was close the door.

He kicked out a foot and wedged it in the doorway. I stared at it, wide-eyed.

"Look, I've called and called. Tried to be patient. Now I've come all the way here, and I'm not leaving until I see her."

He pushed open the door, and I wilted toward the wall.

"Who is it, Jackie?" Daddy's voice filtered around the corner.

"I'm looking for Katherine King!" The man strode past me to the archway. "Well, well, there she is." His thin lips pulled into a satisfied smile.

I edged behind him to peer into the dining room. Katherine's lips slowly parted. Her face blanched white. "Wh–what are you doing here?"

Daddy rose from his chair. "Who are you? What do you want?"

Greg ducked his head, as if embarrassed to be caught in some private family matter. Clarissa's mouth formed a round O. She started to say something, and Robert shushed her.

The man drew to his full height. "I've got business with Katherine." Each word sounded precise, dripping with arrogance.

"No." Katherine pulled to her feet. "I told you, Trent—I don't want to see you again. I can't believe you came here!"

Daddy hurried to her side and grasped her elbow protectively. "Whoever you are, you need to leave."

"Not without my ring, I'm not." He sneered at Katherine. "As for this piece of trash, you can have her."

Katherine sucked in air. Daddy's eyes narrowed and his jaw flexed. I'd never seen such an expression on his face. "You are leaving. *Right now.*" He slapped a palm against Trent's shoulder and pushed. Trent's arm shot up and knocked Daddy's aside.

"Trent, stop it!" Katherine cried.

Clarissa whimpered. I shrank through the doorway and ran around the table to her. Greg had pushed back in his chair, unsure what to do.

"Katherine, get out of the way," Daddy commanded. He turned to Trent. "Leave here right now, or I'm callin' the police."

"Bobby, just let me talk some sense into—"

"Quiet, Katherine!"

"What do you mean, talk sense into *me?*" Trent scorned. "Where's *your* sense? You leave your fiancé without so much as a word, with all our bills? A monthly rent I can't pay alone? Least you could do is give me the ring back." His searing eyes dropped to her left hand. "What do you do, take it off when you cheat on me?"

Daddy shot a stunned look at Katherine. "Is this true? You're engaged to him?"

Guilt stiffened Katherine's face. She could not say a word. I watched the color drain from Daddy's cheeks.

"So now she's living with you?" Trent spat the words at Daddy, clearly intending to hurt. "Let me tell you—she'll dump you, too. Just like she dumped me and all the rest before."

Daddy's mouth hung open. Clarissa began to cry.

"Trent, the kids—"

"Shut up, Katherine! Why shouldn't they know your dirty little secrets? How you hop from this place to that? How you hop *beds.*"

"That's enough!" Daddy shouted. He swiveled toward Trent and shoved him toward the hall.

From then on, everything happened at once, spinning out of control like some twisted, evil calliope.

Trent's face turned crimson. Without warning, he lowered his head and lunged into Daddy, knocking him across the dining room. Daddy crashed into the wall, elbows splayed, head hitting hard.

Instantly, Greg jumped from his chair toward Trent and plunged a fist against his jaw. Trent's head snapped to the side, teeth clacking, his skin grazed from Greg's ring.

Clarissa screamed and ran to cower in the corner. Only a few feet from the men, Robert scrabbled desperately for his crutches.

Katherine nearly got hit by Daddy's body. I ran to grab her and jerked her back.

Daddy shook his head hard, trying to focus. I pushed Katherine toward Clarissa, while Robert scrambled out of the way, crutches wobbling.

Trent gathered his strength and swung wildly at Greg. He missed. Greg punched his left ear.

"Aah!" Trent's lips pulled back in fury. Snarling, he bashed Greg's cheek. *Smack.* I could practically feel the impact. Greg ricocheted into the table. One elbow landed on the edge of Katherine's plate, flipping it over. Food flew into the air. Her glass of iced tea tumbled onto the carpet.

Katherine, Clarissa, and I all screamed until I thought my eardrums would burst. Robert never made a sound.

Daddy roared into Trent and punched with both fists. Greg staggered upright, blood at the side of his mouth, then joined in. One of the punches landed squarely in Trent's stomach. Trent's jaw fell open, air keening through his half-closed throat. He dropped to his knees.

"Call the police, Jackie!" Daddy stood over him, arm pulled back, ready to launch. Greg swayed, huffing. His silk shirt bunched at his waist untucked.

"Take Clarissa," I breathed to Katherine. I darted around the table and into the hall toward the kitchen, nearly slipping on the floor. My fingers shook so badly I could hardly dial 911. Bradleyville only has one policeman, and that emergency line is rarely used. Officer Hankins answered on the first ring.

"W–we n–need your help!" I stuttered, my vision blurring with tears.

"Who is this?"

"Jackie Delham. Th–there's a man. He's fighting with Daddy."

"I'm on my way." The phone banged in my ear.

I stumbled back to cringe in the dining room doorway, tears scalding my cheeks. Trent lay in a fetal position on the carpet, arms over his stomach. Someone must have landed a final blow. Daddy glanced at me questioningly. I nodded.

Nobody moved. Clarissa sobbed in Katherine's arms.

We waited.

A minute later, Officer Hankins's car screeched up to our curb. I heard the car door slam, the pound of feet. I ran to our front door and threw it open. "In there." I pointed.

He raced into the dining room, surveyed the scene, the three damaged men. He frowned from Greg to Trent, both strangers to him.

"He pushed his way in here and wouldn't leave." Daddy indicated Trent, voice dripping with derision. "He started to fight."

With no further questions, Officer Hankins dropped to one knee, the leather on his uniform squeaking. He reached back for his handcuffs and slapped them around Trent's wrists. "All right, get up." He yanked Trent to his feet.

Trent's face twisted. He bent forward and groaned.

"I kick him in the stomach," Greg explained. His breath came in puffs. Blood had dripped from his mouth onto his shirt. Food clung to the silk.

"Looks like he got a good one on you, too," the policeman commented. He looked at Daddy, who seemed a little woozy. "And you."

"I'm okay," Daddy and Greg said at once.

Officer Hankins studied Trent. "What's your name?"

No response.

The policeman wrinkled his forehead at Daddy. "Who is he?"

Daddy hesitated. "I don't know."

Officer Hankins swung a narrowed gaze from one man to the other, trying to read sense into the situation. Clarissa hiccuped another cry, and his face softened.

"All right. I'll go lock him up for a while. Then I'm gonna have to come back here, find out a little more about what happened." He pushed Trent past me. I flinched away from the man.

Trent dug his feet into the carpet. "I'm not going until I get my ring back!" he hissed at Katherine. "That ring's worth three thousand dollars."

"Come on, come on." Officer Hankins prodded him. "We'll have this little discussion another time." He turned back to Daddy. "Y'all better call Doc, have him check you out."

Daddy nodded.

Not once had he looked at Katherine.

We all stood practically frozen, hearing the click of the front door shutting.

I didn't know who to go to first. I wanted to hug Greg, thank him. Cry on his shoulder. But knew I couldn't do that. Clarissa still clung to Katherine, Robert scrunched up next to them. Daddy brought a hand to his forehead, closed his eyes. Sadness and shame creased his face. What had Katherine done to him? I ran over and threw my arms around him, pain for him welling up my throat. Slowly, he slid his arms around my back, as if all energy had been driven from him. He rested his chin on the top of my head. I could feel him trembling.

"Daddy, I'm so sorry," I choked into his shirt.

He patted the back of my head.

Clarissa joined us, crying with relief and fear. Then Robert, awkwardly leaning into us on his crutches.

The four of us shook and clung to one another as we hadn't done since Mama's death. I could hear Katherine sniffing from her place against the wall. At least she was smart enough to stay put. I would never trust her again. Ever.

Finally, we pulled apart. Daddy moved to Greg, held out a bruised hand. "Thank you." They shook carefully, flinching at each other's touch. "Better take that ring off in case your hand swells," Daddy noted. Greg edged it off his finger and slipped it into his pocket.

The spilled iced tea lay in an ugly spot on our light blue carpet. I picked up Katherine's glass and set it back on the table. New tears biting my eyes, I surveyed the mess on both the floor and table. So much to clean. So much to make right. Would the stains ever come out?

Weariness surged through me, trailing one depressing thought after another in its wake. What would happen to us now? We'd lost Mama, now this with Katherine. Daddy had to be heartbroken. So much for Pastor Beekins and his sermon, I told myself. At that horrible moment, I felt no hope at all that God could bring good out of past mistakes. Look what Katherine had done. *Lived* with men? Lied to Daddy? Who *was* she, really?

Who had Daddy—who had my family—fallen in love with?

A piece of trash.

I had to turn my mind off. Do *something*. Automatically, I began stacking the dishes to clear the table. Daddy went to phone Doc Forkes, and Greg disappeared into the bathroom. For a wonderful, white minute, I blocked out all, thinking only to clean. To work. To throw myself into a task as I'd always done since Mama's death, channeling my energy away from my emotions.

"Help me, Clarissa," I commanded, heading toward the kitchen with a full load. When I returned, Katherine was picking up plates. I aimed a scathing look at her, and she slipped them back on the table. She stepped away, eyes downcast, a tear dropping on her cheek. Then she turned and left the room. When Greg emerged from the bathroom, she went in and hid.

He'd washed the blood from his face. His jaw had begun to swell and turn color. The food on his shirt was now gone, replaced with greasy spots. They would never come out. I set down the dirty silverware in my hand, searching for words. All I could do was press my lips together, silently messaging how sorry I was. How utterly humiliated. Greg approached me, sadness in his eyes. He placed his hands on my shoulders, his right knuckles battered and red, then urged me toward him.

"I'm so sorry," he whispered, just as I had to Daddy. "So sorry."

Limply, I let him hug me. Was it just an hour ago I'd have died for this? "You shouldn't be apologizing, I should. I can't believe this happened."

Daddy's footsteps crossed the hall from the kitchen. I pulled away from Greg, feeling the guilt on my face. It wasn't right somehow, Daddy seeing us hug in comfort, when he and Katherine couldn't even say one word to each other.

He pretended not to notice. "Doctor Forkes is on his way." His voice sounded flat. "Greg, you stay and let him have a look at you. We'll also have to talk to Officer Hankins when he comes back. Then we'll get you home."

"Yes, sir."

Daddy's chin dropped to his chest. "Dear God. The apology I'm gonna owe your family."

"No, no," Greg assured him. "I'm glad I am here."

Doctor Forkes and Officer Hankins arrived within minutes of each other. I'd cleared the table of dishes, but food still smeared and puddled on the cloth. Without being told, Robert took charge of Clarissa, taking her into his bedroom and closing the door. Katherine sat on the family room couch, face pinched, waiting.

While the policeman looked on, Doc examined Daddy, then Greg. Lots of bruises and soreness but nothing broken. They should ice their wounds. A knot had formed on the back of Daddy's head. "Doesn't look like you hit hard enough for a concussion, though," the doctor concluded.

He smiled almost sadly at Greg as he left. "Do tell Celia hello for me. I got to know her when she was here nursing her dad a year ago. Tell her congratulations on her marriage. Her wedding day was just a

week from mine. And," Doc added, "tell her . . . that I hope she and
your brother are as happy as Sharon and I am."

Greg promised he would.

Once the doctor had left, the four of us gathered with Officer Hankins in the family room. He joined Katherine on the couch. Daddy sat
to the side in an armchair, where he could watch her face. I took the
computer seat, Greg on the extra kitchen chair beside it.

First Officer Hankins turned to Katherine. "Our fightin' friend
wouldn't answer a one a my questions after I locked him up. You're
gonna have to tell me who he is."

Katherine's gaze remained on the carpet. His name is Trent Baxter,
she told us. He had been her fiancé while she was in California. She
had realized he wasn't right for her. One day she drove away from him
for good and returned to Bradleyville. She left him a letter, telling him
the marriage was off. Apparently, he'd tracked down her parents' phone
number and had begun calling two days ago. Katherine had talked to
him more than once, telling him she didn't want to see him again. She
had no idea he'd come here. He did occasionally travel on business to
Nashville, she said. Perhaps once there, he'd decided to come harass
her personally.

"This ring he's talkin' about?" Officer Hankins prodded.

"I sold it." Katherine's voice was barely audible. "I needed money
to get back here and start a new life."

Daddy stared at her, stone-faced. Officer Hankins threw him a
glance. Clearly, he saw there was more to the tale than we were telling.
But I knew Daddy. He'd deal with his hurts privately. By morning, gossip about what had transpired in our home would be all over town. It
was still light outside; most assuredly the neighbors had watched the
policeman's and doctor's cars come and go. Especially Mrs. B next door,
who never missed anything. Still, Daddy would not spread Katherine's
shame any further than our four walls. *Why, Daddy?* I wanted to cry.
*Why let everyone think she's the innocent victim? She lived with this man
and probably others. She hid all this from you!*

How easy it was for me to judge then—when I hadn't lived long
enough to know how easy it is to fall into duplicity. I cringe now,
remembering.

The rest of us gave statements about what happened during the
fight.

"You want to press charges?" Officer Hankins asked Daddy.

The lamplight by Daddy's chair cast a sheen on his pallid cheek. He lifted a hand. "I . . . don't know. Let me think about it tonight."

Officer Hankins studied him, but Daddy would say no more.

"All right." Sighing, the policeman pushed off the couch. "I can keep Baxter locked up overnight. Bobby, you and I'll need to talk tomorrow."

With one last look at Katherine's stricken face, he took his leave.

"I'll take Greg home," I told Daddy before he could offer himself. His scarce acknowledgment bespoke the depth of his shock. I knew his sense of responsibility would have driven him to apologize personally to the Matthews. I looked from him to Katherine. They would need to talk. I hoped he ripped her apart. Told her to never set foot in our house again.

"I'll check on Clarissa and Robert first," I said. "Tell them to stay in Robert's room until I get back."

Greg waited tactfully in the garage while I looked in on my brother and sister. "Jackie!" Clarissa flung her arms around my waist and cried. I held her silently, anger and hatred for Katherine throbbing through my veins. Clarissa could not begin to understand all that had happened, the changes in our lives that this night would bring.

She tilted her tearstained face up at me. "Jackie, Robert wouldn't tell me. Why did that man call Katherine a piece—?"

"Shh." I pressed fingers against her lips. I could not bear to hear the phrase spoken from this innocent mouth. Robert turned away to hide the sick expression on his face. What the words must have done to him—a young boy, looking up to Katherine the way he did. Surely they crawled and wriggled and slimed inside him, just as they did within me. I wondered how we could ever look at Katherine again and not think of the label Trent Baxter had prescribed with such apparent accuracy.

"Clarissa." I sat on Robert's bed and pulled her down with me. "Everything's going to be okay. I need you to stay in here with Robert now while I take Greg home. Don't go to Daddy now, hear? Let him and Katherine talk. I'll come in here and get you when I get back."

She nodded, resting in assurance upon my lie that all would be well.

Before leaving, I hugged Robert, whispering, "Are you all right?" He nodded, his forehead creased and eyes averted to the carpet.

As I joined Greg in the garage and we got into the car, I silently begged God to see my family through the next few days.

chapter 22

I can walk," Greg said as I backed our Ford Taurus out of the garage. "It isn't far."

I managed a smile. "Yeah, right. A stranger walking through town with a bruised face and a stained shirt. You have any idea how many people would call Officer Hankins?"

"Oh." He touched my shoulder. "Then we can talk before I go back?"

I could not believe this night. Greg Kostakis wanted to be with *me*—alone. The thrill I once could have taken in that. Now I felt only weary gratitude. "We can take a few minutes." I reached the end of our street and turned right on Main. "I can probably find a spot outside town to stop."

Instead of turning left on Minton toward the Matthews', I drove on straight through the stoplight. Two miles past the Bradleyville sign an old logging road veered left. We bumped over ruts and rounded a curve through maple trees until the highway lay out of sight. I rolled to a stop and turned off the car. Dust puffed up from the tires to hover, orange-tinted, in the breezeless sunset.

Suddenly, I had no idea what to do next.

Greg shifted to face me, fingers spread on his legs, the knuckles on his right hand puffy and red. I could see the faint indentation from his ring.

"I hope you can put your ring back on soon," I said.

"I'm sure I will."

I searched the corners of my mind for something to say. "Does it mean something? I mean the ring."

The words sounded so stupid. Poor Greg, sitting there with a jaw that looked purple and swollen. It needed ice. I needed a hole to crawl into. My family needed my *mama* back.

"It's the stone for my birthday. A sapphire." Greg felt his pocket, assuring himself the ring was still inside. "My parents buy it for me before I leave Greece. It means much to me."

I nodded. "When is your birthday?"

"September twelve. I am sixteen last year. Yours is when?"

"February tenth. Sixteen for me, too." I drew my shoulders in with a little shiver.

"You are cold?"

"No, it's warm. I just . . ." I focused on my lap.

"Jackie," he said quietly, "Katherine will be okay. Your baba will protect her."

My head came up. "Katherine! Who cares about Katherine?"

He studied me, brows knitting. "Ah, I—"

"She lied to Daddy! She didn't tell him about that man; I know she didn't. I could see it on his face. He can't afford to be hurt again, don't you see? We've already lost Mama. You know what it took for us to open our hearts to somebody else?"

The words tumbled over each other until tears pricked my eyes. I blinked them back. I felt shame enough; the last thing I needed was to cry.

Greg laid his hand on my arm. "I am so very sorry."

The gentleness in his voice cracked something inside me. Slowly, I lowered my head to the steering wheel and broke into quiet sobs. Greg sighed with sympathy. "Here." He pulled me toward him until I listed awkwardly over the console, arms crossed over my chest. Leaning against him, I shuddered air in and out, crying for Daddy, and our family, and Mama. Not to mention the hopelessly shattered night.

I don't know how long I cried, but I do remember what brought me out of it. The sensation of Greg's fingers silking through my hair. I stilled, suddenly aware, focusing on his touch. My back muscles pulled from the strange position I found myself in, but I did not want to move. I blinked my eyes open to focus on a button of his shirt, the silk fabric soft beneath my cheek. The faintest scent of his cologne lingered. I heard his heartbeat and closed my eyes again, listening. Until a noisy truck lumbered by out on the highway, breaking the spell. I moved away from Greg then and flopped back against my seat, exhaling a long breath. A blackbird swooped in front of the car, its wings sheening in the waning sun. I watched it fly away.

"You are okay?"

"Yeah." I gazed at him ruefully. "I should be askin' you that. Your face looks terrible."

One side of his mouth curved. "Thanks."

"No, I didn't mean . . ." Carefully, I touched his cheek. "It must hurt."

He folded his fingers around mine, easing them away from his face. "It is fine."

We managed a little smile at each other. Then I realized my tears must have tracked through my blusher, and my nose probably rivaled Rudolph's. I looked away. "I should get back. Robert and Clarissa need me."

"Of course." He hesitated. "I want to see you again. Maybe go out tomorrow night?"

I picked a piece of lint off the car seat and rolled it between my finger and thumb. This was too good to be true, absolutely too good. Maybe just like Katherine and Daddy. Dueling voices argued inside my head. *Greg really likes me. Greg's got a million girls and is just looking for something to do in Bradleyville.*

"I don't know."

"You don't know if you can, or you don't want to?"

I shook my head at the ridiculous question. "Of course I want to. But I'll have to see. I don't know . . . how my family will be."

He brushed my cheek with a fingertip. My skin tingled under his touch. "I hope we can."

When I let Greg off at the Matthews', he reached for my hand and pressed it between his palms. "Thank you for dinner. I pray for your family tonight."

"Thank *you*," I whispered. "For everything."

chapter 23

Saturday morning we took the phone off the hook. By eight o'clock it rang like church chimes. Everybody knew a few details but not near enough. They wanted to know how we were, and for heaven's sake, what exactly happened?

Most of the calls came from my friends. Even the gossip-minded adults of Bradleyville carry a certain modicum of propriety. I talked to Alison, telling her everything about Katherine, swearing her to secrecy. Then Nicole called, then Cherise. I wouldn't tell them much. Millicent's demand of a minute-by-minute explanation proved the last straw. "I heard that guy was there too, and that he practically saved your life!" she breathed. "Is his jaw broken?"

Daddy heard me mumble an excuse that I had to go. That's when he told me to leave the receiver off the hook. He leaned against the counter looking bruised and worn, his hair still mussed from sleep. More likely, the lack of it. I hadn't slept that well myself. The knuckles on his right hand were swollen and discolored, matching Greg's, no doubt. He flexed his shoulders and arched his back like a football player after a hard game.

"How's your head?" I asked.

"Sore. But I'll live."

Silence. I wanted desperately to ask him about his talk with Katherine but didn't know how. Funny how mere words can seem so threatening, as if tied tongues somehow deaden the hurt.

A tinny voice sounded from the phone. "If you'd like to make a call, please hang up and try again . . ." The annoying off-the-hook signal began, pulsating through my head. I jerked open a drawer and shoved the receiver inside. Even then we could still hear the tone. I glared at the drawer.

"It'll stop in a minute." Daddy inhaled deeply and rubbed his eyes.

I took my time pouring myself a glass of orange juice. Offered Daddy some. He nodded. With a full glass before each of us, we sighed into our seats at the table. The flowers Greg had brought me stood in their vase like multicolored sentinels. I fingered a yellow petal, glad that they had been too tall to set on the dining room table the previous night. As with all else, they would have been knocked over and ruined.

My gaze shifted to Mama's chair. I stared at it, remembering how Daddy had brought it from the garage for Katherine. Only a week ago, but it seemed forever. I wondered if he would put it back.

"Did you apologize for me to the Matthews?" Daddy asked. I hadn't even seen him last night when I'd gotten home. He and Katherine were still talking, their conversation suspended as I walked past the family area toward Robert's bedroom.

"I didn't go in."

Daddy's shoulders slumped. "You should have. Now I'll really need to call them."

"You don't have to call anybody," I declared. "Nothin' that happened last night was *your* fault."

"Doesn't matter. It's the thing to do."

"Daddy—." My mouth pressed shut against any disrespectful words. I wanted to shake his shoulders even as my heart lurched for him. My fingers wrapped firmly around my glass.

Daddy shifted in his chair. "Now listen, Jackie, I don't want a word said outside this house about what you heard last night, hear?"

Fortunately, he'd still been in his bedroom when Alison had called. "I know."

Winnie sidled up to the glass door outside with her forlorn "I'm lonely" look. I ignored her.

"I'll need to call Officer Hankins soon," Daddy said half to himself.

"You goin' to press charges?" A shiver ran through me as I imagined court appearances, the lingering gossip. As far as I was concerned, Trent Baxter could just leave town and take Katherine with him. *Piece of trash.*

"No." Daddy sighed. "On one condition—that he never sets foot in Bradleyville again."

The threat of his tone pulled Greg's words into my thoughts. *Your baba will protect her.* Surely I misread my daddy's meaning. "And Katherine?" I pressed.

Daddy pushed his glass aside and rested both elbows on the table, looking me squarely in the eye as if he knew every murderous inclination I'd entertained about Katherine May King in the last twelve hours. "She'll be goin' to Robert's team's softball game with us at noon. And she'll be stayin' here for supper tonight."

I ogled him, a hundred arguments swirling in my brain. I searched for the ones that mattered, instead grasping only at the stupidest of details. "We can't all fit in the car." The game was thirty miles away. Robert's casted leg would take up half the backseat.

"I'll ride with Katherine. You can drive Robert and Clarissa." Daddy's eyes never left my face, as if he expected an eruption and stood ready to quell it. That same surprised hurt I'd felt the day of Katherine's at-home spiraled through me. Here I sat, looking to comfort Daddy against all Katherine had done to him, to *us,* and he was choosing her side.

I sucked my top lip between my teeth. "How can you still want her around?" I whispered. "She's not . . . she's nothin' she pretended to be. She doesn't *deserve* you."

Daddy shook his head. "She's not pretendin', Jackie. She's simply trying to rebuild her life after having made mistakes. In that way she's no different from a lot of people."

"'A lot of people' don't try to be part of our family!" I retorted. The near-cracking of my voice brought heat to my cheeks. For some reason I did not want to let Daddy see how much Katherine had hurt me personally. I raised my chin. "Are you telling me you've forgiven her for everything—just like that?"

"Did you expect that I wouldn't?"

Were we living on two different planets? Hadn't he looked just twelve hours ago as if his world had caved in? "But you seemed so hurt and mad last night! I thought . . ." I couldn't finish the sentence.

"I *was* hurt. For a whole lot of reasons. Mad, too. Mostly because everything happened in front of you and your brother and sister, not to mention a guest. I knew Katherine was mortified."

"*Katherine* was mortified? *I* was mortified, and so were you when you heard everything about her! She told you she loved you when she was engaged to someone else. She came back here just to get you in her clutches!"

The words leapt from me before I could stop them. Too late, I realized what I'd done. Daddy's eyes narrowed. He leaned back slowly in his chair. "And just how would you know that?"

My face burned as I sought an answer. I could not bear to give myself away. How unfair this was—that any of Daddy's suspicions this infamous morning would be directed at *me*.

"Who told you that?" Daddy spaced out the words as if talking to an errant child.

"Nobody."

"Then how did you know?"

I swallowed, my gaze falling to the floor.

"You listened to our conversation, didn't you?" His voice hardened. "You purposely eavesdropped on us."

What was I to do? I couldn't bring myself to lie. I could only nod miserably. Daddy's ensuing silence spoke more than any words could. "I didn't mean to," I said after a moment. "I was just going to the—"

"Didn't mean to? For how long did you stand around the corner in the hallway and 'not mean' to listen?"

"I don't know," I whispered.

Air seeped from Daddy's throat. I glanced up to see the residue of some momentous thought trail across his features. I knew that he'd remembered our past conversation about Celia, that he now realized just how much I had heard. He pressed his lips, regarding me with a mixture of defensiveness and accusation. I dropped my eyes. Fingered my pajama top.

"Well," Daddy said, his voice clipped. "Since you consider yourself grown up enough to be privy to our personal conversations, you should be able to understand very well why I can forgive Katherine her ..." He cast about for the right word. "... past choices. I haven't exactly been mistake-free myself."

The formality of his tone cut right through me. I felt like some school child being dressed down by the principal. *He has no right to treat me like this*, I railed silently. I'd hardly made the mistakes Katherine or he had. Suddenly, the questions about Daddy and Celia swirled back into my head. How had he loved someone else even as he dated Mama? How could he have hurt her the way he did? And Katherine—how could she so blithely jump from one man to the next? What if that man was right? What if she left Daddy too?

"So." Daddy concluded his little lecture. "When Katherine's with us today I expect you to treat her with respect. And tenderness. Believe me, she feels bad enough as it is."

The softball game would be hard enough, but I could not imagine sitting at the table with her at supper. Tainted Katherine in Mama's chair. I needed some time to rearrange my thinking for that. Like about ten years.

Summoning my courage, I looked Daddy in the eye. "Greg wanted to take me out tonight. I wasn't sure if I could, because I wanted to be here if you needed me. But since you seem okay with everything, I'd like to go."

I felt not the least bit repentant about twisting this absurd situation for my own benefit. Hadn't he done the same thing?

Daddy gazed at me, lines etching around his mouth. "Go then," he said tersely, pulling to his feet and turning his back on me. He exited the kitchen to dress for his day with Katherine, leaving me alone and wondering how on earth, after our horrible night, he and I were the ones who'd ended up fighting.

chapter 24

By the time the next hour had passed, I felt as incensed as a smoked-out hornet, having spent the time mentally telling Katherine everything I thought of her. Only because of her was Daddy so mad at me. Meanwhile I had work to do. I awakened Clarissa and Robert, fed them breakfast, started some laundry, fed Winnie. Then slammed around the kitchen, making sandwiches and assembling them with drinks in an iced cooler to take to the game. High and irritating voices from a cartoon show filtered in from the family room. Clarissa giggled like a nine-year-old without a care in the world. Apparently last night's ills were forgotten, some short-lived fever soothed in sleep. Robert had returned to his bedroom after breakfast to begin the arduous task of dressing himself. Seemed to me the only graceful way to deal with a cast was to have it taken off.

Daddy had driven down to witness Officer Hankins's escorting Trent Baxter out of Bradleyville. Apparently, the man had agreed to Daddy's terms once he learned the ring was long gone. What else to fight for? He'd certainly made it clear he didn't want the likes of Katherine May King back.

The phone receiver still lay stuffed in a drawer. I knew I needed to call Greg about our date, but I didn't want to sound as if I was ready to bite someone's head off. I thought of his wounded face and wondered if it looked better or worse. Probably worse.

I slipped some cookies in a self-seal plastic bag, fleetingly amazed at my own selfishness. Why wasn't I more worried about Greg? What if that bruise took two weeks to heal, as Robert's had, and Greg had some photo shoot right after he left town? I plunked the bag of cookies in the cooler. Well, at least he could leave. Walk away from all this mess while I remained stuck with it. This was my life—and it was about as far removed from his as east from west.

We would be leaving for the game before long. I really needed to call him. Easing open the drawer, I stared at the phone. Took a deep breath and picked it up. I hit the button to connect to a dial tone. Immediately, it rang.

Terrific. I smacked the drawer closed, as if it were to blame. Which titillated friend would this be?

"Hello?" Annoyance coated my voice.

"Hi, it's Katherine."

Katherine. I fixed my gaze on the tile counter, searching for . . . what was it Daddy had demanded? Respect. Tenderness. All I saw were numerous dirty spots needing to be wiped up. Automatically, I reached for the sponge. "Hi."

"Is everything okay? I've been trying to call for the longest time."

Like sure, Katherine, everything's okay. What a moronic thing to ask. "We've had the phone off the hook."

"Oh. Too many people callin', huh."

"Something like that." I wiped furiously. "Do you want to talk to Daddy?"

"Actually, no. I called to talk to you."

One spot would not come up. I flipped the sponge over and rubbed with the scrubber side. "Oh."

She hesitated. "I know the game won't really give us time to talk, and tonight we'll be with the family, so I just wanted to tell you how sorry I am about last night. You have no idea—" Her tone bent. She drew in an audible breath. "I'm really, really sorry, Jackie. Your daddy and I have worked things out, but I feel I owe a special apology to you."

Deep within, a tiny voice whispered that she didn't have to make this call, didn't have to explain herself to me, the adult to the teenager. That, just as she had done the first night she came to supper, Katherine once again graciously recognized my special place within this household.

And well she should. Hadn't she done her best to win me over the first time so I wouldn't stand in her way? And she'd done it too. With well-honed precision, I might add.

The tile glistened beneath the sponge, spots all gone. I moved to the sink, polishing around the edge and the faucets.

"Okay. Thank you." My tone spoke louder than my words. I turned the water on, knowing she would hear it, and rewet the sponge.

"Well. I'll let you go. You sound busy."

"Just getting stuff ready for the game." I turned off the water. "By the way, I won't be here at supper tonight. I'm going out with Greg."

"Oh, Jackie, that's wonderful! I hope you have a great time."

How sincere she sounded. I set down the sponge and wiped my hand on a dishtowel. Maybe she was. Of course she was. Hadn't Greg been her ticket to my acceptance? I could not bear to think of allowing myself any reason to be in Katherine's debt. At that moment I whole-heartedly wished that Greg and I would have a terrible time, that I'd expose all the ugliness and deceit and self-absorption that surely lay within him as some mystical mirror to Katherine's own soul.

"I'm sure we will. I have to get off the phone now so I can call him."

She said goodbye and I smacked the "talk" button off as if it were a hot iron.

Within seconds, it rang again.

I stared at the phone in weary disbelief. Too much was happening at once, and I simply did not know how to keep up. Suddenly, staring at that stupid phone, it occurred to me that for over two years—ever since my mama had first taken ill—life had swept me along at a terrifying pace. I felt like a blind person being shoved down some unknown and obstacle-ridden path. I needed to stop, toe the ground, float my hands in exploration. Take it one step at a time, as I had done that day I walked away from my mother's grave.

The phone rang a second time.

"Hello?" I didn't even try to suppress the sigh that chased the word. Grandma Westerdahl was on the line. Demanding in a shrill voice to hear the truth about the horrible things she'd heard. My frustration piled higher, a growing mound of choking dust and debris in my chest. I told Grandma Daddy's version of the events—the watered-down, Katherine-as-the-victim version. Disneyland meets Stephen King. But she didn't want to hear about Katherine.

"How is Bobby?" she pressed. "How are all of you?"

"Daddy's sore but okay. The rest of us weren't hurt at all."

"But what you saw!" Her tone wavered like a violin player seeking a lost note. She sucked in air. "I knew that Katherine King was bad news the first time I laid eyes on her. Now she's brought you terrible trouble, and you can bet this won't be the last of it. Your daddy needs to get as far away from her as possible."

"Grandma—"

"Where is he? I want to talk to him right now!"

I wasn't all that happy with Daddy myself at the moment, but no way would I unleash my grandmother's tirade on him. Daddy had been through enough. "He can't talk now, Grandma, we're getting ready to go to Robert's softball game." I promised her he would call later, or at least see her in church tomorrow. I did not want to tell her that Katherine would be with us the rest of the day.

By the time I hung up the phone, I couldn't begin to sort out who I agreed with more, Daddy or Grandma. I couldn't sort out much of anything. I'd have been happy to go to bed and pull the covers over my head.

Quickly, before one more intrusion, I dialed the Matthews' number. Celia answered. Shame washed over me as I identified myself, asking for Greg. I couldn't even apologize for returning her brother-in-law looking like he'd accompanied me to a barroom brawl.

"Greg," I rushed when he came to the phone, "how are you? How's your face and your hand? Is your family mad?"

He laughed, unmistakably pleased at my concern. "You are right, I look terrible. But it doesn't hurt much anymore. And no, they are not mad."

I closed my eyes, picturing his bruised face, remembering how quickly he'd jumped to Daddy's aid. I felt about two feet high. How on earth could I doubt his sincerity? How could I think of foisting my disappointment and distrust of Katherine upon him?

"How is your family? Your baba and his head?"

Inside or out? I wanted to ask. "We're all okay."

He hesitated. "And Katherine?"

"Katherine is also fine," I said, an edge creeping into my voice. "In fact she is so fine that she'll be with Daddy all day."

"Ah."

That's all he could say. *Ah.* As if he'd known it, expected it. Was I the only person around here with any sense about this whole thing?

I pushed the thoughts aside. "Anyway. I called to see if you still want to go out tonight."

"Yes! You can?"

I told him we'd return from a softball game around five, and I could be ready by six. I wanted time to shower, put on makeup. Get my head on straight. I wanted time to stare at his picture, recapture the magic of dreaming about being with him. "I'll drive over and get you then, okay?"

He said that sounded great. I hung up the phone, then thought better of it. Punching the "talk" button, I stuck it back in the drawer. As I headed for my bedroom, thinking again that Greg Kostakis was too good to be true, I heard the faint, disembodied voice declare that if I'd like to make a call, I should hang up the phone and try again . . .

chapter 25

Robert's team lost the game, which meant the end of their playoffs and the season. He shuffled back to the car, head down, a glum expression on his face. "We'd a won if I'd been able to play," he pronounced. I had to admire Robert. He could say such things without sounding like an egomaniac. Fact was fact.

"I know." I opened the car door and helped him sit down. He scooted backward across the car until his cast lay out in front of him. Clarissa climbed in front, tired and crotchety.

"I wanted to ride with Daddy and Katherine." She folded her arms and frowned, mad at the world. I felt little sympathy. She'd spent the whole game leaning against Katherine as if her life depended on it, oblivious to the heat of body contact under the sun. Katherine had put up with Clarissa's clinging almost as if she'd expected it, which irritated me no end. If Clarissa needed extra nurturing, it was only because of last night, and I should have been the one she'd come to. On the other hand, Clarissa had seemed just fine as she watched cartoons that morning and as we'd driven to the game, so what was this all about? I didn't care for the thought that perhaps Clarissa indeed worried about something happening to Katherine. Why couldn't she worry about Daddy, for pete's sake? He's the one who got hurt.

Katherine and I had exchanged only chitchat during the game, and as little of that as I could manage. While still sounding respectful. "Tender" proved quite beyond me. "Tender" bespoke memories of Mama and my vague dreams about love. "Tender" spoke of the way Greg had held me last night when I cried.

As I drove, I glanced at Robert now and then through the rearview mirror. He stared sightlessly out the window, lips puckered and sagging at the corners. I could imagine the thoughts banging about his adolescent head. Dreams of hitting a home run to the cheers of his teammates, of leaping to his daddy's aid last night and sinking a fist into Trent Baxter's well-deserving gut.

Our phone shrilled as we entered the house. It was Grandma Westerdahl, announcing that she'd waited long enough to talk to Daddy. "We've just come back from the game," I said, "and he's right behind me. Can you wait a minute?" No trying to rescue him this time. A perverse part of me wanted to witness his having to defend Katherine to his mother-in-law in her presence.

Of course, Daddy found a way to shield Katherine from the storm. He took the call in his bedroom. I flicked her a meaningful look as he disappeared down the hallway. Slowly, she set our cooler on the kitchen table, her expression flattened and drawn. Amazingly, my heart beat one fleeting thud for her. Irritated, I turned away, hearing the orchestral burst of welcome from the computer in the family room. Robert apparently planned to drown his doldrums in a sea of dead aliens.

"Will you play a game with me?" Clarissa asked Katherine as I headed down the hall to dress for my first date.

I chose a simple orange sleeveless dress and heeled sandals. As I fiddled with my hair and put on makeup, Greg's picture smiled at me, reflected in my dresser mirror. I turned my radio on, hoping to hear "Hung Up on You," but was disappointed. Fifteen minutes before I needed to leave, I could find no more primping to do. I sat on my bed and stared at Greg's picture. Stared and stared until fresh amazement and deep disappointment bubbled through my veins.

When you've lost a loved one, milestones in your life are bittersweet, inevitably tainted by the haunting "If only." And so, even as I whispered aloud, "My first date, my first date," reveling in the rhythm of the words on my tongue, a longing for Mama beat through my innermost being. Memories sprang up before me like projected slides. Mama, brushing my hair in this very room when I was thirteen. "Tell me about your first date with Daddy," I said.

She laughed. "How many times have you heard that story, Jackie?" Never enough.

Sitting on the back deck with Mama, shelling peas, the sun warm on my arms. *Plunk.* The peas hit the large pan between our feet. *Plunk, plunk.* "On my first date, I want to go out to supper like you and Daddy did."

"Why?"

"Because I want to sit across the table from him and look at him. You can't do that in a movie." *Plunk.*

"I'd have picked a movie," Mama replied. "But your grandma wouldn't let me go to them."

"Grandma didn't let you do anything."

A winter afternoon three years ago, driving back home down a snowy Route 622 after gymnastics class. "When Daddy first took you out, what did you talk about? Was it hard to find something to say?"

Mama managed a smile in spite of her concentration on the slippery road. "I'd have talked a blue streak, but I was scared to sound too chatty, so I stayed pretty quiet. Your dad forced himself to talk so I wouldn't find him boring."

No, I thought as I waited to leave on my first date, *Daddy forced himself to talk to keep his mind off someone else.* Had Mama known then? I wondered. Did she believe he'd stopped liking Celia Matthews? Or was she just so glad to be with him that she didn't allow herself to think about it?

I ran my palm over my bedspread, feeling the stitches, and stared at Greg's picture. Mama's first date with Daddy may not have been perfect, yet somehow over the years her memories had sifted over the imperfections like gold dust. I wanted that same gold dust now, tonight. Instead of my mama sending me off, Daddy would tell me goodbye, Katherine at his side. *Gold dust.* Greg's bruised face would remind me all evening of what Katherine had done. *Gold dust.* I would never be able to tell Mama about my first date.

Gold dust.

I left my room telling myself no matter what, I would make the most of this night.

chapter 26

My heart fluttered as I clicked up the porch steps to the Matthews' home. I felt downright strange. Never had I expected to be the one ringing the doorbell on this momentous occasion in my life. And I did not care to face Celia or her parents. Greg answered the door and my jaw slacked. His left cheek plumed reddish black, trailing all the way up to his eye. He looked bruised and battered and handsome all at once, dressed to kill in dark pants and a beige shirt, again of silk. The sapphire ring was back on his finger.

"Come." He took my hand and pulled me into their entryway, where I stood tongue-tied, the spicy scent of his cologne filling my nostrils. Greg licked his lips, anticipation and anxiety hanging about him like a fine mist. He gave a self-conscious shrug. "Sorry I look so bad."

"You look wonderful," I blurted, meaning it.

Mr. Matthews appeared, Celia and her mother behind him. My insides cringed. "Jackie," he said warmly, "so nice to see you."

"Nice to see you too," I replied in a small voice, forcing myself to look at him. I saw not the slightest hint of blame in his expression, nor on the faces of Celia or her mother. Instead, Celia smiled from me to Greg with a mixture of tenderness and joy, almost as if she were bestowing some kind of blessing upon us. I felt bared, spotlighted on a stage with no knowledge of my lines. I turned my eyes to the wrinkled, worn face of Mrs. Matthews. "I'm sorry about last night. Everything that happened. And Greg getting hurt. My daddy's really sorry too."

"Well, I'm not," Mr. Matthews declared, tilting his head back to look Greg up and down with satisfaction. "I'm right glad Greg was there to help. Think what might have happened if he hadn't been."

"Good for *you* to say," Greg replied teasingly. We all laughed.

"Have a good time," Mr. Matthews said, putting a hand on Greg's shoulder and urging him toward the door. Gratitude for the man's kindness welled within me.

"Celia's father sure is nice," I told Greg as we drove away from the house.

"They are both very good to me."

"At least bein' at their house has been a little more quiet than bein' at mine, huh."

I made the remark lightly enough, but Greg laid a hand on my arm. "Let's make a promise to not talk about what happens last night, okay?"

"Okay."

We were silent for a moment.

"What did you do today?" I asked.

"Meet people. We eat lunch with Mr. and Mrs. B, and Jessie and Lee. Then we go to the Kings' house. That is already planned," he added. "We almost don't go, but Mrs. King says come."

I threw a glance at him, wondering what he wasn't telling me. Surely that had felt awkward. I could imagine Mrs. King making a fuss over his face. But we weren't supposed to talk about that. "Did you meet Derek?" The thought of Greg and Derek side by side almost made me laugh. Talk about night and day.

"No, he is working." Greg paused. "He is a friend of yours?"

"Yeah. Sort of. He's . . . well, he's Derek. Kind of different."

"Mm." He focused on the tree-lined road. "Sorry you have to drive."

I envisioned all the boys in Bradleyville who could be driving their daddy's cars, taking me out for the first time. Not one picture could begin to compare with this, even with my driving and Greg's wounded face. "I don't mind at all. But you haven't told me which restaurant we're going to."

"Ah. Clayton's Place. Celia says to go there. You know it?"

I bugged my eyes at him. "Clayton's Place, you're kidding me! That's the most expensive restaurant in Albertsville. I've never been there in my life." The restaurant had earned a reputation, and folks would drive a long distance to it for a special night out. It was known as *the* place for romance, the restaurant for making an impression, for proposing, even. Daddy and Mama had celebrated their last anniversary during her healthy days at Clayton's Place.

"That is why I take you," Greg replied grandly. "We are lucky to get in. They give me a table because they have a . . ."

"Cancellation?"

"Yes." He flicked his eyes upward. "Cancellation."

We grinned at each other.

"The restaurant makes you happy?" he asked.

"Greg," I gushed, "just being with *you* makes me happy." Instantly, I felt my cheeks flush. *Great, Jackie, real demure.*

Greg leaned toward me, touched my shoulder. "And I am happy being with you."

Well. What to say to that. Maybe the world wasn't so upside down after all.

"Are you worried about going out? I mean, what if someone recognizes you?"

Greg watched the winding road straighten like a pulled ribbon beneath our wheels. A breeze through his cracked-open window riffed the sleeve of his shirt. "People do know us here in the States. That surprises me. We are known in Athens, as I tell you. But that's home. Even the people I don't know—they are like friends to me because they are from my city. Here, it feels different when people know me."

"Girls, you mean."

"Mostly." He sounded almost apologetic.

The thought irritated me more than it should have. But, glory, fine time to hear that our date could be interrupted by a drooling slew of girls. Most of whom were no doubt prettier than I was. For some reason I pictured Katherine at my age, how forward and charming she'd have been to encounter some singing star in a restaurant. That thought *really* irritated me.

"I should talk before about this," Greg said. Had I spoken aloud? "But we have no chance. Albertsville is not a big city, right? And I ask for a table in the back."

"Mm." We came up behind a slow-moving pickup that had seen far better days. Route 622 offered few places to pass; we'd likely be stuck for a while. I tapped the steering wheel.

Greg waited for me to say something. I could feel his worry over my terseness. I worried about his being worried. "It will be okay," I assured him. "We're hardly in New York. Girls don't expect to see you here. Especially with a bruised jaw. Oops." I cringed. "Wasn't supposed to say that." He smiled. "Even if someone thought she recognized you, she'd probably figure, 'Wow, he looks a lot like that guy from LuvRush.'"

"You mean she will not know my name?" Greg feigned disappointment.

I laughed at that. "Oh, I know! Let's make up a first name, in case someone does recognize you. Some back-hills-sounding name."

He frowned. "What do you mean, a back-hills-sounding name?"

"A name like . . ." I thought a minute. "Willy Ray, Junior."

"Three words? Junior is the last name?"

"No, no, it's all part of the first name. It means he's the second to be called that, and his father was first."

"Ah, I see." He said the name a few times under his breath. "Willy Ray, Junior; Willy Ray, Junior." The "j" sounded like a "ts" again. It all sounded so refined in his accent that I had to laugh.

"Only you could make a back-hills name sound classy, Greg."

He drummed his fingers against his knees, obviously pleased. "So you are not mad at me?"

"Why would I be mad at you?" I shook my head. Guys were sure hard to understand sometimes.

We rolled too close to the truck. I eased off the gas. "Mind if I turn on the radio?"

"Ah, I don't like music much."

I threw him an "oh, ha-ha" glance and punched on my favorite station. Commercials. I turned down the volume. "You know what would be the greatest thing in the world right now? To hear 'Hung Up on You' with you sitting right here."

His lips curved. "You should see the first time I hear the song on the radio. I am getting ready for school. I run out of my bedroom, yelling like a fool. 'Aaahhhhh!'" Greg shook his hands in the air. "My parents think something terrible happened. Mamma is making breakfast, and she pours my little brother's milk on her feet."

I laughed with him. "Hope you helped her clean it up."

"No. I am too busy calling Demetri."

I couldn't imagine what that would be like—hearing your own voice on the radio after years of dreaming about it. Well. I'd dreamed about a first date for a long time, hadn't I? Now here I was. With Greg Kostakis, no less.

Music sounded low on the radio, and I turned up the sound. A lineup of songs played, but not Greg's. Twenty minutes later we arrived at Clayton's Place. It turned out to be all that I expected, intimate, white cloths and a red rosebud in a dainty cut glass vase at every table. Couples and foursomes filled the tables near the front, with about six still empty. "You're the first ones here," the hostess said to Greg with a smile. She looked to be in her midtwenties, with blonde hair and oh-so-straight teeth. I paid little heed to her words, watching her eyes linger on Greg's face, his cheek. Greg may have looked like he'd been in a fight, but it seemed to me all the bruises in the world couldn't hide his incredible looks. I wondered which caused her the most pause.

"First ones?" He glanced at the other filled tables.

"I mean first of the prom bunch." She turned from Greg's puzzled expression to me. I looked down the length of my dress. I was hardly dressed for a prom. Bradleyville didn't even have such a thing. Still doesn't today. A lacking, certainly, that gives Albertsville high schoolers one more reason to look down their noses at our town.

A second later, the woman's words registered. "This is *prom* night?" I demanded, almost as if she were to blame.

"A prom night is what?" Greg asked.

The hostess smiled at him again, indulgently. "You have such a wonderful accent." She laid down her pen. "Sorry, I was assuming. Yes, it's prom night. But you must be the reservation under 'Greg.'" We nodded. "We've saved you a table in the left corner, as you requested, sir. Come right this way." She picked up two menus and led us to our seats as I explained to Greg what a prom was. He pulled out my chair for me, then sat across the table facing the wall, his back to the room, rosebud and fancy china and silverware spread elegantly between us.

"Perfect," he announced with satisfaction. "All I look at is you."

I felt myself blush. "Yeah, and you've got your best side out." I gestured at his perfect right cheek.

We both ordered a salad and the steak. I couldn't believe the prices and would have asked for nothing but soup if Greg hadn't quickly announced what he'd chosen, graciously paving the way for my own indulgence. I wondered if singing had already made him rich. He certainly had more money and better clothes than any Bradleyville guy.

Over salad, he told me more about LuvRush's tour. And, surprising me, he talked openly about his Christian faith—how hard it was sometimes to be a Christian around Alex and Lysander and Demetri, who weren't. "I keep talking to them about it, though. And praying for them. They know I am . . . different for a reason."

He wanted to hear about me, but what was there to tell? I urged him to keep talking, drinking in the sound of his voice, picturing the long hours of practice, the road trips they would take on their special bus. His co-singers, the concerts. Slowly, I felt my worries over Daddy and Katherine slip away.

The waiter arrived to remove our salad plates. I placed my hands in my lap, eyes flicking about the restaurant. Trying to think of something new to say. Fleetingly, I wondered about supper at our house. Had Katherine sat in Mama's chair? Could Robert talk to her?

Greg leaned over the table. "Jackie."

"Hm?" I looked into his warm gaze, sudden butterfly wings sweeping inside my chest.

"You go away sometimes. I don't know where."

"Oh. I'm . . . I just think about a lot of things, I guess."

He nodded. "You think about your mamma a lot?" he asked quietly.

The question surprised me. Greg seemed to flow from easy talk to serious in no time. Maybe he hadn't lost enough to understand how difficult that was supposed to be.

I looked at the rose, picked of thorns and perfect. "All the time."

"You are very close to her."

"Yes." I rubbed a finger along the tablecloth. I could feel his gaze upon me. "Are you close to yours?"

"Yes, very much."

"How about your brother?"

He rested his elbow on the table. "Danny too. I don't see him much now. But Danny . . . teaches me things. Like a big brother, you know? He has a long talk with me before I leave Greece."

"What kinds of things?"

"Ah." He cocked his head. "Things about being a Christian in a world that isn't. Things about traveling. How to . . . watch myself. Family." He smiled. "Girls."

"Really?" I teased. "And what did he tell you about girls?"

"You want to hear what he says before I leave, or what he says this morning on the phone?"

This morning. Oh, glory, I could imagine that conversation. *Hey, guess what, big brother, I got beat up at this girl's house.* "This morning."

Greg fastened his eyes on mine, all seriousness. "He says 'the best girls come from Bradleyville.'"

Well. Of course Greg's brother would say that, having married Celia. But to say it this morning, most certainly after Greg had told him about what happened at our house. For Greg to make a point of telling me . . . Was I reading too much into this?

Oh, hoo-fah, Greg probably talked this way to all the girls. Tried to make them feel special. It was part of his charm.

I rubbed a small circle on the tablecloth.

Greg reached out his undamaged hand to lay it over mine. Then he lifted it up, lacing our fingers. "I think my brother is right."

I stared like an idiot at our fingers, wishing for some witty word. None came. I did manage a little, tight smile.

Sudden voices caused a stir at the front of the restaurant. I glanced up and Greg twisted to look, our hands still linked. Three girls our age, looking like knockouts in formals pinned with corsages, swept into the restaurant, followed by their dates in suit and tie. Greg turned back to me. "The 'prom bunch.'"

Were they ever. Three more girls and their dates followed, filling up the small lobby like multicolored flowers, all fresh and sun-kissed and beautiful. Four had their hair up in elegant twists, adorned with baby's breath. Another's shining blonde hair hung to her bare shoulders in unbelievably thick layers. A pink strapless dress, immodestly low cut, hugged every curve of her body to the floor. The girls chattered with the confidence of the glamorous, laughter and anticipation flowing through the room and causing heads to turn. "There goes our quiet," I commented. Why couldn't I have worn something more fancy? The hostess began leading them toward the three remaining tables near us. They milled about, dividing themselves into quartets, the girls rustling into their seats and setting beaded purses at their feet.

"Doesn't matter." Greg squeezed my fingers.

The blonde shook her hair back and glanced our way, then did a double take, her gaze landing on Greg. From the corner of my eye I could see her brow rise with approval. How nice for her that she found him attractive.

I smiled at him. "So. What else did your brother tell you?"

The girl stared a moment longer, her expression crinkling into puzzled suspicion. If Greg noticed, he paid no attention. She leaned over to the girl on her left, her pink formal meshing with the blue satin of her friend's. They whispered, and I knew what was coming next. Sure enough, both coiffed heads turned to assess Greg once more, then checked me up and down. I felt myself grow warm beneath their dismissive looks. Finally, they turned their attention back to their dates.

"I think they recognize you," I whispered to Greg. He nodded but did not look at them. I felt a wash of gratitude that his eyes remained on me.

The waiter arrived with our entrees. Greg pulled his hand from mine as we were served.

We talked of this and that as we ate, of Greece and Bradleyville and our families. Trying to ignore the increasingly animated banter at the prom tables. After their salads, four of the girls decided to flock to the bathroom, swishing past us with proud chins and lingering glances upon Greg. They caught each other by the arms, exchanging whispers as they flowed up the aisle and around the corner. "I'm telling you," the blonde's insistent voice floated over her shoulder, "he looks just like the picture on my wall!"

Left to their own devices, the girls' dates traded teasing insults back and forth. One pulled at his bow tie, complaining, "How many more hours do I have to wear this thing?"

Greg smiled at that. "Glad I don't have one," he said.

"Glad I don't have a formal dress on." I suppressed a cringe, wondering if he saw through my lie.

The four girls returned. One of them pulled a small camera from her purse and started taking pictures of the others. "Here, do us." She handed the camera to a cohort and leaned close to her date with a sultry smile.

"Want some dessert?" Greg asked as our waiter took our plates.

I hesitated. "Are you going to have some?"

"Sure."

"Hey, you all," the blonde said loudly enough for all of her friends to hear, "we should get a picture together."

"That's too much trouble," one of the guys protested. "We can do it at the prom."

"We'll all get separated at the prom." She pushed back her chair and stood, motioning impatiently for the others to follow suit. "Come on, I'll find someone to take it."

Instantly, I knew that "someone" would be Greg.

She approached our table, dripping with feigned innocence. "Would you take our picture for us?" she asked Greg without so much as a glance at me.

"Ah." Greg forced a smile. "Of course." He accepted the camera with an apologetic glance in my direction. As he stood up, the girl inhaled sharply.

"Oh, my! What *happened* to you?" She reached out a painted fingernail and touched his cheek.

Greg flinched in surprise, then tried to hide it, ever the gentleman. I could have knocked the girl's hand off. "Just a little accident."

If I'd have thought fast enough, I'd have answered for him. The words flowed in his soft and intriguing Greek accent. The girl studied him with unabashed interest as two of her friends appeared magically at her side. "You're not from here, are you?"

My, how perceptive. I'd had enough of her. I'd had enough of all of them. "Willy Ray," I spoke in a clearly annoyed tone, "just take the picture."

A flicker of amusement tugged at Greg's mouth. He played along perfectly. "Okay," he said with an apologetic shrug at the girl.

"Willy Ray?" she repeated with narrowed eyes. I could practically see the wheels of suspicion turning in her head. "With an accent like that, your name is Willy Ray?"

"Come on, Charlotte, let's get this over with." Her date clamped firm hands on her shoulders and pulled her back to their group, her friends following. Greg aimed the camera and they posed, instant dazzling smiles appearing on each girl's face. He clicked and a brilliant flash lit the room.

As her friends reseated themselves, Charlotte retrieved her camera. "Thank you," she purred, her fingers grazing Greg's. "You know, you sure look like the lead singer from LuvRush." She waited for a denial, but Greg didn't respond. His silence etched anticipation into her face. Her blue eyes widened. "You are, aren't you?"

Greg hesitated, then nodded.

"And that accent," she gushed, "I knew it!" Her gaze slid to me and back. She smiled at Greg with sickening indulgence, as if they shared private thoughts. "But what are you doing here? And with a girl from *Bradleyville?*"

The question rained over me like acid. I glared at her in rage and disbelief. What did this stupid girl think—that Greg would be impressed by her snotty attitude? And how did she know I was from Bradleyville, anyway? Charlotte surveyed me snidely, apparently reading my thoughts. "It's the dress," she smirked, her eyes falling to my neckline.

Well, hoo-fah for you, I railed, *at least half my chest isn't falling out.* All the same, her words bubbled right through my skin. Catty or not, she outshone me a dozen candles to one, and I hated myself for it. Greg stood in shocked silence, his cheek mottling deeper red. I pressed my lips and stared at the tablecloth, muscles stiffening. I wanted to melt right through the floor.

A *tsk* escaped Charlotte's teeth. "Greg," she pressed her fingers into his arm, "let me take a picture with you."

"No, thank you," he managed levelly enough, but she paid no heed. She turned her head quickly to hiss over her shoulder, "It's *him!*"

Everything happened so fast. A fluttering gasp rose from Charlotte's friends. Chairs pushed back, excitement springing to their faces. "Could I have your autograph?" one girl called as two more rushed over, spouting questions. Other diners in the restaurant craned their heads at the sudden commotion.

"Wait a minute, wait a minute!" Charlotte fluttered her hands in the air. "I saw him first!" She thrust her camera into the closest friend's hand. "Here, take our picture." She pivoted to press herself against Greg, her cheek against his jaw.

Greg pulled away. "No!" He grabbed the camera from the surprised girl, pressing it until his battered knuckles whitened. Everyone froze. Greg inhaled, as if he didn't know what to do next. In that moment I understood the dilemma that would plague his life. If he'd been a nobody, he could give in to his anger. But how to control himself as fans watched, the same adoring fans whose tongues would surely wag with disdain if he appeared anything less than perfect?

"Come on, Greg," Charlotte wheedled, "it's just a picture."

"Charlotte, leave them alone." Her date shot Greg a look of apology and embarrassment. "They're just tryin' to eat."

"Let me be, Sam." She pouted glossy lips at Greg. "Oh, please. Then I promise I'll leave you alone." She raked a glance at me again, as if she couldn't imagine why Greg would want anything of the sort.

Greg looked at her, his face rigid. Then, slowly, his expression smoothed. Even with the short time I'd known Greg, I knew he'd forced it. He placed the camera on the table. "Sorry," he said with ultimate politeness. "But I have a rule when I am with my girl." He aimed me a quick smile. "If you want to take a picture with me, Jackie is in it."

Sam snorted. Charlotte wheeled on him, nostrils flaring. It took everything I had to hide my vindictiveness. Even stupid Charlotte knew when she'd been put in her place.

With a toss of her head, she snatched the camera from the table. "Never mind," she said sweetly to Greg with a bat of her eyes. "Wouldn't want to waste my film."

Her friend in blue satin sucked in a breath. "As you wish," Greg said, dismissing Charlotte regally. He nodded to the group. "Good to meet you." He held out his battered hand to Sam, who stared at it in surprise, then shook it. Greg winced.

A waiter approached the group's tables with a tray of plates. Sam turned grateful attention to the food. "Looks like our chow's here. Let's eat." The subdued group returned to their chairs, the girl in blue casting a final glance at Greg.

He sat down and reached for my hand, looking mortified. "I'm so sorry," he whispered. "I do not think something like this will happen."

My girl. He'd said "my girl."

Only for Charlotte's sake. He didn't mean it.

"It doesn't matter," I heard myself say. As if either of us would believe that.

He didn't mean it.

"It does matter."

In my peripheral vision I saw Charlotte hunch over her food with fierce concentration. "This is so good!" she said loudly.

Greg's eyes clouded as he tried to read my thoughts. Poor Greg. How the tables had turned from last night to this, no pun intended. I should not even think of my own embarrassment. If that half-dressed witch had treated him the way she treated me, I'd have wanted to strangle her.

"Greg," I declared, "guess what. We're even. Let's just leave it at that. If you keep feeling bad about this, then I'll have to keep feeling bad about last night. And we promised not to talk about that."

He rubbed his thumb across mine. "You are right." He smiled wanly. "You still want dessert?"

I shook my head. "Not here, anyway."

"I—"

"Greg!" a voice called, and our heads automatically turned. A flash popped brightly in our eyes. "Thank you," Charlotte sang as she lowered her camera. She opened her purse and theatrically dropped it inside.

I exchanged a startled look with Greg, a warning about that picture niggling in my brain. Apparently, he had the same thoughts. "Let's go," he said and rose. As he ushered me toward the front, I heard Charlotte call, "'Bye, now!" We ignored her. While the hostess ran down our waiter for the bill, I stood in the lobby looking out the front window, my back to stupid Charlotte.

chapter 27

Dusk had settled over the town with a warm, humid breeze. The air smelled of rain as we crossed the parking lot to our car. Neither of us said a word. Too busy with our own thoughts, I guess. Before he opened my car door, Greg hugged me briefly, his action saying more than words.

"You want to go where now?" Greg broke the silence as I pulled out onto the street.

I had no idea. To another restaurant, so we could meet another Charlotte? Glory, what Greg's life was going to be like. I couldn't imagine dealing with the repercussions of fame day in and day out. People out there were just too crazy.

"I don't know," I sighed.

He laid his head back against the seat. "You want to go home?" He sounded so defeated, tired. I felt achingly sorry for him. This hadn't been his fault.

Annoying voices blathered in a radio commercial. I snapped off the dial. We stopped at a red light, and I turned to Greg, suddenly weary of all the things that had gone wrong. He'd supported me last night; now *he* needed it. "No, I don't want to go home," I told him. "I want to go someplace where we can sit and talk and no one will bother us."

Greg blew out air. "Me, too. But where?" He shook his head. "Right now I wish I never sing in my life. Fans are great, but they make it hard sometimes. I'm so sor—"

"Stop sayin' you're sorry. Good grief, both of us are soundin' like broken records."

"You're right. Sorry."

"There you go again."

"Ah."

A car behind me honked, and we surged through the green light. "There's a vista point between here and Bradleyville that looks out over the hills," I said. "Not always private, as it's not far off the road. But I don't think Charlotte will be there."

Greg smiled in spite of himself. "Sounds good."

Fifteen minutes later we pulled off the highway onto a narrow dirt road, much like the one we'd found the night before. Our headlights washed the darkening path to hover in misty swirls over nothingness as I turned into the vista parking area. No one else was there. Across the valley hills of purple-black stood before the twilit sky.

Greg made an appreciative sound in his throat. "Pretty."

I cut off the engine and lights. The hills disappeared and in the quiet arose the faint *chirrup* of crickets. "Listen." I hit a button to roll down the two front windows, the cricket sounds increasing. "Here that, way in the distance?"

Greg cocked his head. "Water?"

"Mm-hm. It's a creek down there that feeds into the river."

Greg breathed in deeply, basking in the sounds, the feel of the air. A hint of his cologne floated to me. My gaze traveled over his profile, the silk polish of his shirt, and a longing unlike any I'd ever felt before poured through my veins.

He turned his head and caught me staring. I dropped my eyes. I had not the slightest clue what to do. Slowly, Greg leaned over the console. The crickets chirped, and the creek tumbled until it took my heart right along with it. Greg's fingers settled underneath my chin, forcing my eyes up. I looked at him, hardly able to breathe. He slid his other hand to my neck and drew me close until our mouths touched.

I'd seen lots of first kisses in movies and read about them in books. Dreamed of my own countless times, imagining all the feelings. Thought I'd done a pretty good job too. But nothing came close to this. The strangest thing is, suddenly I knew exactly what to do. My hands reached for his shoulder, his hair. I knew to tilt my neck, how to move my head as he did. How to breathe and still kiss. We stopped and hung there, lips still touching, and then he kissed me harder. The world could have ended right there and then, as far as I was concerned, because nothing, *nothing* could ever compare.

Greg moved his mouth away and hugged me, pulling at a strand of my hair. I held on to him, telling myself, *This is not a dream, it is not a dream, it is not.* Then he rested his forehead against mine with a sigh, as if he couldn't believe what had happened either. Thank goodness for the dark. Sunlight would have been too raw somehow, too embarrassing.

When we drew apart, we held hands over the console, lacing our fingers. What on earth to say? I laughed self-consciously.

"What?" Greg smiled.

"Willy Ray, Junior. It just sounds so funny for someone like you."

He puckered his chin. "I like it," he declared. "Willy Ray. You can call me that anytime." He gave me a look. "But just you."

We sat in the car for over an hour, the minutes melting away as we talked and kissed twice more. Seemed like it got better each time. But one thing in the back of my mind kept bothering me. Finally I just came out with it. "Greg, I know we're not supposed to talk about last night. But why did you think about Katherine right off, instead of us?"

He didn't answer immediately. He focused on the dashboard, expression turning solemn. "I tell you about Mamma. That she lives in Bradleyville after she is married. That husband, my brother's baba— he drinks too much."

"Oh."

"Also, he . . . treats her badly." His voice dropped, as if the words knifed his heart. "He beats her."

I drew in a breath.

"I do not want everyone to know this."

Of course not, I thought, then understood the depth of his trust in me. Imagine that information in fan magazines. "Greg, I won't tell anyone the things you say to me. Ever."

He nodded, as if to say, *I know*.

He focused on the blackness beyond the windshield. "He hits her many times. She always is scared. The second time she is pregnant, after Danny, he beats her, and the baby dies. He hits my brother, too. Until Danny gets big to fight back."

I gazed at Greg with a mixture of disbelief and horror. "I had no idea. I mean, I didn't know that kind of stuff happened in Bradleyville."

He smiled bitterly. "Things 'happen' anywhere in this world when people do not know Christ, Jackie. This is true."

Wincing, I squeezed his fingers.

"I first hear when I am ten years old. Baba tells me. I don't forget that day. I run crying to Mamma, begging her to tell me it isn't true. I can not *think* of anyone treating her like that. It hurts me so much."

"Why did your daddy tell you?"

"He wants me to feel the pain. He is very strict, sometimes I think too strict. But when he tells me about Mamma, he puts it inside here"—he tapped his chest—"to make me hate that. So I always treat women right."

I tried to imagine how I'd feel if I heard anyone had ever beaten Mama. I couldn't imagine it. I'd *die* with the thought. No wonder Greg had thought of Katherine first last night. Trent had made him afraid for her.

I hugged Greg hard. "I'm so sorry about your mama. And for getting upset last night when you talked about Katherine."

He burrowed his fingers into my hair. "We don't say 'sorry' now, remember?"

"Oh. Yeah."

He placed his hands on the sides of my face and kissed me again.

On our reluctant way home, we talked about the next two days. Greg stretched his hand out to lie on my shoulder as I drove. "I want to see you tomorrow and Monday," he said. "I want to see you all I can."

I wanted to see him, too. But what on earth would I do when he left? "Are you coming to church tomorrow?"

"I don't know. With my face and . . . everything that happens, Celia thinks maybe I stay home."

Well, thanks a lot, Celia, I thought. People had already talked a blue streak, so what difference would it make? "Come," I urged. "We can sit together. People will be nothin' but nice to you. And you don't have to answer any questions. They wouldn't ask you, anyway. But they'll ask *me*. In fact, my friends will probably bug me like crazy, but if you're there, they'll leave me alone."

"Okay. I will ask."

"Will you call me in the morning? Tell me whether you're goin' to be there?"

"Of course."

"As for the rest of the day, I don't know. I'll have to ask Daddy." I cringed at the thought. Despite Greg's politeness and quick help in the fight, I still got the feeling Daddy would be glad when he'd left town. Seemed like Daddy and I had seen nothing but trouble between us since I'd asked to meet him. Not that any of that was Greg's fault.

"Monday, too, I want to see you." He sighed. "Tuesday, I leave."

I could not think about that. I only wanted to live the last few hours over and over in my head. And that's exactly what I did as I lay in bed that night, the street lamp throwing a faint light upon Greg's picture—just enough that I could see the outline of his face. Felt him hug me. Felt him kiss me again and again. And I didn't let one tiny thought of Katherine May King spoil it.

chapter 28

"Hi, Daddy."

Fortunately, I caught him Sunday morning alone at the kitchen table. We had to talk. He and I had been through so much together since Mama's death, never arguing. Now we seemed to keep stepping into emotional quicksand.

Besides, I'd be needing his permission to go out with Greg that afternoon.

He glanced up from the paper. "Hi."

I edged to the table, tapping on it with a knuckle. "I just want to tell you that I'm sorry for, you know, listening to you and Katherine talk. I'm really, really sorry. I wish I hadn't."

His mouth puckered as he regarded me. "I'll bet you do."

It took me a moment to realize the deeper meaning behind his words. I dropped my eyes to the newspaper.

"We will have to talk about all this sometime, Jackie," he said quietly. "The things you heard."

I nodded, warmed by the concern in his voice.

He sighed. "So much has happened around this house lately, I don't think either of us knows if we're comin' or goin'."

Wasn't that the truth. "It has been rather interesting." I shuffled my feet. "Well, I just . . . wanted to apologize. I have to get Robert and Clarissa up now."

"Okay." He smiled at me. That smile felt very good. I leaned down to give him a hug, and he hugged me back. Which felt even better.

He and I could get through just about anything as long as we stayed close, I thought as I left the kitchen. In fact, hadn't we already in the last two years?

Church felt more like a three-ring circus that day, given the not-so-grand entrances of the Delham and Matthews families. Looking back, I think it's a wonder Pastor Beekins could preach at all. In the first ring, Robert proved quite the popular boy as he clumped down the aisle, every hand outstretched to greet him. Church folk of every generation asked how he was doing. Was the leg healing, did it hurt anymore? And his team certainly could have used one of his home runs yesterday, couldn't they?

Afraid so, Robert replied countless times.

Daddy and Katherine graced the second ring, him with his bruised fingers and head, Katherine with her bruised ego. At least it should have been bruised, although seemed to me she held her head mighty high. "Oh, my, what happened?" fired the inevitable questions as we milled in the fifteen minutes between Sunday school and church. The older ladies clucked about Katherine like hens around a golden egg.

"I heard a man broke into Bobby's house."

"Snuck through the back door, didn't he?"

"One of those stalkers, like on TV!"

"Bobby, are you all right today?" Grandma Westerdahl touched the back of his head with care, purposely turning away from Katherine. "I still can't believe this happened in Bradleyville, in your own home."

And in the third ring, the Matthews and Greg, wearing his clothes from the night before and a tie most likely borrowed from Celia's daddy. His cheek bloomed green and reddish-purple, a stunning sight on his handsome face. He saw me, and his expression lit up. My heart nearly melted.

Celia greeted old friends enthusiastically, blonde hair swinging as she hugged one after another. They all then turned to Greg for introductions, hands on their mouths at the horrific sight of the heroic young man whom God had placed in the Delham's household at just the right moment. Funny, I hadn't thought much about God's having anything to do with it. Mrs. B out-animated everyone, as usual. Her wrinkled mouth hung open in a huge O, her arthritic fingers shaking as she held out her hand to Greg. Mr. B followed her, pumping Greg's arm jovially. "It's good to meet ya, boy, it's good to meet ya. Danny Cander's brother, can you imagine that!"

"Glory!" Alison breathed, clutching my arm as she caught sight of Greg. I wasn't sure what gripped her more—his good looks or battered cheek. "He's gorgeous. And wounded, and . . . *gorgeous.*"

"So—where's Jacob this morning?" I asked her with a meaningful raise of my eyebrow.

"He'll be here. And I was just lookin', so don't be like all protective." She continued to stare. "Are you gonna sit with him?"

"Alison," I whispered, "tell me nobody'll know who he is."

Our school chums Nicole and Cherise attended our church, and I knew they'd be dying to meet the guy visiting from Greece. Fortunately, they hadn't appeared from the Sunday school room yet. They'd probably congregated with the other girls in the bathroom, fluffing their hair and chatting up a storm.

Alison shook her head, still watching Greg. "Don't know. Thing is, nobody would *expect* him to be here."

"Hush, there's Derek."

"So, what would *he* care? The way he walks around like with his head in the clouds?"

I still couldn't get used to Derek without his glasses, although nothing else about him had changed. He sauntered down the aisle in his long-legged way, head tilted and fingers brushing his thumbs. And Alison was right, he forever looked like the absent-minded professor.

Miss Connie introduced Derek to Greg. Now that was a difference in male specimen. They shook hands and spoke for a moment. Then Greg had to turn aside for others waiting to shake his hand. Poor fingers, already bruised. I wondered if they would feel worse after all the pressing.

I watched Grandma Delham greet Greg, introducing him to Grandpa. Ah, my perfect cue to join their group. I sidled toward Greg and his entourage at the back of the church, his voice wrapping around me like warm velvet. He glanced from Grandma to me and smiled, obviously anxious to be with me but too polite to pull away. If I didn't get to him soon, the service would begin, and we'd end up sitting apart. I maneuvered around an elderly couple—and found myself face-to-face with Derek.

"Hi, Jackie." He smiled at me warmly.

"Hi," I replied, distracted.

"Looks like you're on a mission."

Was I that obvious? "Oh. I was just . . ." My hand waved vaguely in Greg's direction. Derek followed with his eyes until they landed on Greg. Understanding and disappointment rippled across his face.

"Well." He jerked his head sideways. "See ya later."

"Okay." I wound past him to Greg, who raised his hand to take mine as if it were the most natural thing in the world. I felt a blush all the way to my toes as Grandma's eyes darted from that hand to me and back. In Bradleyville, couples our age didn't hold hands in church; it just wasn't done. I slipped my fingers into his for an awkward shake, then pulled away. He cast me a perplexed look, then slowly lowered his hand. Grandma Delham, bless her, made a point to turn away and make small talk with Mr. Matthews.

"Will you come sit with me?" I whispered.

"Of course."

I leaned in as close as I dared. "You can't hold my hand here, okay? The old people would talk."

He raised his eyebrows in surprise. I wondered how it would be if we were in Greece. Maybe in his own church, the old folks wouldn't care a bit. Greg would probably sit in church with his arm around me if I allowed it.

Wouldn't that just do it, I thought. Not a person behind us would hear a word of the sermon. Not to mention Daddy would have my head.

As it happened, for the second Sunday in a row, I heard little of the sermon myself. I was far too busy just sitting next to Greg, feeling his presence, watching the way he rested his hands on his knees, hearing him sing the hymns. *Church will never be the same after this*, I thought, *never, ever*. Every movement of his fingers, every shifting of his position, pulled at me. I wished for all the world we were alone, and he could put his arms around me and kiss me. That we could sit in the car again after dark, hearing the crickets chirp and the creek tumble, and I could lay my head on his shoulder.

One other thing I remember so clearly about that church service. The unmistakable hurt on Derek's face when he glanced around and saw Greg and me together. Really, sitting next to Greg, it's amazing I noticed at all. But in order to see me, Derek had to purposely look over his shoulder. Our eyes caught for a second before he pulled his away, mouth flinching. At the time, I felt too caught up in Greg to think much about it. But now the memory pangs me, like bittersweet candy on the tongue.

After the service Greg found himself surrounded once again, this time by my friends, who practically salivated as they asked him a dozen questions about Greece. I caught their envious glances as I stood next to him, oh, yes, I did. I almost wished Millicent attended our church, just to show her I could attract someone like Greg. But then, they didn't know I had, did they? They probably thought he was with me merely because of Katherine.

Suddenly, I wanted them to know. *If only he'd reach for my hand now,* I thought. My friends would fall over dead, every one of them.

Alison and Jacob joined us, and I introduced them to Greg. Derek walked between two pews in an obvious detour to head for the door. He did not so much as glance at me.

Greg and I needed to get going. The sanctuary had nearly emptied. Both our families already stood outside, chatting in the parking lot. I peeked through the open doorway. Daddy appeared in deep conversation with Mr. Matthews, one hand on his chin. Celia talked with Katherine and Miss Jessie. The expression on Celia's face, the way her hand lay so familiarly on Miss Jessie's arm, spoke of a deep friendship.

"My aunt and uncle went to Greece one time," Nicole was saying, then gabbed merrily along about how they'd raved over Athens, and did Greg ever go to the Acropolis, or was that just a tourist thing? And what did he do for hobbies, and what was school like, did he learn English there?

Before I lost my courage, I leaned into Greg's ear and whispered. "You can hold my hand now."

The minute the words were out, I felt like an idiot. Greg would see right through me. What was he, my prize to show off to all my friends? I stepped back, casting about for some action to cover my embarrassment. Nicole's mouth never stopped running. I reached out to Cherise and fingered the stitching on her new purse. "This is nice." She hardly heard me, her eyes on Greg.

He grinned good-naturedly at the rush of questions, his focus still politely on Nicole. Acting as if I'd not whispered a thing.

"Yes, we learn English in school," he replied, "and another language like German or French or Italian." He proceeded to answer Nicole's other questions, vaguely saying he liked music. And then without the slightest break in his words, he reached out and took my hand, as if we'd done it a million times. I watched my friends' eyes widen, including Alison's, their gazes dropping, then springing up again for fear they'd be caught staring. I hoped my throbbing heart wouldn't jump right out of my chest.

After a few minutes we really did have to leave. Greg wisely dropped my hand before we stepped outside. I told him I would ask Daddy about seeing him that afternoon. After apologizing to Daddy, I'd had no more time to talk to him before church, with the usual commotion of getting myself and the kids ready. Amazing that I'd faced the typical drudge of a Sunday morning, after my evening with Greg. The world should have been anything but typical. It should be shining in brilliant, panoramic color.

"Hope he says yes," Greg told me with an enigmatic smile. "I know where we can go."

chapter 29

So much for panoramic color. Katherine went home with us for lunch—our big meal of the day on Sundays—and reality soon came crashing around my shoulders. I still did not trust her one bit even though, after the previous night, I couldn't deny my gratitude that she'd put me and Greg together. Lunch proved a rather interesting venture. For self-serving reasons, I did my best to act glad of Katherine's presence. Couldn't afford to get Daddy upset with me again. Our family made sure to talk about anything and everything but Friday night, finally landing on the subject of Alma Sue. Who, by the way, still hadn't apologized for the soggy coloring book.

"I haven't seen her around here much," I commented to Clarissa. Not that I was sorry.

"She's been sick with a cold."

"Oh. How nice."

"Jackie," Daddy frowned as Katherine repressed a smile.

A canine nose stuck furtively around the dining room corner. "Winnie," I said sharply, "we're still eating. Go lie down." The nose disappeared. We could hear Winnie's sigh all the way from the hall as she cast her miserable, lonely self upon the floor.

Back to Alma Sue. "Well, I don't like her at all," I said, "and one of these days I'm going to give her a piece of my mind. Since *you* won't," I added with a meaningful glance at Clarissa.

"I don't want to give her a piece of my mind, and I don't want you to, either," Clarissa retorted. "I just want her to be my friend."

"Why? She doesn't treat you very nicely."

"Because . . ." Clarissa chased peas around her plate. "Just because."

"Della's your friend, you could play with her."

"I want to be friends with *everybody*," Clarissa burst. "I just want everybody to like me!" Her eyes glistened.

Whoa. What was up with this?

"Clarissa," Katherine soothed, "everybody does like you. Very much."

My sister said no more, her attention focused on the last pea on her plate. Evidently, it was a very important pea. She and I would have to talk about this later. Clarissa's need for acceptance should not relegate her to a doormat for the likes of Alma Sue. I thought of Charlotte, how Greg had ever so politely put the haughty girl in her place. I doubted my emotions-on-the-sleeve sister would ever possess such subtlety. But for Alma Sue and all the oppressive people in Clarissa's future that she represented, a little lack of subtlety would be just fine with me.

"So." Daddy hit the table with drumming fingers. "Jackie, how was your date?"

Wonderful. I got to discuss my first date with my entire family. "Good."

Robert eyed me with interest, which surprised me. I didn't think he cared much about first dates. "Where did you go?" he asked.

"Clayton's Place."

"Clayton's Place, my, my," said Katherine. She and Daddy exchanged impressed glances.

"What's so great about it?" Robert wanted to know.

"It's expensive." Katherine whispered in a conspiratorial tone. "The most expensive restaurant in Albertsville."

"Greg's probably rich." Clarissa seemed very pleased at the thought, as if somehow the money might trickle her way.

"I don't think he's all that rich yet," Katherine told her. "His group's just getting started."

"Well, then, he will be."

"Why'd he take you to such an expensive place?" Robert asked.

I could have strangled him. Why was he so talkative all of a sudden? "Guess he just wanted to."

"Whatdja have for dessert?" Clarissa, ever the sweet-minded.

"Um. Nothing."

"Why not?"

"Because we . . . left before that."

"Why?"

I turned on her, air puffing from my mouth with annoyance. "What is this, twenty questions? We left because we wanted to, that's all."

Katherine and Daddy eyed me, clearly suspicious of the parts I'd left out. Fine, they could think what they wanted. I hardly cared to detail the wiles of stupid Charlotte to my entire family.

"Just so you had a good time." Katherine shook her head the slightest bit to Daddy, as if to say, *Don't press her, this is girl stuff.*

I felt grudgingly grateful for her tact, even as I told myself it was just one more way she worked to regain my trust. Which she didn't deserve.

Later, as we cleared the table, Daddy told me he wanted to take Katherine out for a drive. They'd had little time to be alone since Friday night, he added, and they needed to talk.

Translation: I had to stay with the kids.

"But I wanted to go out with Greg!" I set dirty plates on the counter. "We've only got today and tomorrow and then he's gone. You and Katherine have lots of time."

Katherine entered the kitchen, dirty plates in each hand. Upon hearing the gist of the conversation, she laid the plates in the sink and left. "Clarissa," I heard her call, "why don't you show me another game on your computer?"

Winnie shuffled underfoot, ears up, hoping for scraps. "Will you get out of the way," I complained. "Come here." I walked to the open sliding glass door and pulled back the screen. "Go outside." Winnie withered me with a look—*how can you take your troubles out on your ever-faithful dog?*—and slunk out.

"We've had very little time," Daddy said quietly, not wanting his voice to travel.

"But she'll still be here after Greg—"

"Wait a minute, what exactly is happening here?" Daddy faced me, arms folding. "When we talked about this last week, we agreed you were just goin' to meet him, remember? Just get to know him a little? Now at lunch you're vague about your date, plus you're wanting to see this boy again today and apparently tomorrow."

Here we go again. I leaned against the counter, searching for words. Was this still just because Greg was Danny Cander's brother?

"We talked about this, Jackie," Daddy said almost pleadingly. "About the fact that Greg would not be here long, that I didn't want you to put too much stock in his visit."

Put too much stock in it? What was Greg, the bank? "Daddy, I just want to see him while I have the chance."

"He's leaving, Jackie."

"I know that, Daddy," I cried, "that's just the problem!"

His shoulders drooped. He regarded the floor, mouth pulled in at the corners. "I knew this would happen," he said half to himself. "I never should have let you meet him."

Well, it was a little late now.

"You really like him, I suppose."

The way he said it, as if I'd betrayed him somehow. As if this had anything to do with years ago, when he'd lost his first love to someone else.

Which, let us not forget, had resulted in his marrying Mama.

Daddy looked at me, awaiting an answer.

I could not see then what I see now—that Daddy's feelings had far less to do with resentments from the past than concern for the future. Plain and simple, he didn't want me to be hurt. Not to mention his own side of things. I didn't realize just how much Daddy still had to work through with Katherine. Not a good time for me to face problems in my own love life. As far as he was concerned, our household already had enough to deal with.

All I knew was that Greg would be gone in two days. And the thought of not seeing him before he left was more than I could bear.

"Yes, I do like him, Daddy. And believe it or not, he likes me, too. And when he goes, I'll be sad about it. But let me tell you what else I'll be. I'll still be the one who helps take care of the kids, especially while you're out with Katherine." My voice turned brittle. "Who does the laundry and the cleaning. I'm not goin' to stop doin' all the things you count on me for. In other words, I promise not to be a problem. Okay?"

Briefly, Daddy closed his eyes. "Jackie." He touched my cheek with one curved finger. "You think I'm worried about your chores? I'm worried about *you*."

"I can handle me just fine. I always have."

Daddy's hand fell away. He nodded.

"Do you not trust me, is that it?" I wondered aloud.

"Of course I trust you. You've given me no reason not to."

"Then what is the problem? Greg is very nice and respectful to me. If you trust me, you can believe me when I tell you that." Not to mention Greg had shown nothing but generosity and circumspection when Katherine's ex had burst through our door.

"I'm only trying to protect you," Daddy replied. "I don't want to see things go terribly wrong in your life so soon after you've started dating."

"Like I said, I'll be fine. Please believe that." I didn't believe it at all, but I'd worry about that when Greg was gone. Right now nothing mattered but being with him. I sighed in frustration. "I know what we can do. Let's split up the time. You take the evening, I take the afternoon."

We stood there looking at each other, and from out of nowhere, I laughed. The whole situation seemed just so out of kilter. Never would I have imagined negotiating with my daddy over our dating schedules.

Daddy laughed, too. Then surveyed the ceiling as if searching for an answer to this delicate subject. "How about I take the afternoon, you take the evening?"

"I asked first."

"No, you didn't, *I* did."

"I'm the teenager."

"I'm the dad."

Case closed.

Ten minutes later, Daddy and Katherine happily traipsed out to the garage. Daddy promised me they'd be home by five. I picked up the phone to call Greg with the news.

"So where was it you wanted to go?" I asked.

chapter 30

Greg suggested that we plan a picnic. I didn't think Daddy would mind. Besides, it beat facing who-knew-what at another restaurant. I made sandwiches, gathered chips and drinks. Greg said he'd bring the dessert, seeing as how I'd been gypped out of one the night before. I hardly viewed that evening as my having been gypped out of anything, but I didn't argue the details.

I had plenty to do while I waited on tenterhooks for Daddy and Katherine to return. Most of the time I spent on the phone. Every one of the girls who'd been in our group after church called me, breathless and gushing and seeking details. Was Greg my boyfriend, or did Greek guys just hold a girl's hand for nothing? Had I gone out on a date with him? Where had we gone, what had we done? Questions, questions. They hardly left me room to answer. I hedged as much as possible without lying. Yes, we went out to supper, I admitted. Only to Alison did I tell the whole story. That call in itself took an hour.

"I'm so excited for you," she crowed. "Clayton's Place! Jacob and I went bowling again, big deal."

Jacob would still be here long after Greg had gone, I reminded her. We also talked more about Friday night.

"I don't trust Katherine a minute," I admitted. "She bounced from one job to the next in the past eleven years, and more importantly, one man to the next. She's hardly good enough for Daddy. What if she ditches him and breaks his heart? She'd break Clarissa's and Robert's, too. I swear, I'd strangle her. I mean, think about it, Alison, she doesn't even have a job here. I know she's doin' the cookin' and cleanin' at her parents' house, but how long does *that* take every day?"

"So . . . what does that matter?"

"She's not even settling down!" I exclaimed, annoyed that she couldn't understand. "Doesn't it make you think her bein' in Bradleyville is just another temporary thing, until she gets bored and wants to move on?"

"There's not all that many jobs around here. She probably doesn't know what she wants to do yet. Or . . ." She trailed out the word. "She figures no point in gettin' a job 'cause she's plannin' on marryin' your daddy."

Of course. The thought hit me like a brick over the head. Why hadn't I seen this before?

"And if she wants to marry him," Alison continued, "obviously she *is* plannin' on settlin' down. And you don't have to worry about her hurtin' your family."

"Well, that's just great," I retorted, "but nobody seems to be thinking about *me* in all this, including you. Like what if I don't *want* Katherine in our family?"

Silence. I could hear Alison breathing over the phone. "But if your daddy loves her . . . wouldn't you want him to be happy?"

I focused on Greg's picture. In less than two hours, I'd be with him. Excitement and longing surged through me at the thought. I remembered Daddy's words about Katherine the night we first spoke about his dating her. *Bein' with her has brought me an anticipation I haven't felt in a long time.* Now I knew what he was talking about. Oh, how I knew.

How could I possibly stand in his way, when I'd give anything to have more days with Greg?

❦❦

At 5:30, heart bumping with exhilaration, I trotted once more up the Matthews' steps. Greg pulled me inside the house, saying I needed to hear driving directions to our picnic spot from Celia.

"Do you know where Jake's Rock is on the river?" she asked. "A ways up from the swimming hole?"

I nodded.

"Go to Jake's Rock, turn left, and walk upriver around a bend until you see two large oak trees with thick leaves. It's a great spot, and it'll get you out of the sun."

We drove through downtown Bradleyville and across the tracks, then turned right toward the river. Greg and I had a bit of a trek, since we had to park in a field and trudge toward the Columbia River over a well-worn path. Greg had placed a bag of cookies that Celia had baked for us in my cooler, and he carried it for me. I toted an old blanket. We found the trees without a hitch. Celia was right; it was a beautiful spot. I wondered why I'd never thought to explore this part of the river before.

"How'd Celia know about this place?" I asked as we spread out the blanket beneath the cool shade. The river sparkled in the sun, a wide ribbon of gray-blue.

Greg sat on the blanket, holding out his hand to pull me down beside him. "I tell you if you do one thing," he said.

"Name it."

"Kiss me first."

I scrunched my nose, pretending to think it over. "Well, I guess so."

He pulled me close, and I swear the world stopped as his mouth met mine. Chills marched up and down my spine despite the warmth of the day. *I'd never get tired of this*, I thought, *not if I could kiss him every day for the rest of my life.*

But we didn't have the rest of my life. We had one day.

I pushed that bit of reality away. "Now you have to tell me."

He scooted to sit cross-legged, facing me, and laced both of his hands in mine. "Celia and my brother fall in love here."

I blinked at him. "Oh."

He squeezed my fingers. "They meet here each Saturday. Their special place."

I gazed at Greg, thinking about the past and present. Wondering again if Greg had any idea that my daddy's being third party in Danny and Celia's relationship had almost cost us the chance to meet.

"You are thinking what?" Greg asked.

My head shook slightly.

"Please. Tell me."

How could I? If he didn't know what Celia had done, who was I to tell him? "Your brother knows you've been seeing me, right?" I hedged. "I mean, I know you talked to him on the phone, but did you tell him . . . who I am?"

"Yes. Celia already tell him that you and I meet."

"Oh." I searched his face. "So what did he say?"

"I tell you." He grinned. "He says Bradleyville girls are best."

I focused on our hands, moving my fingers between his.

"Jackie? You are going away again. What is wrong?"

I remained silent.

"Jackie?"

"I don't—. I can't."

"Why?"

"It doesn't have anything to do with us," I said, "so it doesn't matter. I was just thinking about your brother and Celia, and how he left and they stayed apart for so long."

Greg's words from last night whirled like a sudden breeze through my mind. Danny—sitting Greg down before he left Greece, telling him things about living as a Christian, traveling, girls. *How to watch myself.* Maybe Danny had told him everything. Given him warnings about love, using his own past as an example.

"You think about this why?" Greg asked quietly.

Something in his voice—a hint of suspicion? As if I knew something I shouldn't? I thought of Greg's apparent discomfort when we'd discussed Danny and Celia on the phone. Then thought again of his words from last night—and realized the truth. He knew. He had to. Probably more details than I did.

My shoulders drew in. The intimacy of the topic momentarily caught my tongue. "I know about . . . what happened," I whispered.

He eased back, defensiveness flicking across his brow. The expression told me how close Greg felt to his brother and Celia. He turned to gaze out over the river. "Celia is right. People in Bradleyville do not forget things."

"No," I blurted, worried that I'd upset him. "It's not that at all. I didn't know anything until I overheard Daddy and Katherine talking, and—"

"Why your baba talk about this?" he demanded. "Something so long ago?"

"No, no, they weren't really talking about *that*. They were talking about Daddy when he was in high school and what he and Celia did and how Katherine knew about it—"

My words broke off at the look on his face. He angled his head, frowning at me, eyes narrowing. "What your baba does?"

Something clunked solidly in my chest. I stared at him, my mouth still open. He made no move.

"What *your baba* does?"

Warmth flushed through my body. I couldn't hide the horror on my face over what I'd assumed, what I'd done.

Greg dropped my hands and pushed to his feet. He grasped the back of his neck and propelled away from me to the trunk of the oak tree, where he stood, staring right through it. I managed to rise, then hung there, miserably watching. How shocked I had been, hearing Daddy and Katherine's conversation. How shocked Greg must be now, putting the details together, realizing he'd been in the home of his brother's rival.

As if he'd read my thoughts, Greg's hand slid to his battered cheek. My mouth pressed at the movement. What was he thinking—that he was sorry he'd helped my daddy fight?

"Greg?"

He stared at the tree.

"Greg!"

Slowly, he turned to me, jaw flexed. I could see his shirt rise and fall with his breathing. "My brother does not say who. He just tells me his mistake, and then Celia does the same. An old friend in Bradleyville, Danny says, who always loves her. For this Danny and Celia stay apart. For this—*your* baba—my brother pays for seventeen years."

Now wait just a minute, I thought. *Seventeen years apart?* There had to be more to this story, and my daddy could hardly take all the blame. "Celia did it for revenge," I declared. "*She* started it. Daddy was dating my mama, and they'd have been just fine, but Celia apparently got some idea one night. You think your brother's the only one who paid? My mama must have been heartbroken. Think about it! Her boyfriend and her *best friend!*"

His bruised cheek mottled a deeper red. "Your mamma and baba—they get married. All those years my brother stays alone."

"What are you tryin' to say, Greg, that my daddy's to blame for that? Just where was Celia all that time?"

My anger seemed to bounce right off him. His eyes closed, a sick expression stealing over his face. "Why she doesn't tell me? She hears I should meet you from Miss Jessie, but she never says. And Danny—what he is feeling? I go to your baba's house, and I am hit. Trouble again." He ran a hand over his face. "I cannot believe it."

"They didn't tell you because they didn't want you to know," I retorted. "Obviously." Tears bit my eyes. I could not bear to think Celia and Danny had been gracious about our meeting while Daddy had reacted so badly. I hoped they hadn't. I hoped they'd had to fight their own memories just as he had. "And Daddy didn't want me to know, either. But now we both do. So what are we gonna do about it, huh, Greg?" My voice pinched. "We gonna fight each other now, just because the three of them were so stupid?"

His face blurred. Even so, I saw the hurt and shame trailing across his cheeks. With a sudden sigh, he moved to hold me against his chest. "No. We do not fight. I'm sorry, Jackie. I'm sorry."

I grasped the fabric of his shirt, my eyes squeezed shut against the tears.

"You are not mad at me?"

"No," I sniffed. "Just don't be mad at *me.*"

We stood there hugging, my throat all balled up. It occurred to me he'd had to comfort me three days in a row. What a baby he must think I was.

Not until we sat again on the blanket, hands clasped, did we realize the extent of the blessing Celia had bestowed upon me and Greg— telling us about her and Danny's special place. Greg and I talked quietly about what we'd heard of the past, piecing together details from his brother's life and Celia's, and my parents'. So much pain they'd caused each other. Still, they were now letting us be together.

"Danny only tells me so I will be careful," Greg said. "He asks Celia first if he can. He knows I will face much, like him. He says, 'You cannot take your eyes off Christ one minute.'" He smiled. "My brother likes to say that."

I nodded. Now that everything lay out in the open, seemed to me it wasn't such a bad thing for us to know. "I'm so glad Celia shared her place with us. I'm glad I'm here with you."

"Me, too."

He gazed at me, warmth in his eyes. Then a thought flickered over his brow, and he turned to focus distractedly on the river. A few notes hummed deep in his throat. His eyes danced as he hummed it again, mouthing a few words.

I moved his hand gently, recapturing his attention. He shrugged as if I'd caught him at something. "What were you doing?"

"Ah. Sorry. I am . . . writing a song."

"Oh. I see." Not really, but what else was I supposed to say. "I've never seen you do that before."

"Suddenly, it comes. I watch, pay attention to things. Then sometimes—I think something. Usually just words, and the tune comes later."

I realized at that moment, even after all our talking, how little I knew about Greg's world. Soon he'd return to it—a world of singing and concerts and fame. Girls screaming for him. I couldn't begin to imagine it. And I wondered if he'd be the same person then as he was with me. Could he follow his brother's advice and keep his eyes on Christ?

As the sun set, ribboning bronze and red upon the river, we ate and spoke of easier subjects. I wanted to hear every detail of the songs they'd sing on tour, how some of them had been written since their CD had released. He told me about the special effects—the smoke, the laser lights, and the staging. He even pulled me to my feet and showed me some of the choreography to a song. I caught on to the steps quickly.

"Hey," he said, "you are good."

I tossed hair back from my face, pulling in deep breaths. Boy, was I out of shape. "No big deal, I was in gymnastics for years."

He caught me around the waist and kissed me, both of us still breathing hard. "There is much I don't know about you," he said. "I want to know everything."

Darkness would fall soon. We packed up our stuff and trekked back to the car, my heart wanting to sing and wail at once. We had one more day, and I wanted a million. Four days of knowing Greg, and already I could not stand to think of life in Bradleyville without him. Other than his concert in Lexington—*if* Daddy let me go—when would I ever see him again? How could I just live as before in quiet Bradleyville, worrying about whether some boy at school would ever ask me out?

It wouldn't matter, I told myself. If I couldn't be with Greg, I didn't want to be with anyone.

He caught sight of my expression as we placed the blanket and cooler in the car. "What is it?"

I knew that he already knew the answer. He wrapped his arms around me, gentling his fingers into my hair. "I don't want to go. I don't want to leave you."

"I don't want you to go either."

Air seeped from his throat. "We will see each other tomorrow. Promise me."

I promised. But never did I dream how it would happen.

chapter 31

Katherine was still at our house when I returned, sliding a sheet of cookies into the oven. "Have a good time?" she asked, her sad smile betraying just how well she read the answer. *Hoo-fah for her if she can figure it out*, I thought as I threw away the trash from our meal. Did I have a good time? Yes, Katherine, it was wonderful and it was miserable, like falling into the perfect dream world, then being told you must leave.

"Where's Daddy?" I asked her.

"In Robert's bedroom, talking to him." She punched in ten minutes on the timer.

"Why?"

"Robert seems kind of down. I think he's depressed about his leg."

Poor Robert. I'd be willing to bet he was depressed about more than his leg. I wondered if Katherine had any idea how hurt he'd been after hearing the truth about her. I knew Robert would never admit it to Daddy or her, or even to me. He'd hold on to his pain in that place deep within himself, the place that guarded his emotions like a jealous lover.

I leaned down to pet Winnie. Her eyes closed in sheer bliss as I scratched around her collar. Sounds from the television filtered in from the family room. I stuck my head around the corner and spotted Clarissa splayed on the couch, her bare feet on the cushions, knees akimbo.

"Jackie." Katherine laid a hand on my shoulder. "I'd like to talk to you. We haven't had the chance since Friday night, and I think we should get some things out in the open."

Here it came. Her explanations, my expected forgiveness. My mind threatened to burst already with whirling thoughts of Greg and me. All I wanted to do was hide in my room and stare at his picture. Try to figure how to get my life back on keel once he left. "Okay."

If she heard the reluctance in my voice, she didn't show it. "Um, where can we go?"

No place but my bedroom. My sacred room, with Greg's picture on the wall and the remembrance of Mama sitting upon my bed during our talks. I ushered Katherine in and shut the door, inviting her with a reluctant arm to take my desk chair, then perched on the edge of my bed, waiting. Telling myself she would not charm her way back into my heart.

She turned the chair around to face me, clasping her hands in her lap. The neckline of her white blouse contrasted against her tanned skin, oh-so-perfectly-subtle blusher glowing bronze on her cheeks. Katherine's presence fairly radiated in my room, making me feel plain and small. Greg's eyes stared at me from his picture, and suddenly I wondered what he saw in me. Surely he would forget me as soon as he'd gone, as soon as he found himself allured and wanted by girls as beautiful as Katherine.

She tucked her hair behind her ears and regarded me for a moment, as if not quite sure how to begin. I would not help her.

"Jackie, I promise I will be honest with you if you'll be the same with me. It's the only way we can get past . . . what happened Friday night." She searched my face. "Okay?"

I nodded.

"Okay." She focused on her hands. "I know you think I don't deserve your daddy," she began slowly. "You're right. I don't claim to deserve him. I've made a mess of most of my life. He knows about it now—all of it. I don't want to dwell on my past; I just want to go on. But because my past slapped you in the face, slapped us all, I'm willing to tell you anything you want to know. As hard as it is for me, I think lingering secrets and doubts between us will only continue to hurt us both."

I slipped out of my shoes and crossed my ankles, rubbing my feet together.

"Can you do this for us both, Jackie? For once, just come out and say what you're thinking?"

The question surprised me. Robert was the one who hid his feelings, I thought, not I.

So why did my mouth refuse to move?

Here's your chance, Jackie, a voice inside whispered. *Let her have it.* Why not? She'd certainly asked for it.

"Okay." I gazed at Katherine straight on, feeling my indignation rise. "I want to know if it's true that you had lots of boyfriends in a row, like that man said. I want to know why you left them. And why, in those eleven years that you were gone, you moved from one job and one place to another, like you just got bored." My face warmed, but I pressed ahead. "Most of all, I want to know what's goin' to keep you from up and leavin' Daddy the way you did everybody else."

Katherine had the decency to look ashamed. "Fair questions," she said quietly. She pressed back and surveyed the ceiling with a sigh. "Do you know that my daddy, Jason King, isn't my biological father?"

Like this had anything to do with it. "Yes."

She ignored my impatient tone. "My biological father left my mother before I was born. I grew up knowing it, but not until I was fourteen did I really start thinking about it. I love my daddy, and he loves me, too, as much as he does Derek. Still, I wondered about the man who would leave my mother and me and never look back. In my teenage years I felt rebellious and closed in, like there was this big, wide world out there just waiting for me to grab hold of it. I wasn't like most of my friends, and I blamed my thirst for adventure on this unknown man and his blood running through my veins. As I told you, I left when I was eighteen. And you're right, Jackie, I'd stay in one job for a while, and with one boyfriend for a while, and then go on to something else. Always thinking the key to my contentment would be around the next bend. Always afraid that the commitment wasn't quite right for me somehow. I . . ." She hesitated, then pushed on. "I partied too much and ran around too much. But a life like that gets tiring. Finally, I just wanted to come home."

I eyed her, thinking of Greg's mama. "Did any of those boyfriends abuse you? Especially the one who came here?"

"No." She pressed her lips together as though she almost wished for such an excuse. "He had a temper, as you saw. But then, I wasn't all that easy to live with myself."

Live with. The words pulsed. I could only glare at her, Trent Baxter's title for her echoing in my head. Katherine knew exactly what I was thinking.

"Jackie," she ventured, "I'm not proud of the things I did. Shortly after I came back, God really spoke to me in that church service. I asked his forgiveness, and I turned my life back over to Christ, as I'd done when I was a kid, but then had walked away from it. I'm . . . I'm different now. I don't want my old lifestyle."

I didn't doubt Katherine's sincerity. I didn't doubt she wanted to live as a Christian should. If she didn't, I knew my daddy would not have let himself fall in love with her, for Christianity lay at the foundation of his life. But, as much as a trip to the altar had wiped away her sins, I did doubt that it had cleansed her of all her angst. As events had so clearly shown, the past had a way of rising again to haunt us.

To put it bluntly, I saw her obvious pattern: Katherine fell in love, then she fled.

"Do you believe me?" she pressed.

I looked out the window, idly watching a car pass on the street. A part of me wanted to believe that she would do nothing except make my daddy happy, even if she would never be worthy of him. Another part wished she'd never come into our lives, for her coming had only made us vulnerable once more.

But then without Katherine, I may never have met Greg.

"I believe that you don't want to hurt us," I said slowly. "But I don't totally believe that you won't."

She drew back her head, her expression flattening. Something about the sudden stillness of her hands, the drift of her gaze to the floor, told me I'd hit the mark. Hit it right dead center. Katherine, apparently, did not fully believe in herself.

To this day I can almost feel how my nerves tingled, as if I'd just glimpsed a future nightmare. The thought frightened me so badly that I could only push it away. Surely I was wrong, I told myself. Katherine was trying to change. She loved Daddy. She loved Clarissa and Robert. If our family could help put the past behind her, we could make her *want* to stay. Daddy had already forgiven her, as had Clarissa. Robert would never let her know he'd been hurt. Only I stood in the way of Katherine's feeling truly safe with us.

No. Not for the life of me would I take on that guilt.

I stared at the carpet, thoughts pounding me. Hadn't I always sacrificed since Mama died in order to take care of the family? Hadn't I always managed to help Daddy? It didn't matter how I felt about Katherine. What mattered was that my family wanted her, my daddy loved her. Now it fell to me again to make things work. To help Katherine rise above her lingering fears about herself—fears that I doubted very much she'd shared with Daddy.

Tiredness surged over me. It was too much. Just when I faced saying goodbye to Greg, I had to deal with this.

"Katherine." I pushed myself from the bed to kneel beside her chair. "You wanted me to be honest. Here goes. So please listen. Daddy *can't* be hurt again, you get that? Neither can the rest of us, not after losing Mama. We've had all we can take. So please just . . . be happy here. Stay with Daddy. *Don't hurt him.*"

My throat locked up.

"Oh, Jackie—" Katherine leaned over the arm of the chair to hug me. "I won't. I promise I won't."

I hugged her, too, mouth trembling. But I didn't know if I fought tears for her and Daddy, or me and Greg. Or both.

After a moment, we stood, both of us sniffling. I fetched us tissues.

Katherine took a cleansing breath, ending the conversation. "So." She wandered over to gaze at the LuvRush photo. "You really like Greg, huh?"

Instantly, I wanted to circle my wagons. Seemed to me we'd shared plenty for one day. But how would my pushing Katherine away now help her feel wanted?

"Yes."

"He likes you, too. In fact, he's crazy about you."

I blinked at her. "How do you know?"

Katherine cringed a little, just as Alison might upon telling me something she should not repeat. "I'm not sure I should pass it on, but . . ."

"Yes, you should." No subtlety here.

"Greg's apparently real close to Celia. She told me after church how much he's talked to her about you. He says you're just the kind of girl he's been looking for."

Me. *Me.* "What kind of girl would *that* be?"

"Don't sound so surprised, Jackie." Katherine balled up the tissue in her hand. "A girl who's pretty and smart and not stuck on herself. Someone who cares about people. Celia says that, for all Greg's success, he's very much the same way."

My mind blitzed a dozen questions at once. "I saw you talking after church. Miss Jessie was with you; did she hear this, too?"

Katherine sat on my bed, patting the spot beside her. I took it, not thinking that this was how my mama and I used to talk about dating. Not thinking that at all. "I'm sorry," Katherine said. "I don't want you to feel strange, three women gossiping about you. Celia wouldn't tell anyone else, I'm sure, but Miss Jessie's close to both of us."

I nodded, not really caring. Miss Jessie I trusted completely. My fascination lay in the words—*you're just the kind of girl he's been looking for.*

Even after kissing Greg, even though I knew he liked me, it was so hard to believe.

"The thing is . . ." I traced the stitching on my bedspread with a finger. "What does it matter? He's leaving."

She laid her hand over mine and squeezed. "I know." I felt my throat grow tight again. "You can at least see him when LuvRush comes to Lexington. I'll take you."

"What if Daddy doesn't let me go?"

She smiled with secret knowledge. "Don't worry. He'll let you go."

I looked at her face and saw her resolve to fight for me. Katherine most certainly could twist Daddy around her finger. I'd have no worries about the concert. I managed a wan smile back.

"Do you know when it is?" she asked.

I shook my head. "We talked about his schedule today. Greg promised to call his manager and get the whole thing for me. He'll give it to me tomorrow." I eyed her askance. "I *will* be able to see him tomorrow."

Katherine raised her eyebrows. "I've managed it for you every day up till now, haven't I?"

"*You've* done that?" I gave her a dubious look. "When you heard me talkin' to Daddy today after lunch, you ditched us and went to play with Clarissa."

"That's because I won't get in the way of you and your daddy. But that doesn't keep me from speaking my mind when you're not around." She wagged her head in a gesture of self-satisfaction.

I did not know what to say. Had Katherine been fighting for me even after I turned against her Friday night?

Well. Good for her. I'd take her up on the help for one more day. "Will you make sure Daddy lets us go out to supper tomorrow night?"

"I don't know," she teased. "Actually, *we* were thinking of going out."

I pushed her arm. "Fine. You'll just have to find another baby-sitter." We smiled at each other.

I glanced away at my clock radio. "Oh, it's nine o'clock! I have to put Clarissa to bed."

"And I should be getting home. But not until I've talked to your daddy about you and Greg." She touched my hair, then rose. "Thank you, Jackie. For talking to me."

I nodded, wanting to say, *Don't forget your promise.*
Don't ever forget.

chapter 32

Jackie, somebody's waitin' for you!" Nicole announced in a singsong voice after the last bell. She rushed up to my locker, her eyes bright. "I just went out the door, and there's Greg, standin' on the steps! He asked if I'd find you."

Whoa. Waiting to walk me home from school. As if talk hadn't run like a rabbit around the halls all day. I'd heard nothing but "Jackie, tell me!" and "Jackie, is it true?" hour after hour. First, practically everybody in our high school wanted to know about what happened at our house Friday night. I said as little as possible about that. Then they wanted to know about the guy from Greece who'd helped save the lives of me and my family. Was I really going out with him?

Yes, it's true, I said again and again, affecting nonchalance.

"But what're you goin' to do when he leaves?" the girls all wondered.

Why did everybody have to ask that question?

The boys, of course, also heard the talk. "So, Jackie," Billy Sullivan teased, "you like those foreign types, I hear." Billy's groupies hung on his every word, hoping for a reaction. I did not disappoint.

"He's better than anything I could find here." I had stuck my nose in the air and pushed him aside, tingling with satisfaction at the guffaws of his friends.

"Well, get out there!" Nicole cried now. "Get your books and go."

"I'm goin', I'm goin'."

I chose my books in a hurry and banged my locker shut. Nicole stuck by me like glue, her messenger status affording her the right to escort me to Greg. We passed Derek in the hallway, loping along at his usual pace, and I barely noticed until he said hello. "Oh, hi!" I managed, blithely patting his arm as we sailed by. Out the corner of my eye I saw his gaze fall to where my fingers had touched.

Nicole and I reached the propped-open front door of our building. I took a deep breath and stepped outside.

A small entourage of girls surrounded Greg. For a second I nearly panicked, thinking surely someone had recognized him. Instead I heard only questions about his bruised face—did it still hurt? Was that the first fight he'd ever been in? For heaven's sake. Greg's mere appearance caused enough excitement. Imagine if they knew who he was.

"Hi." He dazzled me with a smile that sent my heart tumbling.

"Hi."

My friends shuffled back as Greg moved to my side. He wore designer jeans and a shirt of ice blue that sheened in the sunlight. "Let me take your backpack." I handed it to him wordlessly and he shrugged it on. Then he turned and said goodbye to the girls, who ogled his every move. As we hit the steps, he took my hand.

I did not dare look back. I didn't have to. The envy of my friends practically reached out and plucked the shirt right off my back.

"Grandma will be coming to pick us up," I told him when I could find my tongue. Thinking was it just last week that I'd met him in the dime store? It seemed more like a lifetime ago. "I'll need to tell her I'm walking. She can take my books."

Moments later we stood at Grandma's car, Robert sliding into the backseat with the experience of a casted athlete. Greg set my backpack on the floor. Clarissa ran up, flushed and excited, Alma Sue at her side. "See?" she cried to Alma Sue, "that's my sister's boyfriend that I told you about. And he's a famous singer in a rock band!"

"Ah, good," Greg muttered. I could have strangled my sister. Alma Sue's eyes widened, then turned suspicious as she peered from Clarissa to Greg. She smacked both hands on her hips and cocked her head at him. "I don't believe you," she taunted Clarissa, still eyeing Greg as if he were some specimen under glass.

"Well, it's true!"

"Clarissa, be quiet!" I turned her around and pushed her toward the car. "Grandma's waiting, now get in!" She flounced inside and banged shut the door. I leaned down through the open window and shot Grandma an exasperated look. She raised her eyebrows back at me in an *oh-boy* expression.

"I'll wait for you to get home," she said.

"Well, I still don't believe it," Alma Sue practically sneered at me as Grandma drove off.

Every nerve in my spine tingled as I faced the little brat. I wasn't quite sure which made me madder, that she'd act so disrespectfully to me or that she was calling my sister a liar. "I'm glad you don't, Alma Sue," I announced, "because if you did it just might prove you had a brain in your head."

Alma Sue scrunched her face, apparently trying to decide whether I'd agreed with her or laid her flat. I opened my mouth to say more, but Greg firmly caught my arm. "Jackie. Let's go."

I turned away, still huffing. We'd walked a block before my anger cooled and I could stop to remember I was parading through Bradleyville hand in hand with Greg.

"She'll tell everybody, you know."

He shrugged. "We are lucky it happens only now."

Greg was right. What harm could it do now, when we had only one more night?

Apparently Katherine had worked her magic behind the scenes while I was at school. By the time I arrived home, Grandma had ensconced herself on the couch with Clarissa, clearly prepared to stay so that Greg could come inside. And when I called Daddy, he said we could go out for supper again. For the next hour I happily shared Greg with my family—Clarissa on the computer and even Robert in his bedroom, showing Greg his softball trophies. *If only Greg lived here*, I kept saying to myself, *if only, if only*.

But then, he wouldn't be Greg.

He pulled a copy of the LuvRush concert schedule from his pocket, with his e-mail address at the bottom. I looked at the schedule. Saturday, August 22 was circled for Lexington. August 22. I closed my eyes. *Three months*.

Greg pointed at his e-mail address. "You will write me every day? I will buy a cell phone, too. I'll call you when I can, but after concerts it's too late. An e-mail you can write anytime."

"Yes, I'll write you. But I have to learn how to do the e-mails."

"Come, I will show you. We can write one now and send it to me."

We kicked a pouting Clarissa off the computer. "Come on, Clarissa," Grandma urged, "it's their turn now. Besides, I'd rather play a game with you." They went off to Clarissa's room while Greg taught me what I needed to know.

"Okay, now. You want what for your password?"

I thought a moment. "Willy Ray."

He grinned. "Good. Type it as one word, no spaces."

I did as I was told. Greg showed me how to get into the e-mail system and all its features, explaining that when I received an e-mail I could instantly see who'd sent it and at what time.

"Now you will write what?" Greg wondered aloud as we stared at the waiting cursor, his fingers perched on the keys. "I know." He typed as I leaned in close, my chin on his shoulder. *Dear Greg, Will you kiss me tonight?*

"Don't type *that!*" I gave him a playful punch. "What if someone reads it?"

"Nobody will read it but me. That is why you have a password." He demonstrated how to send it. "There. Done."

"Well, if you send me e-mails like that, I'm really gonna need my password. I can just imagine my family gobblin' that stuff up."

"'Gobblin'?"

"Eatin' it up. You know, enjoyin' it."

"Oh." He stole a quick kiss.

Once Greg left, I tried my best to concentrate on doing my homework. Two hours later, as soon as Daddy got home with the car, I picked Greg up to go out to supper, this time to a quiet little café in Albertsville—one of the few restaurants open on a Monday. We sat in a corner booth, holding hands and talking far more than eating, sans any Charlottes. He had brought me the LuvRush CD. I told him I'd play it until it wore right through. After our meal we drove to our vista point off Route 622 and parked and watched the sun set, dreading the moment when my 9:30 school-night curfew would force us back to Bradleyville.

I can remember that hour with Greg so clearly. The way he gently brushed hair off my forehead while I told him about Mama's cancer and her death. The way he hugged me as he said again that he didn't want to leave. "Hung Up on You" even played on the radio, and Greg sang along with his own voice, the words meant for me.

"Why?" I blurted when the song finished, wanting to hear what he'd said to Celia and more. That I was the kind of girl he'd been looking for. That he wouldn't forget me when he'd gone.

"Because you are beautiful." His eyes radiated sincerity. "Because you are you."

"You're gonna meet hundreds of beautiful girls," I said. "They're gonna fall all over you, and you'll be able to have anyone you want. You'll forget me."

"No, I won't." He gripped my hands. "You don't understand if you think this. I feel things deep inside, Jackie; that is why I write songs. I will work hard on the tour. I will sing. Fans are important, but I don't give my heart to girls who only watch me sing. They don't know me. They don't know who I am on the inside. I need a . . ." He touched his tongue to his lower lip, seeking the word. "Something. When you dial the phone, you get it."

"A conversation?"

"No." He bounced our hands in frustration against the console. "A . . . connection! I need a connection to someone, like I have a connection to my family. When I am lonely, I think of them. Now when I am lonely, I will think of you."

I studied his face, still unable to grasp that Greg could ever be lonely when surrounded by fans.

"Will you think of me?" he asked.

What a question. "Greg," I said, "I don't know when there'll be a minute that I *won't* think of you. You don't know how much I'm gonna miss you."

"Yes, I do. I will miss you as much. More. I love you, Jackie."

The words sounded in my ears, and I could only bask in them, letting them warm me like the sun. Greg watched me almost anxiously, as if afraid he'd said too much. Imagine that. I hadn't known two people could fall in love in less than a week. But after all my dreams of love, if this wasn't the real thing, I didn't need it anyway. I didn't need anything more than what I felt at that moment. "I love you, too, Greg."

He breathed deeply and slid his arms around me. Just held on. Part of me soaked in every sensation—the texture of his shirt against my palms, his smell, the night crickets, the thickness of his hair between my fingers. And part of me hovered, looking down on myself, thinking, *This cannot be real.*

"Jackie." Greg pulled back to look me in the eye. "This is not fair to ask because you can go out with other people, and I don't have time. But—you will be my girlfriend?"

I almost laughed. Not fair to me? "You are . . . too much," I breathed.

"Too much what?"

I did laugh then, a disbelieving, amazed little sound that bubbled up my throat. "Greg." I cradled his face in my hands. "I'd rather be your girlfriend and sit home on Saturday nights thinkin' of you than be out with *anybody.*"

"Yes!" he cried, then leaned back with his arms folded, grinning like the Cheshire cat. "Oh, wait." He snatched his sapphire ring off his finger, as if afraid I'd change my mind any second. "Here." He pressed it into my palm, closing my fingers around it. "Keep this. You can wear it on a chain to tell others you are my girlfriend."

"Oh, Greg, I can't—"

"Yes, take it."

"But your parents gave it to you. It means so much to you."

"This is why I want you to keep it. It's the best I can give you. Except maybe when I write you a song." He smiled again, cheeks glowing with happiness.

I gazed at the ring in my hand. I stared and stared at its gold band with etchings down the side until they blurred, and my throat hurt, and my lips wavered. "Thank you," I whispered, wishing I could find something more worthy to say. "Thank you."

I slipped the ring into my purse so I wouldn't lose it, telling Greg I would put it on the gold chain my mother left me. And I wouldn't take it off, *ever*, even when I slept. I would still have it on when I saw him again at the Lexington concert. Saturday, August 22. I would live and breathe for that day.

When we pulled up to the Matthews' house, both of us silent, already feeling the loss of our separation, Greg kissed me one last, long time. I didn't care that our car sat near a streetlight, that any neighbor nosing out the window—or even my grandma Westerdahl two houses down—might see. I just wanted that kiss to last forever.

"I love you, Jackie." *Tsoky*.

"I love you."

Apprehension creased his forehead as he gazed at me. "You don't forget me when I am gone? And there are other guys here?"

He was thinking of Celia, I realized. The pain she'd caused his brother. But then, hadn't his brother made the first mistake? "No, Greg, I promise. I love *you*. But don't forget *me*." My fingers sank into his arms at the mere imagining. "With all those girls wantin' you, don't forget *me*."

"No. I won't. Do not think it." His eyes glistened. He ran his tongue between his lips. "E-mail me every day. I write you and call when I can. And please—pray for me."

I promised to do all those things.

Five minutes later I trudged into our house, shoulders bent and cheeks wet. Daddy took one look at my face, and his own expression lined with concern for me. Without a word, he hugged me, resting his chin on the top of my head.

Before I dragged into my room, I opened my e-mail on the computer, heart already brimming with words to write Greg. A single e-mail sat in my inbox. A response from Greg, written at 5:30, just before I'd pulled up to the Matthews' door.

>*Dear Greg, Will you kiss me tonight?*<

Yes.

chapter 33

Tuesday morning. From that day on, my life would forever change. *POP STAR VISITS ALBERTSVILLE.* The headline screamed across the front page of the twice-weekly *Albertsville Journal.* Daddy held the section up for me to see the minute I entered the kitchen, his expression black. "Read it," he commanded.

I sank into a chair, heart in my throat, and stared at the front page. Right in the middle spread not one picture of Greg and me, but two. The first had been taken at the restaurant as we'd turned in surprise toward the camera, hands clasped over the table. Charlotte must have snapped the second through the window, catching us by the car as Greg hugged me, one of his hands on my back, the other in my hair. Beside the photos, big black letters spelled out the quote, "She's my girl."

I dropped my head in my hands, mortified. Imagining the gossip already swirling through town, the raised eyebrows at school. I could barely breathe as I forced myself to read.

Greg Kostakis, lead singer of the singing group LuvRush, was spotted at Clayton's Place with his girlfriend from Bradleyville on Saturday night. According to sources in Bradleyville, Kostakis is visiting the town, staying with William and Estelle Matthews, the parents of his sister-in-law, Celia. Kostakis's half brother, Danny, grew up in Bradleyville and moved to Greece after he graduated from high school. All four singers in LuvRush are from Athens, Greece.

Charlotte Deeks, who took the picture, said Kostakis told her and her friends, who were out for prom night, that the girl he was with (later identified as Jackie Delham), was "his girl" and that he would not allow a picture to be taken of himself with any other girl unless Jackie was also in it.

"You should have seen them," Deeks said. "They were practically all over each other in the restaurant, and then they left all of a sudden. That's when I took the picture of them in the parking lot."

Kostakis had a large bruise on his left cheek, as if he had been in a fight. Deeks said he would only explain that he'd had "a little accident."

LuvRush is a popular new band, with their single "Hung Up on You" landing at number five on the charts . . .

I did not need to read further. I slumped over the table, unable to raise my head to look Daddy in the eye, shame and defensiveness like lead in my stomach. Around my neck, hidden by my pajamas, hung Greg's ring on the gold chain I'd gotten from Mama. I could feel the ring's weight as it swung forward against the cotton fabric of my top.

Daddy raked out a chair opposite me and sat down hard. For a moment he said nothing, the headline glaring between us. I turned the paper over.

"Look at me, Jackie."

I raised my head, the rest of me still, wooden.

"Huggin' you like that in a public parking lot?" He threw out the words, his voice harsh. "Tellin' perfect strangers 'my girl' on a first date? He was 'all over you'?"

"It's not true, Daddy, she lied!"

"You got the pictures right there to prove it!"

"But it's not like it looks, and he wasn't 'all over' me in the restaurant, not at all!" My voice pleaded for him to understand. "And Greg didn't mean the thing about 'my girl,' he was just tryin' to—"

"Didn't *mean* it? Sure looks like he meant it to me. Looks like you *both* meant it."

"Daddy, you don't know! That girl was awful, and she was puttin' me down, and Greg was tryin' to be nice, but he wouldn't let her get away with it."

Daddy's jaw worked. "You didn't tell me that someone took pictures. Very private pictures. You didn't tell me that Greg went around braggin' about who he is—"

"He *didn't!*"

"Do *not* interrupt me." Daddy smacked the table. "You did not tell me any of this. Especially about the pictures. All you told me—assured me—was that I could trust you. It was hard enough for me to let you go out with Greg, you know that. I thought from the beginning he'd cause trouble. Now look what's happened. Your name's in the paper for everyone to see. Your picture's in the paper. Sixteen years old, Jackie, on your first date, and the whole town gets to see the way you behaved. I can't *believe* the way you and Greg paraded yourselves around."

"We did not parade around!"

"Then just what would you call it?" Daddy pushed back against his chair in disgust. "Jackie, Greg's life is nothin' like ours. He's lookin' to put himself in the limelight, to be famous. Singers thrive on attention. Well, he got his attention all right, and dragged you into it with him. I'm tellin' you, it's a good thing he's gone, because he would not step foot in this house again."

My head swam with arguments. Greg hadn't left yet, that I knew. He'd be packing, getting ready to drive to the Lexington airport around 11:00. Surely someone at the Matthews' household had seen the paper. I knew he would feel terrible. He'd want to call me, beg my forgiveness. As if he'd done something terribly wrong. Which he *hadn't*.

"It's one thing to let you date," Daddy raved on, "but in Bradley-ville—as you well know—that's done with circumspection, despite how exciting it might be. I never dreamed that on your first date you'd act like this—in front of people who you *knew* were watching you because of Greg. Who would have every reason to spread the news. And now I'm lookin' at what this Charlotte said, and I'm rememberin' how you mentioned you two didn't have dessert. How you left the restaurant far earlier than you came home. And I'm wonderin' exactly where you went, and what you did!"

I dragged in air, my cheeks flushing hot. Dating with circumspec-tion? Wondering what *I* had done? The mere thought that Daddy would suspect bad things of me or Greg made my blood boil. Who was *he* to talk, after the mistakes he'd made at my age?

Daddy glowered at me, waiting, watching my face. I glared back at him. In the next minute, his breath ebbed. He drew back, the lines on his forehead unraveling as he understood my unspoken words. Instantly, then, his expression creased with fresh anger. We faced off, silently spewing.

"Hi, Dad," Clarissa's voice floated from behind me.

"Clarissa, go get dressed," Daddy barked, not taking his eyes from me. I sensed the momentary pause of Clarissa's confusion, then heard her rustle away.

"You care to tell me what's on your mind?" Daddy dared, his voice flint-edged.

I swallowed hard, frayed nerves causing my sense of betrayal over Celia and him to rise bitterly in my throat. Tears pricked my eyes.

"Well?"

I inhaled raggedly. "We didn't do anything wrong, Daddy, please believe that. We were just tryin' to talk in the restaurant, but this girl recognized Greg, and then she wouldn't leave us alone. She was real snotty to me. So Greg put her in her place. That's why she lied. He stood up for me, Daddy, just like he stood up for you the night before. We didn't know she was goin' to take our picture. The minute she took it, we left. Greg hugged me for a second because I was so upset. How could I know she'd take another picture, and go to the papers with them?"

"Greg should have known," Daddy declared. "Maybe at first we all thought he could get by without bein' recognized here. But he's chosen the public life, and he should know how to handle it. The minute that picture was taken, he should have realized what would happen. And you should have told me. The *last* thing you should have done was hug in the parking lot for everyone to goggle at!"

I dropped my gaze, whispering, "I'm sorry."

"Where did you go after you left that restaurant?"

"Nowhere."

"Jackie!"

I heard the fear and mistrust in his voice, and it made me sick.

"We just drove somewhere and parked so we could talk, that's all. Where we wouldn't have to deal with people!"

Daddy's face blanched. "You sat in a parked car, just the two of you, long after dark? What did you do?"

"Nothing! Just talked."

He glared at me, mouth pressed.

"What's wrong with that?" I cried. "What'd you want us to do, stay at the restaurant so they could take more pictures?"

"You should have come home, that's what!"

"It wasn't time to come home!"

Daddy rose from his chair, leaning over the table to sear me with his eyes. "Jackie, you don't go parking with some boy for hours after dark. You know I'd never allow that."

"We didn't do anything wrong."

"Like you 'didn't do anything' at the restaurant?"

"We didn't *do anything!*"

"How can I believe that," he shouted, "when you've surprised me as much as you already have?"

"Because Greg's not *you*, Daddy!"

The words shot from my mouth like heat-seeking missiles. Instantly, I wanted them back. They hit their mark. Daddy hung over the table, lips parted, no words coming, slow pain filling his eyes. Carefully, he lowered himself into his seat.

I could not believe what I had done. Apologies struggled to form on my tongue, then died away. An aching, deep longing for Mama surged through me. This wouldn't have happened if she had been alive.

Some of the longest moments of my life passed before either of us spoke.

Daddy cleared his throat. "People make mistakes, Jackie," he uttered. "And the smart ones learn from those mistakes."

No, I cried inside, *no*. Already I knew where he was headed. It wasn't fair, his using his past to shatter my present.

"Let's talk about you, shall we?" He pointed at me for effect. "I let you see Greg while he was here—even though I never liked the idea. Now he's gone. Hear me when I say I'm fully expecting that will be the end of it. I know you're sad. But this"—he pressed a finger against the paper—"just shows that you are far better off without him. Your lack of judgment and his is goin' to cost us all. I don't want to hear that you're writin' or callin' him. And I don't want to hear about your goin' to any concerts. Is that clear?"

I let my eyes drift, unable to respond. Hugged my arms against my chest, feeling Greg's ring press against my skin.

"As for your going out in the future," Daddy added, "I will watch you far more closely. And it's goin' to be with somebody whose family I know."

The phone rang. Daddy ignored it.

"Do you hear me, Jackie?"

How could I fight him? The barest lifting of my chin answered *yes*.

The phone rang again. Daddy emitted a sigh, then rose to answer it. I knew who it was. My eyes closed, burning, as I listened helplessly to his words.

"No, you cannot talk to her," he clipped. "I'm very disappointed in both of you, Greg, and I blame it mostly on you. You should have known better. Your life has now caused trouble for ours, and we'll have to deal with it long after you're gone. I don't want you contacting Jackie again."

He dropped the receiver firmly back into place.

"Go get dressed for school."

I pushed to my feet and stumbled from the kitchen.

chapter 34

I don't know how I managed to go to school that day. Somehow I got myself dressed and out the door with the rest of the family, eyes red and stomach hungry since I'd had no time for breakfast. I wore a blouse that would hide the chain and Greg's ring. No one said a word in the car as Daddy drove us to school. One look at our faces, and Clarissa and Robert had known to leave well enough alone.

The pain of losing Greg would have been enough. I wanted to slink through the day, wiping my eyes unnoticed by no one. Instead I found myself surrounded and watched like some fascinating pariah.

Alison stuck by me. Most of the other girls did not. They were mad at me to begin with for not telling them who Greg was. I'd hidden information from them, treating them like peons while I played Cinderella with the visiting prince. Then for me to behave on a first date the way stupid Charlotte had said. In a way I couldn't blame the girls, hearing their parents' stunned questions as surely they had. Nicole and Cherise, Millicent and the others needed to distance themselves from me, to let all know that they neither approved of my behavior nor had consorted to keep it a secret. The boys proved far worse, their knowing expressions and under-the-breath remarks telling me all I needed to know. They viewed me with a mixture of awe and judgment. *Well, well*, I could practically hear them thinking, *Jackie Delham. Whoever would have thought?* Billy Sullivan acted the worst of them all. I'd put him in his place a few times, and he clearly enjoyed getting me back. And then some. I will say Jacob did not take part in any of the guys' muted conversations, at least from what I saw. Alison had probably threatened not to talk to him if he did.

Teachers went out of their way to treat me normally. To act as if they hadn't read that article, no sir, wouldn't stoop to believing such gossip. Their tight smiles and averted eyes in the hallway spoke otherwise. Clearly, they didn't know *what* to say. So they said nothing at all.

The irony of the situation was not lost on me. Years before, Daddy had faced days like this, although admittedly his had been far worse. But then, he'd deserved it, I reminded myself. I didn't.

Besides Alison, only one other person at school remained truly kind to me that day. Derek.

He ambled up to Alison and me as we sat on a bench in the yard during lunch. Despite my lack of breakfast, I hadn't felt like eating and certainly didn't want to face our usual table. Derek must have scarfed down his own meal in order to be outside so soon.

"Hey," he said, his head tilted as he gazed down at us.

"Hi." I focused on his ankles, idly wondering about his socks.

"How's your computer?" he asked. The typical Derek question.

If he only knew what that computer would mean to me now. The computer I was not supposed to use to e-mail Greg. And fully intended to use in such a manner anyway. "Fine."

He stood awkwardly, trying to think of something else to say. I felt a rush of gratitude. Derek was strange, but he was obviously going out of his way to be nice to me. "Do you want to sit down?" I asked. Alison shot me a look as if I'd lost my mind. "Come on." I scooted toward Alison, patting the bench slats. Derek plunked down without a word, pant legs rising. My mouth dropped open.

"Derek, your socks are the same color."

He stuck out a foot and inspected it. Then the other. "Oh. Yeah."

"There's Jacob," Alison said. I looked up the yard to see him exiting the lunch building. "I'd better go, okay?" She eyed me, not sure whether to leave me alone with Derek. Good grief. Big, bad Derek. I nudged her off with a toss of my head. Once she'd gone I moved over to where she had sat, turning to face Derek, elbow resting on the back of the bench.

"So why are your socks the same color?"

He shrugged. "I hadn't really noticed. Just pulled two out of the drawer."

Something about the way he drummed his long fingers against his knees, eyes on the ground—I didn't believe him. I picked a piece of lint off my jeans. He studied an ant crawling over the grass. Decisively, then, he looked at me. "I heard about what happened at your house Friday night. I'm real sorry you had to go through that."

I worked to keep the surprise from my face. It wasn't like Derek to say something right out like that. "Well. It . . . turned out okay."

He jerked his head in a nod. The ant caught his attention once more.

Suddenly I wished I could really talk to him, ask him what he thought about his sister's past, and could we really believe she'd changed for good? "Did you know about Katherine's fiancé?" I ventured.

He glanced at me sharply. "No."

"Did you know, I mean . . . Do you talk to her much?"

"Enough, I guess. But she talks to Mama a lot more than she does to me."

I remembered what he'd admitted during the at-home. About not really knowing Katherine, that she'd left when he was six. "Derek, are you glad she came back?"

For the first time he looked deeply into my eyes without flinching, as if trying to read the fears behind my question. "I am now," he replied slowly. "At first it was hard, frankly, because she got so much attention. Mama and Daddy were all happy, which made me jealous. But now I'm glad our family's back together. And that my parents aren't all worried about her like they used to be."

I smiled at him briefly, touched that he would be so honest with me.

"How about you? You glad she came back?"

Wasn't that the question. Had it been any other day, I never would have answered. But I felt worn, my defenses down. Then again, had it been any other day, Derek and I would not have been talking.

"I won't tell her what you say, you know," Derek offered.

Somehow, I did know that. "Daddy's in love with her. Even after last Friday. And she's been real nice to me." I pictured her convincing Daddy to let me see Greg. That was all it took. My words trailed away, my thoughts immediately veering to Greg and where he was right now, how hurt he must be. I focused on nothing in the distance, thinking I *had* to e-mail him as soon as I got home. Tell him I still loved him. Tears seeped into my eyes.

"But?" Derek prompted gently.

I looked at my lap, hoping he hadn't noticed the tears, knowing he had. Surely, he would mistake their meaning, think they were related to Katherine. Well. In a way, they were.

"It's okay, Jackie," he said, and that's all it took to spill the tears right out of my eyes. Once they started to flow I found them hard to stop. I couldn't believe it—sitting in front of Derek, crying like that.

"I'm afraid she's goin' to hurt him. I'm afraid she'll get bored of Bradleyville, and up and ditch one day. And Daddy will just . . . die."

The tears came harder. It was a notion I couldn't bear—that Daddy could hurt over Katherine the way I hurt over Greg right now. Even as mad as I felt at Daddy, even as unfair as he'd been, I wouldn't wish that on him for anything.

Derek said nothing. What could he say? He'd probably never faced a crying girl in his entire life. So different from Greg. When I'd cried in front of Greg, he'd known what to do. Impatiently, I swiped at my tears, feeling foolish. "I'm really sorry." I pushed firmness into my voice. "This has been a hard day, that's all."

Chatter wafted across the yard. I glanced over my shoulder to see more students leaving the cafeteria. Lunch hour was almost over. Better get my act together.

"I need to go get my books and stuff." I threw Derek a wan smile and pulled to my feet. "Thanks for listening."

He stood also, peering down at me with his warm gray eyes, the rest of him all legs and arms and neck. "Thanks for tellin' me." He reached out and squeezed my arm. For some reason, I thought of his words to me the day Robert broke his leg—*You're easy to be kind to*. I remembered the way Derek had looked at me then, as he did now.

I mushed my lips, nodding goodbye, then turned away to leave. After a few steps, I looked around. "Derek?" He hadn't moved.

"Huh?"

"Why are your socks the same color today—really?"

His mouth opened. Closed. He rubbed the thumb and fingers on his right hand. "They've been the same color since church on Sunday," he said. "This is just the first time you've noticed."

chapter 35

Just after the last bell, I stopped Derek in the hallway, asking for his e-mail address, and did he mind if I wrote him? He blinked in surprise as he pulled out a piece of paper to write it down. I gave him mine also.

"Thanks," he said. "I hope you do write."

I promised I would. Keeping my reason to myself, which I knew was entirely unfair to Derek and would hurt him. I needed to be e-mailing people other than Greg. I needed an excuse to be on the computer in case Daddy caught me at it.

I crossed the school yard toward the street corner where Grandma awaited, thanking God I'd survived the day. Well, half of it. I still had to face Daddy that evening. At least the next few hours would provide a brief respite.

So much for positive thinking.

Robert accosted me the moment I reached to help slide his backpack from his shoulders. "Why didn't you tell me about the newspaper this morning?" he demanded, shrugging away from my touch. "All I've done is hear stories about you all day! I near got in a fight four times. If I didn't have these crutches, I *would* have." He faced me, narrow-eyed, for all the world the smaller version of Daddy that morning.

I gaped at him, struck with the realization of Daddy's and my self-absorption. We should have thought of Robert and Clarissa. We should have warned them.

"Robert, I'm so sorry, I just saw it before we left, and—"

"Why'd you *do* it?"

"I . . . if you mean what the newspaper said, it's a lie—"

"I saw the pictures, Jackie! Trevor Caine brought the whole page to school and passed it around the class." Robert's last words bent upward, his eyes glistening.

My legs turned to stone. I so rarely saw my brother cry. "Robert, please. Just get in the car and we'll talk about it, okay? I'll tell you everything."

I reached to help him, but he jerked his arm and knocked my hand away. "Leave me alone!" He wrestled with his backpack until it lay on the ground. Opening the car door for him, I stood back as he threw himself inside. I placed his backpack on the floor.

Before I could turn around, Clarissa hit me from behind, throwing her arms around me and bursting into tears. "Everybody's talkin' about you! Alma Sue said you're bad, and she won't play with me anymore!"

I hugged her wordlessly, feeling about an inch high. When she calmed down, I urged her into the backseat, where she perched beside Robert's casted leg, sniffing and wiping tears with the back of her hand.

"My goodness, what a day," Grandma breathed as we drove away. "I think we all need to go home and have a good talk." She patted me on the shoulder. Her gentle touch made my own eyes fill with tears. I blinked them back. For heaven's sake, that's all we needed, the three of us crying at once.

At home, Grandma came inside and made us all sit in the family room. "We need to talk about this," she declared. "Secrets don't do anybody any good." She looked to Robert. "You want to start?" He shook his head, arms folded. Apparently his outburst had exhausted him. "Clarissa?"

My emotive sister had little trouble spewing all the things her friends had said about me, what she'd said back, and who were now her enemies as a result. By the end of her diatribe her eyes flashed, her feet swinging against the couch. I couldn't tell how much of her anger was directed at me, but even a portion would suffice.

Grandma sighed, loud and long. "Okay, Jackie. Now you get to tell us what really happened."

I told them the sordid tale of Charlotte, how she'd put me and Bradleyville down, what Greg had done in response. Even as I defended myself and Greg to my own family, I felt stripped bare. Never would I have dreamed I'd have to detail my first date like some witness in a court case.

Had Katherine felt like this, explaining things to me?

"That girl said that?" Robert pressed when I was done, clearly peeved. "She said Greg shouldn't be with you just because you're from Bradleyville?"

"Well, that's what she implied."

Robert cut his gaze to the carpet, full lips pressed in indignation. For some softball player's similar sin against him, he had careened into the first fight of his life. I could practically hear the wheels in his head squealing to turn a different direction. We awaited his pronouncement. "She's a jerk," he declared after a moment, giving me a look of absolution. Then abruptly he pushed to his feet and grabbed his crutches. "Can I go now?" he asked Grandma. "I have homework to do."

Poor Robert. First Katherine, now me. We'd probably just about done him in.

Clarissa seemed appeased as well. "I'm gonna tell Alma Sue off," she announced. "I'm gonna tell her if she doesn't want to play, that's just fine with me. I don't *need* her candy anyway!"

She flounced off to play in the backyard with Winnie. I felt a certain amount of vindication at her resolve against Alma Sue. All the same, I wondered how long it would take for it to melt away.

The moment Grandma Delham left, Grandma Westerdahl phoned. And did I hear an earful, worse than anything I'd heard all day. Even worse than Daddy that morning. In between her rants, I tried to tell her the newspaper story told mostly lies and that the "sordid picture" that she so decried had been nothing more than a brief hug.

"What is going *on* in that household?" she demanded. "Oh, I knew this would happen. If only Melissa were there. Bobby just doesn't know how to handle your growin' up. Lettin' you go out with a boy like that! Who sings that loud music and dances. There's nothin' Christian about that, and you shouldn't have a *thing* to do with it!"

"Grandma." I fought to keep the anger from my voice. "Greg is a Christian. There's nothin' wrong with the songs he sings."

"They're full of bad words and talk of love and terrible things!" she wailed.

What, I felt like retorting, *Christians can't fall in love?* "They are *not* full of bad words, Grandma, I don't listen to music like that. I promise you, Greg's committed his life to God."

"You can't be a Christian and play that kind of music," she declared, her feet planted in concrete.

I hung up the phone and dragged a hand over my eyes, wondering if this day would ever be over. Then, gathering myself, I headed for the computer, hoping desperately for something from Greg.

An e-mail sat in my inbox. I clicked on it, brimming with appre-hension.

Dear Jackie,

I can not believe what happens. I am so SORRY! People warn us that these things will happen and that being in the public is not fun always. But I am so sorry to cause you trouble . . .

The e-mail was so filled with apology and hurt and worry that it brought tears to my eyes. He knew he wasn't supposed to contact me, Greg added, but how could he not? He *had* to know if I was okay.

I wrote him back, spilling my heart. *Your ring's around my neck*, I told him finally. *That's what got me through the day. Please don't worry about Daddy. He's mad now, but he'll come around as he learns more about what really happened. I'll write you every day. Don't forget I love you. And don't forget to get those concert tickets. I WILL see you then.*

As soon as I logged off-line, Katherine called. *Good grief*, I groused to myself, *never a dull moment*. "Your phone's been busy, busy, busy," she said. "I don't imagine it's for good reasons."

"I was on the computer."

"Oh." I heard the understanding in her tone and realized how trans-parent my actions would be to Daddy. It was a good thing I'd gotten Derek's e-mail address, I thought. Even so, things couldn't go on like this for long. I'd have to bring Daddy around in a hurry.

"Katherine, you *have* to help me! Nothing's like the newspaper said, and Daddy—"

"I know, Jackie, I know."

I stopped short. "How do you know?"

"Because I've talked to your daddy. And before that I talked to Celia."

"Why would you talk to Celia?"

"She called me, desperate to try to straighten things out before she and Greg left town. Greg had told her what really happened. She'd wanted to go straight to your daddy, but Greg had said he'd sounded so mad that she wasn't sure that was a good idea, and she wanted my advice. I kind of . . . paved the way for her to call him."

I caught my breath. "Did they go see him?"

"Yes. Your daddy agreed to come home for a short while so they could stop by on their way out of town. They didn't want to meet at the bank, with all the eyes watching."

That was easy to believe. "What happened?"

"Well, from what your daddy said, Greg apologized profusely and told him the whole story. I don't think your dad's as mad at you and Greg about the pictures as he was, but he's still upset about the fact that you parked after you left the restaurant. Greg even admitted you'd done it more than once."

Great. Why did Greg have to be so honest?

Clarissa stopped playing with Winnie in the backyard to watch me, worriedly assessing my expression as I talked on the phone. I forced a plastic smile, then wandered into the family room. As I sank into a chair, I wondered if Katherine knew what I'd said to Daddy. Despite all that Greg had done to set things right, Daddy would nurse his hurt from my hateful words. Particularly since it was the second time I'd personally attacked him in an argument about Greg.

No wonder Daddy thought Greg was bad for me. We'd never fought like this before.

"So like what does Daddy think now, Katherine?"

She blew out air. "He thinks that it's still for the best that Greg has gone. He just hopes you all can get back to your normal lives now."

Normal life? I'd never have a normal life again, not without Greg. "Will he let Greg talk to me?" I closed my eyes, afraid of the answer.

"I don't know, Jackie. We'll have to work on him some more."

I focused on the computer, sitting silent and black-screened on the desk across the room. My link to Greg, so easily broken by the mere pulling of a plug.

"Jackie? I want you to know that I'll help."

As she had before, numerous times. That I had to admit. Still, I pondered Katherine's apparent complicity. What might she say to Daddy that she wouldn't say to me? Did she tell him my words, as she now told me his?

"Thank you."

She paused. "Well, I have an idea to start. Actually, though, I can't take credit for it. It was Celia's."

My, weren't we all complicit. "What's that?"

"Take your next-door neighbor some cookies."

Fortunately, I'd had plenty of experience in baking from scratch. Within half an hour, a sheet of chocolate chip cookies lay cooling on the counter, with a second sheet in the oven. As soon as those came out, I could leave them cooling and trek across the yard to Mrs. B's with the first batch.

Mrs. B received me with utmost pleasure, as I knew she would, both for the cookies I offered and the juicy details she might extricate oh-so-skillfully from me. After all, to a much-loved Christian woman whose weakness lay in gossip, I was the hottest ticket in town.

"Fight fire with fire," Katherine had said. "Celia says you need someone spreading your side of the story, and she's right. You need to get folks back on your side so they won't keep talking in your daddy's ear."

The idea had sounded nothing short of brilliant.

"Oh, chil', you shouldn't have," Mrs. B gushed as she ushered me inside, arthritic hands waving in the air. "Frank," she called to her husband, "come see who's here!"

She led me to the couch, clumping across the floor in her solid-heeled shoes. Mr. B joined us, graciously accepting the cookies with a trembling "Bless you, young 'un." He set them on the coffee table, offering me a seat. Both he and Mrs. B eased themselves with care into their armchairs.

"Well, now," Mrs. B breathed, "how is your family after that awful mess last Friday?"

I knew she'd take her time getting around to the more recent subject, but she'd get there all right. All I had to do was follow her lead, the innocent teenager talking to her neighbors. Mr. B said little, his aged, watery eyes moving from his wife to me and back as we talked. As much as I liked him, I almost wished he'd leave us alone. Something about the play of muscles around his mouth—in amusement, perhaps?—made me wonder if he couldn't see right through me.

"Well," Mrs. B said finally, patting the straggling hairs from her white bun, "I just want you to know, dear chil', how upset we are with the *Albertsville Journal*. Filthy rag of a newspaper. You know Jessie called 'em first thing this mornin', said she was cancellin' her advertisement for her sewin' shop. Said they weren't printin' news; that was just straight gossip. She gave 'em pause, I can tell you. That ad's been runnin' straight for four years now."

I blinked in surprise. So intent on spreading information, I'd never thought to glean some myself. Fleetingly, I wondered at the storehouse of Bradleyville knowledge Miss Jessie's aunt must be.

"You know advertisin's the only way that paper keeps goin'," Mrs. B added as if to ensure I understood the import of her niece's action. "Since it's delivered free and all."

I nodded, searching for the right words. "I, um . . ." I dropped my gaze to the floor. "I'll have to thank Miss Jessie for that. I'm glad she realized what that paper said isn't true."

"Well, of course, chil', we know you better than that." She shook her head with righteous indignation, then eyed me expectantly. Mr. B tapped a gnarled hand against his leg.

"If you'll excuse me for a moment, ladies." He pulled forward, placed his hands firmly on the chair arms, and wrestled to his feet. Mrs. B waited for his exit, channeling her impatience by reaching for a cookie. Once up, Mr. B gave me a little smile and shuffled off down the hall, presumably to the bathroom.

"Well, now, that's probably better anyway," Mrs. B remarked. "Little hard to talk with men around sometimes." She tossed me a grandmotherly now-you-can-relax look, then settled back in her chair. "So. You were sayin' that article wasn't true."

With mounting vehemence, I related once again everything that had happened, hoping to goodness this would be the last time I had to tell it. Mrs. B hung on every word, spilling *tut-tuts* and *you-don't-says* and *mercies*.

"And the main thing is," I concluded, "Greg is a strong Christian. Do you know that his parents are so strict that his mama's traveled everywhere with him up till now? He's tryin' to live the Christian life while people all around him aren't, including the other guys in his band. I mean, it takes a lot to stand up for Christ like that. It's just not fair for people to think bad of him, Mrs. B. People should know the truth!"

I huffed forward, grabbed a cookie, and bit into it. Not until I chewed my second bite did I think I may have gone too far with the last sentence. I'd practically invited her outright to tell the town, when she hardly needed my invitation.

Then another thought occurred to me, out of the blue. Surely Mrs. B had known all along who Greg was, being so close to both Miss Jessie and the Matthews family. Goodness sake, she'd been Mrs. Matthews' closest friend for years, despite the difference in their ages. Yet apparently she hadn't said a thing to the townsfolk. I stopped chewing, studying Mrs. B with newfound respect. This woman *could* keep her mouth shut when it really mattered.

On second thought, it was a good thing I'd given her leave to repeat my words.

"Oh, my." Mrs. B laid bent fingers against her cheek. "What a wonderful boy that Greg is. First comin' to your daddy's help like he did, then standin' up for you. Not to mention the town of Bradleyville. If that boy were here right now, I'd just kiss him." She raised her shoulders and gave me a sly wink, as if to say I must know how that felt. That was a bit of bait I would not take.

"Yes, he is," I agreed. "Just think of how long that bruise is goin' to last on his face."

Mrs. B wagged her head, marveling anew. "What a blessed chil'."

By the time I got home, swimming in self-satisfaction, I could practically hear the Bradleyville phone lines burning with Mrs. B's "blessed chil'" declarations.

Now came the worst of all. I still had to face Daddy.

chapter 36

Supper over and the dishes done, Daddy informed me we needed to talk. No kidding. He'd hardly said one sentence to me at the table, his perfunctory response to my welcome-home hug betraying the enduring sting of my words. He sat me down upon the bed in his room, taking Mama's old sitting chair in the corner for himself. His turf, not mine. His choice of location could not be by accident.

"I want you to know I called the *Albertsville Journal* today," he began, his tone stilted and cold. "Threatened a lawsuit if they didn't retract that girl's statements. I imagine they'll embark on a bit more accurate reporting for their Friday edition."

He eyed me, jaw set, signaling his embarrassment at having to stoop to such a lowly task. I said nothing.

"I also talked to Celia and to Greg today."

I widened my eyes, feigning surprise.

"Greg told me what happened, and his story substantiates yours. It was a manly thing for him to do, comin' to see me before he left."

My head nodded. I slid one hand over the other and pressed, waiting.

"You have anything to say to me, Jackie?" His voice implied that if I didn't, I'd better rethink the situation.

"Yes. That I'm so very sorry for everything," I managed, hardly able to look him in the eye. "You don't know how sorry I am. I wish . . . I wish I could take it all back. Especially what I said this morning."

He rested an elbow on the chair, placing fingers against his lips. Clearly, my apologies would take some time to sink in. We sat in silence, my gaze on the floor as I felt his eyes on me.

Suddenly, he exhaled in pure frustration. "I don't know how to do this any better than you do," he declared almost defensively. "No matter what I try, in the end I'm just a dad. I know you need your mama. I know it's awkward, tryin' to work this all out, tryin' to talk to me about boys."

My chest tightened at the weight in his tone, as if he'd failed me somehow. For the first time I realized that part of his irritation was directed at himself. And I saw no fairness in that. "It's not you, Daddy, it's *me*. I did things without thinking. It won't happen again."

"No, it certainly won't."

The way his emotions teetered, seeking which side to blame. I didn't know where he'd land next. "Please," I added, "you do believe me, I mean, that nothin' bad happened? When Greg and I were in the car? *Nothing* bad happened."

"Yes, I believe you."

I could say no more, remembering again my horrible words that morning. My very insistence on what I hadn't done strayed too close to what he had when he was my age. No matter that years had passed since then. I knew Daddy was putting himself in the shoes of a teenager, remembering how easy a "fall from grace" could be.

"Jackie," he ventured wearily, as though he'd read my mind, "it's time we talked about this."

I sat very still, suspended in the awkwardness, wanting to know and not wanting it. Surely this subject proved more difficult for Daddy than my explanations of my innocent actions with Greg.

Daddy turned his head, focusing out the window. I heard a car door slam in the driveway next door. The Bellinghams must have company. Maybe Miss Jessie. "I don't need to belabor the details," Daddy said. "Apparently you heard enough when you eavesdropped on my conversation with Katherine." He threw me a sharp glance. "What I want you to understand is that things can happen very quickly sometimes. That's why I want *you* to be so careful. In a moment of weakness I made a choice that betrayed not only myself but your mama. As soon as I'd done it, I was horrified, but it was too late."

I swallowed hard, thinking, *I know this, I know it already, but it's not what matters.* I could now accept the fact that anybody, even my daddy, could make a wrong choice. What mattered was far, far more important. And if I didn't voice it now, I never would.

"Daddy," I said, "the thing is, you didn't love Mama. She loved you so much and you were goin' out with her, but you were only pretending. You loved somebody *else.*"

Daddy's head drooped. He closed his eyes as if to block out the cutting truth of the words. I envisioned Mama at my age, in love with him as I was with Greg, and imagined what I would feel. She must have been cut to the very core.

"I was datin' her, yes," Daddy replied, clearly ashamed that we would have to discuss this. "But I never told her I loved her. Not until I really did. Not until I realized that she was what I'd needed all along. I was eighteen then, Jackie, not much older than you. And I never looked back. You know that. You *know* I loved your mama. With all my heart."

Yes, I did. And I also knew that this is what Mama had chosen to dwell upon as she and I talked about dating. Not the mistakes and hurt along the way, but the outcome.

"Growin' up can be so hard, Jackie," Daddy offered gently. "There's no such thing as a perfect romance."

My eyes darted to his face. How did he know how I'd dwelt upon that phrase, *perfect romance?* Only Mama would have known that. In quick succession, then, the months since Mama's death unraveled, reweaving a scene of her lying on this very bed, sick, talking to Daddy about all he might face in raising me alone. Suddenly, I saw his side of the tapestry, the tugs and knots underneath, the ungrateful side presenting only challenge.

"Daddy," I blurted, "I'm so sorry for what I said to you. Really, I am."

He smiled tightly. "I know, Jackie. Let's just leave that be, now, okay?" He studied my face. "Is there anything else you need to ask?"

I shook my head.

"Sure? It's best we put this business behind us once and for all."

"I'm sure."

"Okay." He rubbed the back of his neck, as if massaging away the aching topic. "Now. It's time for you to talk to me about Greg. I want to know what you're feelin' about him. You came in cryin' last night, like his leavin' was really hard on you."

My hand nearly drifted to the ring beneath my blouse. I laced my fingers. "It is."

"The way Greg talked today, I got the impression that the feelings between you two are runnin' pretty deep. It wasn't anything he said, really. It was more the intensity of his voice as he tried to take all the blame."

"He loves me, Daddy. And I love him." There. I'd said it, no taking it back.

"Love him? You've known him for less than a week!"

"Yeah, but look at everything we went through together," I retorted. "I got to talk to him a lot. And I saw the way he acted in hard situations and the way he treated me. The way he treated *us.*"

Briefly, Daddy's eyes closed. He focused out the window once more, on something distant and unknown, disappointment flattening his expression. "How things do repeat."

No, I wanted to say, *this is not a repeat. Greg isn't Danny and I'm not Celia. We're us.* Us. *With our own lives and our own love, and we don't need to live under the shadow of what went on before.*

"Jackie, please hear me, as hard as it is. Greg has gone on to a life that's full of travel and lights and action. He's moved on while you've stayed here. It will be much harder for him to . . . remember you as time passes. It's always harder for the one who's left behind."

"He won't forget me," I insisted. "He even gave me his ring. The one his own parents gave him." I pulled out the chain, let the ring rest upon my blouse.

Daddy inhaled slowly. "What's it supposed to mean?"

"That we love each other. And we won't go out with anyone else."

Incredulity flicked across his face. "Until when, Jackie? It's not like he's just off on some vacation. He lives in Greece, for heaven's sake."

"He'll visit. Celia's family is here. And . . ." My voice faltered. "There's his concert in Lexington. At the end of August."

"I told you no concerts."

"Yeah, but you were mad at me then."

"Maybe I'm still mad at you."

"No, you're not!" I pushed from the bed to plead before him in desperation. "You're not mad at me anymore, you're just scared! You're scared I'm goin' to be hurt, and that Greg will ditch me. But you don't know him like I do. He won't, Daddy, he *won't.*"

I grasped the ring, breathing hard, telling myself my insistence was for Daddy alone.

He stood up, placed his hands on my shoulders. "Okay, Jackie, okay. I don't doubt what you think you feel for each other." He pulled away, running a hand through his hair. "I just . . . you're right, I don't want you to be hurt."

"Let Greg and me talk to each other, Daddy," I pressed. "We just want to e-mail each other. And he'll call when he can. If it doesn't work out, well then, it won't. But it's not fair—you not lettin' us talk just because you don't believe it'll last. You can't tell us how we feel."

"Wait a minute, there's plenty of other reasons, beginning and ending with the fact of who he is. And don't forget the whole town is already talkin'. No way am I lettin' you run around wearin' that ring."

"I won't wear it out, I'll hide it!" Swiftly, I slipped it under my blouse. "And the talk won't last, you'll see. Next thing you know, the whole town'll be lovin' Greg, sayin' how lucky we were to meet him. And everybody'll be like all proud that the town can claim him. Bradleyville's own star."

Daddy cracked a smile in sheer disbelief. He shook his head. "That would be some turn of events."

"Just wait, Daddy, you'll see. It'll happen."

His smile faded. "Don't cost yourself good times here, Jackie. There are other boys, other dates."

"I don't want any of them."

He nodded wearily, arguments spent. My daddy had been through enough when he was my age. He knew all too well the stubborn tenacity of a heart in love. "Okay," he sighed. "I'm talked out for tonight. It's been a long day." He arched his back, gaze sliding to the clock at his bedside. "You probably have homework, and Clarissa needs to do her math."

"Will you let Greg e-mail and call me, Daddy?"

"Yes, Jackie. Okay? Just . . . I don't want people seein' the ring."

"Oh, thank you!" I threw my arms around him unabashedly, as Clarissa might do. "Thank you, thank you!"

He hugged me back, then gently pushed my arms away, telling me to go do my homework, and that was no suggestion. "Thank you again," I whispered.

As I left his bedroom, I glanced back and nearly stopped in my tracks. The apprehension on his face shot right through me—as if he thought the day might come when I wouldn't be thanking him at all.

chapter 37

Over the next few days, thanks to the irrepressible Mrs. B, news began to filter around town about what really happened at Clayton's Place, and the way Greg had defended me and Bradleyville. Greg was a Christian boy being maligned, Mrs. B said to anyone who'd listen—which was just about everybody in town—and folks would do better praying for him than talking about him. And let us not forget, people took up the talk, that Greg's face had already been bruised from jumping to my daddy's defense.

Then Friday's edition of the *Albertsville Journal* carried a version of the events decidedly different from its first. The article even included quotes from two of Charlotte's friends who had been present, saying how polite Greg had been and that Charlotte had made a pest of herself and was "jealous." I must admit my gut twisted with vindication when I read that article. Particularly as I saw that one of those friends had been Sam, Charlotte's date.

Of course, some would not come around in their judgment of Greg, including my grandma Westerdahl. To her, secular music on the radio was a sin, and that was all there was to it.

"What do people like that think?" I complained to Katherine one evening as we cleared the supper table. "That you have to be a preacher to be a Christian? That you have to live in Bradleyville? Surely there are people all over the country, in all kinds of jobs, who are also Christians."

"That's true, Jackie," Daddy put in, "but some folks, like your grandparents, feel that certain kinds of entertainment aren't good. God gives each of us a different conscience, you know. If your grandmother believes that certain music is wrong, then you have to respect that—for her. Doesn't mean you have to agree."

"Well, she shouldn't judge, though." I clattered plates into a stack. "She might think pop music and dancin' is wrong, but she shouldn't judge Greg because of her own conscience."

"Maybe not, but you just be sure you're not judgin' *her.*"

"Oh, my, that awful music!" Katherine flipped back her hands in mocking sarcasm.

"Hey, hold it." Daddy shot her a look. "It *is* Jackie's grandmother we're talking about."

"I know, Bobby," Katherine sighed, "but you have to admit, sometimes Bradleyville acts like it's in the nineteenth century. That kind of narrow-mindedness is one of the things that can really tick me off about this town."

Daddy set a dirty plate and glass on the counter. The way he eyed Katherine told me she'd hit on some nerve. "This town," he informed her, "happens to be my home."

Katherine flicked her gaze toward the ceiling but said no more. I looked from her to Daddy, feeling as though a curtain had just been pulled back on their relationship. What was this behind-the-scenes tension?

Well, Katherine was right, I told myself. Bradleyville folks sometimes did seem narrow-minded, even though both Daddy and Mama had told me the town had come a long way since they were teenagers.

All in all, for the time being, I would still need to wear blouses that hid Greg's ring around my neck.

Greg and I e-mailed back and forth once or twice a day. And he'd call me after school if he could catch a minute from all his work. Of course I told him of the news circulating Bradleyville. And he detailed for me his schedule, the hours spent in practice, both in singing and choreography. How he and the group worked on their breathing, exhaling slowly and steadily to keep a scrap of paper against the wall, seeing who could manage it the longest. Demetri usually won.

He repeated his friends' tales of how they'd spent their time off—mostly partying with all the girls they could find and drinking. *Remember to pray for them*, he asked, *and for me, too. I read my Bible and pray every day, but I am alone in this. I want courage to tell others about God.*

I did pray for him. Many times a day.

Friday afternoon, the beginning of Memorial Day weekend, I received an e-mail from Derek. Wincing with guilt that I'd forgotten him, I opened it.

Hey. You were going to write me, remember? So where are you? I'm at work now. Should be fixing a glitch on a software program so I better go.
—Derek
P.S. Notice my socks the rest of the week? Same color.

I couldn't help but smile. Derek really was nice. I could not admit, however, that deep down, I knew his socks now matched for my sake. That thought would have been too searing, exposing my blithe attitude toward him as a knife that could cut. And it would have saddened me. Derek had always been so *Derek*, not caring how others viewed him. Who was I to dampen that independent spirit?

I wrote him back, wanting only to amend my thoughtlessness. But the impersonal screen seemed to loosen my tongue.

Derek,

Sorry, I meant to write. But I'm sure you know this has been a hard week for me. I'm not used to being talked about all over town. Finally things are better.

What are you doing this holiday weekend? Working, I guess. Me, too, except that my work is watching my brother and sister, and cleaning house and all. Gets pretty boring, I can tell you, especially in the summer. Wish I could have a job like you.

Guess I'll see you in church on Sunday. And maybe at the town picnic on Memorial Day? I'll keep writing if you will.

—Jackie

Saturday dragged by, the weather turning hot and muggy until it poured rain in the late afternoon. Missing Greg every minute, I cleaned house, did laundry, gave Winnie a bath, and had a heart-to-heart talk with Robert, who couldn't seem to pull out of his doldrums. He faced another month or so with a leg in an itchy cast, wondering how well he'd be able to run when it finally came off. As for Clarissa, she'd made up once more with Alma Sue and chose to spend Saturday afternoon over at her house instead of with Della, presumably stuffing herself with bribe candy. Daddy and Katherine went to a matinee, then out to an early supper. Katherine "needed to get out and do something," Daddy informed me, even though I knew he'd just as soon stay home and relax after the tough week we'd all had.

It was going to be a long summer, I thought as I wandered into my room for the tenth time that day to stare at Greg's picture.

He called me that night, his voice tossing my emotions about like warm wind. I felt elation and pain at the same time, just hearing him talk. Three months, he reminded me as we hung up. Three months and we'd see each other again. How could we ever last that long, I wondered, when the past five days had seemed an eternity?

That Sunday, Derek ended up next to me in our pew. Katherine's parents had both come down with summer colds and so did not attend church, leaving Derek alone. "Don't sit all by yourself," I told him, thinking, *If only he were Greg.* "Come be with us."

"Sure." He shrugged, and when he plunked down he made a point of pulling up both pant legs for me.

"Oh, Derek," I laughed, "remember when you told me that people who wore the same color socks had no imagination?"

He rested a knobby elbow on the end of the pew, considering. "Well. There's always new things to imagine."

I eyed him, wondering at the remark, but he was too busy shifting into a comfortable position to look at me.

"My brother, Derek," Katherine commented out of the blue that evening as we made sandwiches for a light supper, "I'm going to get him to stand up straight if it kills me. He's got one more year here, then he'll be off to college. I told him he'll never catch a girl walking around with his neck at that weird angle, like someone's pulling him sideways by a chain through his nose."

"That wasn't very nice." I frowned at her, wondering if she always treated her brother so unkindly.

"Well, it's the truth. Nobody else around here would ever tell him, so it's up to me. I want to see him happy."

"I thought he *was* happy, just bein' himself."

She shook her head. "Don't see how he could be, with the quiet life he leads—hardly any friends, and being here in Bradleyville."

My hands stilled, mayonnaise spread across one-half of a piece of bread. *Being here in Bradleyville.* There was that attitude again. But this time I couldn't agree with Katherine, thinking I'd never sensed discontent on Derek's part, so surely she spoke more for herself. Was she getting tired of life here, just as I'd imagined she would? Katherine continued slicing tomatoes as though she hadn't just made a remark that made my mouth run dry.

"Did you have a good time yesterday out with Daddy?" I asked after a moment.

"Of course. No one I'd rather be with." She smiled at me. "Why?"

"No reason."

I lay in bed that night, visions of Greg swirling with vague fears over Katherine's comment. Finally I fell into an uneasy sleep, Daddy's words blowing through my head. *It's always harder for the one who's left behind.*

chapter 38

Looking back upon that summer, I am amazed at how little of the winds of change I recognized. Oh, I did sense them, even smelled the angst in the air from time to time, as on that Sunday with Katherine. But I didn't *want* to understand, nor, I'm sure, did Daddy. Like protecting a house in a sudden storm, we closed the shutters and doors of our minds, capturing the wind into separate little rooms that could be stilled and calmed one at a time. Or so we told ourselves.

In my defense I'll say that I wasn't privy at the time to everything that happened—most notably the arguments between Daddy and Katherine. The smooth sailing of their relationship was about to hit a few waves as the differences in their personalities began to surface. I understand Katherine much better now than I did then. Now I see how much she loved city life—the restaurants and shows and faster pace of living. She loved dressing up and going out to events and parties. She loved the energy of a crowd. We saw little of this the first few months she became part of our lives. But that was to be expected. After all, she'd fled to quiet Bradleyville purposely. "I don't want my old lifestyle," she'd told me that day we'd talked in my bedroom. "I've turned my life over to Christ."

Ah, there. Do you see it? How obvious it seems with the added wisdom of four years. Yet we were so blind then, Katherine included.

Yes, Katherine's "lifestyle" needed to change. Yes, she'd made poor choices. Slept around, partied too much, generally wore her soul out. Bradleyville provided a calm sanctuary for her while she got back on her feet. But Katherine's mistake—our mistake—lay in equating her past choices with city life in general. Christ had changed her, right? So she should just be satisfied with living in Bradleyville.

But deep in her heart was she really satisfied, even though she loved my daddy? As the days passed, I began to wonder if the staccato beat that was Katherine would begin to outpace the languid rhythm of our town.

A week after school let out, Katherine got a job selling clothes in Albertsville's swankiest boutique—a relative description, to be sure. She'd hung around her parents' house long enough, she complained, and cooking and cleaning for them hardly took the day. Daddy agreed that the job was a wonderful step for her. "She's gotten restless, and who can blame her," he commented at supper one night. "She has an active mind and needs more to keep her busy." I agreed. Maybe this job was all she needed to still the waters of discontentment. Besides, Katherine loved looking good, whether dressed for Sunday or a picnic, and her flair for clothes would certainly help her succeed in the boutique.

Katherine worked five days a week, Tuesday through Saturday. The weekend work proved the least favorite detail because it cut into the time she could spend with our family. Still, she would close up the shop around 5:00 and be at our doorstep by 6:00, ready to help put supper on the table. Many nights, she turned right around and went out with Daddy, either to supper or a movie, or both. Not that Daddy really wanted to go out so much, but he was trying to please her. How fortunate for them that Greg was gone, I thought jealously more than once. They could certainly count on my playing baby-sitter every week, couldn't they?

I settled into a routine, taking care of the house and kids, and mostly moping in my spare time. Alison came over often, our usual subject of conversation centering on our boyfriends. She and Jacob were still an item. And my heart remained so achingly full of Greg that at times I thought it would burst. With the town's view of Greg now overwhelmingly positive, save for the few holdouts who'd never change their minds, Daddy had eased up about Greg's ring, and it now hung openly around my neck.

"You *are* going to let me take Jackie to the concert in August," Katherine said to Daddy out of the blue one Sunday afternoon. "Those tickets will be going on sale soon, and Greg will have to hold two of them." She and I both knew Greg already planned on holding two of them in hopes that we could come, but why tell Daddy that?

Daddy eyed her with a tinge of irritation, obviously not happy that she'd challenged him in front of me. "I haven't decided yet."

Apprehension trailed up my spine, even as I suspected Daddy's answer had more to do with Katherine's tactics than the issue. I hoped she wouldn't push him into a "no."

"Oh, for heaven's sake, Bobby," Katherine replied. "I'll chaperone her. How can you let her miss the chance to see Greg in action?"

I had the feeling the last thing Daddy would have chosen was my seeing Greg in action. He still hoped I'd get over this ridiculousness and find a nice Bradleyville boy.

"We'll talk about this later," Daddy told Katherine firmly.

Oh, did they clash about that on Sunday night when they went out for a drive. It was their first major argument, as far as I know. Daddy told Katherine in no uncertain terms she was not to contradict him in front of his kids. "I'm sorry," she retorted, "but what about when you're *wrong?*" The conversation went downhill from there. Apparently they'd worked it out by the time he took her back to her parents' house, but Daddy did seem preoccupied and aloof when he got home.

LuvRush's tour began. I hung a map of the States in my bedroom with pushpins in the cities where their concerts would be held. I also began combing the Internet, reading articles about their concerts in local newspapers. I printed out everything I found, three-hole punching it and placing it in a notebook along with every one of Greg's e-mails.

I miss you so much, he wrote in late June. *I am with people always, and still I feel alone because you are not here. I can't believe I have no picture of you. We forget this how? You think you can scan one into a computer and e-mail it to me? I will print it somehow.*

I had no idea how to scan a photo into the computer, but I bet anything Derek would. He and I had continued e-mailing the whole month, and in my boredom I'd come to look forward to his letters. His sense of humor often came through in his e-mails, and he'd tell me funny stories about the characters at his job. Computer people sure sounded like a strange bunch to me.

Derek worked full-time that summer with weekends off, so I arranged to go to his house on Saturday to scan the photo. I didn't care that much for pictures of myself, but I did have one I liked, taken in our backyard some months previously. Derek took one look at it and raised his eyebrows. "Nice," he said.

"Thanks." I smiled at him, noticing that he was standing significantly straighter these days, his chin held directly over his chest rather than angled. Katherine had been working on him. Derek had also allowed his hair to grow out a little. It would never be as thick on the top as Greg's, but the way it fell across one side of his forehead lent him a sort of rakish look. "You look good, too," I told him. "In fact, you're looking better than ever these days."

I only wanted to say something nice because of his willingness to help me. But pleasure flicked across his face, and one corner of his mouth turned up.

"Okay." He sniffed, taking the picture from my hand. "Let's see what's up with this."

He pulled a chair up next to his for me, and I watched with fascination as he placed the photo in a scanner, then manipulated the image on the computer. "Can you make it bigger?"

He clicked the keys. "I can make it bigger, smaller, I can change the color tone, whatever you want."

"Really," I teased, "how about makin' me gorgeous while you're at it."

"Nope," he said matter-of-factly, "can't improve on perfection."

I glanced at him, surprised, but he focused on the computer, intent on moving the mouse just so.

"Okay," he said finally, satisfied. "I evened out the background tone a little. Like it?"

I leaned over, our arms touching. "Yeah. Looks great."

"So. I'll e-mail it to you now, then you'll have it. If you want to send it somewhere, all you have to do is attach it." He hit a few keys, then leaned back. "Done."

"Thanks."

"No problem. What do you want this for, anyway?"

I hesitated. I never mentioned Greg to Derek. Not that my dating Greg was any secret, what with his ring around my neck, but somehow I just couldn't do it. That should have told me something.

Derek turned to me, searching my face, and knew. "Well," he said, his tone a little too light. "Anything else you need?"

Empathy shot through me. Derek didn't deserve to have his feelings hurt. "No, thanks." I pressed my fingers against his arm. "You've been great, like always."

A week later at the town's Fourth of July parade, Katherine's and my family stood together, pressed on both sides by folks cheering and hollering over the rather ungainly procession of kids on bikes, old cars, and skittish horses. No town can have a parade quite as motley as

Bradleyville. The lead car carrying our mayor had a huge banner down the side—*96 Years Young.*

"He doesn't look ninety-six," Katherine commented, and Daddy doubled over laughing.

"Bradleyville, not the mayor, you idgit." I shook my head. In four years we would be celebrating Bradleyville's first centennial, and the mayor was already promising a stunning day of events. For the last six years the town had taken a collection during the parade that would go for fireworks on the night of July Fourth, 2002.

"Oh." Katherine shrugged as if to say, *How could I know?* She looked stunning in a multicolored shorts and top outfit and a fully beaded visor, all from GreatWear Boutique. Daddy stood with his arm around Katherine's shoulders, the way he used to do with Mama. The sight of them brought a bittersweet taste to my mouth. I wished so many things, watching them—wished that Greg and I could be together as they were, wished that Katherine were Mama, then hoped with all my heart, given reality, that Katherine would never, ever hurt Daddy.

Clarissa rode on Daddy's shoulders, Robert standing with his crutches beside them. Derek and I hung together, cackling like fools over the sawmill men, who were always the hit of the parade. Dressed like women, including wigs and big chests, they pushed grocery carts from the IGA, pretending to fight over food in the baskets. When Derek's daddy sashayed by, donned in Miss Connie's clothes and with bustling hips that had to have required a multitude of padding, I staggered against Derek with laughter. His arm slipped around me to keep me from falling. I clutched his shirt to steady myself, then stayed there for a moment, caught up in the fun.

"Like *what* is up with you and Derek?" Alison demanded over the phone later that day. "I saw you at the parade. So did Millicent and Nicole. We all talked about it."

"What do you mean, what's up with me and Derek?" I carried the receiver into my room and shut the door. "Absolutely nothin'!"

"It sure didn't look like it, the way he had his arm around you and all."

"Alison. We're talkin' about *Derek*. Come on."

She breathed into the phone. "Yeah, but admit it, he looks tons better than he used to. And besides, he's crazy about you."

"He is not."

"He is so. What are you, Jackie, blind?"

"Derek is still Derek," I insisted. "Tall and skinny and Katherine's brother. I mean, a dozen of him couldn't compare to one of Greg."

I stared at Greg's picture, feeling the pull of him, the ache for him, and throbbed with indignation over Alison's idiocy.

"Okay, Jackie, I believe you. Really. I know how much you love Greg. So just . . . I mean, hear a friend, okay? Watch how you act with Derek. It may not mean anything to you, but that's not what it looks like to everybody else. And you can bet that's not what it feels like to Derek."

Dear Alison. She couldn't have put it any plainer. I hung up the phone, realizing she was right. Thinking I'd really need to be more circumspect. Even if no one would *ever* have real reason to believe I'd turn my back on Greg for the likes of Derek King.

I switched on the radio, and by providence "Hung Up on You" was playing. I closed my eyes and listened to Greg's voice, knowing he now sang the song to me, and pretended he was near.

All thoughts of Derek slipped away.

chapter 39

The Monday after Fourth of July weekend, Robert had his cast taken off. He navigated cautiously around the house for the first day, satisfying himself that his leg had mended. Then began the routine that would last the rest of the summer—walking to exercise it, then running, and finally practicing with his friends on the softball field at school.

Clarissa spent her days bouncing from Della to Alma Sue. I can't remember the three of them playing together once that summer, as those two girls continued to fight over Clarissa like cats over spilt milk. Far too much of the time my sister seemed pouty and emotional. She had not taken kindly to Katherine's working, somehow having convinced herself that Katherine should provide ever-present entertainment whenever her friends couldn't play. *Good grief*, I asked myself more than once, *when is my sister ever going to grow up?*

"Clarissa," I sighed one afternoon after she'd thrown herself upon the couch, arms jammed together and lips pulled down, "what is wrong with you now?"

"I am tired of people walkin' all over me," she declared.

"Oh, really. Who's walkin' all over you this time? Alma Sue again?"

"No, Della. I wanted to read comics at her house, and all she wanted to do was watch TV."

"Well, why couldn't you read comics while she watched a show?"

"She wouldn't get 'em for me."

"Did you ask?"

"Yeah, like about ten times!" She frowned at me as if it were my fault.

"So is that why you came home?" I asked.

"Uh-huh." She kicked a heel against the carpet.

"Then it sounds to me like you stood up for yourself just fine. When you didn't get what you wanted, you left."

Truly, that indicated real progress for Clarissa. I felt right proud of my sister.

Her expression lost some of its blackness as she considered my words. "Then maybe if I get mad at Katherine, she'll quit her job."

Quite a turn of logic. "Oh, I don't know about that. I think Katherine needs that job to feel happy."

"No, she doesn't!" Clarissa cried. "All Katherine needs is us!"

I look back now on that outbreak from my sister and realize just how right she was. But at the time, I could only see her narrow focus, and it set off distant warning bells in my head. What if something really did go wrong between Daddy and Katherine? What would happen to Clarissa?

"Sweetie," I plunked down beside her on the couch, "I think—"

"They need to just go ahead and get married," she declared. "Then Katherine could quit her job and stay home like Mama used to do."

Oh, boy. Even if they did get married, Katherine would never be Mama. I could see myself baby-sitting after school and in summers while Katherine worked, just like now. The thought depressed me.

"What makes you think they're gonna get married?"

She eyed me as if I'd just arrived from another planet. "Everybody says so. And I know so."

Slowly, I nodded, remembering Katherine's negative words about Bradleyville. But that had been weeks ago. As far as I knew, she and Daddy were getting along pretty well. Clarissa had to be right; Daddy was going to marry her. I knew Clarissa wanted it; so did Robert. And I certainly wouldn't stand in the way.

So what was Daddy waiting for?

Derek, I wrote in an e-mail later that day, *I know I shouldn't be asking you this. But does Katherine talk about getting married when she's home? Does she seem happy? I know she's used to more of a city life, and I just wondered.*

I'd placed Derek in an awkward position, no doubt about that. He'd been very careful not to play the spy between Katherine and me, which he easily could have done. But the e-mail he wrote back merely said that Katherine never spoke of her relationship with my daddy in front of him, nor did she say anything that would give Derek reason to think she was tiring of Bradleyville. That e-mail set my mind to rest. Derek didn't see a problem; therefore it didn't exist. I told myself that Katherine had found her balance.

LuvRush continued moving from city to city—Spokane, Boise, Salt Lake City, Denver, Kansas City, Des Moines. Greg's e-mails contained news about every concert, how some arenas were better for sound than others, how Demetri fell during the choreography to one song and jumped back up as if he'd meant to do it. How the concerts pulsed with energy, but the days were long and the travel tiring. Greg also told me the news on other bands, supplemented by the articles in my teen magazine. And we talked about the competition from other bands' songs. In July, 98 Degrees had a hit song called "True to Your Heart," sung with Stevie Wonder for the Disney movie *Mulan*. The Backstreet Boys had started their first U.S. tour after making it big in Europe. 'NSync's songs "I Want You Back" and "Tearing Up My Heart" continued to climb the charts in America after that band, too, had become major heartthrobs in Germany.

Funny how the American bands go big in Europe first, Greg wrote, *and we come from Greece and hurry to the U.S.*

As a result of the success of LuvRush's tour, "Hung Up on You" surged back onto the national music charts, pushing to number three. Radio stations began playing another song from their CD titled "All Is Enough," and before long it landed at number nine. *Two songs in the top ten!* Greg crowed. Then at the end of July came the biggest news yet. *"Hung Up on You" is number one!!!* Greg wrote. *We hear the news today!*

I whirled about the family room and out to the backyard, whooping like I'd lost my mind. "Daddy, Daddy, 'Hung Up on You' is number one in the whole nation! The most popular song in the country!"

"Well, that's terrific," he replied, rocking back on his heels from pulling weeds. He wiped sweat from his face, looking nonplussed. The whole music business thing continued to elude him. "Good for Greg."

I seized the moment. It was high time I got the official word that I could go to the concert. "Daddy." I knelt in the grass to look him in the eye. "The concert in Lexington is only a little over three weeks away. Greg saved Katherine and me tickets, right in the front row. *Please* let me go."

He sighed. "I've already decided to let you go. But you and Katherine and I are goin' to have to talk about how I expect you to be chaperoned. Lexington's a big city, and I don't want you runnin' around it with Greg late at night."

"Oh, thank you, Daddy, thank you!" I gave him a bear hug, not caring that dirt flecked his shirt, and knocked him over. By the time we untangled ourselves, I needed to change clothes.

In early August the cover of *Teen Dream* magazine sported a picture of LuvRush, Greg front and center. "LuvRush rushes the country" read the blurb. In the article, Greg stood strong for his Christianity. When asked what gave him energy to get through the grueling days of touring, he said, "I pray each day. My faith in Christ helps me do what I need to do."

I must have read that article twenty times, relishing every word until I knew them by heart, especially those words of testimony. I squealed about it to all my friends, who also were now receiving the magazine, and showed it to Daddy as proof of the importance Greg placed on his faith. Not to mention what a hit the group had become! Some moments I still could not believe that Greg's world—one of music and excitement and adoring fans—had collided with mine and the town's. Suddenly, quiet little Bradleyville had a nationwide claim to fame through Greg. Well, he may have been from Athens, but he *did* have family in Bradleyville.

Even Robert seemed impressed when I showed him the magazine. "Cool," he said. "Even if it's not softball."

Two weeks before the concert, Daddy sat me down in his bedroom one evening as Clarissa took her bath. "I want to know how you'd feel," he ventured, "if I asked Katherine to marry me."

I'd expected the words for weeks now. So why did they root me to the bed? I wished we sat in my own room instead of right here—where my mama had once lain.

"You love her a lot, Daddy?"

"Very much. I don't know at this point what I'd do without her."

"What if she wants to keep workin' after you got married?"

"That would be all right."

A sudden thought struck me. Why had I not considered it before? "Would you have more kids?" My tone wavered in disbelief at the very idea. But surely Katherine would want children of her own.

Daddy regarded me intently. "We've talked about it."

"So you've talked about gettin' married already."

"I haven't really asked her, Jackie. We've just . . . discussed some things in terms of what-ifs."

Well, 'what if' I don't agree to this at all? I argued silently. Why was he asking my opinion now, when the ball had been set in motion? "Seems to me you've already decided. So I don't really see what we have to talk about."

"Jackie—" He leaned forward in his chair. "Please don't do this to me now. I want to hear what you're thinkin'. No decisions have been made yet."

"I wouldn't stand in your way, Daddy." My voice tightened. Great. I did *not* want to cry. "If you love Katherine, I know you wouldn't be happy without her. Just like I wouldn't be happy without Greg. I understand those feelings now, and I wouldn't want you to be hurt."

Daddy rested his elbows on the arms of the chair. I wondered if he felt caught, as I did. He had his love; I had mine. We should just let each other be. "We've had some rough starts, but it seems that you and Katherine are now good friends. She certainly stands up for you, I can tell you that." He smiled ruefully. "But I would never expect her to replace your mama, you know that."

Of course I did. No sense in even discussing such a notion. I could not imagine Katherine's trying to be any kind of parent to me at all. It would feel mighty strange, her telling me what to do.

"I know."

He laced his fingers, then unlaced them, sliding them in and out, in and out. Almost as if he were the nervous child petitioning the parent. "Is there anything else you want to say, Jackie?"

Dozens of questions swirled in my head. Did he fully trust Katherine now? Did he really believe she was ready to settle down? But how did a daughter ask her daddy about such private things? "No."

"Yes, you do. And we're not leavin' here until it's all said. This is the time to say it."

I focused on my bare toes digging into the carpet. I really needed to vacuum in here.

"Jackie?"

My eyes raised to his. "How do you know she won't leave us?" I blurted. "Just like she did everyone else."

He inhaled slowly. "Well, I would expect that if she's not sure she wants to be with us, she won't say yes."

"She's changed her mind before, lots of times. She was even engaged to that man Trent."

"That's before she came back here and gave her life to the Lord."

"Did that change her, Daddy, really? I mean, I know God changes people, but like Pastor Beekins said, sometimes we still have to deal with all the bad results of the mistakes we've made before. And I'm wonderin' if Katherine's habit of jumping from this to that is completely gone."

He stared at me, as if amazed at my perception. "I . . . know what you mean. I've wondered it myself. We've had more than a few discussions about it, I can tell you that."

"And what does she say? I mean, how can you really know?"

"Jackie." He focused on the floor, searching for words. "She says she's ready to settle down. Yes, she's used to a more . . . exciting life than we have here in Bradleyville. We have a lot of differences to work out. But she says she wants to make it work. And I believe her." He paused. "Or I wouldn't be thinkin' of askin' her to marry me."

It occurred to me, then, that maybe marriage was exactly what Katherine needed. Once she'd taken that step, surely she would settle in. A simplistic view of things, to be sure. But allowing myself to think the alternative was just too frightening.

"You can be sure, Jackie," he added quietly, "that I will tell her to think twice before she says yes. For me, once that commitment's made, there's no lookin' back."

"I know, Daddy." I gave a little nod. We sat in silence for a moment as I gathered courage to ask my other burning question. "Um, what about, you know . . . all that she did?" I could feel myself blushing. "I mean, when you found out, you were so mad."

Daddy cleared his throat, clearly uncomfortable with the topic. "I told you I forgave her long ago. I can't hold against her what God has forgiven."

"I know, but . . . well, forgivin's one thing; forgettin's another." I could only imagine how I'd feel if Greg admitted he'd slept with lots of girls.

"Jackie," he said firmly, "this is something between Katherine and me. It's not anything you and I need to discuss."

Not for months would I know how hard the issue had been for Daddy. How he'd lain in bed at night, begging God to ease his mind from the visions it conjured of Katherine's past. How Katherine and he had argued about trivial things, his hurt and her defensiveness from the real, underlying issue spilling over into pettiness.

At that moment, I simply looked at my lap, ashamed that I'd even brought up the subject. Finally, I pushed from Mama's bed to walk over and give Daddy a congratulatory hug. "When are you goin' to ask her?"

The next evening, Saturday, Daddy dressed in a suit and tie and took Katherine to Clayton's Place. I stayed up after Clarissa and Robert had gone to bed, waiting for him to get in. I wrote Greg a long e-mail, spilling thoughts that I could not share with Daddy. Feeling the whole time Mama's eyes on me from her picture on the mantel. What would we do with that family photo if Daddy got married? Replace it with a new one taken with Katherine? The thought made me sick to my stomach.

After switching off the computer, I wandered listlessly about the house, staring at Greg's picture, looking through the LuvRush notebook, listening to his CD. I felt as though I stood in the threshold between past and future, buffeted by winds on either side. Knowing I had to go forward, that the coming days could hold new promise for our family, while wishing with all my might that I could just fall back.

Time ticked by. I waited and waited, my anxiety turning to worry. Then fear. By midnight I could hardly stand another minute. *What* was happening? My mind ran rampant, imagining scenario after scenario, ranging from a car accident to a bitter fight to the more sordid of events. Whatever the circumstance, Katherine was surely to blame.

Daddy finally arrived just before 1:00 A.M. I heard the garage door go up, and a cold relief gushed through me. Then immediately I nearly shook with anger. How could he have done this to me? Kept me up, worrying about him half the night? I hustled to the hall between kitchen and garage like some irate parent, waiting for him, my arms folded and heart beating double time.

"Whoa!" Daddy slapped a hand to his chest when he came through the door. "You nearly scared me to death."

"Why are you so late?" I demanded.

He let his hand fall, slid it into his jacket pocket. "I . . . we had a lot of talkin' to do."

"Talkin' where? Nothin' stays open in Albertsville this long, certainly not Clayton's Place! Where were you, in a parked car?"

"Jackie." Daddy would have laughed were it not for the fury rising from my shoulders. "What is this?"

"It's one o'clock in the morning, that's what!" Indignant tears sprang to my eyes.

His forehead lined. "I'm sorry. I didn't think you'd worry. I figured you'd be asleep long ago."

"Well, you figured wrong." I tried to say more, but all my fears about Katherine whirled through me with a vengeance. Suddenly I wondered how any of this would ever work out. I swung away from Daddy, throat aching.

"Oh, honey." He caught me by the shoulder and turned me around. "I really am sorry. I should have thought of you."

Yes, he should have thought of me, I raged silently. And of Mama. He never, *ever* should have started dating Katherine in the first place.

He searched my face. "Are you all right?"

Who was he kidding? I could not imagine ever being all right again. It hit me then—Daddy's expression showed no sign of grief. In fact, he'd probably be beaming were it not for my ungracious welcome. Which could only mean that Katherine had accepted his proposal. Daddy was going to marry her, bring her into this house. And I'd promised to support that decision. He'd found his love as I'd found mine, and I could not stand against him now, knowing all too well the grief it would cause. Still, the difference in the two relationships could have glared from a mountaintop—Greg did not replace Mama. Katherine would.

"Wh–what did she say?" I whispered, trembling for the answer, not wanting to know.

"She said yes." His face creased into an irrepressible smile.

My head nodded in funny little jerks. I could not believe this moment in our lives had arrived. "I'm so glad."

His smile shrank, lacing with sadness. He pulled me close to his chest and hugged me, one hand patting my back. "Everything's goin' to be all right, you know."

My breath sucked in raggedly. "I r–really am happy for you."

"I know you are, Jackie."

"*Really.*"

"I know."

Clutching his jacket, I burst into sobs.

chapter 40

After Pastor Beekins' sermon the following day, Daddy stood and asked if he could take the pulpit for an announcement. Pastor graciously moved aside as Daddy mounted the two creaky steps, every eye in the sanctuary upon him. From the whispers that fluttered toward the rooftop, I knew folks suspected what he had to say. He'd told Robert and Clarissa that morning. Robert had taken the news stoically, shaking Daddy's hand. "Congratulations," he said solemnly, then burst into a grin. Clarissa had turned somersaults.

Daddy had also made sure to call both sets of grandparents. I heard Grandma Westerdahl sniffle as he reached the pulpit.

"Well." Daddy put his hands on the worn wood and shuffled his feet, suddenly self-conscious. "I stand here today to tell y'all two things, and I'll be brief. First, I want to thank everyone from the bottom of my heart for all the help and prayers you've given me and my family since Melissa's death. You know how much we've needed it. Second. Well, second is this." He looked at Katherine's radiant face. "Katherine May King has agreed to become my wife."

The room erupted into a standing ovation. I pasted a smile on my face. "Glory to God!" Mrs. B cried, and Mr. Matthews shouted, "Hallelujah!" Mr. Luther stomped both feet, then began joyously handing out Tootsie Rolls.

It took us a good half hour to work our way through well-wishers after the announcement. Every one of us exchanged "welcome-to-the-family" hugs with Derek and Katherine's parents. I stood on tiptoe and put a perfunctory arm around Derek's neck, but he held on to me briefly. "How are you?" he asked quietly in my ear.

I pulled away, not able to meet his eyes. "Fine."

Our families planned to meet for Sunday lunch at our house the following week. Grandma and Grandpa Delham would come, too. Mama's parents politely declined the invitation.

All that week in our e-mails and phone calls, Greg encouraged me to tell him how I felt. Which was hard to do at times, because I couldn't quite sort through my emotions myself. *Jackie,* he wrote on Thursday, *you do not know my mamma, I know. The situations are very different. But think about her second marriage. How happy it is. And it causes me to be born!! Your family has much happy times ahead. I know it is hard for you. Do not think you should not be sad for you while you are happy for your baba. You can be both things. So let this be. And soon the sad will be less, and the happy will be more.*

When the Kings came to lunch on Sunday, I shut my bedroom door. I didn't want Derek peeking in on his way to the bathroom and seeing Greg's picture on my wall.

Full of talk about the December wedding, Katherine, her mama, and Grandma shooed me out of the kitchen, saying they'd do dishes. I gladly left them to the mess and their chatter. Derek perched at the computer, giving Robert secrets about playing some new space warrior game, his long arm moving this way and that as he pointed at the screen. He glanced up as I walked by. "Hey. Where ya goin'?"

"I don't know. To my room, I guess."

"Oh." I could see him gathering his courage. "Why don't we go talk somewhere?"

I smiled tightly. "Okay."

No way would I take him to my room. Daddy would frown upon that anyway. The men still sat around the table in the dining room. Nothing left to do but pull some lawn chairs into the backyard shade. We stepped out of the air-conditioned house to a stifling hot afternoon. "Whew," I muttered. Winnie sprawled across the grass under a tree, panting furiously. Derek and I settled in the shaded far corner of the lot, our chairs side by side, out of sight from the cleanup crew. My faithful canine dragged herself over to lie beside me. She was too hot even to nose my arm for a pat.

At first neither Derek nor I could think of anything to say. Finally he broke the silence. "We're all goin' to be in the wedding, I hear. Including Robert and Clarissa."

"Mm-hm. I'm maid of honor. You're best man, so that makes you my escort."

Must have been the tone of my voice. Derek hesitated before saying, "You're not completely happy about this, are you."

"About you bein' my escort?"

I didn't fool him one bit. To his credit, Derek wouldn't let me be. "No, Jackie. About the marriage."

I could have denied it, could have maintained a stoic face, but Derek's voice was so full of concern. I could almost say he sounded tender, if I'd ever applied that word to Derek. So I told him exactly how I felt. I felt happy for Daddy. I felt miserable. Like I'd now been pushed over that threshold, the door slammed behind me, shutting off the past forever. Derek listened patiently until my words ran out.

He lifted his heels off the grass, jiggling one leg. Crossed his arms. "I wish I could do somethin' to make you feel better."

I glanced at him, surprised once more at the tone in his voice. "You make me feel better just by listenin'. Thank you."

"Thank *you*," he replied, "for trustin' me enough to talk."

"I've always trusted you, Derek."

"No, you haven't. You used to think I was a total dork."

A little snort escaped me. "What makes you think I still don't?" I teased.

He turned to look at me intently. "Because I'm not."

Was he talking about his matching socks? His new posture? Okay, so he stood completely straight now. Still, in so many ways, Derek would always be Derek. And then it hit me. Sitting there sweating in the shade, Greg's ring around my neck, Winnie huffing at my side—that's when I first realized who the real Derek was. The Derek I'd come to know had proven kind, considerate, ever-giving. Not even half bad looking. I had to admit his eyes were big and warm enough to swim in.

I laid my hand on his arm. "I know that, Derek. I think you're great for all the things you've done for me. I'm glad we're goin' to be connected by family."

He smiled almost sadly, focusing on my hand. I took it away, and his eyes rose to my face. We gazed at each other for a moment, something passing between us. Words seemed to shimmer on his tongue, begging to be spoken. Suddenly, then, he glanced away with a sigh. He made a point of wiping his forehead. "Sure is hot out here."

Derek had broken the spell, and I would not think of it again for some time. Now this and other memories are precious to me, in ways I never dreamed they would be.

But for that last week—before the lives of our families began to spin out of control—I had other things to think about. Daddy was marrying Katherine, and I had to get used to the idea.

And in just six days, I would see Greg.

chapter 41

Katherine had taken Saturday off. We planned to leave for Lexington before 7:30 A.M., which would put us there by noon. Katherine wanted to "show me the sights of the city," and go shopping before the concert, she'd said. We would stay in a hotel and return Sunday, the drive over dark country roads being far too long and unsafe to undertake after the concert. As excited as I was—almost beside myself, really—Katherine's eagerness ran a close second. All that week she'd come to our house after work, bubbling about two things—the wedding and our trip. Monday evening she and Daddy had gone together to Albertsville to choose a diamond solitaire, which she now sported elegantly on her left hand. Amid all the flurry and my own mounting elation at seeing Greg, my sullenness over their coming marriage began to ebb. How could it not? As each day ended, pulling me closer to Greg, I found little time for anything but trembling anticipation.

Greg and I e-mailed each other two to three times a day—whenever he could find a telephone plug, he told me. And he often called on his cell phone from their bus. He'd mailed me the tickets and back-stage passes, giving me explicit instructions on how to see him briefly before the concert. Thanks to Daddy's insistence that Katherine and I stay overnight for safety, Greg and I would have a chance to be together afterward. I could have kissed Daddy for that.

Daddy sat Katherine and me down in the family room on Friday night for "a little talk."

"Now I'm not worried about the concert," he said, "you all just have fun. Although how you can listen to music that loud is beyond me." Katherine and I exchanged an amused glance. "I'm mostly concerned about after the concert. I know you're goin' to spend some time with Greg, and I've told you that's okay. My concern is *where* that's goin' to happen. And I want you adequately chaperoned."

"Oh, Bobby, I'll take care of her." Katherine waved a hand. "You know we'll be just fine."

"I'm sure you will. But, Jackie, what do you plan to do after the concert?"

I bit my bottom lip. "Mostly just talk. We just want to be together for a while."

"Where? I can't imagine that you can go out to some restaurant without being bombarded by fans. You certainly can't go to his hotel room. Nor do I want you two wandering about Lexington at night. That's a city with a whole lot more crime than Bradleyville, I can tell you."

Judgment crept into Daddy's voice. Katherine pressed her lips. "I'll be close by, Bobby," she insisted. "We'll find a way for these kids to be together without being too alone, okay?"

Uh-oh. I could sense the tension underneath the surface. Daddy didn't mean to sound distrustful of her abilities, I told myself. All the same, she had never been a parent, while he'd carried that responsibility solely since Mama died. If he appeared overbearing on my account, I could understand it, even as I felt a bit of indignance for Katherine. Now, looking back, I realize part of his anxiety lay with Katherine herself. She'd played through city nightlife alone in the past. Now she'd pledged to be his wife, and he wasn't thrilled with the idea of her going to Lexington without him. Especially when she seemed so excited about it.

Daddy opened his mouth to say more, but the defensiveness on Katherine's face held him in check. He would not argue with her in front of me. Instead, he managed a smile. "You two are goin' to have a terrific time," he said. "Just . . . don't forget who loves you at home."

I learned a number of things about Katherine on that drive to Lexington—not so much from what she said as the way she said them. She talked about Mama, and how she knew we all continued to miss her very much. She talked about my daddy's loyalty and stability. Daddy was a man to be counted on, a man good to his word, Katherine said. She could trust him. I think she told me these things to help put my mind at ease about the marriage.

I watched her profile as she gauged the curves in the road, her long red nails firmly around the steering wheel. Her lipstick matched the nails, her dark hair sleek against summer-tanned skin. She wore white slacks and a blue satiny blouse, gold bracelets on her wrist. I'd laid out three outfits the previous night, finally deciding on a white skirt and pink lace-trimmed top. I'd put on makeup, fussed with my hair, done everything to look my utmost. But I would never come close to Katherine, not in a million years. I felt mighty glad she was my daddy's fiancée and not one of my girlfriends, or surely she'd have turned Greg's head.

But then, Greg found himself surrounded by beautiful girls every day, didn't he?

Katherine's exuberance grew as we neared Lexington. I was simply too excited about seeing Greg to be concerned by it. In fact, her attitude made me feel closer to her than I ever had, for I read it as an empathetic reflection of my own feelings. We checked into our hotel, then shopped at the downtown stores. "No time to go all the way over to Fayette Mall," she told me. She oohed and aahed over one outfit after another, and spent over three hundred dollars at one boutique. "Don't know where I'll wear these in Bradleyville," she commented as she handed the salesgirl a credit card. "Your daddy and I will just have to go out more, I guess. Maybe come here overnight sometimes."

"Oh, Jackie," she exclaimed at another store, "look here! This is the *perfect* outfit for you to wear tonight."

I glanced down at my clothes. "I thought I'd wear this."

"No, no, I've figured all along I'd buy you an outfit. You haven't been to a concert before; you don't know how the girls dress. They wear glittery stuff, you know, clothes that are really fun."

She held up shimmery black pants and a matching sleeveless top that swirled gold and green into the black. A small purse, beaded and fringed, hung across one shoulder and to the other side of the top. "Wow," I said.

"Try them on." She pushed the hangers into my hands.

The outfit looked sensational on me. I stood before the mirror, ogling myself. Greg would just die.

Katherine paid for the clothes, all grins, shunning my effusive thanks. "Just you wait till I do your makeup." She winked.

I could barely eat our early supper, excitement tying my stomach in knots. All I could think about was Greg—the feel of his hair in my fingers, the way he kissed, his smile. Back in the room, Katherine told me to wash my face and get dressed. Greg's ring proudly hung against my new shirt, golden and blue. Then she put makeup on me as I perched on a chair, my back to the mirror. "Don't want you to see till we're all done," she declared.

"What's that?" I asked as she pulled off the cap of some shiny stick.

"Glitter."

"Glitter?"

"It's the new thing to wear, Jackie, especially to a concert." She rolled it high on my cheeks and patted, then across my shoulders. Finally she pulled out glitter hair spray and applied it with wide sweeps of her hand. She stood back and looked at me critically. "You're done," she announced. "Glory, do you look incredible."

She pulled me up and turned me around to the mirror. I gawked at myself. High cheekbones, even skin. Glossy pink lips.

"Move a little and you'll see the glitter."

I angled my head left, then right, watching the light play subtly on the silvery bits in my hair and on my cheeks. "I thought it would look like, you know, *glitter*. That thick gold stuff we used for crafts in Sunday school."

"Not at all. It just gives you a little sparkle."

I gazed at myself again, hardly believing my eyes. For the first time in my life, I felt truly beautiful. Gratitude surged through me. Even Mama would not have known how to make me look like this.

"Thank you," I breathed, hugging Katherine with all my might. "Thank you!"

"Okay, okay," she laughed, pushing me away. "Don't ruin your makeup." She fetched my purse, putting inside a tissue, the lipstick, and glitter. "Put this over your head carefully; don't mess up your hair." I slipped it onto my right shoulder, the bag resting against my left hip.

Six o'clock. Time to go. I could barely breathe.

We took a cab to Rupp Arena. Katherine insisted it would be easier than driving ourselves. She was right. I couldn't *believe* the traffic jam. Girls hung out of convertibles and car windows, honking, singing, the cars streamered and plastered with pictures of Greg and his group, messages written in soap across the windows. "We luv LuvRush!" The group's music blared from CD players, and girls called back and forth, fairly jumping up and down. The air pulsed with excitement and energy, and we hadn't even entered the arena yet. We paid the cab driver and walked the last few blocks, swept along with the crowd of laughing girls, many with their mamas. Amazing, but the parents seemed almost as wound up as the teenagers. I felt a momentary twinge inside, seeing them and their daughters having such a good time together.

Katherine couldn't stop smiling. "This is so fun!"

We pushed through long, chattering lines until finally finding ourselves inside. The arena looked huge to me, its seats already filling. Fans milled and yelled to one another, bouncing oversized balloons across the crowd. A long, high ramp stretched from the stage to a platform in the center of the arena, surrounded by lights and sound equipment and cameras. Above the stage was suspended a large screen. In forty-five minutes the show would begin.

Katherine and I wound our way down front and showed a security guard our backstage passes. He pointed toward a corner door where other personnel stood. Once through that door, we were stopped by a huge man, his orange security vest tight across his chest.

"Greg Kostakis is expecting us in the dressing room," I told him. "Jackie Delham and Katherine King."

He looked us over suspiciously. "Hold on a minute." He pulled his walkie-talkie off his belt. "Gary. You know anything about a Jackie Delham and Katherine King seeing the group?"

I waited on pins and needles. What if something went wrong?

The walkie-talkie crackled. "Yeah. Bring 'em on back."

Katherine and I sighed in relief. "You'd think we were going to see the king," she breathed.

The man gestured with his head. "See all those girls out there? To them, you are."

He handed us off to Gary, who escorted us to the dressing room door. "Wait here. Let me make sure everyone's decent."

I stood with hammering heart and knocking knees as he disappeared inside.

"Do I still look okay?" I whispered to Katherine.

"Honey, you're gorgeous."

The door opened. "All right, you can come in. You'll need to leave in fifteen minutes." He stood aside, and somehow my feet moved over the threshold.

Clothes hung everywhere, long lighted mirrors running the length of one wall. I recognized all of the band members at once—Demetri on a couch, Alex before a mirror, Lysander singing as he buttoned a shirt.

"Jackie!" Greg materialized from behind a partition, and his face lit up. He rushed across the room, then stopped before me, grabbing my hands. "Ah," he breathed, drinking in the sight of my face, my clothes. "You are so beautiful."

I couldn't say a thing. Not one tiny sound. He looked better than I'd even remembered, the bruise long healed from his face, his brown eyes reflecting the gold sparkles in his shirt.

"Ah," he said again. He put a hand against my cheek, brushed back my hair. I knew his friends watched, and somewhere behind me stood Katherine, but we didn't care. I laid my hand over his. "Greg."

He cupped my face with his hands and kissed me.

"Whooo, Kostakis!" rose a chorus of cheers from his friends. I only half heard them. Greg's lips lingered, and I wound my hands around his neck, thinking I could die right then and there.

Greg pulled away, murmuring, "I love you."

"I love *you*," I whispered.

He smiled at the ring around my neck, picking it up to admire it. "Looks good on the chain."

Then, grinning like the Cheshire cat, Greg introduced Katherine and me to his friends. Katherine raised her eyebrows at me, most assuredly over the kiss, and I looked away, embarrassed.

"Such lovely ladies!" Demetri pronounced, kissing Katherine's hand with a flourish. She laughed, clearly pleased.

"I see why Greg talks about you much, Jackie." Alex swiped playfully at his shoulder. "You are more beautiful than your picture."

Our fifteen minutes practically flew by. The door opened and closed as people began hustling about with last-minute details. Greg introduced us to the stage manager, who breathed a harried "welcome," then gathered the group to talk over various points about choreography and microphones. Katherine and I sat on the couch and watched, fascinated. Greg broke away from the others, and we rose to meet him.

"Sorry you must go." He spoke rapidly, his expression almost preoccupied. "We have little time, and the warm-up band does not play long. We must do things."

"Are you nervous?" I asked

"Always before a concert." He slipped his arm around my shoulders. "Tonight I am more nervous because you are watching."

"You shouldn't be! You know I'll love everything you do."

He smiled. "I have a surprise for you. I hope you like it."

I nodded, and Katherine said, "She will."

"Hey, Greg," someone called, "they still riding with us afterwards?"

Greg hit his forehead. "You drive here?" he asked me.

"We took a cab."

"Good. Come here after the concert, and you can go to the hotel with us in our bus. I will let Gary know, okay?" He looked to Katherine for approval.

I could only imagine what Daddy would say, but Katherine gave him a grand smile. "That will be great."

He clasped his fingers around my neck. "I hope you do not mind the bus and everything. It is . . . the fans are everywhere. This is not like Bradleyville, Jackie. But it is my life." He searched my eyes, his own begging for acceptance.

"I love your life, Greg," I assured him. "I love *you*."

I would not understand until later that night why he thought my acceptance may be so hard to give.

chapter 42

It feels so good to be back here!" Katherine exclaimed, turning around from our front-row seats to sweep her gaze over the arena. The place was almost full.

"How are the people way up there going to see?" I asked, pointing to the topmost level.

"They can see close-up by watching the monitor." She pointed to the giant screen above the stage. "But believe me, the closer you can get to the front, the more exciting it is."

Soon after 8:00 the houselights dimmed, and the warm-up band took the stage to play four numbers. Their music was fast with a heavy bass that beat right through my heart. I had never heard music that loud in my life. The crowd applauded, yet somehow I sensed they held back, their enthusiasm waiting to spill for the band they'd come to see. Still, I had no idea then just how much enthusiasm that would prove to be. After the warm-up band, a clock appeared on the screen, ticking down the minutes and seconds until LuvRush would take the stage.

Twenty-nine minutes and fifty-nine seconds.

I swiveled this way and that, watching people. Katherine was right— the girls had spiffed themselves up, glitter and all. One large group of friends wore matching white shirts with "LuvRush" spelled across the front. Others wore LuvRush T-shirts with a photo of the group. Such a strange feeling I had, seeing Greg's face on the clothing of all those girls.

Vendors came by, selling soft drinks, candy bars, and glow-in-the-dark wands.

Nineteen minutes and twenty seconds.

"It's a good thing *I* brought you, by the way," Katherine teased. "I don't think Greg would have kissed you that way in front of your daddy."

Not in front of Mama either. But that wasn't a thought I cared to dwell upon.

"Yeah." I could feel myself blushing.

"It's all right, you know." She grinned at me. "I had boys kiss me at sixteen, too."

Boys, plural. I just bet she did. Dozens of them.

I pushed those ideas from my mind. Katherine didn't deserve that, not after all she'd done for me today.

"What will we do about goin' to their hotel room?" I asked. "Daddy will get all mad."

"Don't worry. They'll have a suite of rooms, living area included. You'll have a place to sit with Greg, and I won't be far away. Even your daddy won't find reason to complain." She gave me an impish smile.

I went back to watching the crowd, thinking I couldn't wait for the concert to start, and I didn't want it to end. And I couldn't wait for it to be over.

Eight minutes and forty-six seconds.

By that time I checked the clock every minute. When it reached five, the very air in the stadium bristled with expectation. Every nerve within me hummed. Four minutes. Three. Two. One. Thousands of voices took up a joyous chant, counting down the seconds. Electricity surged through the arena, the hair on my arms rising. The girl on my right hung on to her seat, back arched, shouting the numbers. I could barely distinguish her voice amid the noise.

"Ten! Nine! Eight!"

"Here goes!" Katherine poked my side.

"Three, two, ONE!"

The arena cut to blackness, dotted by glow wands. Four spotlights flooded the stage, each lighting a figure completely covered in a hooded robe. "Aaahhh!" I couldn't see behind me, but I could hear the sound. Every fan in that arena rocketed to her feet, yelling. I scrambled up, heart thudding, fingers pressing into my palms, the corporate scream of thousands of teenagers sizzling like a live wire in my ears. Music crashed into play, and the hooded figures glided into motion. Suddenly, the lights cut out on stage. When the lights came up again, the hooded robes were gone. LuvRush posed theatrically, lit in silver.

Screams multiplied until my very being shook with the sound. A song from the LuvRush CD crashed into play, and Greg's voice rose above it all. The group danced their way across the stage, singing.

I will never forget that concert. The pulse of music through my body, my very heart thudding with the beat. Girls shrieking the names of the band members, tossing flowers upon the stage and ramp. Girls reaching to touch the group members as they sat on the ramp in the midst of the crowd, singing "Hung Up on You." Song after song, both fast and slow, of which I knew every word. Close-ups of the guys on the screen above the stage. The synchronicity of laser lights and music. Confetti, pink and green smoke, fireworks. Flashing costumes and constant, constant sound and motion. An *energy* such as I've never felt in my life. No one in the crowd sat the entire hour. Greg and his band strode, danced, and rubber-heeled across the floor as they sang, microphones positioned in front of their mouths and attached to headsets. The agility of their movements. How did they *do* it? I wondered— never a ragged breath amidst all that choreography. Mostly I remember the way Greg exuded such easy confidence, as if born to sing.

I'd met the quiet, gentle Greg in Bradleyville, the Christian who listened with patience, who loved family, and who cared with his whole heart. Now I saw the public Greg, the only one his fans saw, the Greg destined to be a star. And my chest filled with a love for him—all of him—that spilled into my eyes and down my cheeks.

A fast song ended amid wild shrieks from the crowd. Slow music began. "Now," Greg spoke over the noise, "I want to sing a new song for the first time tonight, called 'Love Will Begin.' This is for Jackie." *Tsoky*.

My breath sucked in and held. Katherine hugged me, elated. I clutched my fingers under my chin, fresh tears filling my eyes. The spotlight turned golden on Greg as he moved to the front center, just feet away. Girls on our row jumped up and down, reaching toward him, but he sang only to me.

> The skeptics say that dreams are just the tales we spin at night.
> And wishing for things we do not have won't bring them to our
>   sight.
> It's true I knew that all these words from wisdom could be traced.
> But then you spoke your heart to me, and all else was erased.

On the chorus, he tipped back his head and closed his eyes.

> I can't believe you look at me the way I've looked at you.
> I can't believe you stand so close, the way I want you to.
> If you take my hand and I tremble, a leaf before the wind,
> Just hold me close till I am still, and our love will begin, yeah,
> Our love will begin.

After the final song, we all roared and yelled and stomped our feet until LuvRush materialized in plumes of smoke for a smashing encore. Then, suddenly, the concert was over, the music silent, my ears ringing. Katherine hugged me, practically shaking. "Did you like it?"

"Like it," I breathed. "I'll never be the same!"

As everyone else crowded up the aisles, Katherine and I made our way back through the door down front. From there we were escorted to the dressing room. We stood outside for some time, waiting for the guys.

"Greg says to tell you he's getting cleaned up," Gary said as he emerged from the room. "They're always pretty sweaty after a concert."

Soon Greg appeared in jeans and a T-shirt, looking exhausted, his hair wet. I rushed to hug him, barely able to talk, feeling his ring between us. "Thank you, thank you," I whispered against his neck. "I love the song. I love your singing. I love you."

I couldn't believe the throng of fans who'd crowded at the back of the building, waiting to see the group as they trotted for the bus. Greg held my hand tightly as security guards on all sides protected the band from screaming, pushing girls. Demetri ran beside Katherine. We jumped into the bus, and my jaw dropped open at the layout, complete with bunk beds and seats along the sides like couches. "My home." Greg smiled. He pulled me onto a seat and slid his arm around me.

As the driver started the engine, girls pounded on the windows, calling the guys' names, begging for them to peek outside.

"How do you *ever* walk down a street?" Katherine wondered aloud.

Alex lifted his hands. "We don't."

"They don't really know us," Lysander said. "They think they do, but they know only what they see. This is why Greg is so fortunate. He has someone who *does* know him."

Greg caught my eye, clearly surprised. His e-mails had been full of tales about his three friends—how they loved partying with girls and all the attention. They'd even teased him about tying himself down to "one girl."

"I told you guys you do things wrong." He raised his chin at Lysander.

"Ah. Yeah, but *you* have Jackie."

At the hotel, security herded us off the bus and into an empty elevator. "No girls," Alex commented. "How long before they find us?"

I aimed a shocked look at Greg. Did their fans pursue them even to their hotel rooms? He gave a self-conscious shrug. "They will have to sneak here to come up," he told me. "The floor is closed."

LuvRush had two connecting suites, both with large living rooms. Greg and I took the couch in the sitting area he shared with Demetri, while everyone else tactfully trooped to the other living room next door. Katherine made no bones about leaving the door open between the two suites. All evening people would come in and out as others traveling with the band arrived for the gathering, sometimes going through our area to reach the other one. And before long we heard security in the hall, forcing excited girls to leave. The girls protested, calling the guy's names. "Demetri, come out! Lysander, kiss me!" But most of them called for Greg. "Greg, I love you! Greg, I want your body tonight! Greg!"

Once I recovered from my shock at their boldness, I wanted to go out and slap each one silly. I aimed a stunned look at Greg, wondering how he lived like this, wondering how he could possibly be faithful to me amidst all the temptation. Stupid Charlotte's aggressive tactics were nothing compared to this. He pressed his lips in embarrassment. "I'm sorry," he whispered.

"Does this happen every night?" I asked.

He nodded. His expression begged for my understanding.

"And the guys usually let them in, right? You said they party a lot." My voice turned edgy. "I didn't know you meant in your own hotel room."

"I go into a bedroom and lock the door."

"Greg—one door, that's it? One little door separates you from—all that?"

He turned to face me squarely, his knee on the couch cushion, and grazed his palm across my cheek. "My heart separates me from that," he said gently. "My heart is with you."

Remorse tugged at my chest. I shouldn't judge him. He couldn't control what his fans did. I smiled wanly, reaching up my hand to place over his. "I'm sorry. I just . . . I didn't realize . . ."

"I know." He breathed deeply, making me wonder if he'd almost been afraid of this evening, of my seeing this side of his life. "Do you forgive me?"

I shook my head. "There's nothin' to forgive."

We pushed the subject aside then, focusing on each other, on *us*. For the next two hours, we talked, barely stopping to eat the pizza that soon arrived. I'd have thought, given all our e-mails and phone calls, that we'd have little left to say. But we couldn't seem to spill our hearts enough. I told Greg in low tones how I was feeling about Katherine. How I dared believe that now Daddy and she were engaged, she would not change her mind. "She's been so excited all week," I added, forgetting to mention that part of her excitement had centered on coming to Lexington.

Greg talked more about his tour—everything from the dozens of people who traveled with them in order to put on the show, to the promising moments when his three friends had seemed more open to talk about Christ. "You know we all pray before each concert now? We get in a circle and pile our hands together. I pray and they listen. At least they do that."

If only they behaved as well after the concerts, I thought. Suddenly I realized how much strength it took for Greg to be outspoken about his faith. "I'm still so proud of you for what you said in that *Teen Dream* interview," I said. "It must take a lot of courage."

He blew out air. "I think it is a reason God puts me here. The more people know me, the more I can talk about Christ. Of course, magazines do not always use those quotes. But sometimes."

"And your tour is goin' great," I added.

"Yes, so good. Stations play another song from our CD now, you know? Maybe we will have *three* in the top forty!"

I brushed hair off his forehead. "You probably will, Greg. LuvRush is gonna be a huge success. You know it, and I know it."

"I do. I feel it here." He thumped his chest. "But I hardly believe it still. Sometimes my head goes around, and I think it is a dream."

I squeezed his knee. "It *is* a dream. A real one."

Out of nowhere, a knot formed in my throat.

"What is it?" Greg laced his fingers in mine.

"I just . . . You're a big star. And you're goin' to be even bigger. I don't want you to leave me behind. All those girls—"

"I *never* leave you behind," he said fiercely, pressing my fingers. "You see? The more star I am, the more I need you. Like Lysander said, we all need someone like you. Someone to talk to. Who knows us—inside."

"But with all the girls, you could find somebody else—"

"I *won't*. I promise you." Hurt creased Greg's face. "This is why I am afraid sometimes. That you don't believe me. And so you will find someone close to you in Bradleyville. Someone whose life is like yours, not like . . . this."

"No, Greg." I bit my lip. "I wouldn't *ever* do that."

He looked at his ring around my neck. "You wear it always? You don't take it off?"

I pressed my palm over it. "I never take it off. I promise."

Later, I asked him how he wrote the song for me. And did he start thinking those words when we'd sat under the trees at the river? He looked a little embarrassed.

"Yes. But you must see I had much help. I want the words to be . . ." He looked away, frowning. "I don't know the word . . . it means like a poem."

"Poetic?"

"Yes! I want them to be poetic, and so I need help with language. But it is not like speaking. I can take time, you know?"

"I loved it," I told him. "I love the song."

Our time had passed too quickly. Katherine and I would have to go soon; the guys needed a good sleep before hitting the road in the morning. Tomorrow night they would play in Nashville. I didn't know how to leave Greg, every moment that ticked by draining more of my elation, filling me with dread. "When am I goin' to see you again?"

He hesitated. "I hope after the tour. I do not want to tell you until I know for certain. But I want to come again to Bradleyville, and now Celia and Danny talk about coming. Celia wants to have early Christmas with her mamma and baba. She wants Danny there."

I raked in a breath. I could see him again in a little over three months? "Oh." I wanted to smile and cry at the same time. "I can't *believe* it!"

"Just—I must be sure. Danny . . . he does not come to Bradleyville usually. He does not like it much. But he will maybe go for Celia."

My smile diminished. Suddenly I remembered Daddy. How would he feel to see Danny Cander again? How would Danny Cander feel to see *him?*

"Greg." I hesitated. "Will your brother . . . I mean, does he not want to come to Bradleyville because of my daddy?"

"No, no. He lives there before, remember? With his baba? Not a good time."

"Then—"

"Hey, you two." Katherine called from the doorway, and we both jumped. She tapped her watch. "Ten minutes."

Greg squeezed my hands until they hurt. "Okay."

I couldn't go. I couldn't leave him. "Tell me now when I'll see you again," I begged. The next time, the next date to mark on my calendar and hold on to.

"The last concert is November 28. We will be busy for a few days after that, talking about things. We have to think about the next CD."

"Will my song be on your next CD?"

He winced. "I don't know. I hope so, but I don't decide that. Our record producer must decide if it has a strong enough hook."

What stronger hook did it need? I thought rather indignantly. It was about me, wasn't it? "Okay, anyway. Go on."

"The other guys will go back to Greece then. I want to come to Bradleyville."

I thought a moment. "So around the first of December? Daddy's getting married on the twelfth. I don't suppose you'd still be there?"

Greg shook his head. "No, I don't think. Wish I could."

At his answer, an unexpected thought flashed through my head. I felt almost glad Greg would not be at Daddy's wedding, for Derek would be escorting me down the aisle, and the thought of Greg's seeing me on Derek's arm made me uncomfortable. Derek would be uncomfortable with Greg there, too, and I didn't want that for him. He didn't deserve to be hurt.

The thought vanished as quickly as it came. But later I would remember it—Derek, springing to my mind out of nowhere, while I was with Greg.

We had to say our goodbyes. Greg and I couldn't hold each other tightly enough, say we loved each other enough. Katherine nearly had to pull me out the door.

When Katherine and I returned to our hotel room my whole body still pulsed with remembrances of the night. On the telephone by the bed, the red message signal was flashing. It would be Daddy, I figured, worrying about why we'd been out so late. I sailed into the bathroom to take off my makeup, sharing incredulous glances over the evening with myself in the mirror. I paid little attention when I heard Katherine talking on the phone, even though it was after 1:00. She appeared in the doorway a moment later, face white, palms pressed tightly to her lips. One look at her and I froze.

"We have to go right now," she said, her voice raw. "Derek's been in a car accident. They don't know if he's going to make it."

chapter 43

That drive to Albertsville would mark a dividing line in our lives, separating all that had gone before from the rapid changes to come. I look back now on the months that followed and see the grace of God at work. Then, all I could see was confusion and sorrow.

Within ten minutes of hanging up the phone, we'd checked out of our hotel, stopping only to change clothes and throw our things into our overnight bags. By the time we arrived, gritty-eyed and exhausted, at the Albertsville Hospital, it was after 5:30 A.M. Hearts in our throats, we hurried to the waiting area for intensive care, begging God as we had for the entire drive that Derek was still alive. We stumbled into the room, Katherine's parents pulling to their weary feet. Katherine rushed to throw her arms around them, choking on a sob. Her mama sagged against her.

"How is he?" Katherine searched her parents' faces.

"Still alive, thank God," her daddy managed. "Looks like the surgery did all it was supposed to do."

"You have to tell me everything, you have to tell me what happened!" Katherine sank down on the edge of a couch, holding tightly to her mother's hand. Old tears and new tracked through her smeared makeup.

I lowered myself into a chair, ankles trembling. How could such a magical night turn into such tragedy? I could not believe that Derek would die; I *would* not believe it. Over and over during our harried trip to the hospital, I relived all the moments in which he'd been so kind to me. The moment when we'd sat in our backyard, his expression saying what words could not. Derek needed to keep writing me funny e-mails. He needed to escort me down the aisle in my daddy's wedding. He needed to *live*.

"I never should have sent him," Katherine's mama intoned, her face ragged, old. "I needed some things from Albertsville, and Derek offered to go."

The winding and narrow Route 622 between Bradleyville and Albertsville had proven dangerous to many over the years, especially to those unfamiliar with its curves. With vivid horror I could picture the truck, stacked high with wood, its new driver taking a turn too fast, losing control. Derek, coming around the curve from the opposite direction and swerving to miss the truck, plunging down an embankment. The car must have rolled over numerous times, Mr. King said. Rescue workers found it on its side, crunched against a tree. Derek lay crumpled and unconscious in his seat belt.

I raked my hands through my hair, listening to the strange medical terms that had become so suddenly, intimately real to the King family. A subdural hematoma—intense pressure in the brain caused by internal bleeding. A ruptured spleen. Doctors had drilled burr holes in Derek's head, alleviating the pressure from the hematoma. They'd operated to remove his injured spleen and put a cast on one leg. Ribs were also broken. He lay in intensive care in a coma.

"Can we see him?" Katherine whispered.

"They let us in for a few minutes every hour," her daddy replied. "Only the immediate family."

At 6:00 Katherine and her parents went to see Derek. I slumped in the chair, head resting against the pale yellow wall, stomach churning. Praying to Jesus to save Derek. At 7:00 the family visited Derek again. He remained unconscious. In between those times we sat in vigil, mostly silent, Mr. King often pushing to his feet in desperation to pace the floor.

At 7:30 Katherine called Daddy. I knew he would be here for her if he didn't have to stay with Robert and Clarissa. She returned, saying he would soon be on his way. Grandma Delham would take the kids to church. "He says the whole town's praying." Katherine aimed an exhausted smile at her mama. "They've been praying through the night."

My thoughts swirled like dust before the wind. Would Daddy and Katherine postpone the wedding? If Derek lived, *when* Derek lived, would he ever be the same? I promised myself that I would do everything I could for Derek. I would visit him, sit by his bedside while he recuperated at home if I had to, bring him homework from school. He deserved as much selflessness from me as he had shown himself.

Then I wondered when Greg would get up. I pictured security loading LuvRush onto the bus, heading for their next concert. I envisioned the arena from last night, the music, the excitement. Now it all seemed a planet away. Greg in his wondrous world, I in Bradleyville. Facing death—again.

Daddy arrived, heading for Katherine, then her parents. I shoved to my feet to hug him, hurt that he would leave me for last, disappointed with myself for having such a selfish thought.

We stayed at the hospital all morning, the Kings continuing to see Derek every hour. I memorized the worn, blue fabric of the couches, spots in the multicolored carpet, a gray streak on the far wall. The covers of the unread magazines on the wooden coffee table. Derek did not waken. Each hour, our fears ran higher.

"All those machines!" Katherine wailed into Daddy's shoulder after one visit. "Everything pumping and clicking. I can't stand it, Bobby! All the years I was gone, missing his growing up. I come back and look what happens!"

"Shhh." Daddy held her, his dark hair crushing next to hers. Miss Connie's chin trembled as she watched them. "He's goin' to make it," Daddy soothed. "What counts is, you're here now. You're here when he really needs you."

Daddy proved a rock of strength all morning, never letting on how hard it must have been for him to be back in a hospital. When we found ourselves alone once the Kings had shuffled down the hall again, he quietly asked me about the concert and Greg. Yes, I told him, it was wonderful; you wouldn't believe it, Daddy, how great the show was. But the words flattened with insignificance, spilling away like water over a cliff.

By noon I felt like a walking scarecrow. We all did. Little food, no sleep. All the anxiety. My legs literally shook.

"You need to go home, get some rest," Daddy said to me. "You, too, Katherine."

She moved her head side to side almost like a puppet. "No. I can't leave him. My parents have been up all night too."

A doctor appeared in the doorway, white-coated and solemn, one hand in his pocket. Our eyes riveted to his face, searching for answers, begging for good news. Mr. King stood.

"He's holding his own," the doctor said. "You have a miracle boy in there. He appears stable, and so if you need rest, which I know you all do, you ought to go home for a while. You know we'll call you if anything changes."

Miss Connie brought fingertips to the bridge of her nose and dragged in a sob. Her husband squeezed her shoulder. "Thank you, Dr. Namon. For everything you're doin'," he said.

As soon as we arrived home, I fell into bed, descending into sleep with tears tracking down my temples for Derek, Greg's picture the last thing I saw. I awoke after 6:00 P.M., immediately frightened that something had happened while I slept. Then I realized I hadn't e-mailed Greg. He'd worry that Katherine and I hadn't made it home safely. And now he would have no time to turn on his laptop until after the concert.

I rubbed my eyes and stumbled out to the family room. Robert played on the computer. Daddy flipped halfheartedly through the Sunday paper. "How's Derek?" I demanded.

"The same."

I flopped down on the couch, chin practically to my chest.

"You need to eat something," Daddy said.

"I know." Sighing, I focused on Robert's profile, his arm jerking as he fired lasers on the screen. "Robert, I need to write an e-mail real quick. Could you pause the game?"

Daddy shifted his position. "To Greg, I suppose."

Did I imagine the judgment in his tone? My chest twinged at the thought that I could be so self-absorbed, wanting to write Greg while Derek lay near death in a hospital. "It'll only take a minute. I want to tell him about Derek."

Daddy studied me for a moment, as if seeing right through me. "Robert, let her have the computer."

My brother grumbled but did as he was told.

Minutes later my fingers hung over the keyboard as I tried to think what to say. Except for that brief conversation on our first date, I'd never mentioned my friendship with Derek to Greg, even though I knew they'd met briefly. I felt suddenly caught between them, which made no sense. Plus, I could practically feel Daddy's eyes on my back. At that moment the realization hit me. "Derek is crazy about you," Alison had said, and she barely had any contact with him. If *she* could see how Derek felt about me, surely Daddy and Katherine and her parents knew too. Had they felt sorry for him because of that? Had they wished for his sake I would turn from my "foolishness" over some singer to him?

I stared at the computer screen, wondering at that. Wondering particularly about Katherine. She'd never breathed a word about Derek's feelings to me, never done anything but encourage me with Greg. Did she think she'd betrayed her brother now? That she should have done more to push me toward him?

Slowly, I typed, telling Greg what had happened. And how kind and generous Derek had always been to me. That I counted him as a good friend.

If I don't write as much as I usually would, I concluded, *it's because I'll be back and forth to the hospital. Daddy and I need to support the Kings and Derek all we can right now.*

Don't forget, Greg, how much I love you.

—Jackie

After a long rest, Katherine and her parents returned to the hospital that evening. They would keep vigil for the second night in a row. Daddy drove in also for a few hours, leaving me to stay with Clarissa and Robert. When he returned with the news that nothing had changed, our family sat around the kitchen table to hold hands and pray for Derek. Clarissa cried crocodile tears. For the first time ever, I heard Robert pray aloud, asking God to please heal his friend. Hearing his mournful plea, I cried too.

At 1:00 A.M., I found myself wide awake and slipped to the computer to check my e-mails. Greg had written of his sadness at the news. He was praying, he said.

The following morning, just after Daddy pulled out of the garage for work, Katherine called. Derek had come out of the coma and was talking. Clarissa, Robert, and I all leapt with joy. *Thank you, God, thank you, thank you!* I prayed, rushing to the computer to write Greg. All that day Derek continued to stabilize, his family seeing him every hour. That night the Kings returned home for a full night's sleep, rejoicing that Derek was going to pull through. The town of Bradleyville rejoiced with them.

Katherine called me from home Monday evening. "Derek's asking to see you," she said.

I drew in a breath. "Can I do that? I thought only family could go in."

"You *are* family. Maybe not immediate, but I don't care what the nurses say. If Derek wants to see you, I'm getting you in there."

I thought of the promise I'd made to myself about visiting Derek, to do anything I could to help him get better. I would stay at the hospital day and night if I could.

"Come to the hospital tomorrow evening as soon your daddy's home to watch the kids," Katherine urged. "I'll get you in then."

"Okay." I hesitated. "You sure your parents won't care?"

"Jackie," she said, and I heard the raw honesty in her voice, "my parents want anything that will make Derek happy right now. And that happens to be you."

chapter 44

I'd judged Daddy. I'd judged Katherine. Easy to do when you're sixteen and have yet to fall on your own face. Now would begin my own complicity. It would start in the smallest of ways—so small that I would not even recognize it. Isn't that often how it is. A choice here, a choice there, each one rationalized as worthy under the circumstances. Then before you know it, you're in over your head.

To visit Derek, I chose to wear a short-sleeved blouse that could hide Greg's ring around my neck. Nothing new in that, was there? I'd hidden the ring before, when the town was against Greg. Besides, *I* knew with whom my loyalties lay. But for Derek's sake, I simply could not envision myself leaning over to talk to him with that ring swinging between us. I buttoned up the blouse and slipped the ring inside.

Sometimes I still wonder—if I hadn't made that first small choice, if Greg's ring had been a visible reminder to Derek, and to me, of whom I'd pledged my heart to, would things have been different?

"Jackie." Mr. King rose to greet me when I entered the now-familiar waiting room that Tuesday evening. He pressed my hand between his roughened palms. "Thank you for comin'. Derek's been askin' about you all day long."

"Yes, Jackie, thank you," his wife agreed. "I think he'll get better just seein' you." Miss Connie looked like she'd aged ten years in the past few days. Her tired eyes held mine for a brief moment, unspoken words hanging between us. I knew then that she understood her son's feelings for me. No doubt Mr. King did too. Half the town probably knew. Suddenly I felt caught in a spotlight, as if I were supposed to *do* something. Self-consciousness made me turn away from Derek's mama.

I perched on the couch next to Katherine. She reached over and patted my knee. That small action shot straight to my heart. She knew what I was feeling. She *knew*. Katherine understood as no one else could, not only because she'd seen me with Greg, but because she was Katherine.

Without thinking, I laid my head on her shoulder, just as I might have done with Mama. Her fingers tightened on my knee.

Ten minutes later we all slipped in to see Derek.

"I'm not supposed to let you in there, you know," a tall, nononsense nurse informed me.

"She's—"

"She's no sister, if that's what you're fixin' to tell me," the nurse cut Katherine off. "But I'm lettin' you go in because Derek, weak as he is, threatened me within an inch of my life if I didn't." She pressed her lips into a knowing little smile. "So go."

I avoided Miss Connie's eyes as we shuffled past the nurse.

The intensive care unit was one huge sterile-smelling room, beds curtained off from each other. As sick as Mama had been, she had never spent time in intensive care. My chest tightened at the feeling in the room—everything solemn, weighted. Our shoes squeaked across the floor. I was not prepared for the sight of Derek. He lay in the second compartment, gray side rails up on his bed, surrounded by machines and blipping monitors displaying heart rate, oxygen saturation, and a dozen other functions I couldn't begin to understand. Lines ran from his body to the machines; thick cords plugged into the wall. One whole side of his hair had been shaved, apparently for the holes they'd drilled in his head. *Oh, Derek.* I pressed my fingers into my palms, hanging back while his family said hello.

"Look who's finally here, Derek." His mama's voice lilted, overbright. "Jackie."

He moved his head the tiniest fraction, seeking me. Katherine nudged me to his bedside. Derek's face looked so bruised and battered, far worse than Greg's had ever been. Stitches ran across the right side of his forehead. Tears bit my eyes. "Hi, Derek."

"Hey, Jackie."

Even in the weakness of his voice, I could hear his pleasure. I laid a hand on his upper arm, feeling the soft cotton of the hospital gown. "I can't believe what you've gone and done to yourself."

His lips curved. "Guess what," he rasped.

"Hm."

"Can't wear socks. But my feet are the same color."

I laughed softly, holding back the tears. "If they look anything like your face, they're probably purple."

He swallowed carefully. "I like purple."

"Me, too, Derek."

It seemed no time at all before the nurse stuck her head in, telling us we had to go. "Come back next hour?" Derek asked me.

I nodded. "Sure."

Twice more that evening I saw Derek, crowding into the small space with Katherine and their parents. I promised him I would return the following night, which I did. Derek continued to improve amazingly, given his injuries, and he was talking better. By Thursday any lingering doubts about his pulling through were put to rest. Mr. King returned to work at the sawmill, and Katherine went back to the boutique. Miss Connie phoned from the hospital after 12:00 that day, saying she was exhausted and had to go home for a nap. Could I possibly visit with Derek that afternoon so he wouldn't be alone?

Good thing she called when she did, I thought. I'd just been sitting down to the computer to e-mail Greg, which would have tied up our phone line. "I'll see what I can do," I told her.

Grandma Delham was not home. Grandma Westerdahl sounded all too happy to come over so I could visit Derek. In fact, she sounded downright pleased.

At the hospital, the day nurse gave me no trouble, apparently expecting me. I saw Derek five times that afternoon, about ten minutes each visit. Twice, when the nurse was preoccupied, we stretched it to more like fifteen. Derek had gained some strength in his voice. We gently teased one another, and talked about school, which would start the following week. I became used to the intensive care room, with all its scary equipment. And I had to admit, it was a lot less crowded in there without the Kings around.

"Jackie," Derek said on our third visit, "when I get home, I'll be all bored to death. Long recovery. Will you come see me?"

"Of course, I'll come see you. I'll bring you your homework."

"Gee, thanks."

"You're welcome."

He attempted a mischievous look. "Would you come even if I didn't have homework?"

"Yes, Derek, I'll come."

On the fourth visit, I made another small choice, barely giving it conscious thought at the time. I reached over the side rail to lay my hand upon his.

He smiled. "How come you never did that before I near killed myself?"

I looked at our hands, almost startled. "I . . . don't know."

"Mm. Will you stop if I get better?"

What a question. Suddenly I realized the boundary I'd crossed. Alison's voice echoed in my head—*Watch what you do with Derek*. But how to back out now? I didn't want to bring him down at a time like this. "Just get better, okay?" I managed. "Then we'll . . . talk about it."

"Promise?"

"Promise."

I told myself I would not make the same mistake again, but I'd hardly reached Derek's bedside on our fifth visit when he raised his hand from the covers, silently demanding mine. What to do but take it? I hesitated, then laced our fingers, trying to convince myself it really didn't mean anything. "This is our last time today, you know," I told him. "I've got to get home and make supper for Daddy."

"You've got people wanting you everywhere, don't you," he said. I couldn't think of a response. Something told me he included Greg in that remark. For Derek's sake, I was glad Greg's ring once again lay beneath a blouse.

We soon fell back into our banter. But before I left, Derek turned serious. "Jackie." He paused. I knew he fought with himself over something he wanted to say. A sigh escaped him. "I'm kinda tired." He closed his eyes for a moment. "Will you come back tomorrow afternoon by yourself? We can talk. I'll tell Mama; she needs to rest anyway."

I nodded. "Okay, Derek, I'll find a way."

His fingers pressed against mine ever so slightly. "Don't ditch on me, now."

That night I lay on my bed, looking at Greg's picture, sliding his ring back and forth across its chain. Remembering the concert, his kisses, his promise that he wouldn't leave me. My promise that I wouldn't leave *him*. Then I thought of Derek—his long road back to recovery, his obvious pleasure each time he saw me, his fingers in mine. I thought of the boundary we'd crossed that day, and that *I'd* taken the first step. Why had I done that? What's more, I'd promised to visit him at home, seeing him day after day. While Greg traveled far away from me, performing and surrounded by fans.

Watch what you do with Derek.

My parents want anything that makes Derek happy right now. And that happens to be you.

As the voices of Alison and Katherine swirled in my head, I wondered what on earth I'd gotten myself into and what I would do.

chapter 45

The following day I wore yet another blouse. I had to.

"I want to see Derek!" Clarissa complained just before Grandma Delham arrived to take over baby-sitting. "Take me with you, Jackie."

"You can't go, Clarissa."

"Why?"

"Because."

"Because why?"

"Just because, that's all!"

My sister stomped off. Robert watched her go, his face placid. He seemed to be the only one in our family that week who remained on even keel. Sometimes I wished I could be like Robert.

"Tell Derek I miss him," my brother said. "Tell him I have a new computer game, and I can't wait to show it to him."

I tousled his hair. "Okay."

He regarded me silently, eyes falling to my blouse and the ring that he knew lay beneath it. Then he mushed his lips and focused out the window at nothing. Robert didn't miss much. I knew what he was thinking. I opened my mouth to try to explain. But I didn't know the explanation.

I sought shelter from my brother's eyes in my bedroom. I stood staring at Greg's picture, remembering the concert and being with him.

Alison, Millicent, Nicole, and other friends had phoned during the week, wanting to hear all about the concert. But I'd lost half my enthusiasm for describing it. Somehow it didn't seem right, talking about all the fun I'd had during the very same evening that one of Bradleyville's own had been so bruised and broken. Looking at Greg's face, I felt cheated that I couldn't enjoy those anticipated conversations with my friends. Then I thought of Derek and felt guilty for my selfishness.

In my daily e-mails to Greg I'd been giving him updates about Derek—no trying to hide the fact that I was visiting every day. Greg also called whenever he could. He understood about my seeing Derek. At least he claimed he did. It was good of me to be willing to spend so much time in a hospital, he'd said just the day before. Then came the call that Friday afternoon while I was in my bedroom, staring at his picture. Bad timing. I felt awkward—admitting to Greg that I was waiting for Grandma to come so I could go see Derek. I chided myself that I had nothing to hide. So why did I feel like I did?

"His parents are there too?" Greg asked casually—almost too casually. Had he heard a tone in my voice?

I hesitated. "Usually. But I don't think so this afternoon."

"It is just you and Derek?"

"Uh-huh." Lightness in my response, as if to say, *So what?*

A pause. "Yesterday they are there?"

A chill stole over me. How I wished I could hang up at that moment. "No, they couldn't be. But they'll be there tomorrow."

"Ah."

He said no more. He didn't have to. I could practically hear his worries tumbling through the phone line.

"I love you, Greg," I said. "Your ring's around my neck."

"I love *you*, Jackie. Don't forget."

Grandma Delham arrived. I told Greg I had to go, hoping he would hear the reluctance in my voice.

She eyed me as my hand lingered on the phone. "You all right?"

"Fine. I'm just . . . it's been a hard week."

"Yes. I know." She patted me on the shoulder, making me wonder just how much she perceived things. "Give Derek our love," she said. "Tell that boy the whole town is prayin' for him, so he best get better in a hurry."

"I will."

I drove to the hospital, forcing thoughts of Greg and Derek from my head. I had to admit I had another worry—Daddy and Katherine. Daddy had driven to the hospital in the evening for the past two nights to sit with Katherine and her parents, but they'd had no time alone. Which they badly needed, as far as I was concerned. In the back of my mind I couldn't help remembering what a good time Katherine had spent in Lexington, before and after the concert, and how she'd chattered like a jaybird about it on our way back to the hotel. I'd sensed tension between her and Daddy for the past few days. I wanted to believe it was due merely to Katherine's concern over Derek, but something told me it was more than that. Seemed to me she needed to get herself regrounded with Daddy and Bradleyville in general, and facing such tragedy in her family was hardly helpful. No time to work on any problems with Daddy in the midst of that.

No way around it—Derek had to get better soon. For the sake of a lot of people.

Miss Connie had already gone by the time I reached the hospital. I wandered into the waiting room with a few minutes' time before my first visit with Derek. An older man sat forward on the couch, head down and elbows on his knees, hands pressing the sides of his head. A woman—perhaps his daughter—sat next to him, arm around his shoulder. She and I nodded to one another. The sight of them unnerved me. They represented some recent tragedy, a new patient in the ICU. The three beds had all been occupied before. Where had the last one gone? To recovery—or not?

Thank you, Jesus, I prayed, *for saving Derek's life. Thank you for healing him.*

Even in his weakness, Derek greeted me with a smile so warm, so happy with my presence, that it gripped my heart. "Hey," he said. Right off the bat, he raised his hand to link with mine. I could not deny him so little. I slipped my fingers into his.

"Hi. How are you doin' today?"

His face flinched suddenly. He closed his eyes, air seeping from his mouth.

"Derek, what is it?"

"Don't know, just pain from the surgery. I didn't take the pill they offered me. I wanted to be wide awake for you."

"That's no good, Derek, you'd better take it. Want me to get the nurse?"

"No. I can always call her." He squeezed my fingers gently. "Tell me what's up in your house."

"Not much." I gave him Grandma's message, which made him smile.

"Tell me about you," he said. "How are you feelin' about the wedding now?"

Something about the questions—how easily they came. Derek seemed to have lost his reluctance to discuss hard topics. "They need each other," I told him. "Very much. Daddy would die if he lost her now. So would Robert and Clarissa. And she's been so good to me, Derek." I stopped short, realizing I shouldn't have said that. "Good to me" meant helping me with Greg. "Plus, she needs us," I rushed on. "I see that now. Maybe she needs us even more than we need her."

He considered my words, his expression twinged with pain. "Yeah. Think you're right."

We felt silent. The machines blipped, multicolored graphs filling the monitors with his vital statistics. I heard low voices on the other side of the curtain. Probably the man and his daughter, visiting someone. His wife?

"Could you get me a drink?" Derek asked. With my free hand I picked up the cup from the bedside table, positioning the straw into his lips. "Thanks."

Shoes squeaked across the floor. The nurse greeted the patient in the first compartment, behind me.

"Jackie." Derek moved our fingers slightly. "I gotta tell you somethin'. Been practicin' all mornin'. Better come out with it now before I lose my nerve."

A stillness crept over me. I knew what was coming and wished for some way, *any* way, to stop it. "Okay."

He licked his lips. "Here goes. I'm makin' you and myself two promises right now. One, I'm goin' to get out of this hospital and be totally better. Two ..." He hesitated. "Two, I'm goin' to win your heart."

I froze. In the next compartment, the nurse asked her patient in a loud voice how he was feeling. I heard a feeble answer. Metal clinked, something rattled. I gazed at Derek's battered face and held his hand, and could not find a single word to say.

"Surprised you, huh." Derek adjusted his shoulders slightly against the pillow and winced. "Here's the thing. Almost dyin' does somethin' to you, Jackie. Don't know, I may have gone on forever and not told you how I feel, but now I think, well, life's too short. Never know what's gonna happen." He smiled wearily. "Besides, I figure my lyin' in this bed all messed up and you feelin' sorry for me—I might as well milk it for all it's worth."

I couldn't help but smile. "Shame on you, Derek, takin' advantage like that."

The nurse's shoes squeaked away from compartment one. On the other side of us, the voices continued in low conversation. Someone backed into the curtain between the beds, and my eyes drifted to its settling folds, seeking diversion. I did not know how I could look at Derek for one moment longer.

"Jackie."

Reluctantly, I tugged my eyes back to his.

"I love you."

The words pierced right through me. I could not listen to them. Feeling Derek's fingers in mine, I thought of Greg, and the way he held me; I heard his voice say the very same words. Then I thought of Derek's vulnerability, and the trust he had in me, in himself, to say what he did. Of how much he needed me right now.

"I love you, too, Derek," I said lightly, as if I misread him, thinking he spoke only as a friend. Instantly, I regretted my tone. Derek didn't deserve that from me, not at all. Not after he'd bared his soul like that.

He moved his head. "No, don't. Don't say it till you mean it like I do."

"I'm—"

"Don't say anything, Jackie. Just . . . listen. *Please.*"

My throat fluttered. I pressed my teeth together.

Derek gave a long sigh. Swallowed. "I need another drink."

I fetched the cup for him. He drank slowly and long, as if sucking in courage. When he spoke again, it was almost as though he'd read my mind.

"Jackie, no matter what you feel right now for somebody else, I'm the one you should be with." I noticed he could not speak Greg's name. "You don't need someone who's travelin' all the time, someone whose life is a world apart from yours." He squeezed my hand with what little strength he possessed. "You need somebody more like you, who understands your life, and who can *be* with you. That someone is me."

His words ran out. He sighed again, relieved and, I think, proud of himself. Then he turned down the corners of his mouth, twitched his head as if to say, *So there.*

His face blurred.

"Aw, I didn't mean to make you cry. Uh, tell you what." He tried to tease. "I'll let you pick out my socks."

"Oh, Derek." I shook my head. "If I picked out your socks, they'd be like one orange and one green. That was definitely your most interesting pair."

"Huh?" His brow creased in surprise, whether feigned or real, I couldn't tell. "You mean I've been wearing the same colors for nothin'?"

"Guess so."

"Why?"

"Because . . . because mismatched socks were *you*, Derek."

He studied my face. "I thought you didn't like that me."

"Well, I . . ."

"See. You didn't."

"Okay, maybe not. But now I do."

He blinked his eyes in a *good grief* expression. "Girls. They make no sense at all."

Wasn't that the truth.

"How 'bout this," I ventured, trying to draw out the teasing. Thinking surely it was time to go. "Could we just talk about the sock thing later? I mean, with your cast and all, it's gonna be a while."

Our curtain pulled aside, metal loops slinking against metal. The nurse stuck her head in. "Time's up." She disappeared, leaving the curtain partly open. I tried to hide my relief.

"Come back next hour," Derek said, anxiety tingeing his voice, as if he was sure he'd frightened me away for good.

I wiped my eyes, my heart twisting for him. "I'll be here, Derek. Don't worry."

I couldn't bear to sit in the waiting room for the next forty-five minutes. Emotions rattled inside me, forcing me out the door of the hospital into the sun-baked parking lot. I trudged to Grandma's stifling hot car and drove the short distance to a park. There, I wandered aimlessly under the maple tree shade, watching kids play on the swings and trying to clear my head.

I wished I could go home. I wished I'd never promised Derek to see him all afternoon. I wished I could see Greg. How could I put a stop to this? Derek *needed* me.

Fortunately, the second time I visited Derek we talked about anything else and nothing at all. Looking back, I think both of us had said enough for a while. At 3:00, on my third visit, Derek was woozy from a pain pill, his words slow, long breaths in between. I stroked his forehead, avoiding his stitches, saying maybe he should just sleep.

"Mm, feels good," he mumbled. "Don't stop."

He slept through my fourth visit. I stood by his bed anyway, one hand resting lightly on his arm, staring at his face. Praying that God would heal him completely. Then maybe by some miracle, a new girl would come to Bradleyville, turn his head, steal his heart. I told myself that's what I wanted for him. But the oddest thing happened. At the mere thought, jealousy slunk through me like some predator in the night. Of course I denied the feeling. Why on earth would I be jealous?

Five o'clock. Our last visit of the day. Derek was surprisingly alert, the pain momentarily masked by the pill. "Oh, no," he said, "did I miss one?"

"Don't worry." I took his hand. "I was here."

"What did you do?"

I gave a little shrug. "Watch you."

"Oh." He winced. "Did I snore?"

"No," I laughed. "That would be funny."

"Yeah, real funny. How'd you like to be asleep and tied to this bed, and me watchin' *you* snore?"

"No, thanks."

"Well, then."

I shook my head at him. "Derek. Sometimes I don't know what to do with you."

He inhaled deeply. "Yeah, know what you mean."

For a moment, we simply looked at each other. He wiggled my hand. "Jackie."

"Hm?"

"Kiss me."

My smile wavered. Talk about surprising me. Fleetingly, I wondered just how bold this new Derek would be once he was well. What would I ever do then? I couldn't even handle him in a hospital bed. "Um. Right here? Right now?"

"Like I'm goin' anywhere."

"I know, Derek, but I mean it's just so . . . sudden."

"About as sudden as a snowmelt in Siberia."

I had no comeback for that.

He tugged my hand. "Come on."

I could feel Greg's ring hanging against my chest.

"If you don't, you're going to leave me lookin' like a total idiot for askin'. Would you want that?"

"I . . .'course not."

"Then come on."

Do it, some foreign voice in my head urged. *It won't matter.*

"Okay, how's this," he said. "I'll close my eyes and wait." His eyes shut. "See, I'm a sittin' duck."

It won't matter, Jackie. Just make him happy.

Thinking nothing more, nothing at all, I leaned over the railing and down, feeling Greg's ring swing out from my chest to lie against my blouse. Slowly, I lowered my face to Derek's. His mouth twitched as he felt my nearness. I touched my lips to his, thinking to break away quickly. Instead, inexplicably, I hung there, not breathing. Then I pressed against his lips. He responded, his mouth warm and soft, unshaved hairs tickling my skin. Derek's fingers tightened in mine as we kissed, his chin rising a fraction from the pillow as if he didn't want to let me go.

When I eased away, his eyes remained closed for a moment. Then a lazy smile spread across his face. He sighed with contentment. "That just made everything worth it. I swear I'd wreck my car all over again for that."

"Oh, please, Derek." I chuckled shakily. "One accident's enough."

He regarded me, eyes half closed, lips still curved in that silly smile. He gazed at me for so long I grew self-conscious. "I know," he said finally, tease in his voice.

"What do you know, Mr. Smart Aleck?"

"You liked it."

"Well . . . sure. I liked it just fine, Derek."

"No. You really *liked* it. Me lyin' here in this bed, all messed up, lookin' like a train wreck. And you liked it." For a moment, he basked in supreme satisfaction. Then he raised our linked fingers, pulling mine across his chest. "Do it again."

"Derek, come on."

"Don't make me come outta this bed. You know you want to."

I can't deny it—I did want to. Not just for Derek's sake, but for mine. Before I knew it, I was leaning down to kiss him again. Somehow it lasted longer than the first time. As I pulled away, I couldn't believe what was happening. What was I doing to Greg? How terrible I'd feel if he ever did this to me!

I can't remember what Derek and I said to each other after that. All I remember is that when I had to leave, he demanded a third kiss. *God, help*, I thought, wanting it and not wanting it. *I have to get out of here*. I simply did not know what to do. I kissed him again, briefly, my stomach feeling jumbled and quivery. I just wanted to run to the car and bawl.

"Derek." I ran shaking fingertips down the side of his face. "We can't be alone tomorrow, you know, it's Saturday. Your parents will be here. And on Monday, school starts." Was I glad about this—or not?

His brow knit with sudden anxiety. "You tryin' to tell me you're not comin' back?"

"No, Derek. It's just . . . of course I'll be here."

His eyes searched mine, trying to read answers I didn't begin to have. "Thank you for comin' today," he said finally. "Don't forget my promise. I mean what I said."

My chest clenched. I had to get out of there *right now*, before I broke down in front of him. "I won't. See you soon, Derek," I breathed, my voice catching. "Promise." I squeezed his hand, then fled.

I cried all the way home, Derek's and Greg's voices blending in my mind.

You need someone who can be with you; that somebody is me.

I am afraid you will find someone in Bradleyville, whose life is like yours.

I pulled Greg's ring out from beneath my blouse and pressed it as I drove, reminding myself of whom I loved. My head pounded, and my throat felt like it would never let loose.

Daddy was pulling into the garage from work just as I drove Grandma's car up to the curb. He got out and met me on the sidewalk. I didn't want to talk to him. I didn't want to talk to anybody.

"Honey?" He cradled my quavering jaw with his hand, fear in his face. "Is Derek okay?"

I nodded, shoulders pulled in, eyes on the ground.

Daddy studied me in silence. Then his hand fell away. He sighed deep and long, a sigh full of hurt and love for me. Slowly, he pulled me into a hug and rested his chin on top of my head. "It'll be all right, Jackie," he soothed. "It'll be all right."

chapter 46

I did not visit Derek that weekend. I simply couldn't. But my reasons were so convoluted that I could barely sort them out. Admittedly, guilt proved the overriding factor. I didn't want to talk to Derek in front of his family, especially Katherine. How could I face her in my duplicity, when I had once so judged her own? For surely she and everyone else would see the truth on my face. Then what would they expect me to do—give up Greg?

I was caught, pure and simple, and there would be no easy way out.

"I love you," I told Greg's picture again and again that weekend, tears in my eyes. "I'm so sorry. Somehow I'll fix this. Somehow I'll make it right."

But then I imagined visiting Derek and telling him we could only be friends. I knew the pain he would feel, and I could not bear it. He didn't deserve that, especially not in his feeble state. And there was one more reason—the selfish, inexcusable reason whose very existence caused me the most anguish. A part of me did not want to break off what we had started.

"You don't see Derek today?" Greg asked when he phoned Sunday afternoon.

"No," I replied lightly. "I don't need to see him so often anymore. I mean, at first we thought like he might not make it. But he's gettin' stronger now. Really amazingly fast. The doctors even say they'll probably move him out of intensive care in a day or two."

"Oh, that is good," Greg replied. "God answers my prayers." I could hear his relief that I would not be seeing Derek as much, and it only made me feel worse. He was trying to be so understanding of Derek's need for friends. If only he knew what I was feeling. I *couldn't* let him know. He didn't deserve that.

School started on Monday, and our family quickly readjusted itself to the familiar schedule. By the second day I again faced the unhappy task of helping Clarissa with her math. And studying my own homework, and making supper and doing laundry. I found myself looking forward to the day when Katherine would be around to help with the household tasks.

By Wednesday, I could not avoid Derek any longer. He was asking for me, Katherine told me at supper that night. She looked at me pointedly, and for the first time I saw expectation in her eyes. "He's in a regular room now," she reminded me. "No reason you can't see him any evening. If I know you're going, my parents and I'll stay home."

Her lack of subtlety dragged instant betrayal through my stomach. She was pushing me toward Derek! So much for her wanting me to be with Greg. I could only imagine that Derek's accident had laden Katherine with guilt over not helping him sooner. She'd chosen my desires over those of her own flesh and blood. Now, evidently, she had amends to make.

I flicked my gaze at Daddy. Disapproval tightened his mouth as he surveyed Katherine. A second realization stilled me in my chair. While Katherine was pressuring me for her brother's sake, Daddy clearly empathized with me. Perhaps he was remembering the complexity of his own teenage years. I glanced from him to Katherine. Were my own issues going to cause problems in their relationship?

"Okay, Katherine," I blurted, standing quickly to clear the table. I did not want to look into her eyes another moment. "I'll . . . go tomorrow."

"Good. I'll tell him you'll be there."

The decisiveness in her voice was unmistakable. No way to back out now.

I was surprised to see how much improvement six days had brought to Derek. The bruises on his face had waned, and he had more color in his cheeks. His new semiprivate room was so much quieter without all the blips and beeps of intensive care. The second bed in the room lay empty. My heart did an odd little flip when I saw that we would be completely alone—whether from relief or apprehension I couldn't tell. Maybe both.

The shaved side of Derek's head bristled with new growth. "Great haircut," I told him.

He made a face. "It itches."

We smiled tentatively at each other.

"Where you been?" he asked quietly. "I thought maybe I scared you away."

There went that tug again in my chest. I couldn't stand to think that my mere absence would cause him worry. "No, no," I assured him. "I've just been busy with school and everything."

Derek looked into my eyes and knew I was lying. He dropped his gaze to the sheet.

I moved closer to the bed and took his hand. He searched my face again, as if trying to see whether I'd done it out of sheer pity. I couldn't let him think that. "I've missed you," I ventured, squeezing his fingers.

He nodded. "Yeah, well. I stopped by your house a couple a times, but you were out."

I tried not to wince at the blame underlying his facetious words.

I pulled a chair up beside his bed, and we talked about school, the teachers, my classes. We avoided all discussion of what lay heaviest on our minds. I think at that point Derek knew he had to slow down, that he couldn't push me. And apparently he was prepared to wait me out. After all, he'd made me a promise.

I touched his lips lightly with mine as I left. I suppose because he'd been thoughtful enough not to ask me to. "Come again tomorrow night?" he pressed.

"I don't know. If Daddy and Katherine go out, I'll have to baby-sit."

"Ah-ha." He raised his eyebrows. "Guess I'll just have a little talk with my sister then."

This was beginning to sound like a conspiracy. I could easily guess where that conversation would lead. I'd be back at the hospital the following night, and Katherine and Daddy would stay home with the kids. Which was not what their own relationship needed. Not at all.

Daddy was paying bills at the kitchen table when I got back home. "Don't you need some time alone with Katherine tomorrow night?" I asked him. "If you want to take her out somewhere, I'll stay with the kids."

He laid down his checkbook, absently tapping a pen against it. "Is this about me and Katherine," he ventured, "or you and Derek?"

You and Derek. I winced at the sound of those words. "I don't know. Both."

He considered my answer. "Are you looking for an excuse not to visit Derek?"

"I'm . . . it just seems like you and Katherine aren't doin' so hot all of a sudden, and I thought—"

"Don't worry about me and Katherine. Do you *want* to visit Derek tomorrow?"

I rubbed my fingers over the back of a chair. "No. Yes." I closed my eyes. "I don't *know!*"

"Jackie," Daddy said after a moment, "don't let other people push you into something you don't want for yourself. Do you hear what I'm sayin'?"

I nodded, gratitude welling within me. All these weeks of Daddy's concern over me and Greg, and now he was taking my side.

Whatever "my side" meant.

As it turned out, Grandma Westerdahl insisted on baby-sitting Friday, leaving me no excuse not to visit Derek while Daddy met Katherine in Albertsville for supper. Daddy drove me to the hospital and dropped me off, saying he'd be back in a couple hours to see Derek for himself and pick me up. We talked little during the drive. I couldn't think of much to say.

Sometimes our assumptions can get the best of us. As I would later hear, instead of enjoying an intimate meal together as I'd assumed they would, Katherine and Daddy ended up arguing. Apparently in what little time she'd had to think of herself that week, Katherine had chosen to dwell upon the pleasant memories of our night in Lexington. The night that had reminded her how much she missed city life.

"Do you ever think, Bobby," she said over supper, "that you'd be willing to move from Bradleyville? I don't mean now, when I need to be close to Derek and my parents. But maybe in a year or two. I could work in much bigger retail stores in a place like Lexington, and you can surely find a job in another bank. And we wouldn't be too far away to visit Bradleyville often."

The question sank through Daddy's chest like stone. "You're asking me to leave my home?" Daddy replied, hurt in his voice. "Bradleyville's where I was raised, where my kids have been raised. I can't imagine livin' anywhere else."

"Even if that's what I wanted?" she pressed.

The conversation went downhill from there. Daddy insisted they could compromise on their differences in other ways. Hadn't he tried not to be the homebody, taking her out all he could? But "out" to Daddy meant a date in Albertsville, which hardly fit with Katherine's expectations over the long run. The more he implied Katherine should be content with small-town living, the more defensive she became. He said he loved her, but he wanted marriage on *his* terms. Shouldn't he be placing their relationship above his own desires?

Individual hurts can render grace as elusive as the wind. Feeling guilt over paying too little attention to the brother she'd nearly lost, Katherine, I think, was already struggling with a growing sense of unworthiness. In that frame of mind she easily inferred from Daddy's statements that she wasn't as important to him as she'd once thought.

While they argued their way through supper, I sat by Derek's bed, holding his hand and listening to him talk of his senior year, and how he hoped to return to school in a few months. How he wanted to escort me down the aisle in his sister's wedding. As he talked, my thoughts kept slipping to Greg's visit in December. What the sight of him and me together would do to Derek. I could not imagine how I would act if they ended up face-to-face. Suddenly I found myself almost dreading that visit. I sat there half-listening to Derek, his fingers in mine, awash in horror that I would feel even the slightest sense of dread about seeing Greg again.

That's when I realized just how deeply entangled I'd become.

chapter 47

*G*od *will forgive you but nature won't.*
I think of that line from Pastor Beekins' sermon as I remember the events of the following two weeks. For in those terrible two weeks I would make choices that would push me further into duplicity. Yes, I was caught in a hard situation, one that would progress from bad dream to nightmare. But I should have spoken honestly of my feelings, both to Greg and to Derek. God has forgiven me for my lack of honesty; I cling to that. Still, my choices spawned regrets that would pursue me to this day.

On the following Monday—Labor Day—Derek began to run a fever and have trouble breathing. I probably wouldn't have visited him so often that week had he not taken this turn for the worse. But when the complications of pneumonia set in, I worried and went in to see him daily. Grandma Delham took to coming over after school, staying with Clarissa and Robert while I used her car to drive to Albertsville. I would change shirts from whatever I'd worn to school to one of my three short-sleeved blouses so I could hide Greg's ring.

Often when I arrived at the hospital, Miss Connie would be there with Derek, but she'd always make an excuse to leave us alone. Derek's spirits were up and down, depending upon his physical strength at the moment. As he became sicker, he would insist that I touch him, kiss him, as though my affection were his lifeline. By that Friday I no longer needed to be asked. I pressed my mouth to his as soon as I arrived, lingering there, feeling the softness of his now familiar lips. And I thought, *I can't remember what kissing Greg feels like.*

Greg's seventeenth birthday was coming up on Saturday. Three times that week he called in the afternoon while I was at the hospital. Grandma Delham relayed his messages, and I e-mailed him back each time.

I'm SO sorry I've been gone so much, I wrote Friday night, explaining that Derek was weakening, and I felt compelled to visit. *I miss you, Greg. I miss you, and I miss hearing your voice. I love you.*

On Saturday I was determined to stay home in case Greg called. But Katherine phoned from the hospital in tears, saying Derek was worse, and even with his family around him, he was asking for me. Would I *please* come? And of course I did. Derek was barely awake when I arrived. All the same, he lifted his hand from the covers, seeking mine. I hesitated, then slipped my fingers into his in front of his parents and Katherine. Feeling like a skulking figure in the dark caught by a sudden searchlight. My eyes watered, and Greg's ring seemed to burn into my chest. How would any of them forgive me when I broke things off with Derek?

For surely, I reminded myself, that is what I would do.

The doctors were beginning to scratch their heads. Clearly, the antibiotics weren't working. We didn't doubt that they'd find a way to stabilize Derek once more, but this added illness was sapping his strength. I drove home from the hospital, praying for Derek and feeling more guilt than ever over Greg. Only to hear that I'd missed a fourth phone call. That news drove me to my bedroom in tears, exhausted and feeling torn in two. Not until supper did I realize that Daddy didn't seem all that happy himself. Katherine was noticeably absent. "She's still at the hospital," he explained. But I knew there was more to it than that.

Late that night I checked my e-mails, hoping Greg had written me after his concert. Nothing. Apprehension seeped through my chest. Surely he knew.

He called before church Sunday morning, which he'd never done. With his late nights, usually at that time he was still asleep. The moment he said my name I knew something was terribly wrong. "Greg, what is it?" I demanded, gripping the phone.

"Jackie." His voice caught. "I love you. I need you much right now."

"I love you too."

Silence, then a gasp of air. Greg was crying. "I make a bad mistake last night," he breathed.

My blood chilled. Immediately I thought of his brother's and my own daddy's "falls from grace." Of all the girls outside his hotel room door. No. Greg would never do that to me. "What did you do?" My words were a mere whisper.

"I . . . ." His voice shook. "It is hard for me since I saw you, Jackie. You sound far away when I talk to you, and many times you are not even home. I feel alone. I feel scared. You know I need your help to try to be a Christian in this business because it is hard. And I don't feel it any more." He drew in air raggedly. "Yesterday is my birthday. I think, she will forget. She is not thinking of me now. And you do forget, don't you?"

I squeezed my eyes shut, miserable to the core. He was right. In my worry over Derek, I'd completely forgotten.

"I know you do. And I feel bad. I do the concert, and then I am just mad. The guys have a party with lots of girls and beer. They tell me to forget you and just get drunk." His voice pitched higher as he cried. "I drink and drink until I don't care about anything. I do nothing with the girls, but everyone sees me drunk. Me! The one who tells them I do not get drunk because I serve God. Now what do they think of me? I have no right to tell them about being a Christian anymore, Jackie. The first time things go bad, I fall down!"

He let out a sob, and my heart thought it would break. I leaned my forehead against my bedroom wall and cried along with him, both in relief and empathy. And then thought how selfish it was for me to feel relief that he'd done nothing with a girl, after the way I'd been with Derek.

"Oh, Greg, I'm so sorry. I'm sorry I haven't been there for you. I feel terrible! Everything will be all right. Everybody makes mistakes once in a while, even you. That doesn't mean you're no longer who you are."

"It is too hard to be a Christian in this business, Jackie. I just can't do it right. Maybe I don't sing anymore."

Neither of us could speak for a moment. I knew how deep Greg's remorse must be to cause him to say such a thing.

"Greg, listen to me. I love you. You say you fell down, well, you can get back up. Tell the guys you're sorry, that you made a mistake. Maybe it will help, who knows? Maybe they needed to see you're not perfect."

We fell silent again.

"Jackie?" Greg ventured after a moment.

"I'm here."

"Do you . . ." He hesitated. "Do you still love me, really? Always now you are with Derek. I wonder—"

"Greg, stop it." I could not bear to hear the words spoken aloud, not now, not ever. "I love you, understand? You. And I promise you"— my desperate denial caught in my throat—"you have *nothing* to worry about."

The lie sat like acid upon my tongue. My fingers cramped from gripping the phone. I couldn't believe what I had just done.

We could only talk for a few more minutes. I continued trying to soothe Greg, saying again and again that I loved him, that I believed in him. That he would get through this. And how sorry I was that I'd forgotten his birthday.

I can tell you this: his remorse was no greater than mine. There he was, worrying about his Christian witness. And there I stood, betraying him. Now I'd even lied to him. His mistake was minuscule next to all of mine.

As I reluctantly hung up the phone to dress for church, his voice echoed in my head. *I do nothing with the girls.* Even with his defenses down from alcohol, Greg had upheld his pledge to me. *My heart separates me from that*, he'd said after the concert. *My heart is with you.* If he ever found out what I had done, where I had let my heart go, it would kill him.

I promised myself that morning that he never would.

chapter 48

Sunday, Monday, Tuesday. Derek did not improve. His lungs were filling with fluid, and new antibiotics didn't help. Everyone was on edge. Daddy and Katherine had little time to work on their issues. Greg really needed me as he tried to redeem himself in front of his friends, and I worked to be as attentive through e-mails and the phone as I could. He deserved no less. At the same time, the sicker Derek became, the more obliged I felt to visit. I would drive to the hospital, feeling the pull of Greg, determining not to touch Derek in a way that would betray him. Then I would look into Derek's eyes and see the love for me there. And I knew I couldn't deny him whatever he asked. *When he's better I'll straighten this out*, I kept telling myself. While deep within, I knew I could not imagine that day—for his sake or mine.

I do not know how I stood myself. Even now, these memories wrench me.

On Wednesday Derek moved back into intensive care. Because of the move, I did not see him that day. Katherine stopped by our house on her way home from the hospital that night. She hugged Daddy, breaking into exhausted tears. "I can't stand to think of all the years I was away. How I left him when he was just a kid. Now look at him. He *has* to get better!"

Clarissa cried just from watching Katherine. I comforted my sister, fleetingly thinking it was good to see how much Katherine needed Daddy.

Thursday evening I joined Derek's family for the ten-minute visits every hour. Derek looked so weak and pale, barely able to speak. Dr. Namon stopped by on rounds and promised us they were doing everything they could for him. He expected that Derek would strengthen once more. But by Friday we saw no improvement.

Early Saturday morning, the doctor called the Kings with further bad news. Derek's body had gone into shock. It was a secondary complication—a delayed reaction to all that his system had endured. His kidneys were failing, and they would have to start dialysis. The Kings rushed to the hospital, Katherine taking the day off work. She asked Daddy to come sit with them. I stayed home with Clarissa and Robert, hoping to go in later. The whole town was praying, phone calls going out by the dozens on the Methodist and Baptist churches' prayer chains.

The morning dragged on. I felt miserable for Derek and miserable for me. The sicker he became, the more I knew he would reach out for me. How could I not be there for him in the coming weeks, months?

Greg called on his cell phone around noon. They'd just boarded the bus. I couldn't stay on the phone long in case someone tried to call from the hospital. I'd thought my tears were spent, but hearing his voice made me weepy all over again. "Are things goin' okay?" I asked. "You have more chances to talk to the guys?"

"Yes. You know I pray a lot this week, Jackie. And you are so helpful to me. I don't know what I do without you."

At his words, a sob wrenched deep in my gut. I could not go on like this. "I miss you so much! I need you right now, and you need me, and I *hate* being apart!"

He soothed me, asking if anything in particular had happened. "You do not sound good," he said.

I gazed into the family room. Robert sat on the couch, watching me. I turned away. "It's Derek." My guilt forced the name into little more than a whisper. "We got news today that he's really bad. Would you . . . pray for him, okay?"

"I will." Greg's voice sounded tight, heavy. "I am praying now. I wish I could be with you. Help you."

"Oh, Greg, me too."

He paused. "You still have my ring around your neck?"

"Of course," I replied, stung. "Why wouldn't I?"

"I don't know. I'm silly to ask that. I love you."

I fingered his ring, lying on top of my knit shirt. "I love you, too."

Daddy called some time after 1:00, his voice like lead. At his mere greeting, I sank into a chair at the kitchen table, limbs wooden. I'd heard the tone before—when Mama's health had skidded so badly at the last. Of course that had been different. We all knew Derek would live.

"I have some very bad news," Daddy told me quietly. "The doctors say Derek now has somethin' called ARDS. Acute respiratory distress syndrome. His lungs are failing. They've put him on a respirator. Jackie, there's . . . there's nothing else they can do."

"What do you mean there's nothing they can do!" I cried. "What more does he need? I mean, they'll just help him breathe until he gets stronger, right?"

"It's not like that, Jackie." Pain throbbed in Daddy's words. "Derek's body is exhausted. It's been through too much. And it's just . . . shutting down."

I still could not grasp it. "But he's goin' to be okay, right? He *will* pull out of it."

Daddy breathed into the phone. "Honey. He's dyin'."

"*No!*" The stunning words propelled me out of the chair, across the kitchen. I careened into the counter and leaned against it, pushing the heel of my hand into the tile. "No, he's not, Daddy, no, he is not! We're goin' to pray. God's goin' to bring him through, he *will!*" Air gusted from my mouth. Daddy said nothing. Anger at his silence fisted in my gut. He was supposed to tell me I was *right*. "Is he conscious?" I demanded.

"Barely."

I burst into sobs, loud and ugly and deep. Crying for Derek, crying for me. For his family and for us. *No, God, he can't die, he can't die, he can't die!*

"Jackie," Daddy whispered, his voice snagging, "I'm so sorry."

"I have to come in there, Daddy," I wailed. "I have to see him!"

"I don't know if you can see him now, with all that's happening. Jessie and Lee are here. And even the Kings—"

"I *have* to see him!"

Derek just needed to hear my voice, I screamed to myself. If he saw me, maybe he would find the strength within him to get better, keep his promises to me.

"I'm gonna call Grandma," I declared. "So I can come."

"No, I don't want you drivin' when you're so upset."

"I *have* to come, Daddy!"

"Then let her bring you. Call Grandma Westerdahl to come over. And if she can't, just let Robert stay with Clarissa for a while; they'll be all right."

Grandma Westerdahl came to stay with the kids while Grandma Delham drove me into Albertsville. I scarcely remember the ride to the hospital. Not until we had parked, and Grandma Delham and I were hurrying inside, did I realize what I had done. Greg's ring hung over my knit top, which was too form-fitting to hide it underneath. "Oh!" I gasped, sliding to a stop. Looking down at the ring, thinking what should I do. I grasped the ring, head swimming. Then before I could change my mind, I did what I'd sworn to Greg—and to myself—that I'd never do. I unclasped the chain and slid it from my neck.

"Here." I held it out to Grandma. "I forgot my purse. Would you keep this?"

My wonderful grandma never said a word. She just took the ring and chain, and dropped them into her purse. As if she hadn't just dropped my heart in with it.

Around the corner of the waiting room, I stopped to breathe, rearrange my face. Derek's family was hurting worse than I. They needed my support.

I did not expect the pall in the room. I've known it intimately—that beast that greedily suspends itself over those awaiting a loved one's death. Looking to devour. Sucking up oxygen, stretching faces with disbelief. Somehow in its terrifying presence, hope stubbornly shines, as it did within me. But the beast pulses, making hands rub foreheads, eyes stare at the floor. I knew every feeling and action, every glimmering, wretched one. I'd lived through them once, and I was not going to do it again.

I *knew* Derek would pull through.

Jason King bent forward on the couch, elbows on his knees, his face haggard. Miss Connie spoke softly to Miss Jessie. Derek's Uncle Lee stood like a giant against the wall, muscular arms folded, eyes closed. Daddy sat with Katherine. Without even thinking, I flew to her. She slid her arms around me, shuddering a cry. We held each other, rocking. "He's gonna be okay," I whispered. "He *will.*"

Dr. Namon entered, looking somber, small. Katherine pulled away, back arched, waiting. "He's losing consciousness," the doctor told us quietly. "If you want to talk to him, you should go in now. You can all go, a few at a time."

We sat like statues, trying to absorb the words.

No, I told myself. *No, no, no.*

Mr. King helped Miss Connie to her feet. "Let's go, hon." Katherine rose, too. I clutched Daddy's hand as she and her parents shuffled out the door. Grandma paced the room, praying. Lee walked over to hug Miss Jessie.

The minutes crept by. I focused on the ridiculously bright yellow pillow on the chair across from me, reliving moments with Derek. The day I'd first seen him without his glasses. Laughing with him at the Fourth of July parade. Kissing him. He *could* not die. Because suddenly I couldn't imagine life without him. Daddy said nothing, throat clicking each time he swallowed. Grandma paced. Finally, Katherine reappeared, her parents behind her. Tears tracked down Miss Connie's cheeks. She sank onto the couch, Mr. King beside her. No one said a word. Miss Jessie and Lee sidled out to see Derek next. Then Katherine went again, Daddy at her side, elbow under her arm. When they returned, her face was pale.

"Come." She beckoned me.

At that moment, the truth hit me in one, giant wave, and the hope to which I had clung churned to froth. Somehow I pushed to my feet and followed Katherine into the ICU. The nurse caught my eye, her face etched in sadness, then looked away.

In Derek's compartment, a respirator whooshed, a gut-churning sound added to all the equipment bleeps. Its tube disappeared into Derek's mouth, his lips forced open around it. He did not move, his eyes closed.

"Go on." Katherine pushed me forward. "He's drugged, but he's still awake."

I shot her a look of abject fear, then eased to the bed. "Derek." I took his hand. "It's Jackie. Can you hear me?"

His fingers flinched in mine. His eyes did not open. I drew a ragged breath, looking over my shoulder for Katherine's approval to continue. She was gone. Stupidly, I stared at the spot where she'd stood. She'd purposely left us alone.

I leaned over the bed rail and placed my mouth close to Derek's ear. I told him that we were all counting on him to get better. That I could not bear to think of going to school the entire year without him. That I was mad at him, and who did he think he was, anyway? Telling me he loved me, giving me wonderful kisses, only to go and get so sick? He was supposed to be getting *well*. He'd made me two promises, did he remember? I certainly did. *Both* of them.

His hand twitched. I saw the smallest movement in one corner of his mouth.

"*Please*, Derek." My voice cracked. "*Please* get strong. Don't do this. Don't go! You can make it, I *know* you can."

The respirator whooshed, machines beeping. My eyes were out of tears.

"Derek, listen. I love you. Me, Jackie. Just get better, okay? Do you hear me? I *love* you. Just . . . get . . . *better*."

"Uh," he said in his throat. "Uuuh."

I eased away to gaze at him—his colorless cheeks, the cracking lips, stitches across his forehead. Then, carefully, I lowered my mouth to kiss the corner of his lips. When I pulled back, his eyes fluttered open for a brief moment. He tried to smile. I kissed him again, fresh tears filling my eyes. One landed on his nose, and I breathed a quivery laugh as I brushed it away.

The nurse appeared. "You should go now," she said gently. "In case others want to come in again."

I can't.

Bracing myself, I turned once more to Derek. "They're makin' me go, Derek. Otherwise I wouldn't. Get better now, okay? And I'll see you soon. Remember . . ." My voice caught. "Remember what you promised."

I squeezed his hand hard, not wanting to let go. Memorizing the feel of it. Pressed a palm against the side of his face, reveling in its warmth.

Then I left him.

Nothing to do but wait. I slumped with Daddy and Grandma and Derek's family in the small room. Daddy held Katherine, his voice low and soothing when he spoke. Twice more, Derek's parents went in to see him, though he was no longer conscious. Katherine could not rise from the couch.

He died at 5:46 P.M.

chapter 49

That night, after I'd comforted Katherine and Clarissa and Robert and Daddy, and helped put my tearful brother and sister to bed, I fled, finally, to my room, where I cried and cried, and begged God for forgiveness. Greg's ring hung once again around my neck.

I cannot say which emotion was stronger—my grief or my self-loathing. They tumbled and burned within me like molten rock, until I thought they would crush me.

With the shrieking finality of a loved one's death, elusive meanings and desires inevitably surface. Only now, when I would never see Derek again, did I realize how much he meant to me. I wanted so much to kiss him again, feel his hand in mine. To just see his face. Derek *had* kept one of his promises to me, I realized. He had won a part of my heart.

Don't think I cried only for my own grief. There is enough reason to judge me without that. I was all too familiar with the pain of loss within a family. I grieved also for Katherine and Miss Connie and Mr. King. I prayed that God would strengthen them, somehow bear them through the coming horrible days.

Throughout that searing night, I dwelt purposely upon my grief. How different from my reaction to Mama's death, when I'd tried to drown my sorrow in a sea of busyness. But now my sadness would redeem me, for it was *right* to feel. It was understandable. Expected. It was humane. Derek had loved me wholeheartedly. He deserved my grief.

But underneath the sorrow, deep within the dark recesses of me, a little voice spoke. One utterance, and it echoed through me as a fallen boulder in a canyon. Even now, remembering the first time I heard it, I cringe. I still cannot help but harbor guilt over its insidious words. The truth is this. Even though I had begun to love Derek, I loved Greg far more. My duplicity could not have remained hidden forever. At some point I would have been forced to take the dreaded step—in front of Derek's family—and make my choice. How they would have judged me for it. Because my choice would have been for Greg.

And the little voice whispered, "Now you won't have to make it."

I tried to tell myself that I thought only of Derek. That now he wouldn't have to be hurt. How flimsy, those excuses. Derek deserved to be *alive*. He could have graduated from high school, gone to college, met someone new and fallen in love. Deeper love than he'd ever felt for me. Hadn't Daddy loved Mama more than life itself after he'd lost Celia? So much that thoughts of his past devastation had been long forgotten?

No. That little voice spoke only for me. Selfish, dishonest, cowardly me.

And I could not bear to listen.

And I could not shut it out.

chapter 50

Bradleyville suspended school for two days. Monday the viewing for Derek would be held at the Albertsville Funeral Home. The funeral was scheduled for Tuesday afternoon.

Sunday's service at our church felt like a funeral in itself. My eyes were swollen and lined, my face puffy. Not that I possessed the energy to care. Knowing how Derek's family grieved for him, I did not want to face them, especially Katherine. Surely they saw into my soul, read the horrifying words of that little voice etched upon it.

Pastor Beekins didn't preach. Instead we gathered as a body of believers to pray that God in his mercy would see the Kings through the tragedy. Katherine clung to Daddy as if she could barely stand, remorse over the lost years with her brother carved into her face. Even Derek's parents seemed stronger than she. Everyone cried. At the end of the service, Miss Jessie hugged me tightly, commenting with a shaky smile that if the church had a yearly tissue budget, we'd have gone through it that day.

Daddy went straight from church to the Kings' house with Katherine. I took Clarissa and Robert home, both red-eyed and worn. Seeing my stoic brother cry had torn me in new ways. As soon as she could, Clarissa went out to play with Della, needing to reconnect with childhood. Robert sat halfheartedly at the computer.

Greg called that afternoon, and we talked a long time. Hearing his voice took my own away. "Jackie, I wish I was there for you right now," he soothed again and again. "I love you so much. I'm so sorry."

I clutched his ring until my fingers cramped. The worst part was that he would never be able to comfort the most devastated pieces of me—the pieces that needed him most. "I love you, too, Greg," I breathed. "I love you, too."

After his call I lay upon my bed, staring at his picture, utterly spent. For once my radio was silent. I envisioned the events of the next two days and wondered how our family would survive them. We'd not attended a funeral since Mama's, and instinctively I knew it would bring back all the grief of her death as well. How would Daddy endure it—reliving Mama's funeral while comforting Katherine? I hurt for Daddy almost more than I hurt for the Kings.

From sheer exhaustion, I fell asleep. I awoke with a start an hour later, an implacable knowledge filling my head. There was something I must do for Derek. For me. Compelled to my feet, I shuffled out to tell Robert that I was going to the Kings' house, then I needed to drive to Albertsville. Would he please take care of Clarissa?

Many had gathered at Derek's house, bringing food. It reminded me of the gathering at our own not two years before. I made the rounds, hugging Derek's mama and daddy, unable to look them in the eye. I gave Katherine a perfunctory hug and could have sworn I sensed a chill between us. I knew I had to keep her at an emotional distance. She knew my heart too well.

As soon as possible, I edged down the hall, pretending to go to the bathroom, and slipped into Derek's room.

Memories of Derek instantly pounded me. He'd stood right there the day I first saw him without his glasses. I'd sat there as he scanned a photo of me to send to Greg. I leaned against his dresser, waves of sadness sifting me like sand. After some time, I pulled open his top drawer, staring with hollowed intimacy at its contents. With a deep breath, I reached in to search for the reason I'd come. One orange sock and one green. I flattened and hid them underneath the waistband of my denim skirt, said my goodbyes to Derek's parents, and escaped to the car.

At the Albertsville Funeral Home, I sought the director, closing my mind to the unknown mourners who'd gathered for the viewing of their own. I could not let their grief seep into mine. "I need to give you something for Derek King," I told him. He graciously ushered me into his office.

From my purse, I pulled out the socks. "Please. When you dress Derek, would you use these?"

He looked from the socks to me, smoothing all reaction from his expression. Funeral directors are good at that. "Derek's mother has already given me the clothes she would like to use." He paused. "Are you part of the family?"

"I . . . not really."

The man shook his head. "I'm sorry. But I always comply with the family's—"

"Please." Tears sprang to my eyes. "They won't know. Who will ever see? No one else ever needs to know, but I *need* to do this for Derek!"

He hesitated, then raised a reluctant hand for the socks. Before he could change his mind, I shoved them into his palm. "Please tell me you'll do it."

His gaze fell again to the ugly, mismatched colors. "I need to know who you are."

"Jackie Delham."

He repeated the name. "A friend of Derek's?"

I hugged my arms to my chest, searching for an answer intimate enough to give this perfect stranger. He studied the tears in my eyes.

"We . . . he loved me."

The man's eyelids flickered, and in that tiny movement I saw his empathy over the death of a boy he had not known, and all that could have been. His hand lowered.

"Thank you," I whispered.

He nodded.

⁂

Greg and LuvRush sent a flower arrangement to the funeral home. The largest one around Derek's casket.

Two things got me through the next few days: prayer, and focusing on my secret, symbolic gift to Derek. When the guilt rose as I laid my palm against his cold, hard skin, I thought of the socks. When we stood at the grave site, Katherine sobbing into Daddy's chest, his own eyes filled with pain, I remembered the socks. I said a final goodbye to Derek as the *chink chink* of metal gear lowered him into the earth, and I pictured the socks. What a hit they would be in heaven. How the angels would grin.

No theology or logic in that, I know. But at funerals, you do what you can to survive.

chapter 51

Raleigh, Charlotte, Charleston. Jacksonville, Orlando, Tampa. LuvRush continued their tour through the south, then began looping back toward the west as the Indian summer of September gave way to the chill of fall. Greg was busier than ever, studying in earnest on the bus and in hotel rooms now that his own "school" was back in session. "Hung Up on You" would stay number one on the charts throughout September. When it fell to number five, "All Is Enough" took its place at the top. Every concert proved a sellout.

Greg, now aware of his frailties, spent even more time reading his Bible and praying. "I have to," he told me. "I am so weak without that."

He remained loyal to me and loving, comforting me over the loss of "my friend" Derek. In my sorrow I needed to hear Greg's voice daily. I ached to see him. Yet I wept with the knowledge of the profound change between us. I had secrets now that I could never share. A part of myself that forever would remain locked away from him. I know he sensed this. Sometimes when Greg and I talked on the phone, the questions hovered almost tangibly between us. But never again did he voice them. I think he was afraid to hear the answers.

In those days I thought often of Pastor Beekins' sermon. That God could work through the mistakes of our past for his own glory. And I prayed that somehow, some way, God would do that for me.

Derek's parents held up amazingly well in their mourning. At least it appeared so from the outside. But then, what else can you do? Life goes on, even when your insides feel like they're wasting away. I prayed for them every day. I *knew* what pain they endured.

Katherine struggled terribly under the weight of her grief and remorse. Emotionally she flailed herself for her perceived failings with Derek. Amidst her own pain, the distance between us grew. Guilt bends one's perceptions as surely as water bends light. I thought in her disgust of me that *she* had drawn away. Now I know how wrong I was. Now I see that when she needed me most, I refused to help.

She and Daddy continued to plan their wedding, set for Saturday, December 12. But Katherine's enthusiasm had gone. At first we merely thought the obvious—Katherine's pain over her brother's death overshadowed her joy. Then I really began to worry. All the stress made her and Daddy short-tempered with one another, particularly Katherine, the smallest of things tripping irritation across her brow. I'd catch Daddy gazing at nothing, anxiety lining his face. Sometimes he had little appetite for supper. I fussed at him like a mother hen, telling him he hardly needed to lose weight. Clarissa took to pushing around the vegetables on her plate that she didn't like.

"Eat 'em," Daddy commanded her.

"Well, you're not eatin' yours."

"This is not a suggestion. Eat 'em."

One month after Derek's death, Katherine and Daddy had a major argument. Thank goodness it was Sunday afternoon, with both Robert and Clarissa at friends' houses, because I certainly heard an earful. I balanced on the edge of my bed, biting my lip, the door cracked open, listening.

"All I want to do is go to Lexington for overnight, Bobby. I could get Saturday off work. You and I need to get away."

"Like I told you, I don't think we should go anywhere overnight," Daddy said. "Separate hotel rooms or not, it just wouldn't look right to the folks here."

"Who cares what the 'folks' think?" A pause. "Fine, then, maybe we could at least take a drive for the day. Go *somewhere.*"

"Katherine, please. We've talked about this enough already. I just don't want to go anywhere next weekend. Let's do it later in the month."

Next weekend? I thought. *She picked a fine time.*

"I need to go soon. I'm stifling here! Nothing but grief and pain in my parents' house. Everywhere I go, people are asking how we're holding up. I'm tired of the questions."

"I know." Daddy's voice softened. "I know how hard it is, believe me."

"Then let's go."

Daddy sighed loudly. Then said something I could not understand. I eased back my door and crept out to hover in the hallway.

"I don't—" Something rattled, like newspaper under a hand. "Why don't you want to just have fun for a day?" Katherine demanded.

"I have fun every day, with you around."

"Oh, stop it. Stop trying to play Mr. Perfect."

"I thought I was."

"Bobby, I'm serious, I'm going to walk out the door in a minute."

"Okay, okay, I'm sorry."

A pause. "Will you take me next weekend?"

"Katherine." Now my daddy sounded peeved. "I thought I just said let's do it another day."

"Why?"

"Katherine. It's not a good weekend." Daddy emphasized each word. Silence.

"I just don't understand you sometimes," she declared. "I know you don't like big cities, but Lexington is hardly L.A. I haven't been to Lex since the concert."

"Well, maybe you should go to another one." Anger edged Daddy's voice.

"Maybe I should." The newspaper rattled again, followed by footfalls pacing the carpet.

Daddy said nothing. I pictured his face, lips pressed and eyes darkening. Katherine most likely glared back at him.

"Maybe I should go to Lex all by myself for overnight. *And* see a concert and a movie, then go shopping and out to dinner. Oh, *supper*, as they say in Bradleyville," Katherine added with sarcasm. "Excuse me."

"Katherine. Stop it."

"I don't want to stop it." Her voice tightened. "I want to *do* something, go somewhere. I don't understand why it's such a big deal, just getting you out of Bradleyville!"

"How old did you say you were?" Daddy shot back. "You're actin' like a whiney teenager."

Katherine sucked in air. "Well, that's just fine, Bobby. This teenager's out of here."

I heard her stomp around the couch. I jumped back toward my bedroom, ready to slip inside.

"No, you're not," Daddy commanded. "You're not leavin' this house mad."

"I'll leave this house any way I want to!"

"Katherine!" The couch squeaked.

"Let go of me!" Clothes rustled.

"Will you *stop* it?" Daddy tried to keep his voice down. "Will you *listen* to me?"

"I'm tired of listening to you! All you're thinking about is yourself."

"I don't think that's quite fair," Daddy retorted. "I think I've done an awful lot of thinking about *you* in the last month."

"And well you should. It hasn't exactly been a great month for me." Katherine sounded near tears.

"I *know* that." Daddy lowered his voice. "And the next weekend isn't a great weekend for me. I need to stay here with the kids."

"Why?"

I closed my eyes.

"Do I really have to remind you, Katherine?"

No answer.

"Saturday's the twenty-fourth. The day Melissa died."

Silence.

"Oh, Bobby, I'm sorry. I . . . had forgotten."

"Obviously."

"But I . . . maybe that's all the more reason to go. To get away, together."

"I just don't think so," Daddy said quietly.

"You'd be in good company."

"I know. But," he added reluctantly, "I'm thinkin' of the kids. They just might need me."

"Of course. The kids." There was no mistaking the hurt in Katherine's voice. "And you too. Remembering how things were. How they should be now. Why should you want to be with *me?*"

"Katherine—"

"What else would anyone expect? Of any of you."

No response. I imagine Daddy didn't know what to say.

"Well." Her tone mixed defensiveness and bitter disappointment. "I picked a bad day, no way around it. We'll just . . . do it another time. Maybe next month. Maybe next year."

Her footfalls hit the wood floor leading into the kitchen. I stepped into my room, listening through the cracked open door.

"Katherine." Daddy sounded miserable. "Where are you goin'?"

"Home."

"Please don't."

I heard her keys slide off the kitchen counter. "I'm not mad anymore. See?"

"I know you're not, that's just—"

"In fact I'm . . . nothing."

Before I knew it, she'd hit the hallway, mumbling, "I'm nothing at all." Daddy's footsteps followed behind her, then stopped. I moved to shut the door but too late. Katherine saw me down the short corridor. She slowed momentarily, then tossed a look over her shoulder at Daddy. Pulling in a deep breath, she headed for the front door. I heard it open. Close.

Not another sound from Daddy.

Concerned for him, I crept toward the entryway hall. He stood staring at the door, face pinched. When he saw me, he turned away.

I bristled in delayed reaction. "What's *wrong* with her?"

Daddy shuffled back to sigh onto the couch. I pursued him, indignation rising. "Really, Daddy, doesn't she—"

"Hush, Jackie."

"But—"

"*Hush.*" He clasped his arms wearily, staring at the coffee table. "You shouldn't have been listenin'. Again."

"I didn't have to try very hard."

He gave a little snort. "Guess not."

I eased down next to him. "Is she goin' to be okay?"

"She'll get over it."

"But, I mean, is she goin' to be *okay?*"

He pushed his tongue under his upper lip. "She'll be fine."

Of course, she would. It had only been a month since Derek's death. Katherine was still mourning. For heaven's sake, what were they doing fighting when they needed each other more than ever? They obviously were both on edge and worn. Weren't we all. "Yeah," I whispered. "She will."

As I rose from the couch, Daddy flicked on the television with the remote and stared sightlessly at the screen.

Greg phoned me that night, and we talked for over an hour. The group had a couple days between concerts and were resting in a hotel in Little Rock, Arkansas.

"This is where Celia lives all the years she and my brother are apart," he said. "You can believe it? Seventeen *years.* What a waste."

"I could never be apart from you that long," I breathed.

"I could not either."

I spilled out my concerns over Daddy and Katherine's argument. Greg soothed my worries, reminding me what a tough time Katherine had gone through. Was still going through.

"You try to help her?" he asked. "She is hurt over that fight. She thinks she is not loved like your mamma was. You have to show her she is needed."

I hesitated. "I know, but she's . . . we're not as close as we used to be."

"Why? She needs you now especially."

"She acts like she doesn't want to be around me. And frankly, she's been so irritable that I haven't wanted to be around her."

"You have to give her extra patience. She is very sad over her brother."

"I *know* that, Greg," I replied testily. "I know she's hurting. We're all hurting. But she's just being so unreasonable."

Greg sighed. "I need to be with you, help you through this. A little over two months, and you and I can be together."

For one week. A blessed week, ending just one day before Daddy's wedding. But after that how long would we have to wait? How many weeks, how many months?

"Jackie?"

"I'm here. I can't wait to see you, Greg. I just . . . I hate bein' without you. And once you leave, then how long do we have to wait till the next time?"

With the success of the LuvRush tour, the group's manager and record producer had told them he wanted the group to work with fury on cutting their next CD. They all believed it would be a major hit. The final songs had to be chosen. The group had to practice them, then record. Months of work, all done in Los Angeles.

"I will be in Greece not long," Greg told me. "Then we go to L.A. I will visit you all I can, just even for a long weekend. That will be so good for us. Poor Mamma, though, she has to leave Greece so soon. She does not want to do it."

The group had been talking for the past few weeks about a move to L.A. They knew they couldn't stay in Greece much longer, at least not year-round. As much as they loved their home, it was too far removed from everything they needed to do. L.A. was certainly closer to Bradleyville than Greece, I had to admit. Still, it seemed a world away.

Greg's parents were not thrilled with the idea of his moving. He would not be eighteen for another year. Still, what to do? Break up the group now, just when they were rising to fame? Last week, his parents had told him what they had decided. Until he turned eighteen, during the months the group lived in L.A., Greg's mamma would stay with him.

"You hear, Jackie? We will not be apart for months anymore. It will not be more than . . ." He thought a minute. "Two months. How is that? Not more than two months apart. I promise."

I slid his ring on my chain. "You really promise that?"

"I do."

"Okay. Two months, Greg. We can do that. Two months at a time is worth it—for you."

chapter 52

Daddy's face looked thinner. For good reason—he'd lost eight pounds. Folks at church started to notice. "You losin' weight?" Pastor Beekins teased. "Maybe you're plannin' ahead to all that fine cookin' Katherine's goin' to do for you."

Months later I would ask Daddy—When did you know? When did you allow yourself to admit that something was really wrong?

It was the weekend before Thanksgiving, he would reply. When Katherine announced that the owner of GreatWear Boutique was moving to Lexington to open a larger shop and wondered if Katherine could come for three to four days every month to help her run it.

"Sylvia's moving into her two-bedroom apartment next week," Katherine said. "The Gardens, right near Turfland Mall. I can just stay with her when I go."

When I go. It wasn't a question. No discussion about whether or not this would be a good choice month after month, once she shared the responsibilities of a house and three children. Just—when I go.

Wedding plans were fully laid. The tuxes were chosen; Miss Jessie had made the dresses, including one for herself. Clarissa would look darling in hers as a "mature" flower girl, as Miss Jessie put it. I liked the term. Any reason for "mature" to be tacked onto my sister's name sounded good to me. Perhaps the sound of the word would goad Clarissa into finally growing up a little. Robert would escort her, and Miss Jessie would be on Lee's arm. Lyle Roth, one of Daddy's friends from childhood, had been asked to take Derek's place to escort me.

Every time I pictured that wedding without Derek a needle drove through my heart. I admitted to Daddy once that I couldn't be sure I'd make it down the aisle without crying. He'd thought I was talking about crying for Mama. Funny, but that hadn't crossed my mind.

We spent Thanksgiving with the Kings at their house. Katherine insisted upon cooking. At the time, I thought her offer a promising sign of familial instinct. Now I know she merely sought to channel her mounting anxiety into something she enjoyed. She and I were more distant than ever. I simply couldn't talk to her about Derek. And frankly, I'd grown less empathetic of her pain with each argument between Daddy and her. Seemed to me he tried to be patient, but she'd become too wrapped up in her grief to be anything but selfish.

Now I see the cause and effect that I could not see then. Now I realize that Katherine's uncompromising attitude wore Daddy down until he could not always give her what she needed. And in her hurt, she lashed out more. Such is the vicious cycle of a stressed relationship after the death of a loved one. After a time the hurts from the fighting build such a wall that you forget its very foundation was poured from your shared pain.

Mr. and Mrs. B came to the Kings' that day also, plus Celia's parents. Daddy tried his best to eat and hide his worry. During the entire meal, even though Katherine and he sat together, they hardly said a word to each other. With all the folks and conversation, that wasn't particularly obvious, unless you were watching. I certainly watched. And once I caught Miss Jessie's keen studying of Katherine's face. Miss Jessie is one of the wisest women in Bradleyville. Plus, she knew her niece. I did not like the look of concern in her eyes.

Clarissa insisted on sitting on the other side of Katherine. She told the entire table of adults how pretty her dress looked on her, and how she couldn't wait for the wedding.

"And you should see this boy in his tux." Daddy smiled at Robert. My brother shrugged, but he couldn't hide his pleasure.

Holidays are a difficult time after a death in the family, and this was no exception. Oh, yes, we laughed and chatted and ate. But every once in a while I'd catch Miss Connie staring at nothing, her mind far away. Or Mr. King with a glisten in his eye. Emotions don't play fair when you're grieving. They creep and hide; sometimes they even lull you into believing that they've retreated to some distant corner, and maybe, just maybe, you can let down your guard a little. Then they pounce from the most unexpected of places, teeth bared, claws out.

Holidays are prime pouncing times.

After our meal, I found myself beside Miss Connie, clearing the table. We were the only two in the dining room. "You miss him, don't you," she said out of the blue, her hand stilling against a half-empty glass of iced tea.

I froze, a plate in each hand. Guilt sloshed about in my stomach as I forced myself to look at her. "Very much."

She gave me a sad smile. "I know you visit him every Saturday. Folks tell me they see you at his grave."

Those Bradleyville eyes never did miss much. Maybe half the town guessed about Derek and me. Did they know about that horrid little voice inside me too? I placed one plate on top of the other, reached for a third. "He was . . . very dear to me."

She ran her hand up and down the glass. Then straightened her back to look me full in the face. "I know about the socks."

Her stunning statement brought heat to my cheeks. *No*, I wailed inside, *she took away the one thing we could always share!* All those weeks that I'd taken comfort in the socks—how they'd symbolized the part of me I'd given to Derek. I focused on the dirty plates, suddenly heavy in my hands. Stiffly, I put them back on the table.

"Mr. Henks called me. The funeral director. He wanted to carry out your wish, but he just didn't feel right without getting my permission."

My eyes would not rise from the tablecloth. If he'd told her this, surely he'd relayed to her my reason. She had to know everything, all I'd done. The depth of my dishonesty. What she must think of me.

"I told him yes, of course."

I blinked at her in surprise. The way she spoke the last two words, as if denying my request would somehow have denied her precious son. The gratitude that flooded me nearly weakened my knees.

"Thank you," I whispered.

"Derek wouldn't have wanted it any other way. Because they were a gift from you."

I nodded again, unable to say another word. Her eyes glistened as they told me things she wouldn't speak. She took a deep breath, blew it out. "Well. Guess we'd better get these dishes cleared." She reached for the glass.

"Miss Connie," I blurted, "does anyone else know? About the socks, I mean." *Please no! Please not Katherine!*

"Just Derek's daddy. No one else will ever know."

My eyes closed. I felt almost sick with relief. When I looked at her face once more, I saw no judgment there, only regret for things that would never be.

Miss Connie slowly exhaled, then picked up the glass. I stood rooted to the spot as she disappeared into the kitchen.

We did not speak of the socks again.

chapter 53

Thanksgiving weekend wrapped up the LuvRush tour. Greg phoned me on Monday, elated over their final concert. "It is wonderful!" he exclaimed. "We sing very good. We are so tired, we think we will be happy it is the last, but then we do not want it to stop."

They would spend a few days in L.A., discussing future issues with their manager. On Friday, Demetri, Alex, and Lysander would return to Greece. Greg would catch an early morning flight to Lexington that day, then drive to Bradleyville. Celia and his brother, Danny, also were coming.

I couldn't stand the waiting. Everything within me reached toward Friday evening, when Greg would appear at my door. After all the heartache and guilt of the past few months, and with the unsettled atmosphere between Daddy and Katherine, even as they counted the days until their wedding, all I wanted to do was cling to Greg. Tell him in person how much I loved him. Try to get my life back to some sense of equilibrium.

In that final patchwork of days before I saw Greg, the last worn threads of Daddy and Katherine's relationship unraveled.

Tuesday evening, Katherine would not come to the phone when Daddy called her parents' house. "She's just pullin' away from everybody," Miss Connie worried to him. Daddy clicked off the receiver and stood wordlessly in the kitchen, staring through the back glass to the cold night beyond. One look at his face, and a trapdoor opened in my stomach. I hadn't seen such fear in his expression since Mama's approaching death.

I put my arms around him, feeling the new slimness around his back. "Daddy, I love you. Everything's gonna be okay."

He barely returned the hug. "I love you too, Jackie."

Later I would hear the details of the events that followed. On Wednesday, Daddy tried to call Katherine at the boutique numerous times. "I'm too busy to talk right now, Bobby," she said every time, her voice preoccupied, aloof. "I'll call you later."

That night Daddy showed up unannounced at the Kings', demanding that Katherine take a drive. They *had* to talk. Reluctantly, Katherine acquiesced. Not until then did Katherine admit she was having second thoughts about the wedding. So much had happened. So much within herself had changed. Yes, she loved him and the kids, she said. But how could she take Melissa's place? She'd begun to realize in October that she never would. "Jackie's now acting like she doesn't want me around," she added. And she had no strength to fight me. She did not admit then how deeply my indifference cut her. How used she felt. She'd done all she could to help me with Greg, overlooking the desires of her own brother. Now I had Greg completely, and Derek was dead. Now I no longer needed her services.

Finally, Katherine told Daddy, he'd made it clear that she was not first in his eyes. He would never move from Bradleyville for her sake. Didn't even want her working in Lexington a few days each month. She felt unwanted, unappreciated, and yes, trapped.

They could work out their problems, Daddy insisted. They *loved* each other. Daddy placed a hand on her cheek. "I don't think any of these things are the real reason," he said quietly. "I think you're lettin' your old fears rise up. 'Trapped' is a word from your past. This is the present. We love you. We need you."

Katherine shook her head. "You think you do. But I'm not good enough for you. Deep inside you believe that. I'm not good and perfect like Melissa was."

"That's not true! How can you say that?"

"It is true, Bobby. And it will only become more true. I need more than you can give. And besides, we are so completely different! We'll only end up hurting each other."

They talked for two more hours until Daddy believed he'd convinced her how wrong she was. Katherine finally waved a tired hand at Daddy, mouthing shallow assurances—you're right, you're right. Take me back home now, I'll be fine. I just haven't been thinking straight.

I don't believe until that point she had planned to leave that night. But Katherine now hung like a drop of dew on a spiderweb—clinging, balancing, ready to fall. She knew in her heart the marriage would not survive, and she couldn't stand to witness its slow demise. And for all their talking, she didn't feel Daddy had heard her. Best to cut things off right now, she told herself. Less pain for everyone in the long run.

As her parents slept, she quietly packed her car.

Thursday morning, the day before Greg came, Katherine went to work as usual. She called her mama at the end of the day, took a deep breath, and told what she'd decided. She knew it was the right thing to do, so don't try to talk her out of it. She was headed for Lexington to stay with Sylvia. If she was going to break things off with Bobby, she needed to get completely away. Next, she would call Bobby to tell him the wedding was off.

Miss Connie, her heart already broken over one child, begged and begged Katherine not to go. Her daddy threatened to drive to the shop and force her home.

"Don't," Katherine retorted. "You can't force me anywhere, Daddy; you think you can live my life for me? Think you can make my decisions?"

When she phoned our house, I answered. In a worn and distant tone she asked to speak with Daddy. And somehow I knew. She could not be home yet, I realized. She had to still be at the store. I pressed the receiver to my ear, gripping the edge of the kitchen counter, trying to think of something, *anything* to say. I could not call Daddy to the phone. But he'd heard the ring from the family room and now stood in the doorway, his body going rigid at the sight of my own. Silently, he held out his hand.

My feet cemented to the floor as I watched Daddy's face. I could hear Katherine's voice as she told him how sorry she was. How she wished it would have worked out. That she loved him, but there was simply too many differences between them to overcome. Please tell Clarissa and Robert goodbye for her.

She did not mention me. I winced at that, thinking how much she must despise me. I now know that she simply did not think I would care.

Daddy pled with her, but she would not listen. Finally spent, he fell into stunned silence. He showed no anger. That would come later. Shock comes first; I know that. I've lived through death before.

He did not hang up the phone, even as the dial tone clicked on. I had to take the receiver from his dangling hand.

Clarissa wandered in, tipping her head and frowning as she studied our faces. "What's—"

"Nothin', Clarissa, go on." I gave her a little shove.

"But—"

"*Go.*"

Daddy blinked, then looked right through her. Apprehension widened her eyes. Abruptly, then, she trotted away and down the hall, as if the very act of leaving would protect her from whatever new bad thing had happened.

I placed the receiver on the table. "Daddy?"

He came to life with a rasp of breath and stumbled from the kitchen. His bedroom door smacked shut. I crept after him on shaky legs and listened at his door, my heart hammering. Nothing. Then a groan rose from deep within him, a groan of such despair that it ripped my chest in two. My knees went weak. At that moment, I honestly was afraid of what my daddy might do.

I ran back to the kitchen and with shaking fingers dialed my grandparents. "You better come over," I choked to Grandma Delham. "Katherine's left Daddy, and I'm so scared. He needs you." Then in desperation I called Miss Jessie, begging her to *please do* something, talk some sense into Katherine, as if she had wings and magic to fly across space and land in her niece's fleeing path.

Grandma and Grandpa rushed through the front door without knocking, their faces pale. Grandpa headed to Robert's room to "keep the young 'uns occupied," knowing instinctively that Daddy needed a mama's touch.

I hustled behind Grandma past the kitchen to the master bedroom, then hung back, palms pressed, fingers to my lips. A low moan filtered through the door. Grandma's eyes squeezed shut.

She knocked gently. "Bobby?" She eased the door open. I caught a glimpse of Daddy on his knees, face in his hands. Grandma hurried to him, knelt down. Put her arm around his shoulders. Daddy sagged against her like a lost child and broke into the wracking sobs of a man in agony. "Oh, Bobby," Grandma crooned. "Oh, Bobby."

Sick to the core, I turned away, unable to bear the sight.

chapter 54

Friday. Greg would arrive around suppertime. Not that we'd be eating. Our entire family was numb. I think the town felt numb. By Thursday night, everybody knew, the phone lines buzzing, people gasping at the news, everyone resolving to pray.

Daddy did not go to work. Not since Mama died had I seen him so immobilized. That morning, he barely dragged himself from his bedroom. Determined to keep an eye on him, I refused to go to school. I'd thought to get the kids off, but Robert would not go either. And Clarissa couldn't stop crying long enough to get dressed. I gave up and let them stay home.

My brother proved the small version of Daddy, breaking down in my arms before the morning had passed. "Why did she go?" he demanded over and over. *"Why?"* I held his thin shoulders and patted his hair, seething with anger at Katherine, decrying the day she set foot in town. I should have done more to stop her then. I'd known from the very beginning, hadn't I? I'd let her wheedle me in, wrap me around her finger like she had the rest of the town. I should have done *something*.

The phone rang constantly. I answered, knowing that Daddy had unplugged the receiver in his bedroom. Folks wondered if there was anything they could do other than pray. They assured me Katherine would come back. I knew better. Katherine did not "come back" to anything once she'd left.

Miss Connie came over, shoulders drooping, her eyes rimmed and puffy. Daddy put listless arms around her, and she heaved into tears. She'd come to apologize for her daughter, she said. On her knees, if she could. She was so, so sorry and ashamed. As if what Katherine had done somehow reflected on her own motherhood.

"Don't you worry, we'll keep prayin'," Daddy soothed her. For the moment, he was out of tears.

She wiped her eyes, drawing a deep breath. "I have to . . ." She blinked tears away. Reached for her purse. Drew out a small blue velvet box, her fingers closed around it as if it might break. "I found this on her dresser." She held it out to Daddy, unable to look him in the eye. "The ring's inside."

Daddy stared at it in disbelief. I think until that point, even in his grief, he'd held on to the hope that Katherine would return, that the wedding could go on as planned. He took the box from Miss Connie without a word.

Twelve o'clock. Six hours before Greg arrived. He'd called the night before, excited about coming, only for me to throw a wet blanket on his entire trip with the news. I couldn't help thinking how unfair it would be for Daddy to see us together. I wanted to cry over that thought, but I couldn't. I wanted to cry my pain over Daddy's hopelessness, and my anger over Katherine's foolishness. I wanted to cry for how much I'd missed Greg, and for Derek, and for Mama. And I desperately wanted to cry over Katherine, for now my emotions had swung from wishing we'd never met her to fervently wishing she hadn't gone. Despite the recent distance between us, despite what she thought of me or I thought of her, I knew how much my family had come to rely on her. She had brought them happiness. Now that their joy had been snatched away, I couldn't help but think I was partly to blame. I began to realize how my own guilt had pushed Katherine away. For my family's sake, I should have done something to close the gap that had opened between us. Maybe, just maybe then, she wouldn't have gone.

But I couldn't cry over any of these things. Tears had forsaken me when I needed them most, puddling in some deep, unreachable place in my chest.

I tried to keep busy, doing laundry, cleaning. But even my old standby method could not relieve me. For lunch I made sandwiches for Robert and Clarissa, and tried to eat one myself. Daddy didn't want anything. On automatic, I cleaned the few dishes and put the food away.

The inevitable turn within Daddy hit after lunch, the immobilization of shock crashing into anger. Gathering his resolve, he rose to control the situation. He called Miss Jessie to get Sylvia's phone number in Lexington, then punched the buttons with purpose. When no one answered the phone, he called again and again, knowing Katherine was there, listening to it ring. Finally she picked up.

They talked for a long time. Daddy paced in his bedroom, out of my earshot, but I now know much of what was said. After almost an hour of rational argument, Daddy's anger got the best of him until he out-and-out demanded that Katherine return. If she didn't, he'd hop in the car right then and get her. That was the worst thing he could have said. Katherine merely dug in her heels.

"See how selfish you are?" she retorted. "You can't even give me some space when I need it."

"*Space!* Is that all you call this? Katherine, you left your ring behind! Our wedding's supposed to be in a week; this is a fine time to decide you need some space."

"Bobby, you're not listening to me. Like you haven't been listening for the past two months. I'm too messed up inside right now. I can't give you what you need. And you obviously can't give me what I need. So please, just . . . let me be."

Daddy's voice fell to cold fury. "So you can do what—decide to pick up and move across the country again? Take up with somebody else?"

"Bobby, don't—"

"Trent Baxter was right. He warned us what you would do."

Katherine sucked in a breath. "I'm *not* the same as I was then. This is different."

"Really?" Daddy's tone dripped with sarcasm. "Well, you couldn't prove it by me."

He slammed down the phone.

After he'd calmed down, he tried calling back again and again, but Katherine would not answer. She finally took the phone off the hook. Daddy sank again into despair. He remained mostly in his bedroom, praying and begging God to do *something*. Hadn't he lost enough in his life?

One bright spot shimmers from that stained and worn afternoon. For some reason—I suppose because she'd finally had all she could take—Clarissa chose that auspicious day to stand up to Alma Sue.

About an hour after school let out, Alma Sue banged on our door. I almost refused to let her in, irritated that her mama had let her come over when our household lay in such disarray. But Clarissa needed a diversion, and so I relented. Daddy remained in his room with the door closed. Robert had retreated to his bedroom as well and lay on the floor with his chin on his stacked fists, reading a softball magazine. "You two can play in the family area until 5:00," I told Clarissa. "Then it'll be gettin' dark, and I'll have to send Alma Sue home. Keep it quiet."

I retreated to my own bedroom and turned on the radio, leaving the door open. Clarissa had not had an easy day. I wanted to keep an eye on her, make sure Alma Sue behaved.

Lolling before the picture of LuvRush, I stared at Greg. Two hours. A shiver ran through me. He was really going to be here. *Here.* For the first time that week, real exhilaration brushed my nerves. I closed my eyes and envisioned holding him, heard his voice say, "I love you." Suddenly I realized just how very much I needed him.

I don't know how much time had passed before the raised voices of my sister and Alma Sue attracted my attention. Sighing, I headed out to the hallway to put a lid on whatever trouble brewed. "You cheated!" I heard Clarissa declare.

"I did not."

"You did too!"

Something in Clarissa's voice—a tone I had not heard before. I pulled up, then edged against the wall to listen, much as I had listened ages ago to Daddy and Katherine.

"You moved those two dominoes," Clarissa insisted. "I *saw* you."

"I did *not!* You're just mad because I'm winning."

"Well, for your information, I don't care if you're winning. But I *am* sick of you cheating. You do it *all the time!*"

Alma Sue made a disgusted sound in her throat. "You're such a baby, Clarissa, you just make things up. Forget this."

"Fine, I will!" Dominoes hissed and rattled. I peeked around the corner. Clarissa had swept them off the coffee table. She and Alma Sue faced each other, their profiles to me.

As my sister would tell me much later, that one unexpected act on her own part fueled something inside her, sort of like striking a match. Boldly, she glared at her nemesis.

Alma Sue drew to her full height and stared down at Clarissa, hands on her hips. "You wanna fight?" she challenged.

"Yeah," Clarissa sneered back, chin jutting.

Alma Sue blinked in surprise. Then recovered. "Okay, fine. I'll count to three, and we'll start."

Some things had not yet changed. Alma Sue still knew how to take charge. And apparently she felt not the least bit intimidated. That thought almost prompted me to intervene, but I held back, waiting. *Come on, Clarissa.*

"One," Alma Sue called.

I watched the expression on my sister's face focus, gel.

"Two."

Clarissa raised a fist. *Uh-oh*, I thought. *I really should stop this.*

"Thr—"

Clarissa let loose her arm with fury, balled fingers slamming straight into Alma Sue's nose. The girl's eyes nearly popped out of her head.

"Waaaaah!" Alma Sue wailed. "I wasn't reeeaaaadyyy!" Her hands flew to her bleeding nostrils, and she ran out of our family room right past me, down the hall, and slammed out of our house.

I stood in her wake, mouth open, and ogled the door. Then swung back to find Clarissa equally frozen. She stared from her fist to a glistening drop of telltale blood in the domino box, and back to her fist, clearly wondering what on earth she'd done, and would she now have Alma Sue after her but good.

Then a slow smile spread across her face.

"What is goin' *on* out here?" Daddy demanded as he appeared in the hall, frustration hanging about him like a black cloud.

"Nothin', Daddy. Clarissa just punched Alma Sue in the nose, that's all."

He twisted his face. "What?"

"Never mind, it's okay, everything's under control." I hurried to Clarissa's side and started gathering the dominoes off the floor.

Daddy hung there, only half seeing us.

"Go on, Daddy, it's okay. Really."

He put a hand to his forehead and retreated back to his bedroom.

I picked up the domino box, smiling wickedly at the bloodstain. "Proof."

Clarissa giggled. It was a joyous sound.

"Daddy." I knocked on his door at 5:30.

"What is it?"

I stuck my head inside his room, my stomach quivering both with anticipation of Greg's arrival and with guilt. Daddy sat in his chair, Bible on his lap. I could see circles under his eyes.

"Are you . . . okay?" I asked.

"Fine."

I slipped over to sit on the edge of the bed. "Daddy, we know where Katherine's stayin'. Maybe you should go there tomorrow, talk to her."

"I've tried and tried to talk to her this afternoon, Jackie. She won't ever answer the phone now. And she certainly wouldn't let me in the door."

I focused on my lap. "I know she loves you, Daddy."

"Well, she has an odd way of showin' it." He ran a thumb up and down the side of his Bible. For a moment I watched him in silence.

I drew a deep breath. "Greg's goin' to be comin' over soon."

Daddy's eyes closed. "Yeah."

"We were goin' to go out to a movie or somethin'. Is that still okay?"

"How will Greg keep from bein' recognized?"

I fingered the edging on his bedspread. "He probably won't, Daddy, not anymore. We'll try to find an out-of-the-way place. But this is just . . . somethin' we'll always have to deal with."

Always. I regretted the word the moment it left my mouth. It could only remind Daddy of what he'd lost.

Daddy sighed deeply, then gave me a wan smile. "Jackie, you don't need to feel guilty. I know you've been through a lot of upheaval. I know you've missed Greg. Just let yourself be glad he's back."

My throat tightened. I walked over to hug him, and he patted my back. "Thank you."

"Now listen." He pointed his finger at me. "You're either in a restaurant or a movie, or you're comin' home, understand? You're not—"

"I know, I know."

We exchanged a weary smile.

"Go on now and get ready." He nudged me away. "I'll take care of makin' supper for Robert and Clarissa."

For the next half hour, I paced the house, waiting, watching the street. My anticipation built until I could hardly breathe. "You're gonna wear out the floor," Robert commented. When I thought I could bear it no more, I heard a car pull up to the curb.

"Oh." I waved my hands. "They're here."

"Lemme say hi first, lemme go!" Clarissa trotted down the hall and threw open the front door. I sailed up behind her, cold air whisking into the hall. Greg was climbing out of the car, a black leather coat over his jeans. At the mere sight of him, something within me cracked open like a fissure. I pushed past Clarissa and stepped out onto the porch, chest fluttering. "Hi!"

"Jackie!"

He hurried up the sidewalk, and I ran down the steps until we flung ourselves into each other's arms. I pressed my face into his neck, not ring that his brother and sister-in-law looked on, not to mention Clarissa. "Greg," I breathed into his skin, smelling the leather of his coat. "Greg." He pressed the back of my head, fingers clutching my hair until it pulled.

"I am here for you now, Jackie."

I burst into tears and clung to him, shivering, not wanting to let go. Greg could not let go either, his hands sliding from my hair to my shoulders to my head again, as if he couldn't quite believe he held me at all.

"You still love me?" he whispered.

"*Of course*, I still love you; I never stopped."

The ache in his voice bore a hole right through me—that he would have to ask that question *again*. My released emotions flooded through my limbs. How could I ever have betrayed him? How had we gotten through these last months apart? And how would all of us—Daddy especially—get through the coming days now?

I dug my fingers into the back of Greg's coat and shuddered against the cold.

"I am here for you now, Jackie. I am here."

chapter 55

Daddy tried again and again Friday night to call Katherine. With each vain attempt, his hope dwindled. For the third time in his life, he'd lost the woman he loved. He'd once have thought the past two times had tempered the steel within him. Not so now. Celia's betrayal years ago and, far worse, Mama's death, had compromised his strength, weakened it, and now he felt he just might break. But he couldn't. He had children who were also hurting and who needed his care. He needed to focus what little energy he possessed on them.

And so he ceased his desperate pursuit of Katherine May King.

That's when the town intervened.

Over the course of that Saturday, an idea was born, conceived through numerous conversations between Miss Jessie and Celia. I knew at least the main points of Celia's story. I had not known that Miss Jessie nearly left Bradleyville herself when she was twenty-four, walking away from Lee. She had turned around only by the grace of God.

Like Pastor Beekins had preached, God can turn our mistakes from the past into good. I'd clung to that belief for myself over the last few months. Now I would see it put to the test.

Amidst our sadness, Greg's presence pulled our family through that Saturday. He spent the day at our house, doing everything he could to help. He took time with Robert—played computer games with him, sat in his room and asked one question after another about softball, which Robert gladly answered. Greg watched TV with Clarissa and listened in awe to her tale of punching Alma Sue in the nose. When she got the notion to bake cookies, Greg aimed a pleading expression my way. What did he know about baking? Clarissa got him into an apron, which she thought hysterically funny, and the three of us made cookies together. The heavenly smell brought Robert out of his room, and we all sat around the table making pigs of ourselves while Greg told us about his tour.

Daddy wandered in from the garage, which he'd suddenly decided needed some cleaning out. While I heated some soup for him and made a salad, Greg engaged him in conversation, asking him about the banking business, about growing up in Bradleyville. Anything to try and get his mind off Katherine. Daddy, in turn, asked him about the LuvRush tour and how did Greg keep up with his studies, and what challenges the group faced next.

They got to know each other more that day than they had in all the previous months put together.

In the evening, we gathered around the television. Daddy focused sightlessly on the screen. One week from now was to have been his wedding night. The thought churned in my head like stormy waters. I squeezed Greg's hand, anchoring myself only by his strength.

Sunday morning, Daddy decided not to go to church. "I don't want to face people right now," he told me privately. "I just don't want to deal with the questions and everything else. You take the kids and go."

Although I hated to think of him alone in the house, part of me felt glad he would not be in church. What bad timing for him to lay eyes on Danny Cander for the first time in nearly twenty years. I knew that old rivalry had long since died. All the same, he represented more unpleasant memories Daddy did not need.

Before the service, Celia hugged me hard the way she'd done the day before, when I'd picked up Greg at her parents' house. I thought Danny a strikingly handsome man, but in a far different way than his brother. Danny's hair was light brown, and his eyes were the greenest I'd ever seen.

"How are you all today?" Celia whispered.

"Daddy's really tryin', but he's not doin' too well."

Miss Jessie joined us, and she and Celia exchanged a look. Miss Jessie ran her fingers over my hair. "We'll talk after the service, okay?"

"Honey, honey." Mrs. B shuffled over to rest her fingers on my shoulder. "Chil', I've been prayin' so much for your family. That Katherine May. I'd just like to strangle her."

One by one, it seemed as though every person in that sanctuary asked about Daddy, many with eyes misted for Katherine and him. Even my friends, who'd been dying to see Greg again now that they knew who he was, merely greeted him quietly, then turned to see how I was doing. Folks hugged the Kings, women clutching Miss Connie's hand as they spoke of how they'd been praying. I felt a rush of guilt, watching Katherine's parents. So worried over my own daddy, I'd forgotten how much they had to be hurting, losing Derek and now Katherine.

Derek.

I sought Greg's eyes, a sudden lump in my throat. They gazed back at me, full of love and trust.

I herded Robert and Clarissa into the pew with the Matthews family. Clarissa just had to sit on the other side of Greg. Pastor Beekins preached a muted sermon. I tried to sing the hymns, but the words caught in my throat. Just before the benediction, Pastor sent up a special prayer for Daddy and Katherine, for us and the Kings. The moment before he prepared to dismiss the congregation, an amazing thing happened. Celia Cander stood up.

"I'd like to say something," she announced. And in her own pew, Miss Jessie also silently stood.

You have to remember the independent, fighting spirit that has always described Bradleyville. The way it was founded—settled in the middle of nowhere by Celia's great-granddad, an upstart Christian man with the dream of building a Christian town. The way its people have stuck together for almost one hundred years. Bradleyville folk built the town, ran the town, took care of the town. And the town took care of its own.

"Except for perhaps the young people here, you all know my story." Celia's fingers worked a tissue, and in that action, I saw the courage it took for her to speak so freely. "I fled this town in a weak moment, and it cost me seventeen years with the man who is now my husband. Seventeen *years*. I don't want that for Katherine. And . . ." She balled the tissue, nails pressing it into her palm. "Bobby's been through enough."

She looked to Miss Jessie, suddenly helpless.

"I tried to leave, too." Miss Jessie took up the speech. "Many years before Celia was grown. Now, I'm not as stubborn as Celia, mind you." Lee snorted. She gave him a look as the congregation tittered. "Well, I'm not. Only took me a little over three hours to come back. And I've been stuck with this man ever since." Her husband aimed an innocent look at the ceiling. "Thank God. But it seems to me that each time, this returnin' business gets harder. Me at three hours, Celia at seventeen years, and now Katherine. She called me yesterday, talked to me for quite a while. And I can tell you somethin'; I know my niece. *She* won't come back at all."

Miss Jessie's eyes traveled over the congregation. "Unless we give her a little help."

Reaction buzzed through the pews. Katherine's mama lowered her head, mouth trembling. Mrs. B breathed an "amen."

Miss Jessie lifted her chin with determination. "So I say we do somethin' rather unprecedented, even for Bradleyville. I say we go after her."

My mouth fell open. Church or not, my hand scrambled automatically to find Greg's as the buzz through our sanctuary grew louder. Clarissa leaned over Greg to whisper to me, her eyes wide. "Jackie—"

"Ssh."

Jason King pulled slowly, almost painfully, to his feet. Everyone fell silent. He gripped his wife's shoulder. "It's true. I don't think she'll come back. It's not that she doesn't want to. It's just that, with all that's happened, Katherine's not thinkin' straight. Plus, she's forgotten what God has done for her. She's fallen back into bad habits, lettin' the past pull at her, and she's runnin' scared. Katherine's overlookin' how much she really loves Bobby and his family, and even this town. So—what I'm tryin' to say is, I agree with Jessie."

Folks all began talking at once, throwing out questions. How? When? What could they possibly *do?*

"Wait a minute, wait a minute!" Pastor Beekins held up a hand. "All right, now. Jessie, tell us your plan."

"We know where she's stayin'," Miss Jessie told the congregation. "It's a long drive, I realize that. By the time we got there and came back, it would be late. But today is our chance; tomorrow we all go to work. And the longer we wait, the further Katherine's head's goin' to turn from here. Who knows how long she'll even stay in Lexington."

Pastor Beekins drummed his fingers against the pulpit. "Seems to me, though, we can't do this without Bobby's consent. Goin' after Katherine is really something *he* needs to be doin'."

Almost instinctively, then, all eyes snagged on me—the daughter who'd done so much to help her daddy. Who knew him so well. I looked around at all the faces, tongue-tied, nerves tingling. Suddenly, I felt like a tiny child. After all I'd done, was God giving me the chance to help make things right?

"Tell them, Jackie." Greg tugged my hand, nudging me to rise. "Tell them he needs help."

If Greg hadn't been there, I never would have spoken. But with his encouragement giving me strength, I pushed myself out of the pew.

Clasped my wrists. "The thing is . . ." My voice wavered. *Oh, Lo[rd,]* *please help me.* I did not want to cry in front of the whole church. If [I] started, I might never stop. Greg gave me a little nod, urging me on. "The thing is, well, as you can see, Daddy's not here. He's not doin' very well. He's talked all he can to Katherine, but she won't change her mind. So now he's . . . given up."

"Do you believe that?" Miss Jessie asked gently. "You know better than anyone how Katherine's been with your family. Do you think she really wanted to leave?"

Tears pricked my eyes then, no way to hold them back. I shook my head. "Mr. King's right. I just think she's . . . mixed up and afraid. And the longer she stays away, the less ties she'll feel with us. She needs to be reminded of what she's left." I pressed my lips together to keep my mouth from quivering. "She needs to see Clarissa and Robert," I declared, my voice rising. "She needs to see *Daddy.*"

"Then we'll just have to persuade Bobby to go," Danny Cander spoke up. "We'll go by his house and get him, no taking 'no' for an answer."

Imagine that. Danny Cander speaking up to help my daddy.

And that's just what we did.

I drove home first with Clarissa and Robert and Greg to give Daddy fair warning. The folks who decided to go hurried to their own houses to change clothes, then began to line their cars in our street. Katherine's parents, and Grandpa and Grandma Delham came inside.

"No fightin' this, now, son," Grandpa told Daddy matter-of-factly. "We've already decided. This'll teach you to miss church."

Daddy appeared more than speechless. He was downright flabbergasted. When he found his tongue, he threw out one argument after another. He'd already tried to talk to her and nothing had worked. What was the point? He'd drive all that way, and she wouldn't even let him in the door. Besides, maybe he'd decided he *didn't even want her anymore!*

"Oh, peanuts, who do you think you're foolin'!" Grandma grabbed him by the elbow and steered him toward the door. "Fetch your coat now, it's cold."

chapter 56

We made quite the procession, winding through those Kentucky hills. Woodenly, still not quite believing what had happened, Daddy drove our car, hemmed in—Lee and Miss Jessie before us, a dozen vehicles behind. Robert sat in our front seat. An excited Clarissa shared the backseat with Greg and me. "We're gonna bring Katherine home, we're gonna bring Katherine home," she sang, bouncing up and down. "I can't wait to tell her what I did to Alma Sue!"

Fiercely, I shook my head at her, warning her to be quiet. Daddy did not need the commotion. The creases on his face bespoke the nausea in his stomach. He'd found himself at the wheel only because he'd been so pressured. Now, surely, he deplored what he'd agreed to do. How could he face Katherine, just to be told no all over again?

Celia and Danny rode with the Matthews. Both sets of our grandparents went, Grandma Westerdahl fuming all the while, so I later heard, about Katherine's unreliability. Saying her son-in-law would just be better off without the woman except that he seemed intolerably miserable, so what could she do but try to help? The Beekins joined our group, and Lyle Roth and his wife, and, of course, the Kings, who rode with Lee and Miss Jessie. Mr. and Mrs. B wanted to go in the worst way. "But honey chil'," Mrs. B shook her chin at me, "if I sit that long in a car, I'm afraid I'll never get out." Mr. Luther, who'd always admired Katherine so much, said he'd ride along with the Clangerlees. He'd managed to get home first and grab a new bag of Tootsie Rolls to hand out "when Katherine changed her mind." Numerous other friends came with us too.

The drive took over four hours. Clarissa fell asleep on my shoulder. Greg and I entwined our arms and fingers—and prayed.

"Daddy," Robert asked when we were about halfway there, "do you think she'll come back with us?"

An interminable moment stretched out as I waited for Daddy to answer. "I don't know, son."

"Yes, she will, Daddy!" I burst. "She *will.*" I could not bear to think of anything else. The mere idea of her denying Daddy a second time—in front of all his friends and family—left me cold as ice. Daddy would not survive it.

Still, Daddy's answer got me all riled up. The more I envisioned the scene of Katherine's turning away, the more panicked I became. What had I led our family into? We'd all rushed like idiots, not thinking this through. It really could turn out very badly; Daddy was right to think we shouldn't come. We could be *worse* off than before.

I checked the clock. Three hours. Somewhere in this area years ago, Miss Jessie had turned around. I wondered why. Some day, she would have to tell me her story.

Please, God, help us. Please.

Daddy's shoulders drooped. He flexed them tiredly. I leaned forward to rub them. "I love you, Daddy," I whispered.

He managed a smile.

We hit the interstate, heading north. The last time I'd been on this road, Katherine was driving me to Greg's concert. The memory knifed through me, cold and clean. What a fun companion she'd been that night. Spontaneously, I squeezed Greg's hand, bringing it to my lips. How very much I owed her.

Darkness was falling by the time we entered the city of Lexington. Lee knew the general direction of the apartment building. Near Turfland Mall—not far from New Circle Road. Our lineup meandered a bit looking for the building, having to turn around at one point like some ungainly caterpillar. I could hear Daddy deep-breathing. I perched on the edge of my seat again, pressing fingers into his shoulders. By the time we pulled into the parking lot and turned off the engine, his hands fairly trembled.

He spotted Katherine's car. "Well, at least she's here."

I floundered then, not quite sure what to do. "Do you want everyone to go with you to the door, Daddy? Maybe you want to do it alone."

He slipped the keys out of the ignition. "I'm . . . not quite sure yet."

Car doors opening, people getting out, stretching, breath misting in the frigid air. Streetlights washed the pavement in pale yellow. Apart-

...ment twelve, Miss Jessie had said. Our group straggled together, a motley crew of stiff backs and stubborn hearts.

"Who's goin' in?" someone asked.

"We should ask Bobby what he wants."

"How we all gonna fit in one apartment?"

"Well, that's what we came for, isn't it?"

Daddy stood gazing at the apartment building, a grim look on his face. My pulse kicked into high gear. How would he stand it if Katherine refused him now?

Surely God's providence intervened at that moment. The door to the apartment house opened, and Katherine May King walked outside, hands in her coat pockets, purse over her shoulder. Headed somewhere.

We all fell silent like some trapped flock of birds. Katherine stepped down from the porch onto the parking lot. Someone in our group sneezed, and her head came up. She slid to a halt and froze.

Nobody moved. I couldn't tell which of us had frightened the other more. Her mouth opened, but no words came.

"Katherine!" Clarissa tore from my side and bounded to her, throwing both arms around her chest. The hit pushed Katherine back like a puppet. Robert followed Clarissa, flinging his arms around her from the side. A cry escaped Katherine's lips. Slowly, almost as if in a dream, she moved to hug my brother and sister. Then she nudged them away. "Clarissa. Robert." Her voice shook. "What . . . why . . ."

"Katherine," Daddy called gently. He emerged from our crowd but did not approach her. "We've come to take you home."

Katherine made a little noise in her throat. She tossed her head and faded back.

No! I cried and threw a glance at Daddy. He watched her with pain on his face.

"Come on, Katherine," Celia called. "We know—"

"Stop!" Katherine raised her hands, palms out. "Please don't do this to me. You don't know what you're doing."

"Katherine." Clarissa reached for her again.

"No, Clarissa." She spread her fingers. "Just . . . I . . ."

I hugged my arms against my coat, sickness welling in my stomach. Greg steadied me. This could not be happening. Neither Daddy nor she was moving toward the other. I needed to *do* something.

"Katherine!" her mama said sharply. "Now you're gonna hear us out."

"No!" Katherine raked in air. "Stop telling me what to do! All of you! Bobby, *why* did you bring everyone here? I've already told you—" Her voice pinched off, high and flat.

"I didn't bring them, Katherine; they brought me." Daddy started walking slowly toward her. "They know as well as I do where you belong."

"Bobby, this just isn't right! You can't come here with half the town and force me to change my mind on the spot."

I could see her muscles tensing, as though she prepared to bound away like a deer at any moment. Daddy stopped. Raised his hands at his sides, palms up. "Katherine," he said simply, "we all love you."

Her throat convulsed as she swallowed hard. Clarissa tilted her face up at Katherine in a sudden grin and pulled on Katherine's sleeve. "Guess what I did when you were gone. I punched Alma Sue in the nose!"

The statement rang through the air like wind chimes in a freshening breeze. Nervous laughter sputtered from our group. Katherine turned a nonplussed look upon my sister. "You did? Well, that's . . ." She lifted her hand to smooth Clarissa's hair, then let it drop again.

We all fell silent. I gripped Greg's hand.

"It's getting kind a cold out here," Daddy ventured. "Let me help you get your things, and these good folks can head on back."

"Katherine," Miss Connie jumped in, "now you listen to him. 'Cause we're not movin' till you do."

"Mama, please. There are so many reasons why I can't. You don't know everything—"

"I know all I need to know. I know that the grief over your brother's death has clouded your thinking. We let you run before. You were an adult and there was nothin' we could do. Well, you're still an adult, but you're thinkin' like a child right now. Honey—" Her voice broke. "When you're hurtin' and scared and feelin' like you made too many mistakes in life—that's when you need the people who love you the most. This is not the time to leave, Katherine. This is the time to cling. To your friends, to this family who loves you. And most of all, to God."

"I haven't run away from God, Mama," Katherine retorted defensively. "You don't know how much I've been praying!"

"Talkin' to God is wonderful, daughter, but have you done any listenin'?"

Katherine turned away. "This isn't the time, Mama, in front of so many people."

"Why not?" Daddy demanded, anger edging his voice. He still had made no move toward her. "Your actions were certainly in front of a lot a people. You left a week before our wedding, Katherine. You knocked me to the ground, then left me to pick up the pieces, to tell the kids and the town. To cancel the wedding." His anger mounted, propelling him a few steps forward. "Now you can't so much as talk in front of your friends and family, after they've come all this way?"

At the tone in his voice, Clarissa started to cry. Robert moved to Katherine's side and slid his fingers around her arm. "Please come home with us," he said matter-of-factly, as if he were a grown man talking to a child. "We need you. Daddy can't eat. Clarissa's gone off the deep end, fightin' with somebody twice her size. Jackie's not happy, even with Greg here. And I just . . . miss you a lot. The house isn't right without you anymore."

I stared at my brother in amazement. For him to sound so mature, so insightful. For him to not only express his feelings, but in front of so many.

Before I knew it, I'd let go of Greg, pulled across the pavement toward Katherine like tide over a beach. I stepped out from the crowd, passed Daddy, then drew to a halt before Katherine. Her eyes found mine, a pleading, exhausted look flicking across her face. "Jackie," she said, so quietly that I barely heard.

She waited for me to speak. I sensed that she was bracing herself, as if I had the power to cut from her what little strength she had. Suddenly I saw how unfair this was to her—the public airing of her private pain. If Derek had lived and I'd had to make my choice for Greg, would I have wanted a confrontation such as this?

In that moment, all my judgment and anger slipped away, and I saw in Katherine a reflection of myself. Two stripped saplings in the wind, barren and weathered and clinging to shore.

"Robert, Clarissa, leave us for a minute, okay?"

They eyed me questioningly, then moved away. I sensed them joining Daddy, watching, wondering, but I did not look back.

"Katherine." My voice was low enough for only her to hear. "Look. I . . . know you're hurting. For lots a reasons. I know you miss Derek and that you think you failed him. I failed him too. And I miss him more than you can know." I exhaled raggedly, my breath fogging in the chilled air. "Now we have to go on. I'm goin' to make it with Greg. I have you to thank for our bein' together in the first place. With God's

help, I'm not gonna let my past mistakes ruin my future. I'm goin' t
love Greg. I'm gonna be *loyal* to him, Katherine; do you hear what I'm
sayin'?"

Her face pinched, tears welling in her eyes. I knew she understood
the confession behind my words.

"As for the differences in his life and mine—and that's a lot—we'll
work through them." I reached for her, laying a hand on the sleeve of
her coat. "And you can do the same with Daddy. Because you love him
and he loves you. Together, you can work through your problems. And
all the stuff you're feelin' underneath—the confusion and hurt and
guilt—they'll . . . well, they'll get better in time. They have to." I
breathed a half laugh, half sob. "At least, I'm sure countin' on that for
myself."

She puffed out air. I tried to say more, but the words had run dry.

I heard shuffling behind me. *How bizarre is this night,* I suddenly
thought. *Daddy hanging back while I try to convince Katherine to come
home.*

Now I realize that he understood how much she needed to hear my
words.

Katherine could not find a response. She opened her mouth, then
shook her head helplessly. A sound rose from deep in her throat, and
she reached out to pull me close. My arms went around her, and we
held on to each other, bodies quivering.

Time blurs at this point in my memory. I know only that after some
moments, I sensed Daddy beside me, pleading etched into his forehead. I let go of Katherine and slid away, Daddy before her. "You know
I'm not leavin' without you," he uttered. For a moment Katherine
stilled. Then her fingers sank into his coat until her knuckles blanched
white. She sagged against Daddy's chest as he pressed his face into her
hair. I left them then, drifting back to Robert and Clarissa. The three
of us shuffled to our crowd of friends and family, allowing Daddy and
Katherine what little privacy they could muster.

Greg slipped an arm around me and held me tightly. I leaned against
him, gratitude and love welling within me like a sun-warmed spring,
filling me until I thought I'd drown. He whispered words against my
head that I did not catch. No matter. I felt their meaning.

Vaguely, I registered the sound of crinkling paper. Mr. Luther began
moving through the crowd. I heard a tiny, relieved chuckle, unmistak-

oly Miss Jessie's, followed by a giggle from my sister. Everyone began to whisper and mill, as if passing a secret amongst themselves. I held on to Greg, immersed in my emotions, and paid little attention.

Until Celia sidled over and pressed a Tootsie Roll in my hand.

~ July 4, 2002 ~

epilogue

Fireworks *rat-a-tat-tat* in the summer sky and burst into color, fizzling long fingers back toward the earth. "Ooooh!" The crowd's appreciation drifts heavenward.

Bradleyville's first centennial. It seems everyone raised in the town has returned for the wild celebration. Well, wild for Bradleyville. This morning the parade had to continue around a broken-down farm wagon. Somebody's runaway horse scattered participants like bowling pins. The Methodist and Baptist women held a much anticipated and highly competitive pie-baking contest, only to tie in the end. And this afternoon at the all-town picnic, a makeshift table collapsed under the weight of the food.

Whoosh! A multicolored snake bursts into life and writhes through the sky. "Aaaaah," the crowd responds.

I lean back against Greg, feeling the strength of his chest, his arms around me and clasped at my waist. For months we have looked forward to our visit here, a break from the mad dash of concerts and touring. Only in Bradleyville can the lead singer for LuvRush, relentlessly pursued by fans around the world, be simply Greg, my husband. Here we joy in seeing old friends and family. When we visit, we stay with Daddy and Katherine in my old bedroom, where I used to gaze at Greg's picture. The tack mark has longed been filled, the wall repainted. The memories linger. Memories of falling in love with Greg.

And memories of Derek.

I do love visiting Bradleyville. Still, I have an admission to make. There remains a part of me that cringes when I come back. In the rush and cacophony that has become my life, it's far easier to drown out the thoughts that insistently thrum upon my return. Here I come face-to-face with old regrets.

As always when we visit, this morning I stole away alone to the cemetery. Greg knows I go to Mama's grave. I expect he also knows I visit Derek. Invariably, I return to the house red-eyed and quiet. Greg holds me, his expression tinged with sadness. He asks no questions about my tears, and I offer no explanations. Such is the wordless agreement surrounding the secrets I wish I did not keep, and Greg wishes not to know.

Clunk, POP. *Clunk*, *pop*. More colors paint and whistle through the sky. Everyone cheers, our upturned faces reflecting red, green, purple. Perched on Daddy's shoulders, my pudgy two-year-old brother starts in fright and breaks into a bawl. Daddy swings him down and presses him to his chest. Little Jason struggles, demanding his mama, and Katherine takes him from Daddy's arms.

"I remember when you used to do that," I tell Clarissa. She makes a face at me, far too mature at thirteen to be reminded of such nonsense. Robert emits a knowing laugh, then seizes the distracting moment to reach for the hand of his new girlfriend with feigned nonchalance.

"And I remember when you wanted me to do *that*," Greg whispers teasingly in my ear. I give his arm an affectionate slap.

Jason finally quiets. "Look, look," Katherine urges him, pointing to the sky. "The big noises make pretty colors."

I smile at that, watching them. Jason appears unconvinced, but I know how true her statement is. Daddy and she certainly made enough noise to scare us all for a while.

They did not marry on December twelfth. Daddy wisely suggested they put off the wedding until they'd worked through some of their issues. Some in town thought him crazy. Mrs. B told him flat out to "catch Katherine quick" before she bolted again. But Daddy and Katherine remained firm in their decision. The town had helped them; now they needed to attend to their business—without interference. When the wedding did take place in April, a lot of folks in our church expelled a collective sigh of relief.

Boom, boom, boom! Myriad colors sparkle, then melt against the darkness. Jason starts to cry again. Behind us, I hear Danny and Celia's little girl, Patty, scream with delight. Greg and I turn as one to smile at her. She is riding on Danny's shoulders.

"Geg, Geg." Patty abruptly leans over toward her uncle. Greg catches her at the last minute. She claps chubby hands on Greg's cheeks while he blows at her belly, and she giggles with abandonment.

"Let me have that ball of fire." Lee smacks his huge fist twice against his palm, urging Patty from Greg's arms. She mushes her lips at him, digging a finger into his cheek. Miss Jessie laughs. "Oh, Celia, when she's a teenager . . .," she says with a prophetic tone of warning.

"I know, I know." Celia sighs. "I'm going to have my hands full."

"And now for the graaaand finaleeee!" our mayor announces through the bullhorn. And in wild response the sky lights and sputters and zings and swirls. We all oooh and aaah until the last hue fades, then we break into catcalls and applause. Lee sticks two fingers in his mouth and whistles a piercing scream, nearly breaking my eardrum. Jason cries at that, too. Patty giggles, showing new teeth.

"Sounds like one of your concerts!" I yell at Greg over the noise.

He shakes his head. "Nah. I can *hear* you!"

"Well, that's the end of our celebration, folks," the mayor declares. "One hundred years! Hope I'm still around for the next centennial. We'll have double the blessin's then to be thankful for."

Sudden tears sting my eyes. I look from Lee and Miss Jessie, to Danny and Celia, to Daddy and Katherine. And finally to Greg, who squeezes my hand. Double the blessings? Hoo-fah. Seems to me we have a mighty lot to be thankful for this time around.

Author's Note

Greg Kostakis is a fictional character, but I'm glad to say he's based on a conglomeration of real people in the secular entertainment world. I always feel heartened and blessed to come across folks like Greg. Sometimes it's in the most amazing of places. As Greg does in this story, on MTV I've seen a young Christian member of a "boy band" lead his manager and group in prayer before a concert. Seen him study the Bible with his girlfriend and talk about how important it is to date someone who shares his faith. Numerous times I've bought a secular CD of pop or R&B music and have been surprised to hear one or even two songs within it giving unabashed glory to Christ. Or I'll read an interview of an actor or actress and find words of testimony.

I think God has given these believers a unique opportunity to share their faith in ways that many of us cannot. So when I find people like Greg, I pray for them—that they will remain strong against the temptations that most assuredly come their way. That they will continue with the courage to speak out for Christ. And I thank God that he's placed them where they are as beacons of light for his kingdom.

— Brandilyn

Dread Champion is a
Novel in which
Appearances Can
Deceive!

Dread Champion

Brandilyn Collins

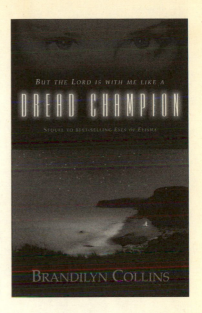

Chelsea Adams has visions. But they have no place in a courtroom. As a juror for a murder trial, Chelsea must rely only on the evidence. And this circumstantial evidence is strong—Darren Welk killed his wife. Or did he?

The trial is a nightmare for Chelsea. The other jurors belittle her Christian faith. As testimony unfolds, truth and secrets blur. Chelsea's visiting niece stumbles into peril surrounding the case, and Chelsea cannot protect her. God sends visions—frightening, vivid. But what do they mean? Even as Chelsea finds out, what can she do? She is helpless, and danger is closing in. . . .

Softcover: 0-310-23827-7

Pick up a copy at your favorite bookstore!

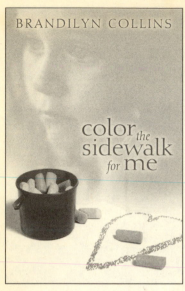

We want to hear from you. Please send your comments about this book to us in care of the address below. Thank you.

GRAND RAPIDS, MICHIGAN 49530 USA

WWW.ZONDERVAN.COM